The interrogator switched languages. "P.... you like to story, yah? Tell lah. Tell us," she ....
No clipped, controlled ....ongue, learnt in schools. They we.... .... with questions of what P.... ....hey knew hurting her, ... as not going to work. So the.... ....r to this one who spoke with famili.... ...., the lingua franca of the Layeptic region, i.... ....ie colonial-born Ro''dal; breaking words, shortenin.... sentences, barely obeying the laws of grammar.

In the light-hearted music of the new interrogator's voice was the indulgence and comfort of a glutinous rice and coconut milk dessert. Ria could almost forget the tight cap suffocating her hair, the immobility of her clamped-down limbs, and the collar that was fitted just tight enough to remind her where she was every time she swallowed.

She'd pissed herself a few times and had been constipated for days. She could not see, for her eyes, too—her eyes *especially*—were bound. Judging from the hollow ring of the space, she guessed that she was in a too-large room with an ominously high ceiling.

"Tell lah," the interrogator said again. In colloquial Sce' 'dal, the word *cerita*, for "story", was shortened into *c'ita*, "create".

Ria smiled, lips cracking. To tell—no, create—a story like hers, was to tell of regrets from first beginnings, perhaps even when the country was called by a Tuyunri name that linguists could only transliterate as Ma(an) TisCera—The Land(of) SkyHills.

And what a peopled land it was.

Early records called the scaly, reptilian Scereans the "dragons of the waters" and the first book written about the pre-Human history of the land spoke of them as if they were devil spawn. Back then, most of them had inverted knees and leg spurs, and long snouts filled with sharp teeth that they used to snap up fish in the Su(ma) Uk'rh, or Lower Marshlands, where the soft ground ate boots and plant- and animal-life ate everything else. It was a time when everyone kept to their dwellings and settlements: the Scereans in the northeastern side of the island country, near Su(ma) whence they came; the agile, cat-like Feleenese to the northwest where they fought wars with their canine Cayanese neighbours for control of the fertile land around the Anur Delta. The river systems ensued from a convergence of the clear streams within the land's rainforest centre. Ma(an) TisCera's first inhabitants, the Tuyuns, existed to and past their decline there, atop mouldering, ancestral ruins. The Tuyuns were almost Human-looking, but they wore scales of *tur* and *yun*—rock and wood—upon their skins, so that they might camouflage into the land that was theirs by right of precedence.

The Humans only arrived much later, coming from lands high up in the north and far west across the seas, though they were quick to take things for their own. No one noticed the pig-fleshed things in their villages, or how their centre in Krow City grew as time went by, forcing the other races into tight, defenceless corners. But in no time their arrivals were forgotten and it was as if they had always been there: raising buildings, laying down pipes, making laws and governments,

"*The Gatekeeper* is a marvellous blend of home comforts and pains, and the strange treasures of other realms. It's a skilled writer indeed who can make fantasy sing with so much real-world truth and delight."

—Jen Crawford, Assistant Professor, University of Canberra

"I love how Nuraliah has created this imagined but totally plausible world which is both strange yet familiar. An impressive piece of writing—confident and effortless."

—Haresh Sharma, Resident Playwright, The Necessary Stage

"A great Singaporean and politicised twist on an old myth with a moving—even romantic—storyline."

—Cyril Wong, author of *Ten Things My Father Never Taught Me*

The Gatekeeper

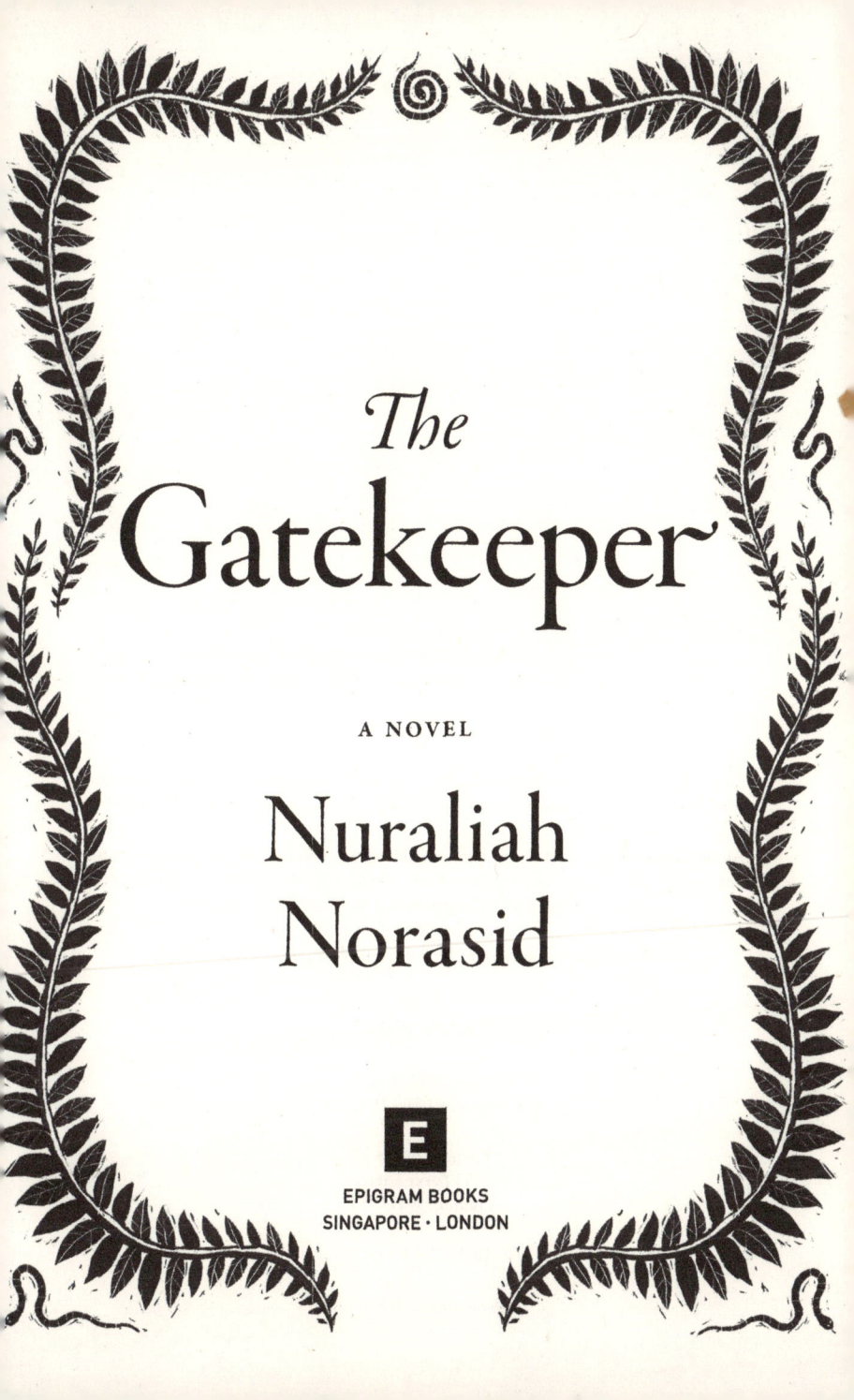

A NOVEL

Nuraliah Norasid

E
EPIGRAM BOOKS
SINGAPORE · LONDON

Epigram Books UK
First published in 2017 by Epigram Books Singapore
This Edition published in Great Britain in May 2017 by Epigram Books UK

The moral right of the author has been asserted.

All characters and events in this publication, other than those clearly in the public domain, are fictitious and any resemblance to real persons, living or dead, is purely coincidental.

All rights reserved. No part of this book may be reproduced, stored in a retrieval system, or transmitted by any form or by any means, mechanical, photocopying, recording or otherwise, without the prior permission in writing of the publisher.

A CIP catalogue record for this book is available from the British Library.

ISBN
978-1-91-209868-2

Printed and bound in
Great Britain by Clays Ltd, St Ives plc

Epigram Books UK
55 Baker Street
London, W1U 7EU

10 9 8 7 6 5 4 3 2 1

www.epigrambooks.uk

*For my Mama who has survived so much
and looks set to survive still more.*

ria I: gembira, girang, riang, sukacita
(Translation: happy, cheerful, carefree)
—from *Kamus Dewan: edisi keempat*

What is life's greatest illusion?
Innocence, my brother.
—Dawnstar Sanctuary riddle from *The Elder Scrolls V: Skyrim*

And to this day, Minerva, to dismay
and terrify her foes, wears on her breast
the very snakes that she herself had set—
as punishment—upon Medusa's head.
—from Book IV of Ovid's *The Metamorphoses*

and getting things done the way they saw fit.

When the country was populated enough and important enough in the larger scheme of *dinya*—the world—someone declared its birth as if it had never been there before. The country was later named "Manticura", for a poisonous flying Human-headed lion made for a much stronger symbol than disappearing skies and deflating hills inhabited by savages.

Scerean (me-tura). In official Manticurean records, that was what Ria would be named, though her being was more than a composite image of a snake and a woman.

Ria had only seen herself in reflection once. Her widely-set, slanted orange eyes with their starved pupils and her flat nose made her more Scerean than Human. And yet, the oily black serpent coils falling to her shoulders made sure all of that didn't matter.

Once again: "Tell lah."

Ria conjured for her listener a memory of rustling undergrowth and a lone attap hut on stilts in a small jungle clearing. Chickens pecked in the courtyard dirt and in the shaded kolong beneath the hut. A few times she had darted in among them from behind the moss-covered roots of a meranti tree, dragging cans strung on a length of white twine, to watch them scatter in a flurry of clucks, wing beats and feathers.

Sometimes her Nenek, grey hair in a snail knot, sat on the short flight of steps that led up to the veranda, chewing on her sireh while she watched Ria play. Sometimes Nenek wore her baju opah; most times, Nenek wore only her sarong, hitched up high over her freckled and wrinkled breasts, her ankles skinny and her veins tracing bulging courses across the tops of her bare, rough-soled feet.

Barani never watched, but when Ria did something wrong, her sister was always there, waiting just inside the veranda and frowning at the top of the steps. Tall Barani, with her serious eyes like brilliant purple stones, her pupils tiny triple knots and the slight jut of cheekbones that seemed to trace their way to her full lips; different, beautiful—"Enchanting," as Nenek pointed out to Ria once.

Ria had none of that beauty. All Ria had were the laughter and smiles, and the silent feet that let her creep about the kolong unnoticed, above which Barani could be heard screeching, "Ria! Where are you, you little devil? Come inside now!"

To be quiet, Ria would have a hand pressed over her mouth, cupped to keep her voice in as her sister screamed again:

"Ria!"

Then, Ria, who was named for old, forgotten joy, would open her hand and let her laughter ring out for all nearby to hear.

~~~

It was joy that Eedric tried to remember, as the hours, perhaps even days, in lockup started to feel like months. He sat in a large crowded cell, caged in by bars with white paint peeling off, revealing grey metal in places. The dark walls were nothing but ravaged, windowless expansions of those bars, keeping him packed in with the other men awaiting second judgment.

He leaned his head back and glanced about at the other

occupants of the cell. They were a threatening mixture of almost every non-Human race that existed on Manticura, reeking aggression and menace as they squatted or stood clustered in their groups. One man was taking a piss in the far corner, either oblivious to the guard banging the bars with his truncheon, or deliberately ignoring him. Behind the man, two others—a midnight-coated Cayanese and a Tuyun, his grey, rock-like *tur* scales rough and scratched, the row of spikes along his arms blunted—were going at it, their foreheads mashed together as they argued, their respective hodgepodge band of "members" adding to the cacophony with trash talk.

Eedric didn't see how it would be a fair fight, because the Cayanese, like all of his kind, was a hulking figure, twice the Tuyun's size. Granted, he was not a pure-blooded Cayanese. There was a Human face seamed into his canine features: his brown eyes large, furry brows drawn low; nose protruding and pert though not like a snout, beneath which his mouth was drawn into a tight line. Eedric saw how, within offspring of mixed blood, the Human bits always struggled to be present amongst those of the *anir*, or for want of a better Ro' 'dal word, the "creature".

The midnight Cayanese's ears were perked into tall triangles. A mane of grey, darker than the rest of him, swept back from around them and down to where his chest began. His legs grew straight down to flat Human feet with small toes, which were quite likely the only Human parts of him that managed to really assert themselves.

A group of Feleenese men sat against an adjacent wall near Eedric. They watched the fight with disinterest. They wore their shirts with the sleeves rolled up high on their upper arms and Eedric noticed the matching triangle of spirals burnt into their short brown fur. One of them saw Eedric watching and shot him a look, calm yet confrontational. Eedric turned away, to the austere, white walls of the corridor outside.

So far none of them had picked on Eedric yet. Strange, seeing how his was the only Human-looking form in the room.

Perhaps the whispers had got around about what he really was: a *Human-minora (survivalist)*; meaning "minor Human", signalling a mixing of blood, that last bit tacked on like a warning or an insult. And no one was desperate, angry or bored enough to provoke him into a fight. He wouldn't have minded though. It would certainly beat waiting about for a verdict, or for a next-of-kin to care enough to bail you out. Occasionally, a guard came around to open the gate and announce a name, and Eedric would watch the person depart to a rapacious display of spread arms and small cheers, as if freedom was around the corner rather than prosecution and punishment.

He closed his eyes and let his mind wander to a certain medusa. Ria, with her name like smiles freely given, and her half-moon eyes the colour of the sky at sunrise. He recreated his mental image of her with the single-minded purpose of remembering only the best of her in quiet hours. He could forget the reek of urine around him and smell instead the salty musk of the valley between her breasts, the fullness of them in his hands; the valley that began the invisible line down her stomach, to the pubic triangle wedged between warm thighs, which sloped to perfect knees. Her laugh had its own characteristic timbre, resonating in his head long after the last note had floated away in conversation. He thought of the two moles on the left side of her face—the one in the corner of her lips, a hint away from the dimple that appeared when she smiled, and the bigger one at the corner of her eye, bisected by her ragged scar. The snakes that frequently touched her face on the side with the moles seemed to have a single white mark on the backs of their heads, as if in a conscious effort to match.

He got to thinking of the way her hair was attached to her head: not like hair with roots, but extensions of her skin, growing out into each serpent body. The scales were sparse where the strand began at her scalp, closing up into tight patterns, nearly imperceptible in the uniform green-sheened black over the whole of the visible creature.

How did one explain what seemed like a lifetime of presence? It struck him that she could have been there, all that time: the mother by his bedside, his first love from days of innocent youth, a remembered act of kindness and—at the same time—of complete and utter cruelty.

In spite of his best efforts, every one of her faces in the album of his mind—in laughing moments, and in the sad and distant ones—were sombre black-and-white snapshots, her eyes averted just a little so as to not dazzle and petrify. It was not memory, not really. It was the desperate creation of one from the starbursts of joy that her presence had once brought him as the pain of her recent betrayal threatened to flood over him once again.

UPPER F'HERAK

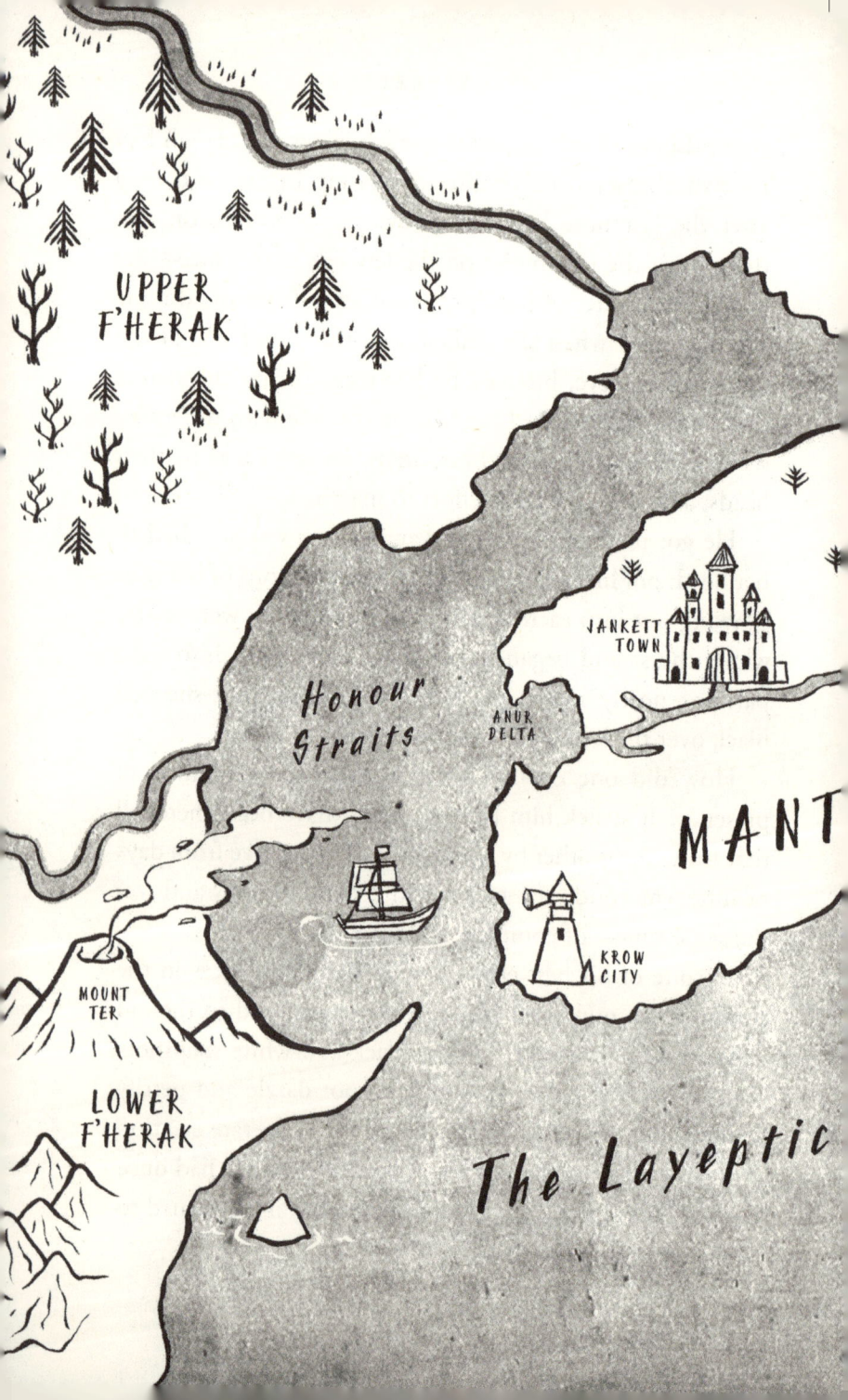

JANKETT TOWN

Honour Straits

ANUR DELTA

MANT

MOUNT TER

KROW CITY

LOWER F'HERAK

The Layeptic

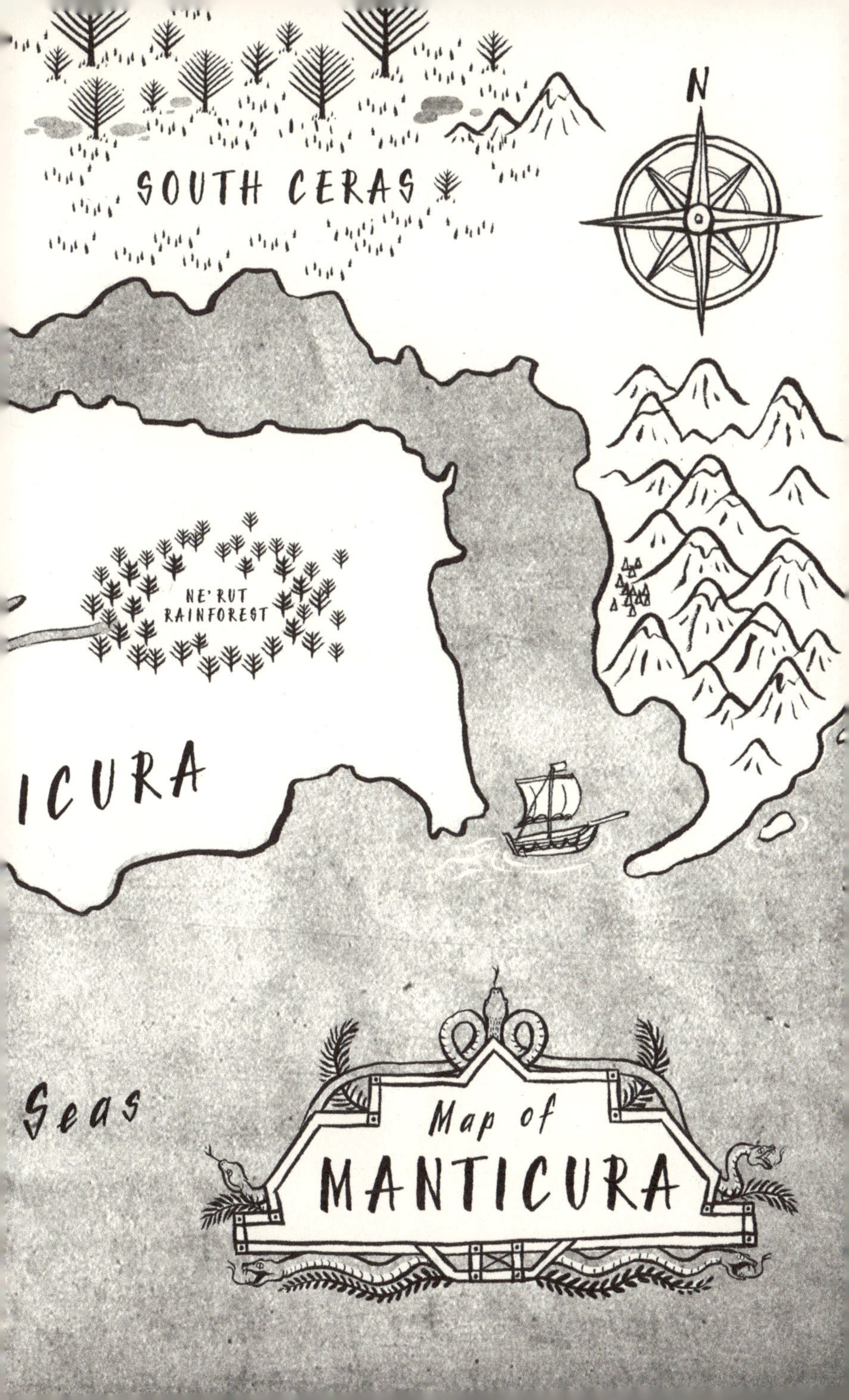
SOUTH CERAS
N
NE'RUT
RAINFOREST
ICURA
Seas
Map of
MANTICURA

5064-5068 CE

Wash Feet

Ria raced past the earthen container with its wooden cover, up the steps and onto the veranda before entering the house to sit across from Barani and Nenek at the woven tikar. She held out her enamel green plate to her sister. Barani did not even give it a glance, scowling at Ria's feet instead. Ria looked. They were dusty from the outside. Something was stuck to the sole and in between her toes. Might be a leaf, or a squashed fruit; *as long as no smell*, Ria figured and took a sniff just to check.

Holding the rice spoon high above the steaming pot, Barani admonished Ria with a loud, "*Kan* dirty!" extending the last syllable until she sounded like an annoying trilling bird.

When Ria didn't move to wash her feet, Barani went around the tikar and took the younger girl by the ear and forced her to stand. Ignoring the violent, protesting hisses from Ria's hair, Barani marched her to the container at the bottom of the steps.

Ria clutched at her tender ear as she scooped water onto

her feet. She rubbed the soles against her shins to get rid of the dirt and the unfortunate specimens she had picked up earlier, muttering the entire time—about Barani being a monster, a devil, a no-good busybody. She never saw the logic of this foot-washing regimen. What difference did it make if she were to wash them only right before going to bed? All in one, no trouble. She was only going to get them dirty again anyway, when she had to go out later to get the chickens back into the coop beneath the house and to take in the laundry. Foot-washing was a stupid rule someone had made up—must be Barani who was too lazy to sweep the house. One of those silly bits of nonsense that stated you could do something, but not something else, all for someone's benefit—must be Barani's. "This cannot. That cannot. All cannot."

Barani shouted at her from the top of the steps, "Eh, what you muttering about?" And she went on—"Just now just come back don't want to wash, now suka-suka take your time to wash, you think what? Time your mother make is it?"—such that even if Ria wanted to tell Barani what she was mumbling about, she wasn't given a chance to.

Nenek always said Barani had a beautiful voice: lemak manis, they called it; coconut milk rich and sweet as sugar—like that singer, Salo… Salom… somebody. But right then, Barani's voice grated on Ria's ears. Not nice at all.

Walking damp-footed past Barani, Ria remarked, "Voice not nice *tu*, be quiet only lah."

Barani flared into a new temper and, hitching up her sarong with one hand, snapped her body around. "This child!" she exclaimed. "So insolent already! Come here!" And gave chase.

Ria, small and lithe, sprinted into the house, screaming with gleeful panic, "Nek! Kakak want to beat Adik, Nek!" Barani was red-faced. Her hand was raised. She had taken five unsuccessful swipes at Ria, who had counted.

Nenek, who liked to begin meals with sireh, was in the process of spitting out her chewed clump of leaf and betel nut into the spittoon by the time Barani got inside and settled back down, seething, beside the elderly woman. Barani spooned rice for Nenek first, who serenely took her plate, before snatching Ria's out of the girl's outstretched hands. While she waited, Ria sniffed at the dishes served in their little bowls: cassava leaves cooked in coconut milk, sambal belacan to make it spicy and boiled sweet potatoes for afters. It was rare to be having rice, and rice was always Ria's favourite.

Later, Ria would ask for seconds. Barani, scolding, "Later you fat, then you know," would always give her another helping. Fat or not fat was of no concern to Ria, who was small and so thin everywhere that Nenek had once thought she had stomach worms.

～

Everything was routine around the house. Barani and Nenek woke up early every morning to cook and pack lauks, to make kuihs and some shell ornaments for sale. Then, while Nenek trekked to the coastal village to sell their goods, Barani tidied their home, which was the easiest part of the morning. The hardest part was getting Ria to wake up. Often Barani had to grab the girl by the ankles and heave her off the sleeping mat. Ria, still sleeping, protested by lashing out arms and feet at her sister, all the while shouting like she was battling sea monsters in a dream. When she finally woke, it was with her face partly on the mat, partly on the floor, and Barani very close to kicking her out onto the veranda and down to the courtyard where they would have their morning baths.

Ria hated these baths because mornings were cold, and the girls would be shivering in nothing but their sarongs. Ria's sarong kept slipping off her flat chest, so she had to hold it up while she splashed water over herself. Barani had no such concerns. *Dasarkan tetek besar*—breast big, always no problem.

Nenek was used to them fighting. She rarely ever reacted to it. What Nenek would not tolerate, however, was when they turned their gazes to each other; both locked in a battle of who would channel that petrifying energy better—Barani, obviously. Those were times when Nenek, who was always benign and understanding, would roar, "Don't play with eyes!" and twist both girls' ears until they stared back at her, red-faced, red-eared and ready to cry. Those times when Nenek got angry, not even Ria could laugh at the double meaning of "playing with eyes". No matter how much they tried to deny it, Nenek would have caught the twin clouding of their eyes and the raising of their hairs. To the old woman, it did not matter that their gazes would not affect either of them, or even Nenek (not that they had ever tried). She did not want them to make a habit of it.

"Because you live with people now," Nenek explained later when all the sniffling subsided. "They may not like you. They may not want you near them. They may not want you near their children or their chickens, whichever is more important.

But you cannot stone people."

It was the year of the "Mati-kura Tra-jadi". Ria didn't know much about what a "tra-jadi" was, but from the way Nenek was so strict about things, Ria guessed it had something to do with girls like Barani and herself getting into trouble for the things they could do with their eyes. There was also "Mati" in that "tra-jadi" somewhere, which meant "die". So that "trouble" likely involved dead people.

"But what if they deserve it?" Ria asked. She was already bright-eyed, sitting straight, fingers of one hand picking at the nails of the other.

Nenek slapped her hands apart without having to look. "Don't argue. People don't do anything to you, you don't do anything to them. In life, you must be patient. You must accept. Be kind and some day, someone will be kind back."

Whatever Nenek might say, Ria was sure they did not live among people. They lived among chickens; chickens they let out of the coop every morning. Into their clucking fray, Ria would secretly throw the clumps of rice that she knew had weevil larvae in them. They had many hens and this one cock Ria wanted so badly to kick for the way it walked, breast out, tail feathers arced and shaking.

Ria could if she wanted to—kick the cock, that was. Unless it was something she did wrong, no one in the house really paid attention to her. Nenek placed all her hopes and expectations on Barani, raising her to take charge of the household and to set a good example for Ria. After Nenek's lectures Barani would be quiet for hours, sitting on the veranda with her back to the entrance. Ria could not even think of anything annoying to do. She could only watch her sister silently, nothing but her eyes peeking past the rough-hewn wooden doorjamb, body crouching on all fours just inside the ibu rumah. She wanted to call out "Kakak" to her older sister but the words always withdrew, back into some far corner of her mouth.

～

When Ria turned seven—"Count-count, about seven," Nenek told her, holding up one hand, fingers splayed, and another to resemble a pair of scissors—she climbed her first tree.

They were to have tapioca again because their rice had finished. Ria had caught a caterpillar—the fat, furry kind Bara was always afraid of. This she put down the back of Bara's baju when the older girl wasn't looking. The sight of Barani twisting and squirming, all while she screeched and cried, was funny right until she rounded on Ria who was laughing behind an open hand. Ria thought she was going to get it then, but instead of beating her, Barani issued a dare: "You see that tree?"—Bara pointed at a tree—"You so smart, you climb lah. I want to see."

Bara was herself an expert tree-climber and kept goading Ria with, "Scared right? Scared right?"

To prove herself not scared, Ria hitched up her sarong and climbed the tree Barani had indicated. The branches were thick and the first of them were low enough for her to grab and hoist herself up with. She clambered up with some difficulty, legs spread too wide and sarong pushed scandalously high around her thighs, until she reached a broad branch some way off the ground. She stood on it, trumpeting her success while Barani looked on, unimpressed.

In time, Barani turned to go, saying, "Come down lah. Go home."

It was then that the distance Ria had climbed caught up to her and became terrifying. The ground seemed so far away and everything below her so small.

Barani turned back after a bit, saw Ria still up in the tree and needled her with, "Ah, climb so high, and then don't know how to come down."

Torn between a fear of falling and the pressing need to return to the safety of the ground, all tangled together with the determination to not be shown up by her sister, Ria shouted even as she began to cry, "Kakak ask Ria to climb, Ria climb lah!"

Barani, still amused, held out her arms. "Jump!"

"Don't want!" Ria cried out, hugging herself closer to the tree.

"Jump! Kakak catch!" Barani called out again. She made a motion with her hands—jump, come down. Don't worry. Kakak catch. There was no uncertainty in her countenance or bearing. So Ria finally closed her eyes and leapt. And Barani did catch her. The impact of the drop and meeting bodies sent Barani into a half spin as her arms closed around Ria. Ria held on to her, taking in the smell of the jasmine oil that her sister liked to dab in the crevices of scalp between the serpent bodies.

"Alah...not so high also..." remarked Barani, smiling.

After that, Ria had no problems climbing trees. Whenever Ria found flowers, she held them to her nose, trying to find a matching scent because back then she didn't know what jasmine flowers looked like.

∽∽

When Nenek decided that they must have an education, Ria wondered if it had anything to do with how much time she had spent playing in the forest lately. Barani said it was so that they could read the words in the newspapers. Ria didn't argue.

One day Nenek had them dressed in their nicest baju kurungs and wrapped their heads with the new shawls she'd got for them, before trooping them with her along a narrow dirt path that cut through a long stretch of forest. Barani held Ria's hand throughout the walk. Ria kept trying to tug herself free, so that she was angled away from Barani the whole time.

She saw a troop of macaques sitting on their haunches and watching them pass. One had a baby clinging to her, its large eyes in a tiny face staring at Ria. Nearby, a group of young monkeys were engaged in a game of mock wrestling. Ria bared her teeth at the lot of them. Barani pulled at her hand so hard that Ria collided into the taller girl's body as she jerked upright. But Barani was not looking at her. Rather she was keeping her eyes firmly fixed on the oversized basket strapped to Nenek's back. Ria looked back and saw that some of the macaques were frozen in place, and those that weren't were bounding about the stone ones in the beginning stages of a frenzy.

The path they were on led to a perpendicular tarred road. It ran along the back of a row of conjoined ground houses, each one thatched-roofed, marked by a barred window and bigger than the one she'd known all her life. A rusty bicycle sat propped against a wooden wall, its front wheel squashed into an eight that was fat around the middle. Its seat was missing, though its bell was still intact. Ria wanted to reach out and ring it, but Barani did not slow her stern pace. Discarded paraphernalia lined the path, pressed up against the houses. She lifted her nose to the smell of fried banana fritters, trying to detect which house it came from. Ria peered into each window but save for a hint of light from one open door or other, the houses' interiors were dark and offered nothing more than glints of pots and woks, outlines of things kept and the occasional silhouette of their tenants.

To the other side of the path was open ground covered in patches of dark grass stretching out to a line of distant, but familiar forest.

Nenek went down the path, and the sisters followed. At one point they came alongside a group of children—all boys, dressed in buttoned shirts tucked into shorts worn high on skinny waists. One boy wore shoes—too big for him—with white socks. The others wore slippers, the blue-and-white rubber kind like hers. Too big on some. Too small on another. Soles too thin on one. Like hers.

They watched goggle-eyed as Ria passed them with Barani and Nenek. Ria snapped her eyes away when her sister reached down to grasp the point where the two ends of scarf were knotted under her chin, so that it was pulled tighter over the undulating mass on her head. She wanted to cry out in protest but saw that Barani was doing the same to her own scarf, seemingly unaware she was only making her hair more visible through the cloth.

When they came to the end of that dirt road, Nenek went around the corner of the last house and it was not long before Ria got her first glimpse of Kenanga.

The whole village was set on a huge clearing of dusty dry ground which the sun bore down upon, unimpeded. Tall sticks of coconut trees rose between the houses. Ria bent a little while she was being pulled along, so that she could look into the kolong of the raised houses—no chickens, but there were more children, playing together, squatting about, returning her wide-eyed stare in kind. She peered into the houses with their broad areas of veranda; wondered at the legged furniture and the bits of patterned curtains she could see in a few of them. Near the village centre, there was a sheltered area with a dark green awning held up by thick poles. Two bicycles and a motorcycle stood slightly tipped beside one of these poles. Further in, within the sheltered space itself, a group of men sat at a long table while someone appeared to be pouring drinks at a metal stall behind them. Their voices rumbled over to Ria, though they stopped altogether as she came near with Nenek and Barani. They turned their heads in sync, to watch Barani—Ria, too, but Barani more—as they passed.

There was a discomfiting quality to their gazes that Ria couldn't pin down. So she stared at them instead. Or tried to, because Barani placed her hand on Ria's cheek and turned her face away.

"Enchanting", or "*menawan*": Ria remembered the word Nenek used. Barani was like that; Ria too, perhaps, but Barani more.

The schoolhouse was a single-storey building, raised on a concrete platform. There were two doors—front and back—and an ample amount of windows, their shutters opened so that Ria could look into the classroom. A long dark board spanned the whole of one wall, while another board, a green one tacked with papers and drawings, spanned another. Students sat on high stools around the rectangular tables they shared. One or two tomes—*kitabs*, she thought Nenek once called them—lay opened at each table, shared between eight students. The younger ones sat near the front, while the older ones—some adults too—sat in the back. Each only had thin, bound folds of paper, into which they were inscribing, Ria guessed, the symbols that were written on the board.

Ria saw the tall, pretty Cikgu with her thick, close curls and plain, off-yellow baju kurung, smiling at them from behind big black-framed glasses. Feeling suddenly shy, Ria scratched at her hair through the scarf. Barani nudged her to stop. So she stopped.

Cikgu beckoned them in, saying, "Ah! There you are! Arrived already! Come in lah. Don't be shy." Ria stumbled slightly from Barani's push as they entered. Once inside, Cikgu introduced them to the rest of the students in the class. The students all slouched forward a little more on their stools, eyes wide with fascination, as seemed to be the common reaction amongst people in the village when they saw the sisters.

Ria heard Barani draw in a breath as she returned the students' stares. Ria waited for the tell-tale clouding of her sister's eyes, preparing to turn her head and find all the students cast in stone.

Cikgu assigned them their seats then and Ria took relief in that.

Barani took her seat at the back among gaping boys who would not stop staring at her, while Ria was made to sit in front, so close to Cikgu that she could reach out and touch her if she wanted to.

Midway through class, Ria glanced to the back of the room to look over at her sister. Barani's scarf-covered head was bent over a table much too low for her, as she laboured over the small board Cikgu had given out earlier, her grip on the chalk awkward, white-knuckled. A persistent pair of eyes watched her from a corner of the classroom; some stupid boy with ears that stuck out too much through his head of tumbling hair. Stubborn, *degil* ears, Ria remembered Nenek calling those types. So, in class, she tried her best to keep an eye on him.

Grasshopper Army

By what Ria could discern of the calendar and the way time and days were marked by it, she and Barani had been in school for a few weeks, probably nearly a month. In that time, Ria picked up on symbols and numbers, and their set sequences that were not supposed—she was told—to vary even as the moments or the reasons for their use changed.

Cikgu was always kind, always patient; always wearing her simple baju kurungs over her small-chested, big-hipped frame. And Ria would try to do things right just for the warm smile Cikgu would give her.

But there came a morning when Barani did not ask Ria to pack her board and the homework she had prepared so meticulously the night before, and did not pass her a packed lunch of fire-baked cassava to take to school. Ria sat folding grasshoppers out of coconut leaves by the door, eyeing her school things and her sister, who was sweeping the house with all the air of a brewing storm during monsoon time. It was the same sort of air that would hang the smell of rain around them and point a warning finger at Ria, telling her that she couldn't play outside. So vigorous was her sister's sweeping, and yet so brooding, that Ria tucked her feet away without being told to.

Finally she dared ask, "Kakak, not going to school *ke*?"

Barani replied without looking at Ria, "School? People like us, what for need school? No need school!" Every word sounded like Barani was biting into it, vicious as an attacking roc, those reptilian pets that people liked to keep to guard their property and chase innocent school kids up trees. Her hair hissed a drawn out chorus, ready to attack and spit their venom at anybody who came too near. Barani continued to sweep the dust and dirt out the door, her face set neutrally. The broom scratched at the wooden floor, seeming to scrape the words "sweep, sweep, sweep" all out the door. Ria could only pout, but turned her face away so Barani could not see. Secretly she wondered if them not being able to go to school was her fault, because whenever she tried to talk to one girl, the girl proceeded to cover her work with a shielding hand. And no one would lend her their eraser when she asked.

∿

Ria missed learning. She was just getting good at addition: one leaf grasshopper add one leaf grasshopper was two leaf grasshoppers. She badly wanted to know how to read and write, and every day she would look to Barani, hoping to see her sister change her mind about "people like us" not needing to go to school.

In answer to her wish, a day came when Ria, sitting on the veranda, spotted Cikgu walking down the dirt path, an umbrella over her scarf-covered head. Ria saw that Cikgu carried a bag in her free hand. Before Cikgu could reach the house, Ria dashed into the house, crying out breathlessly, "Nek! Nek! Kak! Kak! Cikgu come!"

Nenek continued to chew calmly on her sireh, instructing Barani to go prepare coffee and something to eat for Cikgu. Barani flitted back and forth from the ibu rumah to the kitchen, getting ready to serve the guest even as she tried to throw on her scarf and help Ria put on hers at the same time, scolding, "Do work a bit faster can or not? People come, no drinks, no food..." Ria tied a firm knot under her chin to secure the scarf. She thought Barani was going to have a seizure from all the worrying about the state of the house and whether Cikgu liked her coffee black or with milk. Amidst Barani's flurry, Nenek rocked where she sat on the floor, her red-stained mouth chewing and chewing.

Nenek met Cikgu at the top of the stairs and invited the young woman in. Cikgu spoke to Nenek and then to Barani for what seemed like a long time before she sat down and took out books from her bag to spread on the tikar that had been rolled out on the veranda for her. Ria was made to wash her face and then sit across from her. She watched, chewing on a fingernail, as Cikgu slipped her own scarf off to let it hang around her shoulders. Her wavy locks were glossy black, loose and free. Looking right at Ria, she asked gently, "Do you want to learn, Ria?"

Ria glanced at the books. She had never held one before. In class, no one sharing her desk would let her. She looked up at Cikgu and wanted to be just like her: hair big-big and curly, bespectacled, poised and smart. And pretty. Not beautiful like Barani but pretty in a way that felt just right. She quickly removed her finger from her mouth before nodding. Cikgu reached out and pulled off Ria's scarf with a smile—"At home, no need to wear. Hot outside, or raining outside, then wear. Don't worry." Which was how Ria became the first of the two sisters to receive home-schooling.

In time, symbols—those curves like smiles, lines like tree stems, diamond marks and tiny snails that hung mid-air—gained meaning, pointing at things. Even her name became tangible, contained in a page she could give to anyone. She wrote her name first on the chalkboard and then made meticulous copies on slips of lined paper. She gave the slips to Nenek, Barani and Cikgu. When those symbols became something called the "alfa-birds" after the school system changed, the words she spelled still sounded the same. She was still "Ria" and for that she was glad.

Cikgu taught her another language too—made of squarish symbols of whorls-and-dots, and branching twigs with crowns of eyes—a language she said no one had any use for any more because the people who used to speak it were quickly dying out of their traditions, forgetting their language. There were not many books to teach it with, but "there's value in Tuyunri. If you don't speak it, who will?" Cikgu said. "You are special and that is why I will teach you." Ria wanted to ask Cikgu how she came to know the language in the first place, but wasn't sure it was at all right to ask anyone how they knew anything. However, what Cikgu had told her made Ria feel extra special and she took to learning the language with zeal, knowing to spell her *apis* for "fire" in Sce' 'dal, and her *krik-eks* for the same in Tuyunri. She was happy—happy to know the many ways to speak the same.

∿

Cikgu was not the only person to venture down that path from Kenanga to the isolated house. For all of their isolation and for all of the sweeping that Barani had done, there was one unpleasant thing that persisted in coming.

He first came on a bicycle, meandering over the unevenness of the path, and almost falling more than once. Ria saw him while working on her penmanship at the veranda. His bicycle jolted sideways. He twisted the handlebars as he shot out a leg to stop his fall. He looked up and, seeing Ria, smiled, righting his bicycle before pushing forward until he was just below the veranda. He must have been sixteen or so. The teeth in his smile were very white against his brown skin. His *degil* ears still stuck out and his hair was still ruffled. When he greeted her, Ria felt like throwing her pencil at him. Useless Boy. But before she could think about not answering his greeting, she had to remember to pull her scarf from around her shoulders to throw it over her head. By that time, Barani came out with her own quiet greeting. Her scarf was already in place and she appeared so composed that Ria suspected she must have spotted the Useless Boy from a distance. The Useless Boy handed Barani sweet potatoes wrapped in tempeh leaves—his excuse for being there.

He always visited when Nenek was not around, his arrival announced by the grating of wheels over the sand covering their small courtyard and then affirmed by the sharp chirp of the bicycle's bell. Barani would fumble for her scarf, throw it over her hair, tuck in any that tried to wriggle free and rush to the door to greet him. He didn't seem to mind that Barani's scarf undulated like a sack full of pythons. He also never asked about the colour of the sisters' eyes, or why they lived all the way out here. Never. He wore a wristwatch with straps made of "ladder", like the thing people climbed in the village; an actual watch with moving hands, unlike the one Ria had tried to make out of drawing block paper, which always showed 3.30 morning, afternoon, or evening; a watch he was always consulting when he was with them.

Once Ria carried a pot, ladle and wooden spoon to the veranda, where Barani and the Useless Boy were sitting close together and talking. She drummed a steady "pom-pom" rhythm on the bottom of the upturned pot as she belted out medleys she'd heard before. The Useless Boy clapped for her, which only made Ria sing worse. Barani tolerated it for a while before she snapped her head back and shouted, "Noisy lah!" Other days she wedged herself between them. Still others, Ria spent her day inside the house, reading or writing, sometimes telling stories to herself or folding and lining up armies of coconut-leaf grasshoppers.

Maybe he sensed her boredom and pitied her, because the Useless Boy would at times turn away from Barani long enough to teach her how to make matchbox cars and ice-cream stick guns that shot rubber band bullets. He was attending a public school in a town an hour and thirty minutes away by then, the one with windows that had open-shut glass panes, many classrooms with ceiling fans, a great thing called electricity and a big man named

Principal. When he came bearing toys and fascinating new gadgets like ballpoint pens with tube ink encased within hard, transparent outer bodies, Ria decided she liked him a little. Those times, and that time when she had managed to cycle his adult-sized bicycle into a mangrove swamp.

He was smart, Ria often heard Barani praise him in a gentle voice that made Ria's hair shiver. But Ria recalled the way he had struggled through the swamp mud at low tide to get his bicycle and didn't think she could agree with her sister. Still, he said a great many things to Barani that Ria, crashing matchbox cars and throwing sticks to bring guava down from trees, did not understand. He would gesture excitedly as he spoke and Barani would listen, watching his face intently. He spoke and she listened, listened until he glanced down at his watch and said he had to go, because he had homework to do and because Nenek would be home soon from her market stall.

Once Ria saw them approaching the veranda after feeding the chickens, and she saw the boy take Barani's hand. Barani pulled away, staring at him in shock. Ria was watching from the open door, just peeking over the doorjamb, and saw the boy lean in to say something to Barani. Whatever he said, it made Barani run up past Ria into the house. The Useless Boy followed at a leisurely pace, his hands clasped behind his back, chest pumped out full of air. Barani stopped and stood just inside the house, wrapping her scarf tighter around her head, trying to catch her breath.

The boy stared at Barani, as if he wanted to memorise her. Before he left, he said to her, "Ani, wait for Abang eh? When Abang become a doctor, Abang will come back and cure Ani."

Ria turned away from the scene, mouthing "abang" like it was distasteful question. *Disgusting lah*, she thought. She popped her head back out. Barani might have replied if Nenek wasn't suddenly seen hobbling down the dirt path towards the house. Barani threw him a quick glance before darting across the ibu rumah to get to the kitchen. Ria watched the boy mount his bicycle and push off, riding past Nenek with a nod and a greeting. He probably action-action asked Nenek, "Nek, back home already?" but Ria could not hear.

It came to be that he did not return for a long, long time. He was away furthering his education. Some place where they could give him even more homework. Barani pined for him, Ria knew. The older girl seemed to have lost all of her purposeful briskness and went about her chores so distractedly, pausing to gaze out the door so often, that Nenek yelled, "Like there is no other boy *tau*!" For all the boy's watch-consulting, Nenek knew about him anyway. But not from Ria. Ria had kept quiet, swarming matchbox cars with her grasshopper army and bringing down still more guavas with her well-aimed sticks.

Stone People

Sometimes, Ria wished that the Useless Boy would return, if only to make Barani smile again. Barani went through mute periods where she scratched at her arms, as if plagued by rashes, until blood ran. Ria often watched her cook, cry and scratch herself in the gloom of the kitchen. Ria would be on all fours as she peered down the steps, the rest of her body in the ibu rumah and her heart, it seemed, held between crab pincers. If Nenek was home, Nenek would shoo Ria and her questions of "Kakak why, Nek?" away from the kitchen entrance before going down to speak with the older medusa. Those nights Nenek patted Barani to sleep like the latter was still a child. Ria would lie on her side, her hand cradling her head through the flattened pillow, and watch her sister fall asleep in the light from the small oil lamp. When Barani finally lulled into slumber, Ria inched closer and snuggled into her sister's side, because it was only in sleep that Barani would not push her away.

When Nenek took ill and could no longer go to the market to peddle her wares, it was Barani who undertook the task, strapping a basket to her back and winding her scarf tightly over her head, as if to suffocate her snakes into stillness. Maybe it was because she was a good businesswoman or maybe it was because she was so beautiful, but her returns were always enough for them to live on, albeit simply. Ria had to give up her childish play so that she could be at home in case Nenek needed anything. There were days when she wasted soap while washing clothes, and days when she was too slow in taking out the firewood, so that the rice at the bottom of the pot ended up a blackened crust that she would later spend hours trying to scrape off.

During the afternoon quiet, while waiting for her lessons or for Barani to return, Ria liked to unroll her sleeping mat beside Nenek's, and lie on her back to be made drowsy by the empty attap roof and the quietude of the jungle sounds. If Nenek was awake, she would ask Ria for stories: "Ria like to story right? Ria story-*kan* Nenek." So, Ria told her the stories she'd made up and the ones she'd read. And always the happy ones: those about Feleenese princesses and Scerean princes who would sweep the former off their feet, and about foreign families who lit special, non-cooking fires in their homes and who always had lots of cake to eat.

Nenek died in her sleep.

Every night since Nenek fell ill, Ria woke up to put a saliva-wet finger under Nenek's nose to check her breathing. And still Nenek had passed away without her knowing. They only found out after their morning baths when they could not wake Nenek up to be washed and fed breakfast. While the sun was changing into its burning afternoon skin, Nenek's was cold. The old woman lay in repose, hands clasped over her stomach the way they always did when she slept. Neither of the sisters had known that Barani's usual leave-taking—"Nek, Ani go first eh?"—and Ria's gift of a leaf grasshopper that had her best saga seeds for eyes, would be their last. Nenek had never complained, never lamented her lot, never spoke of pains. She had expired in the same quiet, a leaf grasshopper arranged by her head.

The sisters found themselves orphans. They stared at their lost parent before Ria started to cry. Her voice rang from the silence of the small house to the surrounding forest bathed in the light of a bright afternoon.

Nenek should have been buried near their house, where her grave could be taken care of and read to every day. However, things were changing far beyond the spaces they moved within, radiating from a centre and reaching towards the peripheries of the land they lived on. Cikgu told them that someone called the Gavermen would have none of it. Strange, fancy name this "Gavermen", and stupid, Ria thought, to not allow loved ones to be buried where loved ones wanted them to be buried. Gavermen had set aside land with plots for every dead body. Plots, Ria thought. A great big collection of stories for passed loved ones, which did not feel quite as comforting. Not knowledgeable enough to argue and with a grandmother waiting to be buried, they agreed to let Cikgu get them a plot number for Nenek. She also helped them arrange for the cleaning of the body and the imminent burial. She advised them to stay at home while some men from the village bore Nenek's body to her plot. The body was seen into the ground by people who claimed blood relation by husband's mother's sisters or brothers, but who had never come to visit, or even liked her presence in the village, let alone that of the two strange creatures in her care.

The day the burial was to take place, Ria threatened to wail, turn Gavermen to stone. However, Barani told her, patience. *Sabar*. Accept. Some things in life we cannot change, and others don't do anything wrong to you, you don't do anything wrong to others.

Because that was Nenek's moral lesson, Ria listened, slipping her hand into her sister's as she stood in the shadows just inside the doorway, watching the last of the funeral congregation disappear around the bend in the dirt path. And she accepted.

Then *he* came, when Ria was crying into Barani's lap, soaking the material of her sister's sarong. Barani was stroking Ria's head, letting the strands slide over her hand, not saying a word. Positioned in that way, Ria almost did not hear the quiet wish of peace upon them. She felt, however, her sister give a start. Ria sat up; wiping her wet cheeks with her palms as she automatically pulled the scarf from around her neck over her head. Eyes heavy and nose feeling swollen, she saw that Useless Boy from years ago peering in from the veranda. Ria glanced to Barani, who stared at the young man like she did not know him, before recognition swept across her features and confused them—with sadness from Nenek's passing and gladness from seeing him after a long time. She slowly got to her feet as she bade him to enter.

He was dressed in a pressed white shirt, through which his white singlet was visible, all of it tucked meticulously into ironed dress pants. He wore his hair parted to the side, oiled and combed so severely that it looked fake. He wore only his socks into the house, his footsteps feline-like, quiet as a stalking traac's. He asked after Barani—"Ani *baik?*"—and hearing the familiar voice was enough to make Barani's defences crumble.

Ria watched her sister's face crumple up as sobs racked her body. The man went up to Barani and broke an unspoken house rule when he embraced her. Ria stood rooted while Barani towered, crying into the Useless Boy's chest. It left Ria feeling a little nauseated. The beginnings of a migraine caught at the areas around her eyes and the top of her head, threatening to culminate at such a point that she had to pick herself up and leave.

Ria walked across the courtyard and ambled into the jungle where she proceeded to pluck fruits she would never eat and to frighten animals on a whim. However, always mindful of Nenek's rule to never be in the jungle at twilight, she returned home when the day was nearing dark to find the man gone and her sister looking freshly-bathed and smelling of talcum powder. Barani did not scold her for being out so late, but Ria found herself wishing that she had.

For days after, she found it repulsive to be near her sister. He came every day. No longer wobbling down the dirt path on a bicycle, his arrival was now always heralded by the steady sputtering of his motorcycle, still on two wheels but moving fast enough so that he could balance himself. He called her "Ani", sometimes "Sayang", and Barani called him "Bang", like she was already his. Ria had never seen the ocean, but if she was to describe it based on what she had read of it, the Useless Boy would be like the ocean, drowning her sister in murk and birthing an alien woman in her place: soft, fragile and silent as a corpse.

∽

Change came to the household suddenly, when the Useless Boy came one day with five other men, one riding pillion with him and the others on their own motorcycles. Barani heard the furore of motors and hurried out, only to halt at the top of the veranda stairs when she saw the strangers. Ria stood in the ibu rumah, her head peeking around the threshold of the front door, watching their approach from behind her sister. Barani eventually descended the steps to meet them, slow and wary.

Two of the men were dressed like the Useless Boy, in short-sleeved shirts tucked into pants, while the other three wore shirts with too many metal buttons and too many pockets, tucked into shorts that fell to just above their knees, with black boots and berets. Ria recognised that they were policemen and she tried to recall any bad thing she had done to have them coming for her. Stretching her neck out, she saw the policemen standing at the back of the group, feet apart and hands clasped at their belt buckles.

All the men were staring at Barani, to whom the Useless Boy was excitedly speaking. Barani listened, shaking her head for the duration of the conversation. Soon the two other men started to speak to her as well, first earnestly, then furiously, showing her papers that Barani would not look at.

In time she turned and stormed up to the veranda. Her scarf had come loose, some of the snakes slipping out from under it to dart tongues about her ears. The Useless Boy came in moments after Barani, forgetting to remove his shoes. Ria scrambled further into the ibu rumah when she saw the others come up as well.

The Useless Boy motioned for the others to remain outside as he reached out and grabbed Barani by an elbow to make her turn. "Ani! Don't be stubborn, Ani. This is all for Ani's own good!" Ria listened as he spoke about a shelter for them—her sister and herself. He made promises: *You will be happy there. It's better there, and it's safe. Got electricity, buses and cars, schools!*

"Is that where we are going to live? A shelter?" Barani asked in a quiet voice. Looking up to face the Useless Boy squarely, she added, "You said we live with you! In *your* house!"

The anger in her tone shocked him. It even shocked Ria, who had been on the receiving end of Barani's disciplining for a long time. After a bit, he relaxed, shaking his head and smiling as if he found it all very amusing.

"Wah," he replied, appearing impressed as he leaned back to assess Barani from head down. "Ani so smart now. Talk back to me. Where did you learn all this?" When Barani did not answer, he went on, "Ani, we discuss that later. Abang have a deadline. Development is coming. Everyone is going. The shelter is only temporary. You can work and then buy a house for you and Ria. The city is a place of opportunity, trust me. You don't have to worry."

"You promised," Barani said through clenched teeth, "to cure me when you come back!" She took him in with disbelief before continuing, bottom lip quivering, "I let you—I let you because you said you were going to *marry* me!"

It frightened Ria to see her sister so angry and so desperate in the way she tried so hard to keep herself from crying. It frightened her even more to know the implications of those words. There was a pause, long and uncomfortable. The Useless Boy made noises in the back of his throat that could be laughter or questioning "uhs" as he kept glancing over his shoulder at the others.

"Life is not that easy, Ani," he said finally, gripping both of Barani's arms, his voice hardening as he shook her, as if he was trying to sift into her the complexity of that life. "Ani, you have to understand! I know—Abang know why you can't go to school. With these ears, Abang hear what the kampung people say, about you, about Ria... Not everyone is like me, Ani. You like or not they will take you away. Better I do than they do. Over there, there will be many people you can be friends with, all really nice people."

"People like us," Ria remembered her sister saying when she first found out she couldn't go to school. It dawned on her why that one girl's parents said she shouldn't speak to Ria, and why no one would lend her their eraser. There were no others like them, with snakes for hair that they had to constantly hide, and eyes with which they had to be careful in how they looked at things, especially at people.

The Useless Boy cried out in a last ditch attempt to convince the older girl, "Come on! You will be protected there, Ani!"

"With guns? By people like your friends? People like you?" Barani shot back.

For all the revelations emerging, Ria only saw the way the Useless Boy was treating her sister—holding her, spewing anger at her. Ria wanted to reach out, remove his hands from her sister's arms and tell him that he had no business using that tone on Barani. But there was only Ria's uncertain silence.

The Useless Boy caught sight of her. He let her sister's arm go—just one, not the other—and instructed Ria, in a voice an adult would often use on a child they thought should not know any better: "Ria, be a good girl and go to the kitchen, eh?"

Ria did as she was told and made for the dark depths of the kitchen. There she could hear a rush of voices, but refused to make them out. Her chest rose and fell fast but the air could not catch up. Her eyes fell on the square of light on the kitchen wall and it drew her to the window, its single shutter propped open by a metal prong. She remembered the policemen. The shelter couldn't be anywhere nice if policemen were involved. When she was being naughty in the past, the three things she was told could carry her off were the devil, jungle people who only came out after dusk, and the policemen—devil to a hell palace, jungle people to another realm and policemen to a square hole underground called the jail. No way home from any of them.

There was a table underneath the window where her sister kept packs of salt, sugar and dried spices. She pushed these aside, cramming them into a corner. Bracing her feet on the wall, she managed to haul herself up and climb out through the window. The shutter slammed shut just as she came to a painful, crouched landing on the ground outside. The prong ended up beside her but the window was too high up for her to replace it.

Going around the house, she saw that the rest of the men were no longer at the veranda. One of the policemen had also left his post to join them inside. The other two guarded the dirt path to the inland village. They were still in the same pose as before—feet apart, hands clasped—neither of them speaking as they idly watched the house. There was a pompous air about them, and the handcuffs they wore at their belts had the same evil gleam as the shiny black bodies of their batons.

She walked up to them. Seeing her, one of them held out his hand telling her that everyone must stay inside until the business had been concluded. What business-business, she didn't care. All she knew was that they had no business wearing their handcuffs, harbouring plans to haul her and her sister off to the jail when they didn't do anything wrong.

When she came near, the policeman who had been warning her froze, hand out, eyes and mouth opened wide in surprise. She didn't have her scarf on, so maybe that was why. Every strand of her hair was clustered around her face as if they all wanted to take a harder look, weighing her head down as they did so. She felt the tug of migraine again, though not so intense this time that she had to close up around herself and grit her teeth, and the policeman greyed over, outwards from his face to the rest of his body. His upper body had already hardened, but his feet continued to move towards her, so when they, too, became stone, he fell over. His companion watched his body fall, saw parts of it break on impact, before he raised his own eyes to hers— only to meet the same fate.

Ria stepped around their stone forms and made her

way down the path to Kenanga, where children were taught that *people like her* were not to be spoken to, or to be associated with, and where someone had decided that people like her did not deserve a roof over their heads, by marriage or by birth.

∿

Barani vaguely heard the kitchen window slamming shut but couldn't move herself away as all the men around her tried to convince her into signing an agreement to give over Nenek's land to their fancy urban development plans. It wasn't that she hadn't expected it. On her odious errands to Kampung Kenanga, she had already seen the beginnings of the plans creeping in with surveyors and the officials going from door to door, talking to people, taking photographs of various paths and corners. People at the outskirts were already being moved out. The coastal village was still largely untouched but no one could ignore the increased number of tugboats and cargo ships on the water's horizon. It was a sign of things to come, the mostly-Scerean villagers would say as they stared out to sea from the rickety verandas of their homes, and in low rumbled whispers near her corner stall in the marketplace. Even Cikgu had left shortly after Nenek's death to take up the post she'd been offered at a government school in the city. Barani remembered Ria clinging to the teacher, pleading with the woman not to leave, as if she, her own sister was not good enough company.

She had thought—no, hoped—that she would be married, that Abang would have a home for her and Ria. The way she saw it, that was not happening. He was not the doctor he said he would be when he left her those years ago. And two girls with snakes for hair were not the family he'd imagined, and that was what really pained her. She was beautiful, yes, but she was not good enough to be a respectable wife.

He'd taken hold of her arms when he began shouting again after Ria left. Barani shrugged them off, the force of her action sending him reeling slightly. Giving him one hard stare, she turned to check on Ria in the kitchen.

She had expected to see Ria: if not helping herself to the boiled bananas under the straw food cover, then at least sitting in a corner narrating stories, or just generally talking to herself the way she always did when left on her own. She found only an empty room. Nothing seemed disturbed at first, but then her eyes were drawn to the window with its single shutter down and the packs of cooking ingredients out of place. There were marks on the table's surface that looked like they had been made by grimy feet. Barani rushed to the table, her breath in her throat, and pushed open the window to see the unstirring forest.

Barani ran back up to the ibu rumah, pushing past the men to get to the veranda. She could sense Abang behind her; heard him above the cloud of noise in her head, demanding she tell him what was going on. She saw the two policemen with the mark of her sister's gaze on them.

She did not bother with the steps when she made her way down. Instinct told her that she would not find Ria anywhere in the compound. Trying not to look back at the house, she hurried down the bald path towards Kenanga.

She peered into houses and under kolongs, over crude

window stalls and into houses that had been improvised into shops, later around the newspaper stand located in the village centre. She went up several sets of stairs to several verandas before she slowed down in the courtyard of the final house, staring out at the patchy grass field that stretched to an empty horizon.

All the people were frozen in place, as if they were entities in a photograph. Barani walked back to the village centre where she spun herself round, staring up at the moving roofs and the circling clouds on the sheet of blue. If she shouted, she was sure her voice would echo back and so affirm what she was trying not to see, even though every shadowy interior of every home, every open veranda, every courtyard and kolong told her the same story.

Men and women stared, some surprised, some appearing like they were just looking up to see who was greeting them at the door or the foot of their steps. A woman still held in her hands a long bean stalk she was breaking into smaller pieces for cooking. A man had a chicken ready for slaughter on a large cutting board, the edge of his knife at the edge of its throat. An umbrella still shaded the head of a young woman who had been walking alongside her bare-headed friends.

She found Ria halfway down the single tarred road that ran along a row of ground houses at the eastern edge of the village. She was clomping around on homemade stilts made out of tall milk cans, manoeuvring them with the twine strung through holes punctured into the bottom. Stillness reigned around her, making her movements strange and out of place. She played by herself among children, all stringy in build and uniformly grey from head to toe, and even to the clothes they wore. Some stood watching her as if in amazement and others peered up at her over their shoulders from where they squatted. Those children would never move, would never grow to adulthood. Ria raised her eyes to her sister and even as she smiled at Barani, the cheeriness she had always kept in those eyes was no longer there.

Barani saw what her sister was capable of, but could not comprehend it. She tried to see if the smile held malice, a reason perhaps for turning the villagers to stone, and how, *how* it could have taken place as fast as it did, how Ria had not missed a single person and raised no alarm. Yet, as if her vision had tunnelled, all she could see was a deep regret that could not muster itself into a proper expression. She didn't know if the regret was her sister's or really her own.

Barani bent over and grabbed her sister by the shoulders. She wanted to ask, "Why?" but the word died in her throat and she knew from Ria's steady eyes on her that she was staring. Instead, giving the girl an unrestrained shake, she asked, "Ria, are you mad?"

Even as she asked it, she retracted. Madness? This was not madness. Angry shouting manifested in silenced heartbeats and scrutiny in unseeing stares. The authorities were going to build roads and erect clean housing on the land where Nenek's house stood. This was Ria's way of trying to stop all that.

If Barani did not have snakes that would bite her, if she had real hair, strands of them to pull, she would have pulled them. If she could have just turned anyone in Kenanga to stone, she would have. She had been tempted. Every time she had gone to the inland village on errands, women had moved their children out of her way and men had stared at her openly. As she protected her family's money cent by precious cent, she had been met with derision from those she bargained with for home necessities. They said her mother had sinned and sometimes Barani even believed them because she did not know who her mother was.

After Ria, Nenek had been the closest thing she had had to a real family. A few times, wishing to right any sins she might have committed, Barani had asked Nenek if she had ever tried to turn Nenek to stone in a time she could not remember. The old woman's reply was always the same: Have or don't have, not important now.

The fear, the hatred—both hers and those of the villagers; the responsibilities of dealing with the world they knew and the one that was fast approaching from newspaper pictures—the riots and the roads, the tall buildings in close proximity: these were the things Barani wanted to protect Ria from. When Nenek was alive, she had reminded Barani over and over that she was to be a good influence on the much younger girl. Nenek had revealed once, over the pounding of chilli and shrimp paste in a mortar, that under that vexing, scrappy exterior was a little girl who thought the world of Barani.

Barani wanted Ria to always remain the same—always with her eyes big and innocent, always to make epok-epoks too big even though she'd been shown countless times how to make them the right size, and always to be frightened of the dusk because of the tales they told her about the jungle people.

Perhaps Nenek had seen what Ria could become, what

she could do. Like an omen, a single chilli seed had jumped from under the pestle into Barani's right eye. It burned, and Barani, hissing, "Ah, it hurts! It hurts!" groped for some water to wash her eye with and the conversation was pursued no further.

In the present, months after that conversation, Barani looked down into the eyes that peered up at her. She saw tears welling in them. She thought she heard a tin plate drop and drum its spinning rhythm on the floor of the distant house, before Ria heaved in a deep breath and let her eyes dart around her. Barani, too, let her eyes wander; taking in the stone forms of what was once alive. She often wondered what kind of curse was placed on their ancient predecessor, so that their eyes could make still what moved, immortalise what aged, and—she turned to look at Ria again—blind what once could see?

Ria was distraught. Barani, while groping for a way to comfort her, suddenly remembered the men who were still at their house. They would have found the petrified policemen by now. There was little time. She could only think to get Ria away.

Nenek had once told her that if anything went wrong, she was to take Ria to the old, abandoned quarry. Nenek never gave further explanations, only mentioned an old Tuyunri tribe still living within its depths and that she was to look for a door. "Humans can be an unobservant bunch. They won't find you there." And she would fold the betel nut into a single sireh leaf before popping it into her mouth, then say nothing more.

Barani took hold of Ria's small hand and with a gentle

tug got her down from her tin-can stilts. She'd just turned around to go back up the path to their home when the rest of the men rounded the bend and ran towards them.

"Kakak..." she heard Ria say fearfully.

Barani kept Ria behind her as the men came to a halt at the sight of the stone children, Abang at the head beside the one remaining policeman.

"Ani!" Abang cried out, turning horrified eyes to her. "What—"

He cut himself short when he spotted Ria. The horror became mixed with fear and as a policeman reached for his holster, Barani heard Abang say, "What? No—"

At the first silver flash of the revolver, Barani struck. All who looked at her—all the men who'd come to her house—greyed over instantly.

She noticed that the stone forms she'd created were a few shades darker than Ria's. She might have wondered why, but Abang—no, no, this Useless Man—stood before her as a statue. She remembered how in her bright-eyed youth he had promised to find a cure for her "condition"; remembered the way he kept telling her how beautiful she was, though it was with his eyes closed and his sweat-covered body pressing—gyrating—into her. In a flood of sentiment, she raised a hand to touch him but clenched it into a fist just short of his face. She could not afford to cry or to regret what she'd done. Turning back to look at Ria, she noticed her sister's own hand was raised to touch her, and knew like the hand, Ria's expression of alarmed pain was a mirror of her own.

Nelroote

Back at the hut, they packed what little they had into an old suitcase Cikgu had given them right before she left. Ria knew they were criminals now and that they must be gone from the house before more policemen came, so she did everything she was told without the usual arguments. She kept glancing furtively at Barani as they worked. Barani would not look at her after they made for the house and guilt rose in Ria like a putrid stench from a dead animal. She knew it was her fault that Barani had had to turn the Useless Boy to stone, her fault that they were running around the house grabbing clothes and what few belongings they had, and prying off the floorboard in the corner of the kitchen to take the emergency money kept hidden in the nook. But every time she tried to apologise, the words found no way of expressing themselves to Barani's averted face.

The heavy suitcase held everything they needed to bring. Ria had some books that Cikgu had given her for the day she would be able to read books without pictures. These she wrapped up in her scarf. She held on tight to the bundle as Barani took her free hand and hefted the suitcase. They released all their chickens and chased them around the courtyard until every single one disappeared into the foliage. As they were doing so, Ria looked back at their old home. The door and the single front window formed an eye and a mouth, blindly staring and screaming. She imagined Nenek and Barani breaking long beans on the veranda, and saw an image of herself wheeling a hoop in the courtyard among the chickens, before the house and all its memories disappeared behind a rush of greenery.

∿

It began to rain soon after, which was strange because Ria had not noticed the leadening of the sky or the drenched smell of the air when they made their run. Barani's shawl was soaked through as the downpour intensified to the point that even the canopy above failed to shelter them. Ria worried more for the books than where they were going.

Barani kept walking at a hurried pace, around buttress roots and over leaf litter, holding Ria tightly by the hand. Gritty wetness got in between Ria's toes and her blue-and-white slippers were slick underneath her feet. Already two sizes too big for her, they threatened to slip off with every rain-heavy step. But Barani kept going as if pursued by hunters with guns and spears, even though Ria knew it would be some time before anyone discovered their house.

Ria tried to say something, but Barani appeared not to hear. Not in the rain, the persistent falling of which drowned out all sounds of the forest. Even if Barani did hear, Ria doubted that her sister would slow down in her search for refuge—for it had to be refuge, for her, for Ria, for people like them whom the world did not want to see. Ria expected that their refuge would be on an island they would swim or take a boat to, and that they would eventually come to a river or a coast. Ria didn't know how to swim but an island would be safe. An island surrounded by blue water, with no road or bridge to the mainland, would be very safe.

Much to her disappointment, however, it was no river or coast that they came to, and there was no boat to take them anywhere either. Instead they found themselves staring down a slope covered in ferns. Below them, level ground had been stripped to reveal red earth turned to mud by the downpour. A sort of vehicle, with a giant rolling pin attached to it, stood near a mound covered in blue-and-white striped canvas. Across the red ravine was another forest, like a distant island behind a rain-streaked blur. Across a stretch of redness, it looked isolated and foreign—safe beneath a barren sky.

Barani had her face partly hidden by her shawl, so drenched now that Ria could see the brown and black of her snakes and their individual long, sluggish bodies moving through the already pale material. Barani turned around and tugged at Ria to follow. Which she did, glancing over her shoulder at the yawning red earth, wondering what was going to be buried down there. What creature could be so big that it required such a massive grave?

In time, they came to a rusty rock face, looming huge over them, higher than even the tallest trees. Barani was always sure of things where Ria only had maybes. However, as Ria looked up uncertainly at her sister, she saw Barani scrutinising it, as if searching for some answer, some message written on its immense face.

Barani was soon muttering, "I see it. I see it. It's here but...how—"

Ria was about to ask her what it was that she saw—just so she could help see too—when a tall rushing mass of dark green came at them from behind some foliage by the rock. Ria started and grabbed a fistful of her sister's baju as Barani pushed Ria behind her. The mass came to a surprised halt and Ria saw that the dark green was in fact a large poncho, the hood drawn so far down that Ria could not see the person's face, and especially not when she was squinting through the deluge streaming over her eyes.

The hood was drawn back, quickly, and the face that appeared was unlike any that Ria had ever seen. It was not Human. If a strand of her hair dyed itself a dark red, grew larger and then grew arms and feet, it might begin to resemble the person standing before them, frowning down at them (if the scaly, low-lidded expression could be called frowning). Even Barani was staring, and she had seen people like this at the coastal village where she had her market stall. The immense amber eyes with their thin convex pupils were focused on the sisters, taking in their every feature. It was a large, strong-looking creature, more dragon- than serpent-like now that she had a closer look. The poncho fell to knees that jutted out at an odd angle, so that the calves appeared elongated, curving backwards away from the body and going down to rather large feet with only three clawed toes on each, and spurs where the heels ought to be.

The Scerean said: "Uh…" Ria jumped at the low voice, male. There was a pause and then he started to speak in a mix of Ro' 'dal and Sce' 'dal, his eyes darting from Barani to Ria and then back to Barani. "It's…what eh?"—he pointed up towards the canopy. "Raining. You no bring…umbrella?"

He spoke slowly, pronouncing the Ro' 'dal words with difficulty, his expression growing more vicious as he went. Ria saw Barani glance down at her before turning back to the strange-looking man. "Don't have," she began in Sce' 'dal, and then asked, "Can I ask if you know… is… is this the quarry…"

It was the first time that Barani seemed uncertain of which 'dal, or tongue, to speak—was it Ro', the new common tongue created by the large Human towns, or Sce', the one from neighbouring Su(ma) and F'herak, which was spoken in most villages. Ria thought the answer was obvious, but perhaps the Scereans Barani encountered at the coast spoke something else entirely—on a rare chance, Tuyunri, and if that was so, Ria was sure she could be of some use. A simple "*bcur'in*", which meant "Day above", or the Tuyunri equivalent of "Hello". It was one of the first words she'd learnt from Cikgu and surely a word of importance.

She tried to muster up the courage to speak when the man gestured a thumb behind him and replied, "Gate…uh… wait, sorry. Uh…wait."

He loped back to where he'd first emerged and was about to disappear through the foliage when he executed a sharp about turn and rushed back to where they awkwardly stood.

He removed his poncho and handed it to Ria with a "Nah" before loping away and disappearing through the plants.

Ria thought he had a funny way of moving and started to snicker.

"Hoi!" Barani hissed, nudging her hard. Silencing any arguments from the younger girl with a warning finger and a stern look, she took the poncho from Ria and drew it over the younger girl's head, bringing the hood down to cover the limp snakes. The poncho nearly reached the ground and was so big it made her feel somewhat smothered. The large hood had a strong plastic smell and was so enclosed around her head that the sound of rain pattering down on it seemed magnified.

The strange man emerged from the foliage and motioned for them to approach. As they did, he indicated the gap he was holding open for them in the plants. The small entrance yawned into an abyss, dark and seemingly impenetrable. Ria regarded it gingerly as she peered in to see if there was any light. Back when she lived in the hut, she was always home before twilight descended and everything became silhouettes against the gradient of indigo to orange sky. When she had to wash her feet before bed, she always got Barani to go down with her and while Barani was washing her own feet, Ria would sprint up the steps and into the house to be on her sleeping mat beside Nenek before Barani came back in. Barani used to say, as she extinguished the lamp, "So naughty and yet so scared," as if it was a common rule that naughty children shouldn't be afraid.

The man plunged into the darkness. Barani hesitated and then followed suit with Ria in tow. Ria did not want to think about what might reach out and grab her in the dark. Tightening her grip on Barani's hand and on the books in her shawl, she let herself be led inside, scraping elbows and shoulders against the rough walls of the crude corridors.

∿

The strange man introduced himself as Acra. He had been a little boy when his family was evicted from one of the villages near the west coast. Ria listened as he explained what it was like before something called a "house in skim" was put in place. ("Skim" is what, Ria also don't know.) Gavermen could pretty much do whatever they wanted to poor folk who only wanted to catch fish and crabs for a living. Unable to afford a place in the city, his family had finally settled underground in Nelroote. He spoke mostly to Barani, although he would caper around Ria, smiling down at her when there was light in the tunnels and even once asked what was in her bundle: "Inside got gold, is it?" In other circumstances, she might have disliked him, but he was helping them and had lent her his poncho. So while his question made her hug the books tighter to her, his antics made her smile back.

Nelroote was at first only a strip of light at the end of an immense tunnel of smooth walls and shadowed enclaves full of occupants she couldn't see. The end was blocked by a solid gate that didn't quite fit the tunnel's width, so light seeped out from the sides without hinges.

As they approached, cold and practically blind, they saw two dark forms attached to necks and shoulders, rising above the top of the gate. A voice called down to them but they could only gape up at the sheer size of the tunnel they were in, and the sheer impossibility of its existence directly under the world they'd known all their young lives.

The voice called again, rough and rumbly, and Acra replied, saying he'd found them outside with nowhere to live.

The two improbable heads disappeared from above the gate and Barani let go of Ria's hand. She dropped to her knees, to Ria's eye level—the first time Barani had looked at her properly since the village. Gripping Ria by the shoulders, she said just loud enough for the younger girl to hear, "Ria, no looking okay?" Ria nodded. *Okay. No looking.*

A creak came from behind Barani and the older girl planted a quick kiss on Ria's forehead, the display of tenderness surprising Ria, before a small door opened, its lit outline growing bigger, momentarily blinding them. Acra stood by the door, watching them. It was only when Barani straightened up to look at him that he motioned for them to enter.

"Not so nice, the place. But this is Nelroote. Uh... welcome," he said, smiling uncertainly.

They were met at the door by the owners of the two improbable heads: another Scerean like Acra, and a fierce-looking Cayanese. Acra introduced them as Mat'ra and Gemir. Ria had thought Acra was a big man, but Mat'ra and Gemir—*especially* Gemir—were even bigger. Mat'ra's snout was shorter than Acra's, almost flat against his face. Ria had learnt from Cikgu that it was a result of time changing the forms of people as bloodlines became increasingly mixed. Mat'ra's scales were a dark green, almost black. Blunt knobs alternated with short spikes down his arms from his shoulders, and he had a cleft at the top of his head that joined to form a ridge which ran along the back of his neck before diminishing into the scales of his body. Gemir looked almost like a man, and his broad nose bridge was scrunched against a wrinkled, leathery face. Coarse, black hair framed his face and covered the rest of him. His brow bones were defined and curved low over his eyes, making him appear as if he were glowering all the time.

Peeking up from under the poncho, she saw that both of the men were shirtless. Mat'ra was even scratching his bare chest as he studied her. Maybe being covered in scales and fur meant they didn't need to wear shirts, Ria thought, and wondered if their women bathed without sarongs out in the open. Ria had the urge to touch Mat'ra, just to see if his rough scales were as dry as the shiny ones on her snakes. He smiled down at her, as if sensing her thoughts, which made her withdraw further into the poncho.

Acra led them towards the settlement. Ria had expected an underground village: familiar houses on familiar bare ground, but with no sky and no guavas growing on trees. They stopped at the top of worn steps cut right into the stone and Ria seized the chance to take a better look at her new surroundings.

The settlement was bigger than Ria had thought. It sat within a great stone bowl with sides that rose up like an arena, surrounded within the cave by natural pillars of joining stalagmites and stalactites. She could not spot the point of a roof anywhere, just stretches of dirty grey walls; the reds, blues and greens of painted, corrugated metal; and tarp covers radiating out from an obscured centre. The homes made of these walls did not seem to have been built according to any design or with any planning in mind. They seemed to have begun as boxes, some alone on ground level, others stacked up to three storeys high, and all pressed into each other so closely that one could stretch out from the window of one's own home and pick food off the table next door.

Around these basic structures the residents had built shacks, extra rooms and fences using bits of spare materials, more often improvising one item for another—such as a door turned sideways made into a low wall, and supplemented with wooden beams that supported a roof made out of tarp, so that a sort of veranda was formed. The extra bits climbed and snaked around each other, merging in some parts, and only accessible on others by rickety staircases and makeshift ladders. Manoeuvring individual clusters of homes was akin to scaling a vertical maze. Between them were narrow alleys either of rocky ground or furrows for drainage, some of which were wide enough to need bridges of plywood boards at intervals. The compact city of dwellings possessed no discernible beginning or end, no distinguishable boundaries. Ria wondered if finding her way around was the same as moving through a jungle—finding landmarks in unusual trees, or tracing the paths in disturbed vegetation. There was no sky to navigate with, to guess at time, and yet everything was also visible. Ria squinted up at the too-bright bursts of white light.

"Generator," she heard someone say in a deep rumble—one of the voices from before. She turned to see Gemir studying her, his arms crossed over his chest and his lips curled up in amusement. He pointed up and added, "From outdoor one, the lights. Same like in stadiums."

She wondered how they had got the lights up and if they switched them off at night, but didn't feel it was the right time to ask. Gemir tilted his head and looked at her, as if waiting, but she turned away to study the massive cave within which the tin-can city existed.

She had expected there to be echoes, sounds of people—living—bouncing off the walls to create a constant buzz with a cacophony of sounds. However, the city was quiet. Every now and then chatter could be heard, growing and then diminishing as if only in passing. She thought she could hear oil sizzling from one of the nearby homes and instinctively lifted her nose to smell what was being cooked.

Within her line of sight in the far distance, three statues loomed in arched enclaves cut into the rock high above the settlement. She could clearly see the silent women in ankle-gracing dresses that began at the tops of their breasts. Each curvaceous figure, right up to their tall, ornate crowns, stood taller than the average tree she had climbed. The statues did not appear to be carved into the rock itself and the material they were made from did not look like it was local to the cave. She could not fathom how the people who'd shaped them had managed to haul them up so high. Each serene face was tilted down towards the settlement as if in fond consideration, undisturbed by the messy and ugly creature of a city that lay below their beautiful forms.

Ria wanted to hold up a snakehead against one of the faces. Perspective would make the snakehead large and she would press the corners of its mouth to make it gape. Then she would release her hold so that the jaws would come snapping down.

As if sensing the thought, her hair began to shift beneath their cover, as if just waking. It was then that she realised that Acra had been watching her from two steps down, smiling as he did. He beckoned to her when she looked at him. Mat'ra and Gemir were already making their way down, Mat'ra looking back every now and then while his companion walked on in a hulking, lazy gait. Ria saw that while Mat'ra's legs looked like Acra's, Gemir's did not.

Barani stood near her. When Ria turned to her, Barani placed a hand lightly on her shoulder and with a nod, urged her to follow. At the bottom of the steps, Ria saw more people with varying degrees of un-Human features. Barani stepped up to them, effectively positioning herself in front of Ria. Ria peered around her sister. There were other children, some very Human-looking, others less so. One end of a skipping rope was in the hand of a Feleenese girl; small like Ria, but in a prettier dress. The rest of the rope lay curled on the floor beside her partner, a slightly older Cayanese girl. A few boys had pockets bulging with marbles and another was holding on to an ice-cream stick gun loaded with rubber-band bullets. Looking up, she saw her sister staring down at her, fear and warning in her violet eyes. Ria dropped her gaze to the stone floor where it was safe.

She thought the silence was going to go on forever and that this was where she was going to be scolded and punished, but Acra was suddenly kneeling in front of her. He peered sideways at Barani before focusing both eyes on Ria and complimenting, "Your Adik is very pretty, eh?" Ria felt Barani stiffen before she came between them. Tugging at the back of Barani's baju, Ria tried to say, *No, Kakak, no.*

Not him. Not them.

Not you, too.

Barani let her shawl drop to her shoulders. Ria pressed her eyes shut, imagining the worst, only to hear Barani, facing all the people who stared at her with a new look of shock, ask for a place to stay and tell them that she would work, any kind of work. Ria expected questions. No one asked a thing.

Ria remembered the books and produced them from under the poncho, unwrapping them from the soggy scarf. They were rain-soaked, the pages already crinkling. At least the linen-bound hardcovers seemed sturdy. She thought they might still fetch a good price.

Just then, the crowd parted and everyone turned to look at a middle-aged man pushing his way through it without hurry. At first glance, his skin seemed to have a rocky texture to it. As he came closer, however, Ria saw that the strange texture was, in fact, formed by a tessellation of diamond-shaped scales, large and visible—not fine like Acra's, Mat'ra's, or her hair's. She remembered seeing a person like him in Kenanga before. Not quite as big, or as kind-looking, but the other person—a man—had had the same rock-like scales, crawling into the face, keeping eyes in sunken hollows with brows resembling hardened geographical ridges above them. The rocky scales extended to his exposed arms and ended at the tips of strangely dexterous though thick-fingered hands. He'd been hunched beside a worn mat, over which was spread a selection of interesting textiles and carved wooden toys, in a lonely corner of the marketplace that she'd had to pass on her way to school. She'd had given him her lunch once—her boiled banana and glutinous rice wrapped in tempeh leaf—thinking he needed it because she never saw him eat anything. He had looked up, had looked so surprised that Ria had to tighten the knot of her scarf just in case he saw. He had smiled, and then Barani came before Ria could ask him questions: *How you make the cloth, pakcik? You make yourself is it? You live where? Are you sick?* From the way no one stopped by his mat and the way they avoided him, she had thought that he must be.

In the present, the same-textured man she would come to know as Pak Arlindi was standing before her, not sick, not hunching. She could guess right away that he was someone important, like a chief. Jerking a chin at Ria he asked Barani, "Is she the same too?"

Barani nodded. She stepped behind Ria and slowly drew back the poncho's hood to reveal their sameness, writhing and looping as if they were excited to be let free. The man swept his eyes over Ria's entire face before taking in the snakes. Ria could feel them acutely on her head, every movement noted and the weight more apparent as if she'd just got them for the first time. There were the compromises of tugs and presses when the snakes were not alarmed or excited, the trails of smooth, slender bodies around her neck and shoulders, and the end of tongues flickering against her skin, tickling her. They fell down in waves, free and uncontrollable. Being what they were, hair and serpents at the same time, made it feel as if everyone's eyes were on them, judging and fearing her because of them.

She wanted to pull the poncho over them again. Maybe she would wear oversized ponchos all her life and be resigned to her ugliness. But the man broke into a smile, one that was sad but understanding, and said, "You are very cute." Ria watched him size her up, unsure of how to react. "But," he added, "you too small size lah. Need to eat more."

A titter ran through the crowd. Barani's smiles had become rare ever since Nenek had fallen ill; the tentative one she wore now was probably the warmest Ria had seen on her sister in a long time.

Nelroote, Ria thought. It was a new way of spelling an old name. It used to be Ne'rut: *ne'*, to, and *rut*, see. Nenek would call the forest the Ne'rut jungle, in memory of the ancient Tuyuns to whom it used to belong. *To see*; even if Ria didn't feel like she'd quite come home, she knew it was the right name for it. And that it was the right place for her sister if she was able to find new reasons to smile within it.

5116 CE

Sketch

The art director called for a time check and was told, "Three-thirty." The photographer directed Eedric to gaze at the red fire extinguisher behind him in the studio space. Eedric focused on it only cursorily while he mentally calculated the amount of time it would take for him to reach the casting later at 4.20. The manager at the agency wanted to write off the casting, deciding that the "timing was too tight" and that this inane magazine Eedric was regularly modelling for was more important than a small, but growing, start-up.

Eedric was not too quick to write it off yet. Not because he had a soft spot for the "small fish in a big motherfucking ocean" type of guys (or that these ones professed more ethical trade practices, because the fuck you think those are real?), but because his greatest folly was that he wanted—and he *believed* that he was able—to do as many things in a day as he possibly could. That he could also do everything right in any one day: ace this photoshoot, then change into his own clothes, sling his sturdy backpack over his shoulder and get to the next casting, *on time*, preferably early, by bus or the CTT, city train—as most efficient urban dwellers do—instead of resorting to the taxi or private hire car service. For the twelfth time that week. And it was not even Friday.

A spot below Eedric's cheekbone itched and he tried to scratch it while the photographer was looking through previous shots in the programme opened on his laptop. He did so subtly and gently, taking care not to upset the foundation that he suspected was the problem in the first place.

The photographer turned back to him, adjusted his camera lens and assured him, "Okay, just a few more shots and I think we're good." Eedric smoothly transitioned into another pose to the snap and whirr of the capturing instrument. He was in a blazer, beneath which he had on a very thin shirt with an extra deep V-neck, so deep that he had to have foundation applied to his chest and "accentuated" by contouring.

With every flicker and whirr, Eedric would change to a slightly different pose, sometimes with artistic direction and sometimes without: tilt head a little further up, down, move to the side; bend arms, cross arms, hands in pockets, hands pretending to adjust sleeves to show off the watch, lean back weight on one foot, lean forward. Shift this here, shift that there.

Change into a different wardrobe a few times.

"Wardrobe" was a rack of clothes just off the white area demarcated for photographing. Two women were stationed as wardrobe assistants, doing the mundane work of steaming and arranging the sets, coming forward with a belt or pins where any were needed. The women themselves were of little consequence to Eedric: fresh tertiary school types, early twenties, in some dress or whatever rag that could pass them off as acolytes of the fashionable and the avant-garde. Which was pretty much every fresh tertiary school type in the country these days. They would not have got his attention. Not a whit, if it had not been for the fact that they had been chatting non-stop since he got there, and as the clock ticked nearer and nearer to the time that he needed to leave, the louder their voices seemed to become.

It was also as if every sound in the space grew increasingly magnified. The responding buzz of every letter that was typed as the art director, leaning now on the table with the laptop and camera lenses, replied to a message on her smartphone. The creak of the photographer's new sneakers as he shifted his weight and position to take the right shots. The rhythmic purring of the cold-as-fuck-Ristrom air-conditioning, just above him, a little past his left ear. The studio walls closing in faster and faster as was what had been muffled became a world of sounds, so unnervingly close, so knife-sharp. There was a buzz, farther out in the mess of cubicles and daily repetition, of voices, phones ringing, fingers typing on keys, people laughing over the coffee machine as the liquid cascaded in a thin stream into a plastic cup that was placed a little off of the circle centre. A car drove away from the pick-up point on a road that was in bad need of re-tarring. And above it all, there were the two girls chatting on and on about a colleague, that shitty service at some vacation and, as it turned out, about him:

"Wow, the model today is a fine piece of…"

"Heard he has a reputation though…"

"Oooh, for what?"

"Bad temper. A bit weird, I heard."

"But he looks all right leh—"

The blood started to pump in his ears as his heart rate accelerated. The photographer was snapping his fingers now—*focus, Eedric, focus. No, no, you're frowning too much. Smile lah, brother, smile.* And there was only that low growling, growing in his throat, emanating from somewhere deep within him. There was a tightness around his face and he knew it was not very much longer before things—no, before *he* was going to be a problem. He bit at the inside of his bottom lip, as if the pain was ever going to help if he did not get to his suppressant medication before he—

"Okay, I think that is enough shots for the spread." The art director's words could not have been spoken by a better angel. She still gave him that wary eye as she and the photographer concluded the shoot with a few quick scans of the photos that had been taken, but at least she knew when they had to stop. Eedric went over to the wardrobe rack, shrugging out of the blazer as he did. The girl he handed it to gazed up at him, fluttering her lashes and smiling, as if that was going to make her endearing. Her shirt was sheer and underneath it she had on a lacy black bra. He tore his eyes away, peeled his shirt off with the swiftness of someone whose clothes were burning him up and, after throwing on the T-shirt he had on when he came in and removing the eyeliner and foundation with the make-up wipes that the other assistant handed to him, he was off. 3.55pm. He was going to need a cab.

The studio shared the glossy Abbett Kros Building with other companies and magazine titles, and the building itself was situated on the outskirts of Manticura's financial district. One would think that a cab would be a common sight in an area of busy people and no sit-down restaurants or cafés, but Eedric could not see any on the roads. He waited, peering up and down the street, until the anxiety and the anger from the waiting and the thrumming in his ears became too much. He pivoted away from the roadside, nearly running into a pedestrian who seemed as much in a rush to get somewhere as he was. Eedric bared his teeth at the man before running off to a narrow side street, not wanting to see the expression on the guy's face—likely one of shock and fear. It would not be the first time. No, no, it would not be the first time.

Eedric ran headlong into the side street and lashed out at the first large rubbish bin he saw. His fist was alien in its largeness as it met and dented the green side of the bin, his fingers elongated into talons and the nails long enough to dig into the skin of his palms. There was a coarse quality to his breathing and he must have rasped a barely discernible curse or two, venting his frustrations on the goddamned marbled wall, before he was calm enough to prop himself up against it, gazing up at the strip of sky between the two high rises he found himself trapped between.

Why does it have to be so bloody blue? He thought that only because he was tired of always asking, *Why the fuck does it keep happening to me?*

It was several determined intakes of breath later before his heart rate was normal again. He took his phone out then, and with a sense of deep shame opened the application to call for a private car service. Something he should have done if he had had any sense of himself at all.

∿

At Sunday family brunch, Eedric felt like an undergraduate in morning lecture again. The words uttered around him meant little as his head and eyes fought off their tired drooping.

His mind drifted. He could be in his room with a tumbler full of coffee finishing that fetch quest in the game he was playing last night, or pushing his Alchemy skill to a hundred and crafting monster sleep poisons with a thousand damage points. His hands felt weighted by the ghost of a console controller. His right leg began shaking to a monotonous hum in his head. And then he stopped himself, remembering where he was.

The doors leading out to the patio of potted bougainvillea and summer lounge chairs were left open, inviting in the heat and still air of the Manticurean dry season. Beyond the glass screen of the dining enclave, the swimming pool glowed in the manicured green like an aurora in the polar night. The ceiling fan spun slowly. A sweat droplet tracked down Eedric's back. Father and Stepmother sat across from him. Beside him, in a pale summer dress, was his girlfriend Adrianne. Conversation was flowing. There were eggs on her plate, sunny side up and sprinkled with pepper.

He took to watching her, this perfect, airbrushed creature. Her complexion was always even and her high cheekbones tinged with pink. No stains on her teacup. Eedric swore her lipstick was tattooed on. Her gossamer hair, which had been recently curled, was pulled back from her face and held by a bejewelled barrette. Her nose continued to remain matte. But she glowed. His eyes drifted back to the pool, face constricting. Eedric was sure that her glow had UV radiation.

"It's very nice outside, isn't it, Jon?" Adrianne asked, turning to him.

Eedric's infant of a yawn died midway in his throat. He had been rocking his chair on its two back legs. His mouth snapped closed and he lurched forward, bringing the levitating front legs down hard on the carpeted floor.

"Yeah," he replied as he straightened up in his chair. *Absolutely, whatever you say.*

He glanced across the table to meet Stepmother's severely lined, staring eyes, and wondered at their colour: burning like the sky on a scorching day, and always staring, always reprimanding.

"What do you plan on doing today, Jonathan?"

Eedric turned to Father, whose own eyes were onyx set in a tanned face creasing into itself.

Father had a way of asking questions so that whatever you replied with meant you were still screwed anyway. "You have homework, Jonathan?" simply meant, "Yes? Let me see you try something harder, something other kids couldn't do," or, "No? No homework? Then there's time for extra tuition sessions or piano lessons, isn't there?"

Father was pedantic about private tutors being only elite university scholars Eedric saw more of than family. And despite the music school graduates being from fancy countries, Eedric continued to play the piano and the violin as if he had Tuyun fingers. Or so Father liked to say.

"It's a Sunday," Eedric pointed out, "so, nothing much."

As if obligated, he added, "Job interview, though. Tomorrow."

He waited for a scoffing exhale of breath from the older man, but Father only nodded behind his cup of coffee, staring into it as he drank. Eedric turned his own eyes away once again, and saw a couple passing through the narrow back gate of the estate. Their brown-and-blue striped su(ma) roc, the semi-amphibious marshland sub-species of the loyal pet, paused to sniff at the hinges. The roc's shorter back legs made it appear squat and its spiked, dorsal fin was drooping to the side, the tips almost touching the animal's body. Its tongue lolled out from a face flattened from years of artificial selection. Eedric wondered what the owners were thinking walking a su(ma) roc in this weather. The animal should be in an indoor habitat, soaking in a pool of water with the right amount of minerals mixed in for it to absorb through its skin. The man tugged at the leash. The roc fought against the tug, continuing to sniff at the gate, before relenting. Then the couple and the roc were gone.

Gone to the rocs, that was what Father thought of him. Getting interviewed for jobs that did not involve selling his backside for men's products seemed to be his only real career. And damn, was Eedric a professional.

Eedric knew what it looked like: all the money Father had invested to groom him for elite society thrown out the window by his vanity. He was, in the old man's mind, every bit his Mama's son.

Eedric had had jobs before, common ones peddling insurance to people on the streets, in underground linkways, or as far inside the CTT stations as he could go before the security guards asked him to leave. Out of a hundred in a passing crowd, one would care to stop, and out of a hundred who stopped and gave their contacts at the end of the survey and a hollow speech about the mileage of a savings plan, there was a twenty per cent probability they'd given fake numbers and fake names. By his calculation, less than one per cent were genuinely interested, though to be perfectly honest, he didn't know if it was in the plan or his flirting ass. The rest turned faces away, thrusting their palms out before he could even utter a word of introduction. Most had their eyes fixed to their phone screens or the floor. And Eedric would have to push his face into their personal space just to get a greeting in.

Being ignored was fine. He was getting used to it. Those smart-arsey, hippie types with their guilt-buying anti-capitalist, anti-government tripe? He hated.

Still, he could handle all of that, the lectures, the ignoring, but one woman some months back made him throw in the towel. Maybe he ought to have stopped his approach when he saw the worn hoodie and the hands that were balled into pockets, and the closed way she had walked as if she was a tightly wound cocoon, afraid of contact. Scerean. Then again, maybe he'd been so close to snapping his tether that he couldn't care less about the "warning signs" that his seniors had advised him to watch out and not stop for.

Her name was Arah—funny name—and she earned about a thousand a month, all paychecks combined. Marital status? Married, she'd said. Three children, husband serving time. All of that alone should have been good reasons to smile and wish her a nice day, but she had regarded him with such tired kindness that he'd felt it only right he returned the favour. She answered him simply. No rudeness, no contempt. Her features were pleasant enough, in the characteristic, latter generation Scerean sort of way: dry, army green scales; large eyes, string-and-knot pupils; flattened nostrils attached to the end of a long bridge that stretched from forehead nearly to the chin; permanently pursed dry lips; distinctive brow plates made out of partially overlapping scales; and high, prominent cheekbones. A pale cleft at the top of her head resembled horns and these closed up into blunted knobs down the back of her skull. She was tall, slim and swaybacked from the inverted knees and elongated calves that were throwbacks to the earlier, more dragon-like manifestations of her race. The worn look of her scales made her appear much older than her proclaimed 25 years of age.

She replied to his questions on her saving habits with: "No savings."

"Oh." He could only stand there, clasping his clipboard against his belt buckle. He felt stupid. "You still need savings, though. Just in case," he tried.

She smiled. "Not easy ah."

"I see," he said.

A corner of her lips curled and she regarded him with a brazen head-to-toe sweep. She shook her head and then asked him, "You have a car?"

"Yes."

"My husband, he broke into five cars before they catch him," she revealed. She paused, considered, then gave him a nod. Lightly patting his arms, she told him, "A lot of bad people in the world, son. A lot of poor people too."

He had been the one to turn away first, in pretence of trying to find someone else to survey.

Son, he had thought and almost spat. Always "son"— child and not relation.

∿

Silence had descended on the table. Adrianne lifted her cup to her lips and kept it there for a longer time than anyone needed to take a sip so dainty. Stepmother was doing the same while Father stared out to the pool, his hand fisted at his mouth.

Finally, Eedric sighed and said to Adrianne, "Do you want to go somewhere?"

He pushed his chair back before Adrianne could answer and stretched his hand down to her. Adrianne lowered her cup. Eedric saw her wince when it clinked with the saucer, before she took his hand and stood up, clutching her tiny purse. Her eyes swept over the table apologetically.

"There are Mist sales going on in town," Stepmother said to Adrianne. "Let me know how low the prices are and maybe we can go check it out."

"Of course! Sure!" Adrianne chirped.

Eedric started to walk away just as Father took a stick out of his cigarette case. From behind him came clicks from Father's lighter, followed by a final resounding one when the ornate cap was snapped back into place.

Sounds could well be amplified in the house because everything about it was large, from the rooms to the sofas, as if it was meant for beings larger than the average Human. Eedric could not help but feel as if his every step echoed and his every reach short of touch. He preferred the closeness of Mama's flat where he used to stay on weekends. It was a small flat with only two bedrooms. One Mama shared with his grandmother. The other was for his uncle and doubled as a place to keep the mattress that Eedric slept on when he visited.

He missed staying over, missed even the fawning of his grandmother who never remembered his name, calling him various others like Rudin, Sultan, even Mariani once. He missed the scents of ginger, cinnamon and betel nut that could be detected no matter where in the flat he stood. There was always sound in the apartment even when everyone was asleep, for a radio was kept on to whisper the oldies throughout the day. His uncle was a big, gruff man who had never married. He spoke little, slinking into his room when he returned from his job as a general worker at the hospital, coming out later to watch the nine o'clock news on television. He built gaming computers as a hobby, sometimes for others. On weekends, the sounds of the games he played to try out his systems intermingled with radio songs and busy kitchen sounds. And Mama would sing along to the radio as she worked.

His visits dwindled in the passing years, to the few public holidays and special occasions that Mama's side celebrated until, when he'd completed his degree, they ceased altogether.

They exited through the front door, opened hurriedly for them by the maid. The same maid ran out to open the main gates as Eedric opened the car door and folded himself inside. Once Adrianne was buckled in, he drove out of the lavish neighbourhood, taking speed bumps carelessly and honking at every man, woman and roc in his path. A few kilometres out, the car ran alongside a ground level CTT track where trains shot past them as blurred streaks of red and green, before they became tail-ends that diminished to nothing in the distance, leaving a vacuum in their wakes.

Motherlands

A glance at his watch face: 3.25 in the afternoon, on a Sunday and the final day of the Mist Sales. Of course, he thought with dripping sarcasm, the Covalence Mall was crowded. Most shops were short-staffed, which only meant a lot more freedom to help oneself to the items on the shelves and try them on. Adrianne was keen on bags (like she didn't already have enough), and when she saw one she liked, she would hang it on a shoulder and, before looking in a mirror, ask him, "Is this nice?"

Admittedly, Eedric had never understood women's bags. They lacked functionality: too small, bloody useless *tiny* compartments, and the paradox of black hole bottoms. But he went, "Nice. It suits you." A slogan good for clothes, shoes, bags, watches, jewellery, cosmetics, and even pets if they were meant to be ornamental. If words could manifest in thin air above him in a cartoon speech bubble, he would make a "Nice. It suits you" rubber stamp for it. And he would use it liberally. *Chop chop chop*.

Adrianne was over it, eventually. They crossed the plaza on

the ground floor and exited into the avenue where the heat was a blow after the frigid cold of the air-conditioning. Shopping malls with their office crown tops towered over congested windpipes of roads. Masses of people trundled along the pavements. Buses carried out their faithful commute, brave in the face of sales-grabbing weekend crowds.

At 1.8 metres tall, Eedric stood above the crowd, looming over that sea of people like a god. In one hand he held Adrianne's shopping bags and in the other, her hand, cold and limp.

Leaning in so that she could hear him, he asked, "Where do you want to go next?"

He meant of course, "Can we leave yet?" But Adrianne never got such things.

"I don't know," she replied, shrugging.

Normally, he would have said that he didn't know either and insisted they go with her decision. The pressing crowd, the shop-hopping that had frankly gone on for hours, the feeling that he was never needed for anything truly important: right then, he didn't know which, but one of the above was agitating him, igniting that dreaded feeling of accelerated heartbeats and cold sweat on his brows.

"Okay," he told her, clenching her hand hard.

He steered her around.

"Where are we going?" she asked.

He tilted his head down towards her, keeping his gaze forward.

"Where are we going?" she repeated, louder and closer to his ear.

"I'll take you home," he replied, walking faster.

Adrianne's resistance was weak and he pulled her on to match his speed.

"So fast?"

"It's getting late."

"Late" was relative, but "late" was what it was starting to become right then. And not just because twilight was descending.

There was not a single building in that stretch that did not have any kind of artificial glow, shine or glimmer in the growing dusk. Lights blinked in drops down the face of one building, a large electronic billboard advertised a facial product for fairer Human skin, and the outer walls of Covalence were a mockery of the bioluminescence found in the deep ocean trenches Eedric once had seen in a documentary on the nature channel. Every few metres along the street stood a mobile ice-cream vendor peddling wares from silver-boxed motorcycles under a large red-and-white umbrella.

Eedric wondered how soon the day would come when these men from a fading past would be required to rent booths in neat, contained rows along the walkway. Manticura was, after all, big on the clean-up. So big, the Jankett Town shopping district bore not a single building from before the "Two-Half" of more than forty years ago. There was a monument to that war, a looming stone obelisk carved with names, in the corner where the district turned into Krow City Capital, where all the embassies and government buildings were. No one gave a shit about the monument until Memorial Day, and that was when Manticureans would commemorate the war by taking pictures with it and tagging them with shit captions like, "In honourable memory of our soldiers!"

The real war existed only in the memories of those who lived it: in Mama, who had her father and a brother taken from her, and waited six years for another to come home; in Father, whose memory of the war was locked on the day he had stood in the mangrove thickets of the Anuri'yun, watching Feleenese soldiers who'd served with him desert the 151 and retreat across the straits to Lower F'herak on the dawn of Manticura's fall to the invading Esomiri forces forty-two years ago in 5074.

But survivors did not live to reminisce. They lived, hoping that living would help them forget.

Where there was no recollection, Eedric mused as he reached the road junction and joined a crowd of others waiting to cross, there was no forgetting. There were only the problems of the day, of myopic weeks and narrow months.

Not ten paces from the junction on which Eedric stood, a young woman sat on the bottommost step of another mall, in front of the orange shop windows of luxury stores. Perhaps not even a young woman—a teenage girl. She sat with her legs apart, her tight top pulled over a pregnant belly. She had the coveted delicate features of the Feleenese: nose a dry, pink inverted triangle protruding a little above an equally small, tight mouth. Her fingers tapered into elegant claw-tipped ends that dangled a bottle of cola between her knees, and she was covered in fine ginger down.

There were four others with her: another Feleenese, two Scereans and a shockingly thin Tuyun with scales resembling bark. The Scereans with their full snouts and horns of hard scale were intriguing enough, for pure-blooded Scereans were rare in the fifth millennium, but Eedric found his attention drawn back to the Feleenese girl. She sat a little apart from the group, enshrouded in her own thoughts and impervious to the raucous laughter of the boys. As if sensing him watching her, she turned her eyes to him and met his gaze. There hers remained, hateful and steely. He wondered which one of the boys she belonged to.

Eedric felt a tug on his hand and moved with the surge of people, each one timed by the blinking green man on the other side.

Adrianne kept her eyes firmly forward as she hissed at him to "Stop looking!"

"What?"

It was only when they were safely across the road that she turned to him and said, "Stop being so obvious."

He stared at her. She stared at the group instead. "You know, I believe everyone has a right to live their lives however they choose." Eedric inclined his head mildly, brows already furrowing. Adrianne didn't see as she went on, "But sometimes they just need to work harder. I mean, there are so many programmes out there to help but—"

Eedric's response was a sharp cut: "They?"

Adrianne turned to him, as if surprised. She made a discreet head movement, gesturing towards the previous group; towards a young Feleenese couple, the mother pushing a pram slung over with a bag, the father walking beside her, empty-handed; towards an old Scerean man with a canvas bag reaching into the "cans" recycling bin; rolling her eyes along the planes of them before turning to him.

"Yeah, you know…people—"

People. It was what Adrianne always called them. "People" was what Adrianne, with her pretty face, and her pretty friends, with the pretty nails they had in common, called "people not like them", but like his Mama.

Mama passed away in his first year of junior college. On that day he had kept his head down in the doctor's office, pumping his foot as if he wanted to drill a hole through the floor. He had not wanted to hear but heard enough to know Mama could not be saved. *Human-minora*— "Minor Human": Human in appearance, but with *anir*-tainted blood. Which *anir*, no one had a proper record of. Something extinct, Eedric would guess. Something happily obsolete.

As a *Human-minora*, Mama was part of the "survivalist" sub-group, a layman's term for an extremely rare genetic mutation that caused her to take on this horrific form when her survival called for it. As such, her body had responded to no medication, no chemical cocktail. No amount of specialist care could allay her of her ailments. From where he had sat, hearing the doctor pause every so often in search of the right words to say, Eedric couldn't tell what the real tragedy was: there being no help for Mama's illness or that she was, for all of her Human appearance, something other instead. Looking up at one point, he had seen the doctor glance his way, cautiously, almost knowingly.

Right at that moment, Father had said, "Maybe it is for the best."

Both men had looked right at Eedric then, masks of sadness worn over what truly went on behind their eyes:

mental tabulations of the medical costs for Father, and something unfathomable for the doctor. Eedric had sat, fists criminal and heavy on his thighs, dropping his eyes to fix them on the shiny floor.

"You should go see her," the doctor had told him gently. *Before we pull the plug*, was loud but unspoken. In his mind, he had raised his eyes to meet Father's, loomed over the older man and said with barely controlled force, "Who made you the Divine? Who put you in charge of how and when a person is supposed to die? Mama lives until her time comes."

In reality, Eedric had only shaken his head, taken his bag and left the hospital that day. Without ever seeing Mama before she breathed her last.

She had already been ill when he was in secondary school. Before her illness had taken hold of and wasted her, he would accompany her to her check-ups in his ugly light blue school uniform, holding her hand in the cab. He remembered sitting at the waiting area outside the doctor's office, leg shaking, never really focusing on the homework he had brought with him. Mama had always preferred for him to stay at Father's home to study. When he insisted on coming along, she had conceded but would not allow him to go with her into the consultation room or any of the treatment clinics.

Mama had always come out smiling and was never forthcoming with the news. He had known things were not okay. But he'd never asked. He had not known how.

He last saw her right after he'd completed his first month of junior college. That day he paused at the threshold to the private ward. As if acting upon an instinctive need to avert his eyes from the form on the bed, he took in the artwork on the blue walls, the flowers on the window sill, the personal bathroom with alternating patterned tiles and then the water dispenser with its red and blue taps. He breathed in the smell of medication and disinfectant, heard the sound of the machines before he focused on the bedridden figure as he moved further into the room.

She did not look anything like the Mama he'd known all his life. No heart-shaped face with its impish smile, plump cheeks pushing up dark eyes into crescents. None of that thrill or that gleeful laugh, the sound of which reminded him of desserts thick with coconut milk. Mama used to have wavy hair she kept bobbed and parted so that most of it fell to one side of her face as if she were from an older era—a better era. In the final stage of her illness, she'd lost her luscious tresses, along with all of her indulgent weight.

Her once black eyes were a new pale grey, her pupils constricted to a single point as if they were rejecting the room's brightness. Uncharacteristically pale skin was drawn taut over her emaciated frame and each finger tapered long, ending in dark nails that looked like they had recently been sawn off. Earlier, the nurse had informed him, rather apologetically, that Mama had to be kept sedated because she had been damaging hospital equipment and attacking staff. The nurse had stood between him and the door, her hand gripping the handle as she peered up at him. He had not wanted to believe her, because the Mama he knew would rather be hurt to the point of breaking than hurt anybody else. But he had nodded anyway so that she would let him through.

It was only when Mama turned her head towards him and weakly reached a hand out to him that he approached. Cautiously, he took the seat by her bed. External veins of clear tubes ran along the length of her thin arms which, like her legs, were clamped to the bedframe. He could smell the stench of urine and Eedric eyed Mama's thin hospital gown, feeling a little angry and at the same time uncomfortable, wondering if the shackles were necessary.

"I got you biscuits," he began, doing his best to sound cheerful. To look at her. "I know this ward, so fancy and all, but they won't have this." He held up a tub of cashew nut biscuits.

"Did not want you to see me like this," she rasped.

"Ma..." he tried. When he choked up and couldn't say more, he took her hand, kissed the back of it the way he always did by way of greeting.

She gripped his hand tight, so tight that blood seeped from the entry point of the needle beneath the clear plaster. "You don't become until like this. Don't become like me, adik. Don't." She always called him "adik", even though he had no older siblings.

"Ma, please, you need to rest to get better. Do you want the bed higher?"

Mama shook her head and made some effort to calm her breathing.

"This is what I look like, fighting it, trying to survive..." she said. "Maybe, this is how I will continue to look after I get better. So ugly already."

"Don't say such nonsense, Ma," he scolded, giving the hand he held a light shake. Cocking his head playfully to one side, he added, "You have a beautiful son, and you know what they say: Beautiful sons come from beautiful mothers, right?"

Mama laughed, but that laugh quickly gave over to a bout of dry coughing. The coughing worried him and the sight of the clamps wrenched at his guts, but he braved a smile.

"So sweet ah your mouth…" Mama managed finally. "You must be havoc with the ladies."

"No," he protested.

"As if I don't know… How many love letters you get every day? Tell me, how many?"

"Nobody writes love letters nowadays, Ma. Modern already!"

He continued to playfully deflect her questions about admirers and girlfriends, feeling almost his Mama's boy again, until the door opened and the doctor came in flanked by two male nurses.

Seeing them, Mama whispered, "Go get those girls. Go!"

The heart rate feedback on the monitor began to accelerate, beeping as if it was a time bomb clicking to its peak. Still, he held on, saying, "Are you feeling okay? They are here to give you your medication."

Mama shook her head again, the movement more a tremor at the pivot of a rigid neck. "Every…time…" he heard her say. She sucked in a breath, her body arching off the bed as her veins grew visible beneath pallid skin. She grimaced before her eyes sought his again. "Your father wanted a son. So much. So, I had you…because I thought…that I could keep him. I was wrong. I shouldn't have put you through this."

The doctor was behind him and he could hear one of the nurses telling him that he had to leave. He ignored them. Mama looked as if she was about to burst out of herself, her pupils almost invisible dots in her pale, suddenly stricken eyes.

"Mama, shh," he whispered back, trying his best to sound reassuring. "We will talk later. After you get well."

"I was wrong. Adik, you are worth…" she struggled to speak and smile at him, "a thousand…of your father. And you remember that. Now, go!"

The doctor was by then trying to get a needle into her, feeling along her arm. Eedric felt her let his hand go, so forcibly and the fingers so stiff he swore he heard the bones in them crack.

"Boy, you really must leave," one of the nurses said, practically hauling him out of the chair.

Mama stared at him as he backed away towards the door. For a moment he thought he saw her eyes darken and crescent into Mama's laughing eyes. It was as if he were a little kid again, carrying a square, dinosaur-brand backpack almost larger than himself, feeling morose as he waved from behind the school gate before morning assembly. Only back then, Mama had been smiling, so excitedly it was as if she were the one attending school instead of him.

The moment was soon gone when she let out a cry and her body tried to rise off the bed just as the doctor pierced her skin, and Eedric was bullied out of the room by the nurse.

The bestiality of the cry had shocked him to a standstill just outside the closed door, and the last thing he remembered hearing was the doctor saying angrily, "Damn it! She broke the needle again!"

Mama had fallen into a coma after that. Father married the woman who became Stepmother even before Mama was brain-dead enough for the grave and Eedric ceased to be anyone's "*adik*".

Remembering, he knew he had failed Mama, not simply with his silence, but with the way he'd dashed away through the corridors and distanced himself after, wishing deep down inside for Mama, the Human, back, and the creature she'd become, dead.

Adrianne… Adrianne wouldn't understand. She was one of those types who got boxed into the SPADs, the Specials A-ducation Programme—not a single non-Human within a five-kilometre radius and so special they couldn't spell "education" right—and who thought virtuous honesty was saying things like she would not go to a particular cinema because it had an "*anjing*" (read: Cayanese) smell or that she tried not to buy from a stall if she saw a Scerean tending it because she was worried moulted scales would drop into her food.

Now Adrianne was saying something to him, and yet again on that day, he found himself looking at her. Somewhere along the way, it'd stopped working for him. He didn't hate her. He'd always thought "hate" was an easily recognisable feeling: that it made your chest heave, no different from impassioned love, which was in turn no different from the exhaustion after a good run. Yet, "hate" could well be silent, drawn guitar-string taut and stretched over a wasted land like a streak of sky. Falling out of affection for someone, while not necessarily caused by hate, had the same silence. That guilty, unhappy silence with which one looked down from the precipice at the end of the wasteland traverse.

He dropped her hand. His first thought was to move, keep his long-legged pace all the way to his car, then drive off to the quayside for a drink and a live football telecast. Threads of obligation and guilt bound him to her and he couldn't, *wouldn't*, just leave. Mama thought he was a better man than his father ever was. Between his violent outbursts and his affair, Father had never told Mama when it no longer worked. Perhaps he had been too cowardly, too frightened to say that it was because she was a mutant, a social outcast, like that pregnant Feleenese girl.

Father was, after all, a very proper man.

Eedric looked back at Adrianne.

So was he.

She was standing in the same spot, clutching at her arm as if she'd hurt it. Her long hair hung about her downward tilted head. So he knew something he'd said had upset her.

"Come," he urged her softly but firmly, taking her hand as he made to move. She resisted. He threw his eyes upwards and clenched his jaw. "You know," he began, "your purse *is* in my car. So want to or not, you won't be able to get home without me."

She started to walk, her arms crossed, hands gripping her elbows, refusing to hold the one he offered. From the tight, rigid way she held herself, he knew that she was going to keep her face averted until he apologised. And he knew that by the time he got to the car, he would have.

Blood History

The phone buzzed in his hand while he was scrolling through a daily laughs site. Eedric saw that it was Miz, replying to a text he'd sent an hour ago about meeting up. The response, a terse, "Ah k. Same place," drew the first crack of a smile from Eedric.

Adrianne stirred in the bed beside him. He set his phone silently on the nightstand, all the while glancing over his shoulder at her. Her bare back was to him. She took nearly all of the covers and claimed further territory with her hair. Eedric felt phantom strands of it in his mouth. It was futility itself to try and remove them.

He wondered why he'd even ended up fucking her last night.

Yesterday's ride home after the impromptu shopping trip had been painstakingly slow. Adrianne had kept asking him if everything was okay, if there was something on his mind, or something he would like to talk to her about, if something was going on with work or family. Basically, the questions she always asked, after every fight, every minor disagreement, every show of "attitude problem" on his part.

Cars had been lined up nose to tail and a voice over the radio told him what he already knew about the state of traffic on the expressway. A billboard had blinked "Heavy traffic". In the midst of the congestion, the chasm in the car had been an ocean wide. He'd opened his mouth to say something, but snapped it closed again.

Finally, he had tapped the sides of the steering wheel and said, "Nope, nothing."

Adrianne had stared ahead at the saturation of vehicles, drawing her lips in a tight line before blurting out, "You know, if you don't communicate, how am I supposed to know what to do?"

Eedric had chosen to remain silent and tried to concentrate on the radio. He'd felt the urge to tune in to the oldies Mama used to listen to, but his hands never moved from the steering wheel. He'd felt the burn of Adrianne's eyes, but did not return her gaze. He'd stared at the road instead, working up every coping mechanism he knew to keep his heart rate steady: deep breaths; feeling the seat beneath him, its leathery solidity, the way it cupped his bottom; and saying over and over in his mind, "I'm here. I'm fucking here." Fool! Though it hadn't all worked out so great because he still punched down on the horn to blast it.

None too soon, he'd managed to inch out of the jam and turn into the neighbourhood of semi-detached houses where Adrianne lived. The day had gone dark by then and the narrow road running between the rows of houses was not well-lit. Most houses already had their porch lights on. A roc's muffled bark could be heard as he'd reached her house. Adrianne had not moved from his car; Eedric didn't turn his head.

"I don't know you any more," Adrianne had remarked quietly.

That had drawn him to face her and before he could stop himself: "You knew me?"

Her expression had been one of hurt and shock at first before she demanded, "So what is this? Why are you being like this? Why are you suddenly acting as if—" She'd paused, lined eyes growing teary. "Is this what it is?" Another pause, then sharply, voice a decibel higher: "Who is she, Eedric?"

He'd stared at her, frowning, open-mouthed. "What? There is no one!"

"I know you have been talking to her—my friend from my risk management class."

"Which one?"

From the way Adrianne had looked, he'd known he shouldn't have said that.

"See?" he'd pointed out. "I don't even know who the hell's in your class. So why the hell would I be talking to them?"

"Then what is it? Why are you being so distant?"

That was as much of the argument that he could remember. What had followed was the usual charade of him apologising for "everything"—for "everything" encompassed all that was wrong with his boyfriending. She had resisted as always, holding fort just long enough before opening the doors to end the siege. To let the making-up happen. Then, because she had always enjoyed make-up sex, the fucking—the motions of it blind from repetition.

In bed, Eedric cast another glance at Adrianne before

slipping one foot carefully over the side, and then the other. Aided by the bit of light that managed to illuminate the room through the semi-translucent pink curtains, he found his various articles of clothing: His jeans were hung precisely over the back of her chair. His socks were paired and folded on the table, right beside the blinged-up laptop computer. He found his shirt on a hanger in her walk-in closet. His shoes were in there too, on the bottom row of her shoe cupboard, heels touching and the toes angled away from each other.

As he dressed, he thought—not for the first time—how he had never once heard Adrianne's maid come in to clean the room in the early hours of the day. The maid was a major-blooded South Ceras Scerean; a slight protrusion of nose and jaw, to give the impression of a snout, and she also had a red frill going from the top of her head down the back of her neck, instead of cleft and knobs. Mouth small, eyes huge and always glazed. Her movements were fast and, as he'd come to know, deathly quiet.

He had his socks on and shoes in hand when he considered Adrianne again, recalling the routine sex with what he could only describe as a profound sense of regret.

He was weighing the repercussions of simply leaving without letting her know, when Adrianne roused.

She lifted her body a little off the bed and turned to look at his side of it. Finding it empty, she turned full on her back. The cover slipped a little down her body, exposing her breasts.

"Sorry, Miz wanted to meet," Eedric explained before she could ask.

Then there it was: the slight furrowing of shapely brows. Sometimes he had to remember that she didn't get along with Miz.

"I have class later at eleven," Adrianne replied. "I thought you would give me a ride."

Eleven was the time he was hoping he could meet Miz. It was already about ten. He was badly in need of a shower.

"If you have to meet your friend," Adrianne continued after a beat, "it's okay. I can go myself."

AdrianneSpeak translation: Warning! It's not.

"No," Eedric assured her quickly. "It's okay."—*EedricSpeak: It's not*—"I have time to drive you over first." He didn't.

Adrianne settled back into bed, not in the centre of it as if she was going to sleep, but on her side of it. She kept her eyes on him, smiled a little.

"You wash up and get ready. I'll see you downstairs," he told her. And then he left, letting the door slam a little behind him.

He met the assassin-footed maid partway down the stairs. He nodded a greeting to her, not meeting her eyes, and kept on walking. Adrianne's mother was doing workouts to a video in the recreation room. There should have been a law against mothers in yoga pants. The woman was doing the backward dog, ass and hint of camel toe pointed to the hallway. He *had* to stare.

She must have sensed him there because she turned. "Is my princess still sleeping upstairs?" she asked.

"No, getting ready," he replied and then excused himself saying he had to check on the car.

Walking out, he reached into his back pocket out of a

force of forgotten habit. He didn't find his cigarettes, and only belatedly remembered that he'd given up smoking a long time ago.

∿

Miz's latest romance must not have worked out if the Feleenese was smoking like a fiend again. Miz's eyes were also shamelessly resting on womanly bums in barely-there shorts passing outside the small café in the Krow City business district. Eedric watched Miz with amusement, in between letting his own eyes wander. He had known Miz a long time, admired him in fact, for simply being the sort of guy who would help you out of any kind of shit, and then ask you for a light by way of payment.

They'd gone through secondary school and junior college together, and were posted to the same camp in national service, where Miz had had it hard. Heck, somehow Miz managed to have it hard everywhere he went. Miz was always the right man for the job, in places people thought wrong for him: too Feleenese to be treated with equality by the Humans, and too Human in his ways and beliefs for the Feleenese to remember him as a brother.

Initial posting into national service vocations was based on merit and Miz had been an exceptional student back in junior college: football team captain and chess club competitive team member with more than 30 per cent of extra community service hours. Not a student counsellor though. His smoking habit made sure he couldn't make it into that. Or get nominated for the valedictorian scholarship. He had excellent eyesight and reflexes—Feleenese gifts—

and as a boy he had dreamt of one day making it into the armed forces sniper division. Turned out, being able to shoot straighter than Humans in basic training only earned him a badge and a little extra pocket money every month. No one escaped Camp Genealogy: that was what they had both concluded when they were prowling together in the haunted parts of the camp's perimeters. They were "with-distinction" certificate holders with some of the best scores in Physical and Marksman, but where they ended up, they were nothing more than bullet fodder alongside the grade-average Humans.

Eedric could write up long complaints, tell anyone who would listen that, "Hey! I am oppressed too! Because my mama's *minora* blood runs in me. Because I went through test after test prior to entering service and none of the doctors would show the reports to me. They said I was fine and that there was nothing to be particularly concerned about." But whatever was written in those reports had made sure he got a shitty posting. It made sure that he had to undergo a psychometric test at the end of every month and be prescribed medication—for "hormonal stability", "stress regulators" to help with "blood control", to "suppress adrenaline over-production"—which he never took beyond a month of their renewed prescriptions because they always made him feel like shit.

But he was still not a Feleenese in a camp full of Humans who thought he was some kind of punching bag, a novelty cap they could wear for street cred. He was not the one who got stripped and drenched before being locked in a room with the air-conditioning on at full-blast by a whole lot of them who thought such initiation rites were funny, even manly.

Still, he had to hand it to Miz. Where any man would have died of hypothermia—and one guy *had* died—Miz had marched back without a hint of a shiver. Eedric remembered what it had been like at the bunks when Miz came back, the way no one had said a word as Miz dried himself off and then got dressed just in time for morning PT.

Most Humans tolerated Miz in the camp; sometimes just barely. A few had asked, "Why put him with us?" There were other camps that had a lot of his kind, probably set up just for them too. Eedric supposed the "Feleenese Retreat" of 5074 didn't engender much trust for the kind.

The official books skipped the part of history where the Feleenese had laid down mines in the swamps, drawn enemy forces into them with their retreat, and for the next four years worked out of rebel camps to try and liberate western Manticura from the occupiers.

"They lost more men to their guerrilla operations than the Humans did to open warfare. Capture, torture and execution were in store for them when they were found. And you know what's more? While the pig-fleshed signed the country over to the enemy, Tuyuns continued to fight in the jungles throughout the occupation period. *That* is loyalty to the country, my friends!"—His old secondary school history teacher used to call the students "friends", sometimes "comrades". Eedric frankly didn't know what to make of it, but he had always liked that teacher even if the latter had obvious biases. He was always so animated that not ten minutes into the class, his famous blue-and-white chequered handkerchief would be out and applied to his red, glistening face. The school had replaced him halfway through the year with someone whose dogma constituted model answers and supposedly infallible textbook facts. Eedric couldn't even remember who it was, so he must have been sleeping at his desk through the rest of that semester.

Miz tapped the end of his cigarette against the rim of the ashtray on the table. His coffee was still untouched, the foam still a mushroom cloud above the rim. Eedric was already halfway through his.

"How's work?" Eedric asked.

Miz nodded, but said nothing. Smoke curled upwards and Miz contemplated some distant vision in its tendrils. Eedric leaned back in his chair and waited.

Finally, Miz was done. Stubbing out his cigarette, he asked, "So you and Adrianne?"

Eedric turned away from the particularly pretty girl watching them from behind the counter in the café.

"Eh, same old."

Miz nodded again, even more slowly this time.

The stretch of the quayside street was quiet. Eedric stared at the stretch of canal across from them, at the tourist boats cruising down its length. What was there to see, he wondered. Concrete, stone, the same walking mass-produced statues everywhere.

"I don't know, man," Eedric added after a while, eyes fixed on a distant boat. "I don't feel anything any more."

Miz half shrugged, half nodded. "It's tough, but if you have to end it, you have to end it." The Feleenese leaned forward, took a drink of his coffee, then settled himself back.

Eedric could smell the smoke on him.

"It's just—" Eedric tried. "How? And going back into the dating game is a hassle."

Miz conceded. No words, as was usual.

"But there's just no...depth. No engagement. She's just..." Eedric struggled to find a word. Turning to look Miz squarely, he said with an ironic smile, "She is probably the *first* right thing I'd ever done."

Miz chuckled. "Does she know?"

Eedric shook his head. He fingered Miz's box of cigarettes. Miz eyed him idly.

"I thought you quit?" Miz remarked.

He had. Adrianne didn't like him smoking.

But right then, fuck Adrianne. He knew he already had. He pulled one out for himself and raised his brows at Miz. The other man waved his hand as a "take it" gesture. Eedric lit up using Miz's lighter and took a long, gratuitous drag.

"What are you doing after this?" asked Miz.

Eedric shrugged and let the buzz and haze of the nicotine envelop him as he took a few more drags. They spent the next twenty minutes or so like that, for after Eedric finished his cigarette, Miz started on another. At the end of it, Miz said, "Have to go soon." Jerking a chin in the general direction of Eedric's body, he added, "How're things?"

"Some days okay. Some days bad." Eedric stubbed out his cigarette.

"No sudden changes?"

Eedric shook his head. "So far so good. Off to work?" He meant Miz's shift at the biomedical laboratory where he worked as a research assistant. The head researcher

Miz was working under didn't start work till after two.

Miz gave a nod as he stood. "You?"

"I'm going for a walk. Give myself something to do… Really don't feel like going home, man."

Miz chuckled and stretched out a fist, which Eedric bumped genially.

Forest Trek

Edric found himself in the open-air car park near the visitors centre of the Ne'rut Rainforest Reserve, hands gripping the steering wheel of his car even though he'd already been there for a good twenty minutes. There was no reason for him to be there, no reason to refill the spaces of his childhood memory bank.

Or perhaps every reason to, he thought as he finally switched off the ignition. He stepped out from the enclosed air-conditioned space, into the dense and humid warmth of the vast outside. He had his shades on, but still had to squint when he looked up at the quarry from which the reserve got its name.

The ravaged face of earthy orange-red tinged in grey rose above a lake, which had formed when rainwater and surface run-off filled the gaping hole blasted out by dynamite. It used to be a site for granite quarrying before mining phased out as Manticura plunged into industry about a decade or two before the war. The rock structure, some people said, was older than all of that, though no one could say exactly how old.

While few trees could gain a foothold on the bare rock face, more crowned the top of the quarry, seaming effortlessly into the surrounding jungle. The largest of Manticura's remaining pockets of rainforest, the nature reserve flanked an entire stretch of expressway and two housing estates. There had been plans once to take down a part of the massive quarry—the only major natural landmark the country had, really—to make way for an expressway expansion. Some people had protested. Others had just thought it was an inevitability and never broke out of their routine. Somehow, however, other sectors of the government had shot down the idea and declared the site a protected area. Strictly off-limits. No discussions were opened after that; no press releases, no newspaper or blog articles; no news, as if the matter had dropped out of existence completely. It was a silence so complete, no one else made a sound after that, not even the loudest, most questioning of the country's dissident voices.

Eedric crossed the near-empty visitors centre to get into the reserve, which began, apparently, with a manicured lawn. The lawn was almost bare save for a few thin trees that grew along the tarmac path. The trace smell of cut grass preceded clipped-off blades sprawled over the walkway.

It was an odd place to be in. And for *him* to be in. If he'd been seeking answers or some kind of atonement, it would have made more sense to visit Mama's grave, put flowers on it and apologise for what he had failed to do for her. But he couldn't get over the fact that the grave was just a filled-up hole in the ground, hiding bones, empty of spirit.

He remembered the burial: how so few had been present because Mama's family was estranged from its extended one and Father's had never really approved of her. The graveyard was a stretching field of tombstones. The well-to-do had mausoleums of marble walls and the others, the ones who would be forgotten, lay beneath a nondescript cover of earth. Mama did not have a marble wall. The only way he knew which square metre of dirt had Mama was by looking at the name on the stone slab that marked it. And even then, Mama wasn't there. Not for him.

The important memories were the shiny shards in the ash piles of past events. A shiny shard must be what had pulled him to the rainforest reserve. When Mama was alive, there had been no path, no manicured lawn. The height of the grass had nearly reached his chest at the time. The visitors centre and the car park had not existed either. On the Sundays when Father was away, Mama would bring him to that same spot. They would spread a woven mat, flattening the tall grass underneath them to picnic. Mama would make pastries filled with spicy, mashed sardines, which went down well with cold milk tea. Encased in the tall fur-tipped grass, she would read while he pretended to be an adventurer, a pirate swimming in a sea of sharks. When he was tired, he napped.

It had been a place far away from the world filled with school, grades, the perfect sonata at the fingertips.

The tarmac path led right into the reserve's rainforest and he kept on walking until the warm afternoon gave way to a shadow-dappled cool. Deeper into the nature reserve the buzz of the main road lost its hold, giving way to forest sounds older than his memory: the wind rustling leaves, cicada calls and bird songs. The drain that ran along the edges of the path was covered in moss. Saplings had pushed through the worn bricks, and the tarmac was cracked and uneven in those places where the tree roots pushed up against it.

The ground sloped up to one side of him and he found himself stopping to stare deeper into that part of the forest. He knew a lot of people who would not set foot into a jungle for the supposed snakes, spiders, monkeys that would claw at your face, and homeless people high on illegal drugs. But not Mama. After their picnics Mama liked to bring him jungle exploring. She would hold his hand as he stepped over roots and showed him which leaves not to touch because they would give him rashes. The only time she had scolded him was to hit his hand when he had tried to destroy a cobweb: "Adik, when you have a house, do you want other people to step on it?" Her rule always was: When people don't do anything wrong to you, you don't do anything wrong to them. Kindness. Acceptance. The Sce' 'dal word: *Sabar*. Patience.

Eedric remembered that Mama could point out where clearings had existed back in her kampong years, before the park management had the areas replanted. She told him stories of who used to live where, what animals they kept and what crops they grew and what they were like down to an odd eye or a stump where an arm ought to be. He remembered the jungle fowl and the way they had run, chicken butts waving, into the undergrowth where they disappeared. He remembered looking up from watching them one day to see the rock wall of the quarry, and wondering if it was really a mountain and if everything people said about Manticura possessing no mountains was in fact untrue. After all, where "jungle met rock" was a part of the jungle that no one dared to go to. Mama and he had never ventured so deep in themselves. It was a supposed burial ground, guarded by beautiful spirits with hair that grew in coils down to their waists. When they were near, flowers of the brightest hues and ethereal scents would bloom. They were not to be looked at because they were known to ensnare men, leading them to their deaths.

Father had never tolerated the stories, of course. "You tell the boy such nonsense. What can a man do with fairy tales?" As always, Father was all hard lines and disapproval, dark brows furrowing over equally dark eyes. "You can't eat daydreams," he was always saying. Eedric recalled the family house, the two cars gleaming in the short driveway and the crystal chandelier in the living room that, as a boy, he thought would some day drop on his head and kill him. You couldn't eat those either.

Their arguments had always started with Father saying something like that and Mama replying with something impudent, which would get her into trouble. People always thought husbands only beat up their wives in poor households afflicted with alcoholism and drug use. The kids of these households had attitude problems and were the ones who always got detention and counselling in school. No one imagined a kid like Eedric, in his big, big house, peeking through the banisters on the upper floor, staring down at the doorway into a side chamber, listening to yelling and tearful screaming. No one thought he would be standing in the living room, fire truck forgotten in his hand, hearing "You make me do this!" to the punctuations of slaps and punches. And running into the kitchen, to his mother cowering against the cabinets, face hidden in her hair, arms limp at her sides, and when his father sensed that he was there, turned, saw and pointed him out, heaving: "Look at what you have done to our son!" The slam of the front door never failed to make him flinch.

The aftermath had always been the same: Mama's cooking was not eaten, her skin would be marked by bruises, even cuts, and her personal treasures—her seamstress-made formal wear, jewellery from her parents, her books—would be thrown away. Later he would get a new toy or game from Father, as if Eedric was the one Father had taunted, beaten up or choked, the one he should apologise to and win back. No child could turn down a new toy, but after every fight, after Father left the house, Eedric would go down to where Mama sat with her face buried in a hand and her shoulders shaking. If the collectors had not come for the garbage yet, he would help her dig her things from out of the green bin just outside the main gate. Eedric didn't know how many instances of Mama saying, "I'm making your father's favourite dish" after that before she finally left; how many times Father came home with a gift that he said some Sandra had picked out for Eedric, before it all became too much. Before Mama went to live with Grandma, who called Eedric by other names than his own, and Uncle, who barely spoke more than two words to Eedric during his visits.

Eedric stepped over the little drain that separated path from wilderness and wandered into the jungle, rolling his sleeves down so that he would not brush against any poisonous plants. He also kept an eye out for monkeys.

Proximity between monkeys and people always ended up with someone inciting some kind of anti-primate right of annulment. He had been in a tug-of-war once, with one of the monkeys populating a forest that his estate audaciously grew up against. He had been about ten, on his way home from school, and had a packet of mee goreng and his wallet in a blue market plastic bag. The monkey had wanted his food. Eedric had wanted his wallet and food (it was not every day that he could sneak home greasy hawker fare), so they got into it—monkey and boy—until the bag tore, spilling the packet of mee and his wallet onto the grass by a dilapidated bus stop. The monkey had left the wallet but cradled the packet in one arm and bounded into the forest, tail up in the air, mooning him. After the incident, mee goreng always tasted like defeat to him. Of course, the area had since been built up further and the forest pushed back behind the new houses. So, he got his revenge, though it was not in the form that he would have liked.

Now he trekked through moist undergrowth, feeling for roots beneath the leaf litter. Above him, the leaves and branches grew in a lattice to form an almost complete roof. A few young plants struggled for the sunlight that revealed the silk threads strung between their bows, fine and golden. A yellow butterfly, no bigger than his nose, flitted in the forest quiet. The pink poui was in bloom, the tree tops lush with them, the forest floor carpeted with their wet mush. In one spot it smelled oddly like a dental clinic, the scent coming from some kind of plant or flower.

Along his route-without-destination, a cluster of flowers hung in Eedric's path from the low branch of a tree that was itself growing nearly flush against a species of strangler. He stopped and took hold of one from the cluster. The radiant yellow flower reminded him of a starfish—six petals, long and slim, thinning out to curling points from a triangular centre. The cananga, he remembered it, known for its perfume. The petals had a rubbery resistance to them but with a silky feel, like soft skin. He withdrew his hand and the whole cluster quivered, bobbing at the end of its bent stalk. In time, it stilled, as if his touch was as inconsequential as a passing breeze.

Eedric would have left it at that. A quick glance at his phone showed the time to be a few seconds past 3.30, nearly time to meet Adrianne after she was done with her classes for the day. They would have dinner somewhere and then it was back to her place. But he looked up and saw how the quarry loomed, seemingly five paces from where he stood. There was a magnetism to it he could not quite put a finger on. Old and prominent as it was, it yet stood, completely isolated and untouched by ever-correcting hands, in Manticura where everything needed to have some form of economic value.

Or perhaps, he thought, not yet.

He took a few steps towards it and then stopped to check the time, to see if he had time to go just a little further in and sate a trivial curiosity he'd always had about the reserve's quarry: if there was a moat of water surrounding the side of it that faced away from the lake. To keep the visitors off. No one seemed to have got close.

Eedric kept the quarry in sight as he picked his way deeper in. There came a point when he could not look up at the top of the quarry without straining his neck. He had never realised it was so tall. There was omniscience to it, as if it watched his every step, both beckoning towards him and warning him away. The vegetation grew thicker the nearer he got to the quarry, before it thinned out again, and Eedric realised that he was no longer stepping through undergrowth or ducking under the occasional slim branch. He lifted his eyes from the ground to see the cascading leaf cover that grew against the reserve's quarry just a few metres ahead of him. He was in a clear space, roughly the shape of a semicircle, fenced in by vegetation that shied away from the quarry even as it created an arching roof to shield the space from sunlight. For a moment he was impressed with himself. To have walked to that spot where "jungle met rock" without any dire encounters: he doubted anyone had ever gone so far into this spot of forgotten legends.

No moat, he thought, feeling a little foolish, *okay*.

He was about to turn, thinking it best to make for the trails again and re-enter the civilised world with all its civilised concerns, when a break in the leaf curtain caught his eye. Vegetation on the quarry's rock face was understandably sparse, with most plants unable to gain foothold given the bare rock face and Manticura's monsoons. The leaf curtain seemed almost deliberate in the way it fell over a single spot and the shadow between the strands seemed far too dark to be rock. When he came in closer, he could hear a hollow humming and feel the briefest touch of moving air.

He reached out, slowly parted the curtain, and found himself looking through a small doorway that led into darkness.

He considered it, and then without knowing fully why,

he called out a cautious "Hello?" into it.

He waited. No one called back and he guessed that was a good thing.

He peered further in, even squinted a little as he tried to make something out—a light, perhaps, or an object, a person. Or something else if he was having the worst of it that day. Nothing looked back. There was only the muted, blind sheet of black.

Drawing the leaf curtain apart a little more gave him enough light to see the rusted remains of hinges, which suggested not only the presence of a door or a gate in the past, but that the darkness must lead somewhere. He activated the torch light application on his phone and it cast enough of a white glow to allow him to see a few metres in front of him, revealing worn patterns carved into the rock that made up the tunnel's walls.

He allowed himself a brief look over his shoulder, before he ducked past the doorway. The tunnel's low ceiling grazed the back of his head even though he was already hunched over as he moved along. The textured walls scraped at his elbows. He could hear his own breathing loud in his ears and every squeak of his rubber soles against the floor grated at him so much he made a conscious effort to lift his feet more as he walked.

He moved down a gentle decline for what seemed like a long time, when the floor started to grow damp and slippery. The air in the passageway grew cool and the ceiling started to drip. The light from his phone trembled in broken bits on the floor now slick with water.

Eedric continued to follow the tunnel. When he shone

light onto the walls, he saw that they were covered in patterns. Squares of about 30 by 30 centimetres contained the visages of men and women, each formed from the mosaics of smaller geometrical forms. Each of the faces had either mouths or eyes, but never both at once. The mouths were all open, showing teeth, sometimes tusks. There was one he stopped to look at more closely because it was the only one with a tongue. He carefully touched the leering organ that protruded from beneath the sharp teeth of what could only be a Scerean before backing away and moving off. The squares without faces were divided into further squares, and within each of these were symbols that he guessed were the letters of a language that must no longer be spoken in Manticura. He could make nothing out, except that the ruins were old and that this wasn't a hoax by some guy in the sewer with the video camera.

The end of the tunnel rounded off into a spiral staircase leading down into an abyss. He peered down at the stone steps. The idea of long gone people from a past, unrecorded civilisation seemed strange to him and raised goosepimples on his skin. *Other* countries had ancient history. *Other* countries had things like catacombs, mummies and ruins of past grandeur that left the modern viewer in awe as they wandered, "How the hell did they do this without cranes and diamond-edged drills?" But not Manticura. Manticura was supposed to be all skyscrapers, digital and new-everything. There wasn't even an old can to kick on the streets, and graffiti would get you fined for more than you had in your bank account (and caned too). Manticura was the antithesis of the messy animal that lent the country its name and that guarded the country's coat-of-arms on everyone's birth certificates. No one existed beyond the system. He swore every Manticurean was implanted with a chip at birth. But here he was, in an ancient ruin, wondering if the spiral staircase would lead to a throne room or a burial chamber. Why, even a toilet with an antiquated flushing system would have impressed him, for it was quite possible he'd discovered a part of Manticurean history that had been lost to the country itself. Lost, because had it been known, there would have been a gift shop somewhere and signs—signs for every corridor, electrical outlet… Signs for every sign already on the wall.

His first thought was to turn around. Admittedly, Eedric wasn't a fan of stairwells to nothingness and the only way he would watch a horror film or play a horror game was in the daytime, with the windows open, curtains drawn back and the volume turned down so low that he had to rely on subtitles for dialogue. No headphones, of course.

However, Eedric's plan to bail was staunched by a sudden flare of orange light from the depths. The way it receded into a soft glow called to him, drew him to descend the stone stairs, one cautious step at a time. As he adapted, his footsteps grew quieter, falling softer and softer as he went. There was a growing clarity as he descended. Sounds he could not recognise but were precise in his ears. Then there were the sounds he found he *could* recognise—the drone of the outside world. (He thought he could hear a moving car in search of parking space, the mumble of voices from the hikers and the runners who could be found congregating at the visitors centre in the late afternoon; was it near four already? If so, he was late to pick Adrianne up from campus.

She was going to be pissed.) And above it all was the nesting quiet of the underground.

Lightness came upon his body and his posture felt as if he was hunching over even though the ceiling wasn't low. He saw the long stretch of his legs and the forward thrust of his pelvis. It was an image—a perspective—he had never welcomed because of what he understood he'd become.

The first rush of anxious, frightened thoughts threatened to wash over him in a sudden surge. He was on the brink of being overwhelmed but for the slightest sound, a touch, of a palm to something smooth. Or was it a gentle exhale of breath? He couldn't tell yet. But he was near the foot of the staircase now, so he turned to it and saw the back of a woman's figure paces away in the corridor that stretched out ahead of him. Her right arm was stretched out, her hand within a hollow in the wall of yet another tunnel.

He took a step down and she looked over her shoulder with a startled hiss.

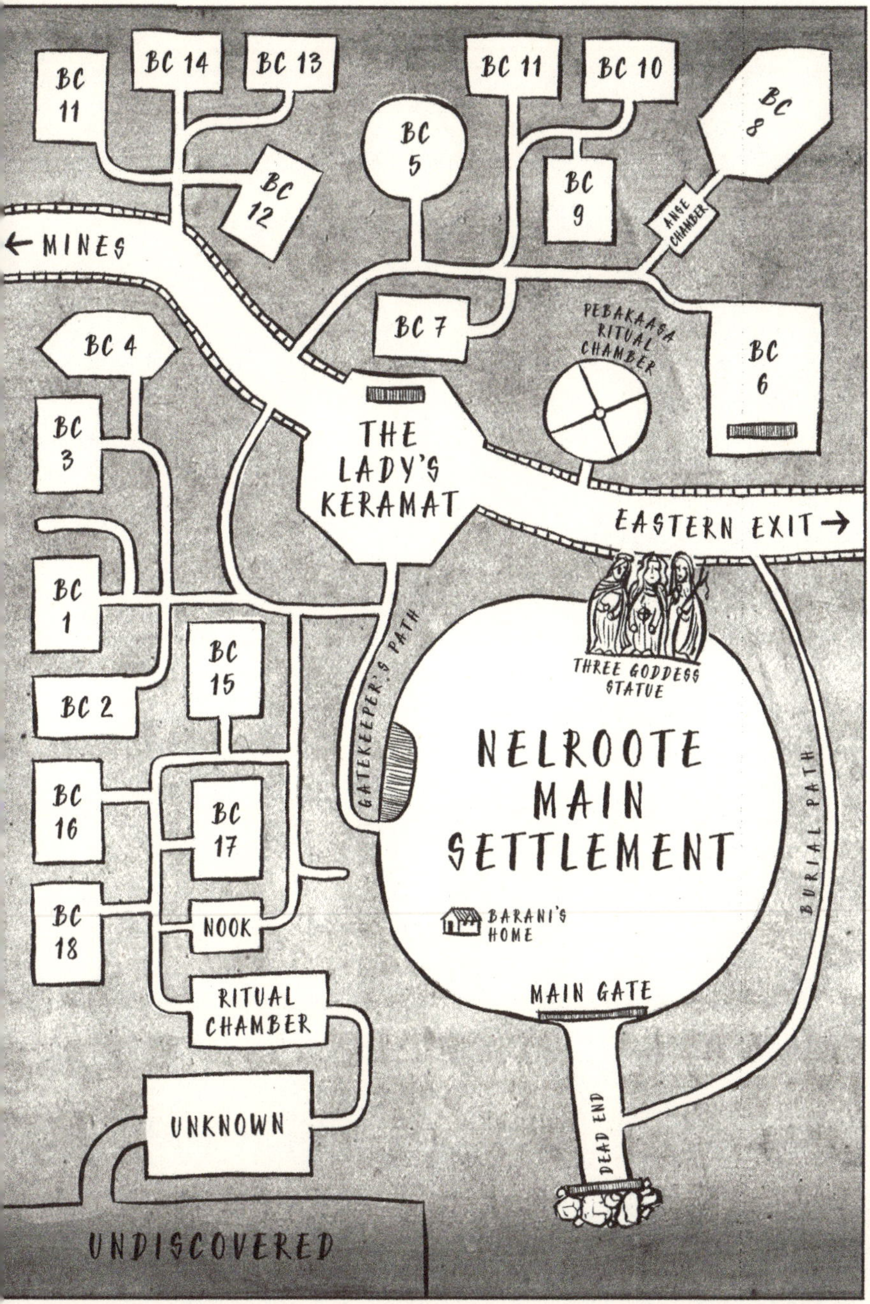
BC 11
BC 14
BC 13
BC 11
BC 10
BC 8
BC 5
BC 12
BC 9
ANGE CHAMBER
← MINES
BC 7
PEBAKAASA RITUAL CHAMBER
BC 4
BC 6
BC 3
THE LADY'S KERAMAT
EASTERN EXIT →
BC 1
GATEKEEPER'S PATH
THREE GODDESS STATUE
BC 15
BC 2
NELROOTE MAIN SETTLEMENT
BC 16
BC 17
BURIAL PATH
BC 18
NOOK
BARANI'S HOME
RITUAL CHAMBER
MAIN GATE
UNKNOWN
DEAD END
UNDISCOVERED

5072-5078 CE

Gatekeeper

The war had burst from pockets of fighting up north in Esomir, diffusing south in scuffles and skirmishes like the toxic gas attack that started it all in one of the countries in the West Continents. It was so close, and yet no one thought it would come to Manticura. There was no conviction at least, but there was the paranoia—in canned food the poor couldn't buy because the shelves had been swept clean of them; in the almost fevered need to stock up on fuel; in the reinforcement of roofs and the marking of windows with crosses of black tape even though underground they were already protected by walls of solid rock.

Barani took to smoking, discarded her kains and bajus for shirts tucked into waist-high denims and mulling endlessly over newspapers as she bit a blood-red bottom lip.

Ria knew hard times were coming when the rice was replaced by tapioca and sweet potato, the lauks dry and rationed—a dried fish a day, only two cloves of garlic, a quarter of an onion to mix in with sambal if there was nothing else to eat. Even before the fighting rolled above them with a shake and a dull roar like distant thunder. When it happened, Ria had been having an argument with Barani about not being allowed to work. Ria thought she could hear children playing deeper in the settlement. It was about three in the afternoon by the clock. The enemy had not even waited for nightfall.

The sisters jerked their heads up, lifting startled gazes to the room's ceiling before Barani had tackled Ria and pressed her down to the floor. Barani's body covered hers and her hands were over Ria's ears. In those first moments of the war's onslaught, it was Ria who froze, her gaze locked with the bit of wall in front of her in the shack behind Pak Arlindi's house that they were occupying at the time.

Later, as the war progressed, and food rations and fuel had to be smuggled in, the black market began its cutthroat trades and, as if everything else had to be shadow-swallowed, the lamps outside were permanently switched off so that travel in the settlement needed to be aided by handheld lights, apertures opened just a slit. Enlistment offices no longer cared what race you were or if your papers were genuine. So long as you were old enough to hold a gun, or at least looked legal doing it. Men like Acra left for the surface in droves to fight.

Ria had no friends among the other children, but Acra had always been there for her. Then he married a Human whom Ria thought very plain-looking. The wedding day had been a simple affair; it was no time to be decadent. Ria had not wanted to go, but Barani made her. And when she'd been dragged to the dais where the couple was seated to bestow their blessings, Barani said loudly to Ria, *"Dah,* enough. He is getting married already. What for face long-long?" Ria could feel Barani's smirk and almost see the gleam in her violet eyes.

Ria had mumbled her blessings to the couple's sandaled feet and would have left for the far end of the tikar if Acra had not called after her. She could not look at him at first, but the gravity of Acra's eyes had forced her mortified ones to meet them. She'd peered up to see Acra and Kak Manyari smiling at her. Something about Acra's smile had made her believe him when he said, "Later, when Ria is big, confirm got a lot of admirers."

Had made her believe he was coming back.

Ria had been with Kak Manyari, helping the latter burp her daughter, when she watched him leave with Gemir. The only reason he gave for enlisting was, "Manticura is my country too." A smile, a cocky two-fingered movie star salute, and he was gone, a simple cloth bag slung across his body.

No news of him came during the two years the fighting went on for. Then Gemir came home, an arm mangled and a part of his face burnt away, leaving an eye blind. Ria was outside Kak Manyari's hut, holding in her hand the single cassava Kak Manyari had told her to bring to Barani as she watched him limp forward. He absently ran his good hand through her hair, either not noticing the serpents or simply not caring any more. Kak Manyari came to the door, tiny now that the rough years had picked her flesh right off the bone and tinier still as she peered around the large man's body. Gemir must have known who she was searching for and in answer, he pressed something into Kak Manyari's hand. The woman stood still for a beat before thanking him and disappearing back into the house.

Ria stared after Gemir as he left, returning perhaps to his own world of pain now that he'd delivered another's right into their hands. Inside, Kak Manyari had her back to the door, and was putting away dried plates into a small cupboard by the makeshift stove, her movements near frantic. There weren't a lot of plates to put away. There wasn't much to clean off of them after a meal either. When she was done, she took them out, even the ones she hadn't used, only to put them back in again.

Ria went over and made to help. Kak Manyari looked and seeing Ria, she pointed to the cassava root, saying kindly with a shaky smile, "Ria, go home lah. Cook the cassava. Later, Kak Bara scold you again, you know?"

Ria didn't reply. She finished putting all the plates away and, once done, took Acra's name badge and sealed envelopes, crumpled and smudged in dark dirt, from where they had fallen on Kak Manyari's floor. She pressed them into Kak Manyari's hands, closing her fingers over them. Ria knew that when Kak Manyari focused on her face, the woman was wishing Ria's eyes would do to her what they had the power to do. Ria glanced at the little girl asleep on the mat, prone on her front and a pudgy fist in her mouth, who appeared very Human save for the body covering of scales and the cleft that ran along her head instead of hair. She was still in the middle of moulting, so there were bits of translucent honeycomb skin stuck to her, just waiting for a good scrub in the bath. Kak Manyari blinked hard once, like a woman clearing her eyes, before squeezing them shut to let herself cry.

Kak Manyari's sobbing recalled Ria to Gemir's limping walk—the sound of his footsteps having been the first tap and stutter of an unhappy message from an already unhappy world.

A few days later, she stood with a crowd in the centre of town, at the settlement's only newsstand, and there it was in a stack under a single lamp: all the soldiers Manticura had sent to meet the invading forces at pocket meeting points, on the frontlines with dead, frozen aftermaths. All those men, and Acra, lost. She gazed down at the topmost paper, making no move to take it. On the front page, in a photograph taking up half of the precious reporting space, the Capital Building flew a flag that was not Manticura's. Ria did not need to read the headlines to know who or what had won.

For years, "Manticura" had meant nothing to her. There were only the immediate spaces: the courtyard and the jungle with no end, the breathy hollows of Nelroote's cave and tunnels. The world, when not in books, was a source of intrusion and the nauseating memories of small statues that were once alive. Another flag meant another government, another set of plots that were really just one big hole to throw everyone into.

Then, she understood. "Manticura" was the bigger space Acra had left to protect, so that the niche he'd carved with his family and the niches he'd helped carve in opening the gate for Bara and herself would be safe.

When she drew back from the papers, she found that she was surrounded by anxious faces. Not directed at her the way anxious faces usually were. People were crowding in close, peering over her at the printed news, commenting on what she had seen and read. They spoke all at once and asked the same thing: what was going to happen to them? Far too many had not heard from sons or husbands.

Out of new habit, Ria kept her snakes close to her head as she pushed through the crowd. No one moved out of her way. For the first time since her arrival at Nelroote, it was as if she was invisible. She might as well be in the dark. She was about to disappear into a narrow alley when she stopped to look back, at the huddled bodies, their spines curved out as if they formed part of a despairing drum. She could hear crying over the buzz and more than one child stood back, unmoving. Ria found herself turning sharply away, looking up at the bit of ceiling between the zinc and plywood awnings. She wondered if this new government was going to tear a hole through and make a sky, a proper sky. Maybe they would all be taken away and made into thralls that smelled of rot and barely had hair sticking to their scalps.

She made her way to Pak Arlindi's, walking the memorised route without the aid of a lamp, and was about to round the house to the shack when she heard Abang Seh, Pak Arlindi's youngest son, say: "I heard the other settlements are going to ally themselves with the Esomiri occupiers."

She had been told countless times not to listen in on adults' conversations, but Abang Seh was practically Barani's age. She dropped to a squat against the house and listened.

"That doesn't mean we do the same," Pak Arlindi shot back. "War is bad enough. We still want civil war? Humans fight the non-Humans, *gitu*?"

There was a loud thud of something blunt hitting a hard surface. "I should have gone out there! With Abang and Kakak when they allowed people like us to fight for the country. I should have joined them!"

"And now they are dead!" Pak Arlindi boomed. Softly, he added, "Your mother will not lose another child."

"Pak—"

"What we have now, we protect. Fight for the home here and not the one that's already lost. Now the problem is we have two entrances. The western one is at least well-hidden and secure. But the eastern one…"

"The one that leads to the central chamber?"

In the pause, she imagined Pak Arlindi nodding. "The Lady's tomb. We should send out a few able-bodied men to set up a guard outpost. They would be inexperienced. We all are, but…"

Another moment of silence passed in which Ria found herself bracing against the wall to stand.

"This is crazy," Abang Seh began slowly, "but what about that snake girl?"

Pak Arlindi sounded surprised. "Ria?"

Abang Seh lowered his voice. Ria could imagine him darting his marble-like eyes from side to side, rocky brows furrowed down, worried. "She frightens me."

"Ria is harmless. As long as we have Barani, she won't do anything."

"That child is possessed with something, I tell you, Pak. Always staring. Always so quiet. What she did to Kenanga…" A pause, then, "Men, women and children too. Young, old, all gone with one look." Another pause to let it sink in. "One look; and government officials too. Before this war, they were looking for her like they did the other one, the one who killed the old president, remember? Heard that was why she ran, and Barani with her. We've been housing a wanted criminal."

"A *child*," Pak Arlindi corrected him. "What she made was nothing more than a child's mistake. The sins of a child are washed off by their innocence. Don't you remember *that*?"

"Innocence don't last very long, Pak. But dangerous or not, not the issue. What I'm saying is with what she can do, we can—"

A clattering reached her from within. Likely plates. "Are you listening to what you're saying? Send one girl out, by herself, to guard an outpost?"

"What is she? Fourteen, fifteen already? The men we're sending are not going to be much older than her. Up there, men and women of nearly the same age are risking lives, getting killed. What difference does it make? How much growing up does she have to do before she understands?"

There was a moment of considering silence.

"But alone?" Pak Arlindi spoke finally.

"Maybe not alone," Abang Seh replied, sounding uncomfortable. "Maybe with Bara—"

The doorknob that she held on to, to heave herself up, felt too large. The door was heavy when she pushed it in to a silenced room and orange faces floating in the dark. She heard the soft slaps of her feet meeting the cement floor as she approached. Once by the table, her voice rang hard and clear: "I will do it."

Pak Arlindi was the first to speak, to tell her that Barani wouldn't want her to do this. Ria nodded. Abang Seh made to speak, his expression becoming guilty, but Ria only turned around and strode back out.

She didn't return to Barani that evening. It was as if she found herself locked out, without a key, and no one at home answering her knocks—locked out, but not panicking because there was some place she could go, some place she should go to instead. She made her way to the gate and out of it into the main tunnel. She didn't even try to remember if she was going the right way as she navigated the dark, a hand out, nursing the briefest fear of her gaze being rendered useless by sudden blindness when it was most needed.

The tunnels of Nelroote hummed a monotonous tune for the dead that resided along their lengths. She had never noticed it when she first came to Nelroote, but the hollows cut into the tunnels were packed with the bones of people, skulls facing out, from a time before numbered plots. There were also detours along the tunnels; narrower corridors that went into small rooms where still more dead were interred.

Her destination was a chamber, the keramat of a dead paragon. She had found it a while back when she was out exploring without Barani's knowledge. She'd come in from the entrance at the far end of the room. A straight walk up an aisle between stone seats, there was an alcove where a large stone sarcophagus was propped up on a slant. On its closed lid, the painted form of a woman stared out with eyes of gold leaf. At the woman's feet were smaller figures, hands raised and faces averted from the glare of her ethereal glow, which radiated out in golden stripes. Before the alcove stood a stone table, empty save for the lichen that dotted its surface. The ceiling was held up by pillars and arcs covered in carved images sporting moss in their crevices. A portion of that ceiling was broken, or perhaps the hole was intentional, for there were no signs of wall sconces or fittings for lamps. Vines hung through it and crept in the spaces touched by the bruised light, specks of dust floating.

The walls on either sides of the keramat contained whole skeletons in deep shelves cut into the rock, each shrouded in linen that must have once been beautiful but was now mostly rotted away by age and humidity. Valuable possessions had been placed in with them, around grinning skulls with indifferent eye sockets. All of them were arranged such that their heads were pointed towards the front of the chamber where the alcove was.

Through the jagged rip of skylight in a portion of the arched ceiling, Ria saw that it was still day. Too bright, the way it always was on terrible days.

The first man arrived moments after she did. She heard him approach and stop just inside the smaller doorway to the outer tunnels which led to the eastern gate. Without hurry, she lowered her gaze from the skylight to him, her hair raised and the throbs beginning to catch at the areas around her eyes.

He was a young Human, perhaps barely even eighteen, his face smeared with dirt and grease, and half of his side a gory mess he was trying to hold together beneath an open hand. She'd never seen a soldier in person before, and maybe this one was not to blame for the darkness Nelroote had been plunged into since the day the war rolled in. Maybe he too was a mother's son, a wife's husband, or a daughter's father. Maybe he too had a young woman in love with him, whose heart he unknowingly broke when he married someone else. But to

Ria, the only good ones were the ones who left Nelroote to fight. The others didn't matter, whatever the colour of the flag on their armbands.

He saw her and his panting ceased with a ravaged gasp. The last grey picture of him wore the open, surprised expression of someone caught in the glare of a very bright camera flash. It was expected. What she didn't understand was why the migraine continued to burn at her temples after and why her face had felt so tight as she looked upon the young man's face, envisioning somewhere in his Humanness the features of a cherished Scerean man.

∽

Nearly fifty years on, and Ria turned her face back to the same skylight, into the downward flow of the floating dust in the sunbeam, and thought how it smelled of morning forest. If she closed her eyes, she could hear the creak and hum of a small hut all alone on a quiet day, the warbles of chickens as they pecked in the dirt outside and voices in low conversation— all those sounds riding upon gentle crests to her as she lay on her sleeping mat, the brightness of the day painting the insides of her lids orange. She breathed it all in, the everyday reminder of the life she possessed that never looked like it was ever going to leave her. She remained creaseless and unaged, even as those she knew from days-back-then folded up into maps of their travelled roads.

She moved from the corner of the keramat to the side of the sarcophagus, where she kept the supplies, and filled a sweets tin with oil before fitting a makeshift spout over its small mouth. From the keramat, she went through the northwestern exit to get into what she called the commoners' tunnel where, like in the one leading away from the southeast, the dead were interred by the numbers, their skulls and other bones making up the walls and pillars with thorny surfaces of protruding snouts alternating with flat faces. The skulls were cool to the touch, and she ran her hand along the rows of them as she added oil to the dying lamps. She often wondered if the ancient Nelrootians had a culture of death, or if these dead had been buried elsewhere before being exhumed and moved to the catacombs. There was a stone altar before the Lady's alcove, upon which Ria's own things were cluttered amongst the spread of offerings—usually alcohol, flowers and fruit.

After the North Coalition forces had pulled out of Manticura, and after the country had settled into a slumbering state of development—cleaning up, burying, forgetting—the old practice of interring the remains of the deceased returned to Nelroote. Ria's knives cut and peeled away strangers' flesh, and her heads extracted their organs. Like ordinary garbage, the whole lot was burnt, bones and all, in special chimney-less furnaces used by the ancients. The ashes she would later place in family urns, to be housed in a smaller chamber, were one and the same with the dust that needed to be swept away to keep the homes of the living clean.

Protecting Nelroote's living from its dead, and later, its dead from the living, seemed like an unceasing task, but there was little else she could do; little else anyone would let her do, even if she were to ask. Hers was the face of stories told to children to get them to behave, and the name incited to quell injustice and violence in the settlement. Where before people had gazed upon her with muted curiosity, now no one would look her properly in the eye. Not even those who called themselves her friends, who thought of themselves as an extended arm of her family—when they really meant Barani's, and Barani in place of "her".

Some days, not even Barani seemed to see her, as the older woman stood in a corner of the home they shared and smoked her way to lung disease. It was as if a wall had been erected between her sister and herself, every brick of it made by a statue from her stone garden.

In that garden, there were scouts, deserters, guerrillas looking for hideouts, the squads that sought to capture her alive. All manifestations of what Cikgu had said to her before the she'd left for Jankett Town: "*Uram'gur nees ru(eis) uram'gur*". Her expression had been pained as she let a strand of Ria's hair slowly slide from her open palm, as if she was already seeing something she loved being destroyed. "Protect what you can protect," it meant. And Ria could, so she had let none of the soldiers find her sister's home, Kak Manyari and her child, or what food they could procure through the black market and had to protect gram by measly gram.

Ria tried not to remember the soldiers' faces but, unlike her eyes, her memory was not one used to blinding. When she remembered, she remembered with terrifying clarity: the darkness of the tunnels, the smell of sweat on the bodies clad in serge, the sounds of footsteps crushing down on the bone-scattered floor, every tug and pull of her hair in adrenaline-rushed moments of fighting and survival. Every gasp and look of horror.

Two of these faces were wont to jump at her—in the sudden flare of a struck match, or in the moving shadows along orange, dead-filled walls and enclaves.

There was the talkative airman, delirious from jungle fever, who wanted her to deliver a pack of letters to a woman named Rafidah. "You see," he'd said as he drew them out from his breast pocket. "Give these to her, 'Dik. Tell her I am sorry. I am sorry." Men sob in ugly ways, she had thought at the time as she stood over him. "I am sorry. I didn't—I didn't say how I lo—" Slurring, pallid and shaking. She had started to leave him. He would not survive the night. But something had made her turn back. She had taken the letters and petrified him in one fell swoop. She still had not read the letters. After all these years, the papers were likely brittle and the faded words meant for someone else.

There was also the one to whom she had lost a snakehead. He had come out of the dark. Unlike the others, she had not heard him until he was nearly on top of her. On sleepless nights, she still remembered the cold of the floor, the uncomfortable stabs from the bones and the small squeal from some animal startled out of its life. More than anything, she remembered the face in the shadows: a Human face, but too pale, too livid, too monstrous. And he—no, *it*—had a hand on her thigh, claws dug so deep she still had the scars to show for it to this day. Her young mind had not known what it wanted to do with her, but every fibre of her being called for her to fight, to survive; told her that it was not an encounter she was going to get out of easily with her gaze.

It had been too dark: the one limitation of her ability was that one had to be able to see her and she the other just as well, in order for the petrifaction to take effect. She had smelt the creature's breath when it brought its face in close. The saliva had been steeped in bloodlust. Then a snake, the one that was always basking on her left shoulder, had lashed out. It spat venom into the creature's eyes before sinking fangs into the side of its neck. The creature drew away, clawing at its eyes and screaming in pain. Ria had taken the chance then to squirm out from under it. She needed to get to the keramat. So she could see. So that the creature would die. She was about to get back on her feet when the creature took hold of the snake that bit it. In the struggle to get free, Ria could not tell what exactly took place, but she registered a sharp tug on her scalp, followed by a wave of excruciating pain that shot through her head. She'd cried out and something about the sound of her cry had caused the creature to stop, blinking at her, its hand gripping the severed head of the snake.

Ria must have got up then and run to the main chamber, for she remembered bursting into its light and coming to a skidding collision with a pillar overgrown with creepers and ferns. She was crying in heaving sobs and her heart felt as if it was beating its last and was going to go all out about it. She could hear the creature clattering through the tunnels behind her. Yet it had been a man standing in the entrance when she turned—Manticurean Human by all appearances; unkempt and ragged, wearing nothing but dirty shorts that hung on his emaciated frame. His chest displayed a prior wound that was green and purple around the edges. The area where the snake had bitten him was swelling up and spreading black with alarming speed. Any lesser creature would have been in agony by then.

A crashing wave of fury had overwhelmed her then. She hated, and she *thoroughly* hated, everything that she thought the surface stood for: force and its concealment, farce and its creation. She gritted her teeth and ground them. She was incomprehensible, tears streaming from her eyes and her mouth frothing as she rushed up to the man. The Human face was begging then. She wouldn't see. She was straddling him, grasping roughly at his face, and then she turned him too.

All that remained of that Changer now were bits of rubble in the threshold to her statue museum. She had broken him right after she'd petrified him, throwing all the rage and sorrow she felt into destroying the statue until she'd broken every bone in her hands. And when all emotion calmed and ceased, she had looked down at her hands and thought with morbid bemusement, "So much for admirers, 'Bang."

5116 CE

Mirrored Shield

The figure down the stretch of dim corridor resembled a ghost-child in a smudged white dress. The thick mop of black hair over her face moved of its own accord in the dim light. Eedric kept himself very still.

There was light enough for him to see the snakes—a whole nest of them, black and hooded with grey underbellies and white eye-like markings on the backs of their heads. Beads of eyes lay nestled somewhere in the gleaming arrangement of scales, heads raised to stare and flick their tongues in his direction. He glimpsed the petals of a tattoo on the inside of her bare arm near the elbow, then the blooming blood spots of a floral pattern on her white dress. Looking back up to her face, as if inexplicably drawn to all things dangerous, he made out alarming eyes, brightly-hued, large wide-set half-moons winging out from her nose towards the edges of her small face and offset by very dark, bushy brows. Staring at him, she appeared as transfixed as he felt.

He recalled a photograph of a medusa, of *another* medusa from Manticura's pre-independence history: the one of the infamous Anten Demaria of the Dinya Uk'rh, who had stirred the country to fight for independence when she assassinated the puppet leader appointed by the F'herak Imperative. There were many dates and details students needed to memorise and regurgitate, of course, but the only thing that stood the test of his memory was the picture of the medusa with her blindfold on, moments before her execution. There was the executioner's spread-legged stance and the gleaming curve of the blade held aloft. Her story was the classroom lesson in staying true to your word and of the power of the media: if you said you're going to give someone the firing squad, give that person the firing squad. And if you're going to fuck it up anyway, make sure it's not caught on camera. After independence in '66, the authorities had said that Anten's head was buried with the rest of her, with the proper rites observed and all her deserved honours. The conspiracy buffs in his old class, however, believed her head was kept somewhere in the Palaçade as clearly as her likeness was displayed on the shield of Manticura's current coat-of-arms. A medusa's head was said to be eternal, though no one knew for sure if the gaze still worked when the creature was no longer alive.

He could not say if any of it was true, but he did know that medusas were treated by governments almost as if they were an endangered species of animal—a *dangerous* species of animal. They were rare and elusive and no two were said to look the same, like the finger prints of Humans and facial scale patterns of Scereans and Tuyuns. So far, none were known to be living among people. Those were the facts anyone would get if they were to run an Internet search of the beings. That, and pictures of wannabes in extreme street culture with plastic hair extensions and scalp implants. The most widely circulated evidence of what a medusa could do was the legend dated 70 years back, in which every single person of a refugee camp, some three thousand strong, had been turned to stone, eyes staring and mouths opened in the immortalisation of silent screams—a resultant tragedy from the biggest refugee crisis the world had ever known. From another time, another country.

His limbs' own lack of feeling at that moment terrified him. He couldn't see much of himself in the shadows, couldn't see if the petrifaction was spreading from wherever it was supposed to begin. He still sensed, still felt the heaving of his chest, but no part of him moved. Perhaps the curse of a medusa's gaze was really an eternity of staring out from within a statue, body given in to the state against the protests of a working mind.

Then, he couldn't see any more, couldn't focus on anything but those glazed eyes which beheld his without expression and, he swore, without blinking. And the beat of his pulse was building up to such a deafening level in his head that he felt riled by it. The surroundings crescendoed into an indistinguishable buzz and in that world of noise the medusa stood in sudden, and perfect, clarity. In spite of the dark, he saw her scars: a few small ones cut diagonally across her lips and a large tear over her entire left eye. One of her snakeheads had been cut off, the remaining body a limp stump over her shoulder. He saw her stare widen right before she thrust her head forward, teeth bared, head of snakes a halo around her face as a cloud came over her eyes.

Yet, instead of backing down, he lunged forward, slamming her into the adjacent wall in an eruption of bones that clattered to the floor. She let out a cry and turned her face away, eyes squeezed tightly shut. Her snakes drew back to coil close to her head with a quickness that resembled a sea anemone retreating into its body. Above her sudden shout he heard a low growl rumble in his ears, resonating from somewhere within himself. The hands that pinned her down weren't his own. Too many veins ran along them in raised expressways embossed in his skin. His fingernails were dark and sharp where they dug into the exposed skin of her upper arms, drawing blood.

Eedric had never been good with blood. The metallic smell of it pervaded his senses making his stomach roil and on top of that his horror was itself a venom that froze him in place for a second time. He noticed then how he loomed over her, body bent, spine elongated and arched in an in-Human manner, his skin stretched far too tightly over his frame. His laboured breaths had the texture of gravel. His mouth didn't feel right—too stretched and gaping with no control. He could feel her shaking beneath him as she held herself very still, her eyes continuing to shut him out. He saw an image of himself reflected in her face; saw that the skin he wore was the same one Mama had inhabited in her time of illness.

He made a sound, trying to utter some word, only to rasp incoherent letters. In his mind he was apologising; in the slew of everything else that followed he was trying to make her understand: "I didn't mean for this to happen. I didn't mean to hurt you."

She snapped her eyes open as if suddenly awakened from a bad dream and started to pull herself out from under him. He saw that she was determined to get free even if it meant ripping the skin off her bones to accomplish it, so he let her go, teetering for a moment, as if he'd been at the end of a taut line that had suddenly gone slack. And then he ran, not for the surface but down another corridor, passing through intermittent light and dark.

Running felt like swimming through not water, but viscous mud that seemed bent on pulling him down.

He must have been about seven or eight when he had first felt that way, struggling to stay alive in a swimming pool. Each time he had tried to surface, legs kicking and arms flailing, the water would close above him, layer upon layer and seemingly thick as mud. More and more. The tiled walls and floor indicated a swimming pool. His lungs began to scream just as he tried to. A reel of images ran through his mind: simple ones, recalling his Mama and Father over and over. His body fought itself from giving over to the drowning and just as it seemed that the water was winning, the world began to slow and the blue of it showed fronds of legs languidly paddling. His body had grown light and strong, and his chest was no longer constricted in pain. In one smooth glide, he shot up and broke the surface.

It should have felt like an accomplishment because he had finally learnt to swim after fearing the water for so long. But all around him, people were moving away from him, staring bug-eyed. A few children cried out in fear and some girl somewhere could be heard asking, "Mummy, what's that?" The lifeguard who had been swimming towards him with a life-preserver suddenly stopped, expression shocked and mouth agape. Mama was standing by the poolside, looking like she was about to cry, both hands cupped over her mouth. And above all, Father, who had been the one to throw Eedric into the pool in the first place so that he "can learn to swim the hard way"—Father had stared at him first, and Eedric had watched as his expression transformed from one of worry to complete and utter disgust.

That was what he felt right then, running away from the woman whom he had hurt: disgust. More than two decades down and he could still feel the stares that would only open him to a world of disdain. Except now his transformation was complete and he had fully become the creature that Mama was, and the creature that his Father feared he would be.

∿

Eedric was only vaguely aware of the dark hollows in the walls the further he went underground. He took sharp corners and went down still more tunnels of uneven turning paths in what seemed to be a massive labyrinth. He could hear himself panting, sharp and penetrating above the pounding of his heart. There was a strange hissing, like water being poured into a heated pan. Perhaps he was growing delirious from the previous shock and the space itself, which widened in places only to constrict again. He was practically running on all fours, bent so low he could see the rough floor streaking beneath his feet. He had the suspicion that he was going to pass out, the way he nearly had when he first ran 1.6 kilometres as a chubby kid in primary school. Yet, he could not stop, for there was nothing but the need to run away from the one he'd hurt and a need above all, perhaps, to lose himself.

The rush of air around him began to sound like the low hum of many voices and he wondered if he was nearing people, even as the noise made the back of his neck prickle. White light burnt against the wall at the tunnel's end. He dashed through a narrow doorway and came bursting into a large chamber, a chamber with shelves carved into its walls and the remains of bodies in repose within them. Eedric skidded and came to a sudden stop when he crashed into a hard stone form. His heart hammered. The nearby sounds—somewhere at a hundred paces, different voices speaking in incomprehensible languages, above ground the patter of running feet, water, traffic—threatened to descend into white noise. He panted hard. There was a sharp itch at the back of his ear, spreading to the rest of him in maddening waves. He tore at the itching skin, his growls growing into a frenzied shouting.

When he managed to calm himself just enough, he looked at what had halted him: the stone sculpture of a man, the top half of him a painted sky with clouds and the other, below, rustling with grass, also painted on. The man's horrified visage stared at him, his features highlighted by shadows in the clouds. His body was turned at the waist, facing the doorway as if his whole form was caught in the process of fleeing.

Eedric huffed and pivoted away from the statue, crashing into another. All the statues seemed to be of soldier folk, and almost every one of them had been ravaged by either carving tools or paint. The one he stood before was of a man with raised arms broken off at the elbows. His entire chest area was carved out into the crude beginnings of breasts, mounds rough but unmistakable. These along with his head were spray-painted indigo and dotted with yellow stars. He went around it and saw that on the span of its back, someone had brushed "Ria was here" in thick red paint, with a date below that went back 30 years. Another aimed down his gun's sight, blooming with roses against the pitch black background of him from his toes right to the crown of his helmet. A small figure of a woman, stone hair short, and her pretty face without expression, had the hips and legs of the man she had been carved out from. There were recognisable pieces of feet, arms and a few decapitated heads strewn on the floor, indicating the existence of more statues before.

Of the few that remained unmolested, one was a tall, major-blooded Cayanese, his figure hulking and his face characteristically wolf-life. His shoulders were hunched, two thick stone arms spread out at his sides to make him appear bigger than he already was. Instead of wearing an expression of shock or horror, he was scowling downwards at some perceived threat far smaller than him, thinking to frighten it.

Another, in an airman's jumpsuit, sat slumped against a far wall. Even the arm he was stretching out seemed to have no strength to it. The way his fingers were curled—thumb slightly up, index partly pointing, partly crooked—it was as if he'd held something in them once. Beneath his stone moustache, his lips were slightly parted. His brows were furrowed, eyes beseeching.

Even in his bestial state, Eedric was arrested by the

images of ruin that surrounded him, taking them all in one at a time, flitting from statue to statue, overwhelmed by the sensory overload coming over him.

He was holding on to his head, trying to quiet it, when a figure in his peripheral vision caused him to turn. He saw the medusa standing in the entrance, a hand braced against the opening. Her snakes crowded in to form an awning, or the brim of a grotesque hat, but she never lowered her hard gaze from his face.

The silence between them was thick. Eedric stood rooted in front of the airman, exposed in the dusty light, feeling ready to run—to fight. He watched the sleek shiny bodies of her snakes glide over one another, past her shoulders. Their movements were strangely hypnotic, sensuous against the earthy burnish of her skin, forked tongues of some flicking at the corners of her lips. He saw that her dress appeared many times washed and mended. Beneath its frayed hem, her bare shins were mottled with welts and picked-at scabs, some of which oozed with dark blood. The blood forced him to look upwards again, to the blood that marked her upper arms. The wounds from which they bled were shapeless gashes that resembled the mauling bite of an animal more than injuries caused by Human—*once* Human—hands. Clenching his teeth, he struggled to speak, only to snarl instead.

With one more unintelligible word drowned in a glob of saliva, he turned and started for another tunnel.

"No!"

There was only dark, on and on, and blooms of orange halos at intermittent distances. Then, after a long time, it all opened into a vast space, to the sound of a heavy latch being lifted, followed by a door swinging on a hinge. He ran towards this door and, with a lunge, threw his shoulder at it. There was a crack, the pinprick of splinters in his skin, before a blinding brightness.

The impact of a large hurtling body brought him to a stop. There was a roar, a grunt and jarring pain when his head met hard ground as an arm came down the back of his skull. When the ringing stopped, he heard the rising furore and that single dreaded question, "*Ibu*, what's that?"

He lifted his head slightly to see the gathered crowd. There was little distance between him and the first set of feet, and the eyes that stared at him with fascinated fear. There were children peeking at him from around the fence of adult legs and bodies. *Anir* children—rock-textured, furred, scaled, all kinds. Somehow, the children were the ones who humiliated and diminished him with those unfiltered stares of theirs.

He escaped the lock of the man who was holding him down and lunged out at one of them: a girl in a short white lacy frock. She screamed. Her mother tried to keep her away. A booted foot met the side of his face and Eedric was on the ground again.

"*Binatang*!" he was called, the Sce' 'dal word for "animal".

More would have descended upon him but for the medusa he had seen earlier dashing into the circle. She stood between Eedric and the man who was about to attack him. Every strand of her hair stood on undulating end. His assailant, a large Cayanese, coloured over in grey, beginning from his face, spreading over to the rest of him.

The medusa turned around and the two men who had

been holding him down released him instantly. The crowd was dispersing quickly now. No backing away or further staring. Just the running of a terrified mob.

The medusa was a petite woman, probably no more than a metre and a half in height. Yet, in that moment, there was no monster who stood taller than she did.

Perhaps save for himself.

The medusa stood deathly still for a few beats before she approached him, still sprawled on the ground. When she knelt beside him and gently touched a hand to his shoulder, he was shaking. He scrunched up his eyes as if needing to unsee. What a mess he was. What a fucking mess.

"It's fine," the medusa said.

He dared to look at her then, eyes smarting a little. She was not smiling at him. Her expression held no pity; it held nothing. As if she herself were made of stone. In an odd way, it quieted him.

She made as if to speak when three new figures came up over the slope that led down to the houses. He had not realised how the slum sat in a massive bowl. He *did* realise that one of the figures approaching them was another medusa, tall and model-slim, dressed in a flannel shirt tucked into jeans. Her expression was both maddened and worried. When she was near, she dashed towards the shorter medusa and started to pull the other away from him. The two men with her were an older Tuyun and another Cayanese with very wolf-like features.

Her eyes widened at the wounds on the first medusa's arms before snapping her gaze to him and asking harshly, "Who are you, Changer? What did you do to her?"

He had never heard that word used before but from the way it sounded, he knew it meant nothing good.

"I—"

More footsteps came from behind him and then he was restrained again. Two Scereans this time, one built like a bulwark and the other spindly. Eedric struggled against their hold.

"He came running through the door, Kak!" one of the Scereans informed the medusa. "Someone from the surface. A spy!"

"No!" protested Eedric, able to form words again. "I'm not—"

The old Tuyun grimaced at him. "If he didn't come with one of the feelers, we cannot have him leave here. He will tell and then what will we do?"

Eedric struggled.

"Changers are always trouble. Look at what happened with the last one," one of the Scereans spoke.

"Locking her up in a container and giving food and water in a pet bowl was not looking after her," the violet-eyed medusa snapped. "Her family left for the surface. Let it be." She turned back to Eedric, her frown deepening. "How did you find this place?"

"I was trekking. I saw the entrance."

The medusa narrowed her eyes at him. "Dressed like that?"

Eedric forgot that he appeared about ready to trek as a woman in a dinner gown was to climb a mountain.

When he could not answer, the Tuyun made to approach him, but the golden-eyed medusa stopped him with a low and steely "Don't."

The Tuyun paused and she said, "You will agitate him again. A man can decide that he needed to clear his head and many have made big discoveries on less." To the other medusa, she said, "He was in the keramat, likely found it by accident. He saw me and ran."

"And the wounds on your arm?" the other medusa demanded.

The first one considered her and then said, rather quietly, "I am not harmless either."

"Ria..."

The other medusa looked at this...Ria, who was the very opposite of cheery despite her name, with an expression that bordered on confusion and concern. They could not appear any less related, with Ria's black cobras and the other's olive-and-brown vipers; the former's petite build and burnished skin a contrast to the latter's tall form and fairer complexion. However, given how few medusas were out there, Eedric thought these two could well be sisters.

Ria shook her head. "Enough."

For a few moments no one spoke, until one of the Scereans stammered, "S-she—J-Johan, there." He pointed his chin towards the stone form of the petrified Cayanese.

That was when the violet-eyed medusa's face sank.

Ria remained impassive. "He was a rapist, a thug and a wife-abuser. I did this place a service."

"Even so..." the Tuyun spoke, "he deserved a trial."

"When have your *trials* ever done anything around here?" Ria shot back.

Not caring for a debate, the Tuyun turned to the other medusa. "Barani?"

Barani's jaw tightened. "Leave it for now. Johan had it coming and you know it." She looked at Eedric and then turned to Ria. "This Changer doesn't come back." It was more a command than a statement. "*Nothing* comes back."

Ria only swept her eyes over the Tuyun and the Scereans, who jumped away from Eedric, releasing him. "As long as none of you leave."

Barani gave a single nod and turned to walk away, the Tuyun following suit with an unconvinced glance back at Eedric and Ria. Eedric heard him say to Barani, "He will bring bad things on us."

Ria waited for them to descend the steps before helping Eedric up. She did so rather matter-of-factly, as if she didn't want to draw attention to the action. She gave him a brief and indifferent once-over, then said quietly, "We can't stay here."

She started to lead him away and he was aware of her hand around his arm. His eyes fell on the wounds, red and angry even though the bleeding had stopped.

"You should take care of that," he said, guilt washing over him.

"Later," she replied, her voice hard. He saw that a small group had gathered below the steps cut into the slope. Every eye was focused on him, anger burning cold in each one.

The two Scereans parted as Eedric and Ria re-entered the tunnel. Eedric half-expected someone to follow them, to make sure that Eedric found his way out and was convinced never to return. However, no one did. Ria continued her hold on his arm and her snakes didn't fall from their aggressive stances until they were well back in the central chamber where Eedric made an effort to speak to her.

"Thank you…for…saving me," he tried, the words feeling strange on his tongue.

She cracked a smile. "Saving you? Maybe."

"But I mean it… Thank you." He recalled the way the people had regarded him—those in the pool and the ones from just now. He felt disgusted at himself, humiliated. Angry.

Ria looked up at him. "I believe you," she said. Quietly, she added, "And I know what it must be like."

"Have you met a lot of survivalists?"

"Changers? Some. They were coveted frontline soldiers during the war because they were hard to kill."

Eedric stared at her, wary suddenly.

"But I have had enough of that," she told him as if by way of assurance. She studied him for a while before saying, "Now you're here, and you shouldn't be."

"I found the entrance and thought…"

She sighed. "That entrance really needs to be resealed, but no one seems to be working any more."

She then reached into her pocket and drew out a strange-looking tool that resembled a small sickle on a short handle. With the point, she began tearing long strips from the dress she wore, cutting just above the hem.

The dress itself was likely a vintage piece, the skirt flowing over and encasing part of her legs in a bell below a black waist. It was ridged and tight around the torso, reminiscent of the days when a woman's body was different: breasts pushed high and stockings on legs, held up mid-thigh by garter belts; when a "bikini bridge" was a non-existent idea.

He watched her split the strip into two, take one end of the makeshift bandage between her teeth, and begin the process of winding it around her arm. Already blood was soaking through, adding new red blooms to the patterned cloth. Her movements were deft and purposeful, as if seeing to her wounds was something she had been doing all her life.

Nevertheless, he moved closer to her and said, "Let me."

Her answer was to shrink away from him.

He took an awkward step back, never feeling more useless in his life. He stared down at his hands, feeling dirty and pathetic. As if she knew, she relented and turned so that her other arm was angled towards him, the wound a puncture that had gone right through. She stretched another strip to him. "You can do the other one."

He took it hesitantly, hoping the rudimentary first aid training he had received in national service would prove to be useful.

"Tie it around the arm as you would a ribbon around a tree. It's the same thing," she directed him patiently.

"Okay."

He started to tie the strip around her arm, going a few rounds before beginning to knot. His hands were shaking embarrassingly and he found himself apologising a lot, as he tried to get over the sight and smell of the blood.

"Tightly, boy," she said.

He redid the knot and pulled the bandage in tight. When he was done, he found her face close. The snakes were within striking distance and he ought to pull away. But he didn't. Instead, he remarked, "Your scars—"

Ria replied, "A bullet that didn't meet its mark." She

made her fingers into a gun and aimed it from the bottom of her chin up. "Young soldier. Crouching and shot up from below."

"Did he—"

"They all did."

They were quiet. Eedric leaned back and looked about him for something to comment on or talk about. He was aware that this situation he was in was not typical: meet a monster girl, get into a scuffle and then talk through calm. Nothing could change what he'd done. Yet, where others had treated him like a gone case when they found that there was a *possibility* of him being like his mother, this medusa, whom he'd attacked, had stood up for him and spoken to him kindly.

"You have—you have quite the collection here."

She turned to look at him and he wondered what sort of first-class idiot he was being. But he felt he needed to talk. To keep talking. "Two-Half?" he asked.

She regarded him steadily and he wondered if this—him feeling strung by the ropes of both fear and hope—was what the last moments of her victims looked like.

Finally, she said, "After."

It wasn't much to go by but he thought there was a shift in the medusa's air.

He swallowed, then asked, "Soldiers?"

"Mostly."

Eedric had never thought he would meet a woman who spoke so little. He glanced at the other doorway, the wider one on the far side of the chamber. "Do you—are you lonely here?" He'd meant to say "alone".

Before he could correct himself, the medusa moved, as if uncertain, before shifting her gaze to the statues. After a while, she nodded. "It does get so."

"Do people ever come here?"

She smiled again. The dark shadows under her eyes made her appear like a case study for drug addiction, or severe insomnia, whichever was the country's bigger problem. However, he also noticed the radiance of those dangerous eyes accentuated by her rather unusual features, which were as alien as they were intriguing.

"No. This is a place for the dead. When someone dies, they are left in a small chamber for me to collect and do my work." She gestured towards the statues. "But I have them."

"Not exactly very conversational though, are they?"

At that, she threw back her head and laughed. The laugh changed the very make of her: it softened edges, added rounded dimensions and caused her to erupt in violent energy that was so contagious he found himself joining in—nervously at first, and then just as heartily.

When they stopped, the wounds on her arms drew his attention once more. He was back in a world of guilt. He made as if to touch her, then stopped when she snapped her head and gaze to him.

"You need to stop feeling guilty," she said. "There is nothing for me to forgive, especially when I was the one who tried to change you at the beginning." She thought a while, then smiled again. "I guess you can say that we're even now."

Her smile dropped and she appeared confused by the situation that she now found herself in. She looked at him a number of times, before turning to the skylight above. Finally, she told him, "We need to go. This is no place for a surface creature like you."

She led him through the tunnels and he followed in silence. She stopped just before the final stretch of tunnel and pointed up to where bits of light came through in little gaps of the leaf cover. She pointed at it, saying, "There," and didn't follow him as he made his way up.

He didn't look back until he was well on the paved pathway of the reserve; up at the quarry that loomed as the largest natural structure in the whole of Manticura. He felt a strange sense of incompleteness.

∿

Hours later, after he had explained his absence to Adrianne—"I...uh, went hiking"—he found himself recalling the way the medusa had spoken to him and accepted him so equitably despite everything that had gone down.

He thought of her for days afterward while trying to convince himself that he had no good reason to return, before preoccupation and obsession drew him back. He found himself pushing past the leaf cover once again and retracing his steps, frequently glancing over his shoulder for anyone from the settlement, before he had his back pressed against the wall by the entrance to the main chamber, peeking in only to end up shocked when she appeared behind him.

Her voice was that breathy, old-timey timbre that had played in his mind for days, one that he thought only actresses in black-and-white films possessed. And with that voice, her face lit in the flame of the oil lamp she was carrying, she asked almost with a touch of fear, "What are you doing here?"

"I wanted to ask about the statues," he told her. "The paintings and the carvings. This whole ruin."

He had with him a camera, hanging from his neck by a thick strap like he was some bloody tourist. He held it up—DSLR, multiple lens changes and all that good stuff he didn't quite understand but wouldn't admit to anybody—grinning excitedly, nodding his head in quick, sporadic taps as if he was trying to convince her. He was quivering a bit from nervousness. He hoped that she wouldn't notice.

She glanced down at the camera warily, before looking back up at him.

"What do you want exactly?" she asked.

He paused, wondering how he would tell her of the nights he'd lain awake, wondering about her, what she'd seen, been through, cared for... More than anything, he wanted conversation; he wanted to hear her laugh. He wanted to be around another person besides Miz who treated his condition like it was as unremarkable as him breathing. More than that he wanted to—

"To know more about..." he trailed off. *You*, he didn't say.

She turned her head and gazed past him into the chamber she resided in, considering it for a long time. Finally, she moved into it, beckoning him to follow her.

"Okay. But no photographs."

Matahari (sun)

She had never wished to be friends with the boy. It would have been so much easier to just let him die. For while she didn't know him, she knew what his kind could do. So much time had passed since anything had taken her by surprise—and then he had come along, an overly friendly and helpful type of surface dweller, all perfect skin, stiffed up hair and clean everything. *Orang suruh pergi*, he don't want to go. *Mati-mati* must try to help. As if he were the model product of a courtesy campaign; at risk of becoming irrelevant if he didn't meet his good-deed quota.

The initial shock of having seen an outsider—and a Changer at that—after years of solitude, eventually gave way to an instinctive focus of eyes—her hair's and her own—and the imposition of warning pain a split second before the transformation. Only, as if the fates had rolled a die that showed no number, the transformation never came. Instead, she had found herself in close proximity to a face that was Eedric's and yet not; his features were seamed into a head that tipped the stalk of a neck, a bulbous growth jerking to sporadic beats as the open mouth full of teeth produced a collection of growls, too thick to be discernible words. But the sentiments of fear, guilt and confusion had, at some point in that encounter, been unmistakable. He had seemed about to burst out of both his clothes and the cage of his creature's form.

In a strange way, he reminded her of Acra—the same good humour and, she would find later, the same simplicity of ideals. He was tall and had a face like a finely-cut gem, on which thick, well-groomed brows were set above intelligent eyes and volatile pupils. Garrulous, and so full of movement: a pulse in the corner of a strong jaw, a stray bit of hair in the valley of his parting. And facial expressions. So many facial expressions—frowns to raised eyebrows, flexible lips, nostril-flare.

She ought not to have allowed him to come back. He was an outsider to her world and to Nelroote. Far too good and too much of a liability to be part of what the settlement had become, where survival meant vice was a necessity. Yet his return always came with a sense of relief, and the growing familiarity made it harder for her to avert herself. Instead, as she started to see more of him, she started to put both a face and a living, breathing person to the name she would rather forget but couldn't.

They moved, at first, within barely overlapping circles. When they were in the chamber, he would keep to one corner where he prodded the skeletons in a *geli*, revolted, but still wanting to touch sort of way. As she moved through the tunnels, he would trail after her at a distance and she could feel his eyes sweeping over her back. When she paused, so would he. He only stopped short at watching her prepare a body for cremation and interment. Perhaps because the first time, the body had only got to her after it had been dead for a while—one of those who had died of overdose in some hidden nook or a closed-up house by themselves—and he had run out of the preparation chamber heaving and retching.

Apart from that, he went where she went in the ancient catacombs. She was sure that wherever he came from, incessantly shadowing a person was illegal, but down here in the catacombs he probably felt that the laws of his surface did not apply. Not to him, no.

Conversation had begun sparsely, and sometimes felt stilted: him wary and always apologetic, Ria either holding back or layering responses with puzzles and obscuring it further with her dry and evasive humour, keeping the gaps of age and era impassable. He never pushed for answers, but was always forthcoming with information about himself: jobs, family, state of the worlds he lived in—Manticura, and the more intimate virtual spaces of his games. Leaning his back against the wall, right beside "Rafidah's airman", he would sit with one leg gathered up to him and the other stretched out, slim and long. In this way, he would run off like a continuous newsfeed, censored only by the limits of his knowledge. Sometimes he watched, living dangerously in the moment, as she lit lamps, painted or carved, paying homage to the sun she saw only in windowed form. He went about like this two, sometimes three times a week. No real schedule; *he like he come, he don't like he don't come.*

Deeper connection didn't happen until about a month

after. It began with the hand-held slab he carried around with him that, as he declared with complete austerity, "contained his life". He'd seen her eyeing it when he looked up from the swiping and the blank staring—left, right, up, up, up, sometimes down; frowning, rolling his eyes, smiling, laughing a little to himself. So he had held it up and asked, "Have you seen this before, Ria? It's called a phone."

He always assumed that she didn't know something. She had seen some of the young people in Nelroote use such a device, though most of them complained that you couldn't get reception so deep underground. Nevertheless, she had shaken her head at Eedric's question.

He had come up to her, close, too close, his proximity a danger to her control over her snakes. "It does everything," he said, but showed her only pictures, mostly of food at first, shiny cutlery and edibles precisely and artfully arranged on pristine porcelain plates. Then of places when she wanted to see how people lived—corridors, interiors, streets and blocks, the countries he had been to, the sets of his photoshoots. People came later: pictures of him, with his friends, at functions, in between shoots, and with a young woman who was as tall, slim and beautiful as he. Ria considered this young woman, with her lush, long hair of black roots and auburn ends. A perfect marble statue with skin so fair and polished smooth, features so evenly placed and eyebrows such impeccable arches. In the pictures that he had shown, Eedric always appeared heavy-lidded as he posed pressed up close to the woman. Ria found her gaze lingering upon this stranger.

"That would be Adrianne," Eedric had explained,

suddenly uncomfortable. "We, uh…are not all right, right now." Perking up, he then suggested, "Why don't I take one of you?"

"Don't. You can't."

"Why not? See this? You can do it yourself too," he told her, and with that, he'd made some taps on the phone's screen before showing it to her.

What she saw surprised her, a strange face, so different from her sister's. Against the allure of both Barani and Adrianne, Ria was strange-looking, almost grotesque: eyes too wide-set, nose flat and ridged as if someone had tried to squeeze it as they would an accordion, face too broad up top and pinched below. Then there was her hair, black as night and moving more slowly than she'd initially thought they would be. She gazed upon her snakes, wondering if she could turn herself into stone if she tried.

"Not now then," she heard Eedric say and he made to take the phone out of her hand, his movements quick as if frightened.

She did not let go at first, so the phone was a bridge between them as they each held on to both ends of it. He stretched out a finger, touched the inside of her wrist. When she finally did let go, he stepped away with what she believed was a puzzled expression.

"She's a beautiful girl," Ria found herself saying as she started to move away from him, feeling the sudden need for ample distance.

But he came, following as he always had. "Not beautiful," he told her. She had looked back to see his mouth stretched downwards and curled into a distinct parabola of disagreement. "Pretty, good-looking. Hot. But not beautiful."

"What do you consider beautiful then?" she asked, starting to move.

She thought she could feel him smile behind her. "Would it be inappropriate if I said *you*?"

She said nothing, but considered it rather odd that a word inscribed upon a fire or warm weather could be used to describe a person too. And she thought about her sister, who had been going lately by "Bara" rather than "Ani". Bara—Sce' 'dal for "ember". "My sister, is she hot?" she verbalised, peering over her shoulder only to have Eedric look at her as if he was in sudden danger.

"But not beautiful," he added before turning the conversation to other things.

∿

His first gift to her was a set of books, a few days after he walked in on her squeezed and curled up in the alcove with the opened sarcophagus, reading one of the old books she still kept. He asked if she liked reading. She said yes, and showed him the book, watched first the purse of his lips as he let out a whistle, then later his blinding white teeth as he told her about the value antique books such as the one she was reading had up on his world. The books he got her had flimsy paper covers, although they were still more expensive in their twenties and thirties of dollars than hardcovers had been in the past. It was about what's within, he told her, and she read the tales of loss and regret, of atonements and love that never ended in tragedy, but never in happiness either. Somewhere in one a broken soldier looked on at a pretty little bird he could never have, and in another a man's long journey ended with nothing but horror.

In their exchange of stories, he got to know about Cikgu, about the life she used to have on the surface, the first time she lamented her lost innocence during Kenanga's petrifaction and how, to remember her deed, she'd tattooed the cananga flower—marquise petals veined—onto her skin using a needle cleaned in fire and dipped in black ink. She recalled how, after the repetitions of tiny stabs seaming the ink into her skin, she became numb to the physical pain. But not to the feelings that came with the memories of what she had done.

She expected judgement from him. She waited for his body to slowly back away from her, wanting nothing more to do with her. She expected words of wisdom no wiser than those from a newspaper, better suited to be made into cotton swabs for cleaning ears. Yet, he only asked, "What do those symbols around some of the flowers mean?"

"They are names," she told him. In tiny letters written closely to the flower's black outline: *Nenek, Kenanga, Acra, Manyari*. There was a gap cornering a petal's tip, and then: *Nelroote, Barani…*

"Oh? And what language is that?"

"Tuyunri," replied Ria.

He looked at the words inscribed into her skin and then to her, shaking his head. "Tuyunri. What's that?"

He was seated next to her, separated from her by the sarcophagus. In spite of the weight of the things she had told him, all she could think about then was how little this man knew; for all of the education he had received up on the surface.

Finally, she explained, "It is an old, forgotten language; the one spoken by the Tuyuns before writing came to them, and before the language of the first occupiers—the Sce' 'dal of the Scereans from Su(ma) and the Cayanese and Feleenese of F'herak, and then Ro' 'dal of the Humans from the West and the North Continents. My cikgu once told me that it's as old as the *kerah*, the dialects, still spoken in the F'herakian north. Interesting, isn't it? How so much of what we say is borrowed?"

He was leaning over, peering around the sarcophagus. "Do you speak it? How do you say 'Hello' in Tuyunri?"

Ria chuckled. People always asked how to say "hello" when they encountered new languages, as if it was at the very core of sentient being to learn to greet another.

"It is not something you can say in a word," she revealed. "The ancient Tuyuns believed that they had a very close connection to the jungle they lived in. So greetings were likely sounds, like animal calls. When they greet each other in very formal settings, they say *bcur'in*, or 'Day above'."

"Why would they say that?"

Ria shrugged and shook her head at the same time. "Maybe life was precious to them. Mortality rates very high among their numbers. So to see day might have been significant."

"Ah, I...see."

Do you? She wanted to ask.

"Never heard of the language before. Is there a dictionary?"

"If there is, I do not know of it. The Tuyun lexicon is understandably small given the way they lived and it was not given time to evolve to be precise, to be relevant in modern communication. Often, it runs circles around things, depending a lot on the context of the moment."

"Context?"

Ria pondered the question. "There was once a town in the marshlands that was populated by early Scereans: Su(ma) Uk'rh, or Lower Marsh(land). 'Uk'rh' is often translated as 'lower' or 'minor', when actually its gestured meaning is 'what it is not, yet could be'. Possibility, I think you would call it. In those days, the Scerean settlement was a home displaced—what is not Su(ma), their land of origin, and yet could be by the little things they did to make it feel like home." A distant look came over her as she continued, "And when the Humans came and spoke of your Krow City, many Scereans left to seek their fortunes there. But, they could only get menial jobs. They were practically slaves, earning very little and regarded even less. As you already know, they lived in that slum. Dinya Uk'rh, they called it—Lower World. Not Su(ma) any more. They couldn't bring themselves to name it after home. Out of shame or disappointment... I don't know."

"Scereans? We were talking about Tuyuns."

"Yes, but due to racial interactions very early on, the Scereans in Manticura used to speak a form of Tuyunri. More words...the addition of Sumean prepositions and pronouns. Sumean is very similar to Tuyunri after all. Sce' 'dal was a... later development, when they had to communicate with the other 'nees'es, namely those from F'herak."

She paused and, smiling, added, "But I admit, my vocabulary is limited. I have only one book on Tuyunri and everything I know is from there. It is thorough but it is nearly two hundred years old and perhaps people who study languages have already come up with something new."

He stared at her, as if she was something he didn't want to forget and Ria realised she had never experienced scrutiny of such a nature before.

After a long pause, Eedric asked her in a quiet voice and with a great deal of care, "Do you remember why you turned the people in Kenanga?"

Ria thought she had reached an age where the events of that day could no longer affect her and where she would be able to approach it with an answer, the clarity of which would show both distance and understanding—a rationale behind the devastating actions of her child self. Yet, Ria found only silence stretching across the turbulent landscape of her mind.

She must have been mute for too long, because Eedric said, "If you're not comfortable answering that, you don't have to."

"I was young," she told him finally. "I thought that was where the enemies were. The villagers were the only ones who knew about us—so I thought at the time—and I thought, with them gone, we could live in that hut in peace forever, my sister and I. It had seemed like the right thing to do."

"When did you know it wasn't?"

"Immediately after."

Silence descended upon them. Eedric studied the empty space of air in front of him, and whatever he saw made him heave a sigh. Ria saw him raise his brows; saw his eyes widen.

"And you have been hiding here all these years because of that?"

Ria nodded, though she said, "Maybe."

"Do you feel...like you should—" He stopped and gestured around him at the statues. "Like, is all this a way for you to make up for it? You know, like an atonement, or something?"

"You cannot make up for killing with more killing, Eedric," she told him.

"No—I meant—yeah. No." He shook his head, eyes pressed shut to rid himself of some image she couldn't see.

"Should I be punished in the court of justice?" she asked.

He looked at her, his expression pained.

"That is only fair," she goaded him.

He turned away. "Not when you—" He paused, then turned back, a smile already adorned. "You know, I still can't wrap my head around the fact that you speak Tuyunri. I bet only a Manticurean historical linguist knows the language... and that's probably one guy, if either he or the title even exists." Turning to her, he asked again, "So what are you? Referred to in Tuyunri, I mean."

Ria scrunched up her face and closed her eyes as she thought. "*Metu'ra*," she said. *Me tuung ra,* it sounded like. Serpent woman.

He nodded, appearing rather in awe now. "Nice. It suits you."

Ria laughed then. She laughed because what he had said was so contrived; and she laughed because he made it sound as if he'd spent a lifetime telling the phrase to someone. Eedric considered her with a puzzled look before joining in.

When the laughter died down, he asked her, "So, what is Nelroote like? It must be quite something, huh? A city beneath a city? Is it busy? How do you keep it ventilated? Lit? Why was it built? And was it always a city?"

She looked at him and felt the urge to reach out and right a hair out of place. She chose instead to give his thigh a light pat. "Another time lah, sayang. Another time."

One more pat and she hoisted herself to a stand.

"How do you know when to leave each time?" asked Eedric, getting up after her.

Ria chuckled. "When you start looking at your watch a lot."

5117 CE

Underbelly

For Ria, the daily move from tomb to home was seamless. She could not think of Nelroote apart from its vast network of tunnels and corridors. For everyone else, Nelroote was solely the flawed city with its narrow alleys, where the dying shared a dim space with the desperately living. The city had got crowded over the years as those finding themselves in Manticura without the proper papers and those who'd been ousted with nowhere to go found their way to the city through feelers working up on the surface. Without a sophisticated sewage disposal system, it had adopted a smell. It was the smell of waste and wasting, but it was the smell of living too: banana fritters being fried in big batches by someone trying to make a living selling them; soap for bodies wishing to be clean in spite of the place they were living in; the flowers people always hung in doorways and windows. There was a woman who lived along the route Ria took. Ria could always smell the scent of the oil she used to keep her dark coat shiny. She oiled herself in nothing but a towel every evening at seven o'clock. And there was a man who burned his incense right across from her doorway at exactly the same time. Prayers, he always insisted when Ria walked by and noticed him peeking into the woman's home. Ria said little to the man. Sometimes the towel dropped off, she knew.

Nelroote was already a shanty town when Ria had arrived with Barani, and it looked set to be a shanty town for all eternity. There was little by way of rent to pay and most people had to scrape by anyway, so anything illegal was generally ignored unless it hurt someone directly. Then justice was whatever Pak Arlindi and Barani said it was during one of their *trials*.

Walking northeast from Pak Wao's shop—the only provision shop in Nelroote—past the homes with walls of corrugated zinc and spray-painted plywood, and the occasional three- or four-family living spaces made out of shipping container walls, one would eventually come to a black door made of heavy wood, a "No Entry" road sign hung up on it. The sign bore the word "Dream" in thick black paint across the white bar. The door opened onto an alley between two rows of stacked houses, lit by red lamps hanging at intervals along one wall. Garbage-lined and with home extensions spilling into the narrow walkway, the alley led to an area the Nelrootians called the "Dream Garden"—a cruel, cruel joke by the drug lords who jointly owned it.

When the Dream Garden was but a hollow of cave seized from a number of families who had been living there, a runner had come to the door to ask if anyone was interested in being a part of it. Ria remembered hovering in the background, at the edges of the shadows within the home's interior, and on seeing her, the runner had started sweating more than he already was. The offer, Ria knew, was not for her, who tended to the sacred dead. Just Barani. "For which job?" Barani had asked as she leaned her shoulder against the doorjamb, unable as always to hide her bemusement. "Prostitution or assassination?"

That was just the kind of place it was.

Every world needed a seedy underbelly—that was true enough—and Nelroote's Dream Garden was an underground within an underground. Brothels, alcohol tanks, gambling and drug dens were kept away from the good folk by walls of welded shipyard steel. Its neon lights could be seen from any corner of Nelroote when the main lights went off, casting their pulsing, pinkish hue onto the three immense stone statues in their lofty niches. Each serene face was tilted down towards the settlement, undisturbed by how much life went on to chase the prevailing desire for instant gratification.

Some years after Nelroote's entertainment district had been established, Ria had walked into the world of pulsing lights and sweaty bodies pressed into coital positions. She had only been an observer, watching in the margins as patrons in various stages of intoxication stumbled down labyrinthine alleyways, as body trades were plied and as addicts slumped against walls in a collective stupor. No one had dared touch her; not even the inebriated. People generally moved out of her way when she came through. The gesture had grown into a reflexive action over the years, done without thought or consciousness. She couldn't decide if that warranted sadness or relief.

Ria had not gone back to the Dream Garden after that initial visit. It was not that she was against it, or the idea of it; rather, what would a place like that offer her? The momentary forgetting of substance abuse? The empty contact of bodies whose warmth was only transient? More reminders of how the world moved while she was but a static object standing in an ocean of regret? Yet following a detour to change her route up a bit, Ria found herself standing in front of the gate again, peering at the "No Entry Dream" sign that no one had changed since the day it was put up on the door. The two burly men standing on either side of it eyed her warily; she didn't know if it was because of what had happened before with Johan or because bouncers were generally suspicious of everyone. One uttered a terse, "Kak."

Ria found that strangely amusing, and the sound of her laughter, rarely heard within Nelroote, visibly startled and worried the men.

She was about to reply when the dark door opened and a familiar voice called to her: "Kak?"

She turned to Sani, the younger of Abang Seh's two sons, crossing the Dream's threshold. Sani was a Tuyun and he had a brother, Lan; four years apart and never more different. Lan was an active boy, big for a Tuyun, the way a lot of them were in Nelroote. Sani was stringy in contrast, though just as tall, and unlike his brother, whose *yun* scales covered his entire body, Sani's were restricted to his right arm, making the appendage appear abnormally large and the hand a menacing claw. The rest of him took after his Human mother—all defined bone structures and pale, smooth skin the colour of new ash. He had been a sullen child with this way of sitting for a long time, hunched forward as he observed people without reserve or restraint.

It was that intense, discomfiting stare that had drawn Ria to the boy when she had first seen him standing at the back of his house, holding a bun in one hand as he returned her gaze with an unfiltered stare of his own. Children generally made her uneasy, but she had gone over and asked how old he was.

"Seven," he had said, a little too loudly, his brows drawn low.

"Why are you not in school?" she asked, referring to the schoolhouse in Nelroote run by a Scerean ex-schoolteacher who'd escaped to Nelroote during the Tuhav. It was where the settlement's children were taught reading and writing along with basic mathematics.

"Father say I cannot go." As an afterthought, he had added, "Because the children beat me."

"Why would they do that?"

He had shrugged, but from the unblinking way he continued to stare up at her, she knew. She had straightened up almost too abruptly, causing a shadow of surprise to cross his young face. She had gone to his house that very same day, and her arrival was met by clattering cups and saucers, and a frantic mother hustling her sons about to make them presentable to the *metu'ra*. When they were finally brought before Ria, Sani's hair had been combed back with cream, so that the flat black surface was furrowed like a tilled field. His face had been washed and powdered—two pats on the cheeks and one across the forehead—clean shirt tucked into shorts pulled up high. No one had fought her decision to tutor him at home, even though she recalled Abang Seh's reluctant expression as the man sat at the dining table while she spoke to Kak Sab, his wife.

And when Sani's intellectual capacity and hunger for knowledge had far surpassed what she could teach him from the books she owned and got from the schoolhouse, she had convinced Abang Seh to send him to the surface to study. With the help of some surface relatives, they had been able to do so, even if the processes involved were not entirely cheap, or legal.

Ria couldn't help but admire him a little right then. Sani had grown handsomely over the years, though the knobs along his back caused his back to arch into a permanent slouch and the dark shadows under his eyes were starker now against his pallid skin.

He had his backpack over one shoulder and a ring file tucked under his elbow. Looking down, Ria saw that Sani had his customised black glove over his right hand as if that was going to make him blend in with the Humans, who were always quick to see when someone was different.

"Back from classes, Sani?" she asked.

He nodded in reply, keeping his face carefully averted and only stealing glances at her through the partings of his long fringe. She felt a familiar urge to push the hair aside, but she remembered the way he'd flinched when she'd done it once, as if her touch was poison. The memory stayed her hand, as it always had.

"I am not a boy any more," he had told her then, and she hadn't had the heart to tell him that to her, he would always be a boy. Until she could look upon him—until he could look upon *her*, could see her properly without fringe curtains or the evasiveness of stolen glances. Or the lies of secret gazes he thought she couldn't feel on her back when she hung the washing out or swept the bit of space in front of her house.

Ria caught a glimpse of a group of men, four or five of them in the alleyway behind Sani, leaning on walls or just standing about. One man called out and stretched his hand to Sani and, with some familiarity, Sani reached back to grasp it with a curt nod.

"Remember to send eh?" the man asked. To Ria, he said, "Evening, Kak," trying his best at a friendly smile and wave that came out feeling forced anyway.

Sani only nodded and closed the door behind him. He ignored the two burly bouncers and started to walk in the direction of home. His strides were long, so Ria had to run a little to keep up. She glanced at his bag, saw the way it bulged and the slight unease with which he carried it.

"Your bag looks heavy," she remarked. "What's inside?"

He pulled the strap further up his shoulder.

"Books?" she pressed.

He nodded. Ria looked back at the Dream door receding behind her. She wondered when Sani had started going to a place like that, lacking a good history with people as he did. Too many times in his teenage years had she found him pushed up by an angry group against a wall, or returning home appearing a little worse for wear than he was before—for staring, always for staring, or being too good for Nelroote, always too good for Nelroote with his better-spoken 'dals—big-big Ro' 'dal words, as if he was too good for Sce' 'dal. She wondered if he resented her for his proficiencies. There were days when he made it seem as if he did resent her; by ignoring her questions, brushing off her help, falling into debates about politics, strife, the "disordered notions" of law. Only to go back to stolen glances, oblique gazes, the shadowing, the early morning visits filled with awkward silences.

"Are they your friends?" she asked, walking fast to keep up.

Sani hesitated, then replied, "Yah. Friends."

"We have not seen you in a while, Sani." Three weeks, nearly four. "You shouldn't live in your dormitory all the time. Once in a while come back lah, to your ibu and ayah."

"I was home two weeks ago, Kak," he said, a little too sharply, "but you weren't around."

Guilt washed over Ria. There was a time some weeks before when Eedric had wanted to spend a night in the catacombs—just for the experience, he had said. "And what about Adrianne?" she had asked, knowing his girlfriend was not fond of being kept out of contact. Eedric had only shaken his head and sank beside the airman who'd come to be his treasured catacomb companion. "She can wait for once," he'd replied. Turning to her, he'd later added, "She wouldn't do these things with me." He had not even asked her if *she* needed to go back home to someone. Barani wouldn't worry, of course. It was likely she wouldn't even notice. Ria had not protested, though. She'd only sunk down beside him and they'd spent the night like that: talking, staring into the dark, telling each other ghost stories they knew as children and seeing whose was more terrifying. Ria had never known more mirth than she had that day, watching this surface dweller jump at every sound he thought he heard coming from the tunnels and corridors.

Right then, Sani was quiet. Ria stole a glance up at him, hoping he couldn't read the reams of memory running through her mind. He seemed a little paler and gaunter than she last remembered. He held himself with great rigidity and unease wrapped like suckered tentacles around him.

While they rounded a corner, Ria cast her eyes back to the Dream gate. The two burly men were watching them leave. Ria noticed they didn't lower their eyes from her face.

When they were far enough from the Dream Garden, Sani spoke up: "You shouldn't go to the Garden, Kak."

Ria turned her eyes to him. Saw how his were full of worry, perhaps even guilt as well.

"It is not a good place," he added.

When he said that, Ria pictured him with a Human girl; fair-skinned, long-haired, black roots gradating into auburn. Tall, slim, pretty... Everything a boy like him—like Eedric—would want. Entangled, folded in, one into the other.

"Then why were you there?" demanded Ria, feeling uncharacteristically miffed.

Something about the cadence of her voice made him stop. He stared ahead at the end of the alley they were in.

"How did you stop, Kak?" he asked finally.

Ria paused and looked at him. "Stop what?"

"You," he began with difficulty, "have not changed anyone in a long time, and I heard..." He trailed off, clenching his jaw.

"You forget about Johan." No one spoke about Johan, but

Ria was not one to let herself forget.

Sani made an annoyed sound, "I heard. I heard about the Changer too. I hope he left without too much trouble." He glanced at her as if there was more that he wanted to ask her about that, but he went on to ask instead, "Did it have something to do with the Two-Half? Did something happen?"

"The war happened. The Occupation happened. People died. That happened too." Ria spoke quickly, harshly.

"So," Sani went on with deliberation, as if he hadn't heard her tone, "it is easy to decide and just stop?"

Ria took a few steps up to the boy. "Sani…" she began, suspicion and worry creeping up on her. "What is this about?"

Sani straightened up, as if in alarm.

"Kak," he said, "I cannot go home today. Y-you tell Mak for me. Or tell Kak Bara to tell Mak."

"Why—"

Sani was already backing away. He ran his Human hand through his hair and for a moment, his fringe came away from his face, leaving it exposed. She saw that his eyes were fully fixed on her, looking as if he was seeing her for the first time.

He shook his head. "I have a lot of school work, Kak. A lot of work," he said. And then he was gone.

Multi-umbilici

Old Waro's shop was a small single-storey shack, with a shopfront made up of a counter and a small courtyard containing a freezer, two ageing refrigerators and wire racks filled with snacks and dry ingredients. It had stood at the centre of concentric circles of houses and tenement apartments for as long as anyone could remember, making one wonder if the settlement had been built around it instead of it being a product of the settlement's need for provisions.

Waro was a wiry old man who had not aged well; his thinning fur clung in patches to leathery skin that showed the tattoos he sported, relics from a younger, more boisterous time. He could always be found watching the small black-and-white television perched in the corner of his shop window, behind clear plastic kuih bottles filled with different varieties of sweets. His father used to own the store and had later relinquished it to Waro when he retired a few years after the war. Barani always thought Waro's father the better shopkeeper, may his soul rest in peace. With Waro in charge, much of the merchandise was covered in a layer of dust. He never bothered to keep track of the expiry dates and took forever to restock. Moreover, drunks had turned the rubbish pile at the back of his shop into a urinal, so his shop always smelled like a toilet, but nothing anyone said could make him improve. *Kalau dah dasar kepala batu.*

"Rolling paper satu packet dengan sabun Trojan," Barani ordered, once she was within earshot of the old Feleenese.

Waro nodded without a word and disappeared into the back of the shop with a jangle of his many earrings. While he was gone, Barani surveyed the shop counter, cramped with shallow plastic trays of little snacks and knick-knacks. She remembered Waro as a young man, crude and crass, a troublemaker who ran with a gang that sometimes risked their activities even on the surface; a Pak to nobody then. He used to give the young women all sorts of trouble with his salacious remarks, sometimes his brazen bum-grabbing, and not even the threat of Barani was able to keep him in check. When the war came, he was one of the first to sign up with chest-pounding bravado, thinking it was some big gang fight he was entering into.

The story went that he'd got captured not long after the surrender and had been put to work at a rail with other POWs. He came home after the liberation of Manticura, trudging behind an impassive Ria, all the while staring at the back of the younger woman's head as if he was seeing the war happen all over again. Ria wouldn't speak of the state that he'd been in when he had apparently stumbled into her chamber of horrors. Trauma was one thing, but Barani always thought adding Ria into the equation was the worst kind of punishment the Divine could impose on him for his wrongs.

"Shopping, Ani?" a voice spoke up beside her.

Barani started and turned to see Kak Sab, Abang Seh's wife, watching her with a gentle smile. The woman was short, wide of girth now that she was getting on with the years, and one of the rare Humans who'd made a home in Nelroote. Barani returned the smile, thinking with amusement how Kak Sab was also the only one around who addressed her by her old name.

"The usual, Kak," Barani replied. "The family good?"

Here, Kak Sab sighed and shook her head, surprising Barani.

"Something wrong?" she asked, feeling concerned.

"Nothing lah," Kak Sab replied, but she was just standing there, instead of examining the basket of potatoes off to the side and complaining about how they were growing shoots big enough to cover the whole of Nelroote, or picking through the snacks to get the dust on her fingertips so that she might accuse Waro with it. "Sani has not been back from last-last week. Call, tak angkat. I ask Lan to message, no reply. Nowadays I don't know what to do with that boy."

Barani smiled. "He is no longer a boy, Kak."

"We try to tell ourselves that, Ani," Kak Sab told her, "but the truth is they never truly grow up in our eyes."

Barani nodded. "True," she replied. "Girlfriend maybe?" she added amiably. "You know how boys are at this age. Want to try. Want to touch-touch."

Kak Sab looked up at her and Barani thought she had upset the woman. For all of Kak Sab's open heart and acceptance, she was still a mother of boys, and mothers of boys always loathed losing their sons to another woman.

"If he has a girlfriend also, Ani…" she began, "I don't mind. But what kind of life can we give that girl down here?"

The words struck a chord in Barani as she remembered the old days when she'd led Ria into the underground settlement. She was about to say something when Waro returned to give her the items she wanted. The transaction ended with Waro's quiet, "Send my regards to Ria," and Kak Sab taking hold of her arm to tell her the same. This was the tradition among people in the settlement. Not that Ria ever received the wishes with much warmth, just an inclination of her dark head and a stony expression.

When she left, Kak Sab was finally starting to deride Waro for the state of his merchandise and Waro was, as usual, keeping his eyes fixed on the television screen. *Buat tak dengar*. The walk to her house was uneventful—strolling past homes, returning greetings with her usual good humour and ease, automatically stepping over rough-shod drains and refuse, and just as automatically reprimanding any wasted youngsters she came across.

She neared home to find it the same way she'd left it, its windowed curtains drawn and gaping doorway dark. There was so little work in the mines nowadays, no overtime to keep her back late and no rosters to go over before heading home. Her day-to-day schedule consisted of idle staring into nothing, smoking her lungs away, reading the news—sometimes Ria's books—and tiring of the routine every time it ended, knowing it was only going to start again the day after. It was not yet ten o'clock, so the lights from the blazing overhead lamps carved out portions of light in the dark interior, revealing a folding table, its mismatched companion chairs, a little of the tiny kitchen and Ria's narrow bookshelf made out of small wooden crates nailed together.

What she hated most about idle days was that they gave her too much time to think about the old days, as if she was some washed up decrepit thing constantly going, "Oh! How great things once were!"

And in truth, they were not.

She didn't know when it was that she became less of a sister to Ria—she didn't know if it was the time she had lost Ria in the crowd on the day when the Tuhav ended and the Occupation began. In the quadrangle near Waro's store where that crowd had gathered as if in candlelight vigil. She had been there with Ria, allowing herself to be taken by the surge and press of bodies, hoping to catch a glimpse of the news about the progress of the war. There had been the fear, attaching itself like a sucking leech onto the stone skin of men; had been the fear that the forces might find Nelroote. She'd felt Ria's hand slip out of hers, remembered herself grasping for it and ended up with only empty air. She'd peered into the sea of people, using her height as a vantage point, hoping to see Ria's distinct head among them. But it was as if her sister had been swallowed by the crowd, and then had drowned in it.

She could not remember the search itself, but recalled bursting upon the sombre faces in Pak Arlindi's home where the man and his last remaining child sat. Abang Seh had suddenly stood, one hand on the back of the chair, body half-turned as if ready to run. After they had told her where

Ria might have gone, for a time Barani could only stare at them in disbelief.

"She's barely fifteen," she had said. Softly, with deepening rage, or sorrow. Who was to say what she had felt at that moment?

No one had said a word at first. Then Abang Seh had spoken up, eyes downcast, "She volunteered."

Barani remembered going up to the man so fast, her hair ablaze, the desire to turn him to stone barely in check. "And you let her? Two able-bodied men?" At the door, she remembered lividly saying to Pak Arlindi, "If you had wanted her killed, *this* is the surest way to do it." Pak Arlindi had only stared ahead, not meeting her eyes.

Later she would find Ria after tearing through the settlement in a state of denial, calling and calling like she was looking for a child, after making every wrong turn she could possibly make in the labyrinthine catacomb. During the search, she had felt as if she was seeking a ghost. And it *had* been a ghost she found when she finally came across Ria. She had seen her sister under the sunbeam, standing again amongst the silence of the dead. Barani had never wanted the innocence of leaf grasshoppers and static time drawn on paper clocks more than she did then.

Ria's eyes had been red and swollen as they looked upon the first stone soldier. Barani had not known that snakes could appear so limp and unwashed until she saw how they hung around Ria's face. The baju Ria had worn on that day was a gaudy yellow piece with puffed sleeves and fake pearls sewn into the lace pattern down the front—a donation from a woman in the settlement. At the time, it had not fitted Ria's small frame, so the girl appeared smothered by it, a bulge showing around the waist pressing through the satiny material where the kain needed to be rolled many times in order to fall to the right length. The ankles that showed beneath the kain had been knobbly; the bit of shin that could be seen thin and covered in scabs.

"Ria—" Barani began, but hadn't been able to continue after that.

For the gaze that Ria had showed turned her cold. What she said after cut far deeper: "Someone had to do it. And if you make me go back, I will kill every single person in that settlement and you know you cannot stop me."

In retrospect, Barani wondered if she should not actually have taken that threat seriously. She couldn't remember if she'd left immediately after. She couldn't remember much of anything from that meeting, except that she had left without saying much else. And she had continued to say little during the times she stopped by with food and supplies for Ria on her way to doing the same for the other watchmen the settlement had posted.

When Ria returned, she was already a woman grown: chest busty, hips filling out the kain so that it was wrapped tight around her form. Her shoulders were stalwart straight. She had lost a snake head and her feet were calloused after having discarded her slippers some time in the four years that had passed. The wounds she had sustained on her face and body, and which she would not talk about even when Barani had asked in panicked concern, had healed into alarming scars.

And she looked, but she never saw. She scanned. She

scrutinised and penetrated with every gaze. But it was never personal. There were even days when those eyes had been blanks. Ria had become a quiet girl since moving to Nelroote; post-war Ria was nearly mute.

Ria had thrown herself into normal living with the blind fervour of the over-determined. But she integrated into normal life with as much ease as would a Scerean in the fur of a Cayanese. Kept a pristine house, maintained the premises and took up the dreadful work of interring Manticura's dead when it was decided that they would have to go back to the ancestral practice. Whose ancestors, Barani didn't know.

After Nenek passed, family life had been the two of them. And for years after the Occupation, family became a threadbare relationship made out of sparse conversations, lowered eyes and oblique gazes; full of questions that wished to be asked, but wouldn't form. At first the thin interactions were discomfiting to Barani, and she had tried: to make small talk, to bring Ria out and let her meet people, bring her gifts in the form of trinkets and dresses—to do her part as Ria's sister after she had failed all those years before. Sometimes there had been gracious sparks: when Ria was fitted for a few new dresses, when she received those dresses after they had been completed, with their fitted waists and the flaring skirts so fashionable at the time. Barani would watch as Ria spun herself in front of the mirror in the seamstress' home.

But never once did Ria look at her reflection. Try as they might, Barani and the seamstress, saying: "Look at it. Is the colour okay?" "Beautiful! Nice colour. Look at it." But no amount of beseeching "look, look" could get Ria to look. She would only keep her eyes down, watching the flare of her skirts with the smallest of smiles.

Over the course of 40 years, there was a point where Barani stopped trying.

∿

Barani went into the house, which was empty as expected, and dropped the items she had bought onto the table. She was about to settle down for a smoke—box in hand, a stick already between teeth, lighter poised—when a shadow spilled from the open door, cutting off the light from the outside.

Barani turned, almost with a start. Though it was one of the settlers she was expecting, Ria stood in the threshold instead, carrying a small basket filled with fruits, dried goods and a bottle of cordial, likely a gift from Hana's family, whose daughter had just passed from a drug overdose.

"You're home early today, Ria," she couldn't help but remark.

Ria stood a while, blocking the doorway and peering over her shoulder as if at somebody. Barani lit the lamp that sat on the table. She did not expect an answer and Ria gave none as she stepped into the house, forgetting as always to wash her feet with the water from the earthen urn stationed by the door.

In continued silence, Ria unpacked the basket. She lit the kerosene stove. Barani lit her cigarette.

The pan went over the fire and then: "I wish you wouldn't smoke when I'm cooking."

Barani was still on her first puff, the cigarette clamped between index and middle finger, about to migrate back to her lips. At Ria's words she stopped and looked to her sister with surprise.

She must have sat there, mute and blinking her eyes as if testing their ability to do so, for quite a while, because Ria added, "It gets into the food. It gets everywhere."

Slowly, and with eyes fixed on Ria, Barani put the cigarette out by dropping it into the cut-off bottom of a plastic soda bottle which served as her ashtray. Bodies of dead cigarette butts floated among water-logged ashes on the surface of the browned water it was filled with.

She almost smiled when she argued, "I have been smoking for, what? Forty years? And only *now* you say that?"

There was a spark in Ria's eyes then. Displeasure it might have been, but it formed a furrow between Ria's brows. Her lips were set in a pert little line. She appeared about ready to burst out with a chastisement. But Barani could only move herself to the window as she tapped another cigarette into her palm.

"I smoke here, can?" she negotiated.

"Outside," Ria told her, indicating the door with the spatula she had taken hold of.

Barani slipped the cigarette into the breast pocket of her shirt and looked to Ria as the latter greased the pan with some oil.

Holding up two eggs, Ria asked, "Do you want eggs?"

Barani waggled her head by way of saying, "Yes."

Ria couldn't abide runny yolks or blinding whites, so she made mata lembu eggs browned with crispy edges. She fried four and gave Barani two. As was her habit, Ria would read at meals: the same few books, over and over, so that their pages had become blotched and crusted with oil stains and sambal. Barani gazed over her plate at her sister's bent head, at sickles of eyelashes cutting swabs over cheeks, always with a sense of wonder at the time that had passed. Ria ate with aged grace but she was always done with her food in the time it took her to read a page, maybe two if the lauk was too hot or difficult to eat. When she was done, her eyes lingered on the page while a finger trailed delicately over the oily remains on her plate. Nenek used to harangue her for reading at meals—"What sort of lady is this? Reading while you eat?"—but had always let her read anyway.

"Rice," Barani said absently.

Ria looked up, confused.

Barani pointed to the corner of her own mouth to indicate the rice that was stuck to Ria's. "You have rice on your face," she said, mildly amused.

Ria caught the rice with the tip of a finger and slipped it into her mouth.

"I…" Barani began. "That Changer from the other time. I hope we're not seeing any trouble?"

For a moment, Ria's expression opened up into one caught by surprise, but it was soon gone and she said, "He—has not given any trouble. But—"

"What's wrong?" Barani asked.

Ria considered her for a time. Barani could almost see the battle in her countenance.

Finally, Ria revealed, "I saw Sani come out from the Dream Garden just now." After a beat, she added, "He said he won't be coming back today."

Barani raised a brow. "Having seen the sun," she remarked with some resentment, "you wouldn't want to go back to the dark. He thinks it's a bigger, better world out there, but it isn't."

She saw Ria lost in thoughts of her own and went on to assure her, "The boy will be fine. Probably has some girlfriend on the surface. It's hard for him, you know, keeping one life here and one up there?"

Ria nodded quickly, eyes shifting and blinking as if trying to rid itself of an undesired image.

That night, Barani didn't fall asleep as quickly as she usually did. They had lived in that home space almost all her life, but she was sure that she hadn't paid acute attention to it before the way she did then, after lights-out plummeted the settlement into a pitch black mimesis of night. Barani could hear one of the neighbours making for the shared toilet nearby. There came the faint sound of water being thrown down the hole from a bucket. Water for washing had to be carried from a centralised public pump that tapped into an underground reserve. The water came out hot, so it had to be left to cool before they could use it. The sisters kept a washbasin under the long table that ran along the far wall beside the stacked up pots and pans. The little kerosene stove sat on the tabletop with a basket of cooking essentials. Their old kettle was in its usual place on the stove, already filled for morning boiling. The plates were on a dish rack on a smaller table where Ria carried out most of their meal preparations. By the dish rack, their kitchen utensils stood in a holder of plastic mesh. The wooden chair leg nearest to her was shiny, the squared edges smoothed over the years and touching it, and Barani could feel the scratch lines. There were a lot of them. She wondered how they had even got there.

Beside her on her own folding mattress, Ria slept on her

side as she always did, facing the wall so that Barani saw only the outline of her back. Ria slept curled so tightly, as if she wanted to fold in on herself or hold an object close for fear of losing it. And so still and stiff. Like a corpse. She had a mind to reach out and shake Ria awake just to tell her how she slept: "Hoi! What's this? Sleep like a dead person!" She did no such thing, only continued to watch as her sister slept the sleep of the dead, whose company she fancied better. Barani shifted, mirroring Ria's pose so that they were spooning without touching. She sleeps so deeply, Barani thought, and yet her eyes were ringed like they'd been keeping eternal vigil.

"Ria," she whispered, trying.

There was no response.

Turning onto her back, Barani stared up at the murk above. She tried to imagine what it would be like to die or be dead. The prospect of no longer walking the earth and stone was one suddenly frightening to her. However, silence and an eternity of darkness were but words, limiting and nothing when the experience itself was beyond description. Worship of the deity, the Blood Mother—the Lady—was bound to an ancient religion, born out of superstition now that the Nelrootians owed their existence to the architectures of a long dead people. No one knew for sure what their idea of an afterlife was. A number of the people she knew believed in the Rion circle of renewals that lasted for as long as time flowed. A constant cycle of rebirths sounded far more comforting to her than the Divine's idea of absolute hell and heaven.

She reached out and tangled her fingers in Ria's curls,

stirring them awake but not their owner. It had been a lifetime ago when she had last done that, before the tough wall of feisty girlhood and painful experience loomed up around Ria, impregnable as a barbed and invisible fortress. She thought about how it would have been if the fairy tale she'd dreamt for herself had come true all those years ago. This moment in the dark world would certainly not have manifested.

Ria stirred then, and Barani lifted her hand just slightly free of the other's hair.

"Ria?" she called, feeling suddenly foolish and old.

Her sister didn't reply, only turned to face her, her forehead resting lightly on Barani's shoulder.

Oblique

Between spinning 360 degrees for no apparent reason, bringing up his sights either too soon or too late and the occasional showman announcement of "Humiliation!", Eedric was not doing too well in the multiplayer map. At all. Targeting took too long with the console controller and felt too clumsy, and for someone getting his ass handed to him a lot, he sure kept checking the leaderboard often to see if he was anywhere near top score. Or at least not too near the bottom. On the other end of the headset mike, Miz was doing far better in the multiplayer game than he was. Good thing Miz was on his team. On the opposing side, some annoying kid was complaining about Miz's cooked grenade suicides, in between telling Eedric how he—the boy—had fucked Eedric's mother last night.

If only the boy knew.

At one point, he could hear Miz's own mother ask if Miz wanted anything to eat—Ria had taught him before: "Eh, you want to eat or not?" in Sce' 'dal—before leaving, it seemed, with the rest of Miz's family for a wedding reception somewhere in the east.

"Not going?" Eedric had asked at the time.

"Need to entertain you, what," Miz had replied, all while executing the perfect sniper rifle longshot from a significant distance away on the map. In that span of time, Eedric had been spawn-killed a few times and then tea-bagged on the last.

"Fuck!"

Adrianne was in his room at that very moment. Had been for some time now. Came to his house, "to spend some time", according to her, and the whole time he had been gaming with Miz, he had felt nothing but her eyes on his back as she sat on his bed.

Finally, she crawled over to sit on the edge of the bed he was leaning against while he played.

"Can you give me some time now?" she asked. "I came all the way—"

At first he cut her off with a noncommittal grunt, then replied, "We'll go eat after this next game."

He barely heard Miz's voice asking, "Girlfriend?" over the headphone, because Adrianne had caused the bed to bounce with the deliberate and overstated gesture of annoyance she made outside his line of sight.

"How long have you been playing that game already?" she voiced. "You asked me to come all the way here just to watch you play a bloody game?"

Eedric whipped his head around to look at her. Ignoring the fact that he had his headset on, he replied, "I didn't ask you to come down. You wanted to come down. And for what? You have nothing to do. I have a match to win." He turned back to the screen; it showed that the match had already begun. Then a hit was indicated by a sudden shaking and reddening of the screen, followed by another, before someone's virtual soldier came up to him and finished him off with a knife. Gesturing at the scene, Eedric very near shouted, "Stop making me lose!"

Someone online pitched in teasingly, "Eh… Don't fight lah." It was not Miz, and Eedric very nearly snapped at the guy too.

He stared at the screen, feeling suddenly defeated. He wanted to speak, but knew some dozen other people were listening in, ready to label him "pussy-whipped", if he so much as tried to apologise. In this game, with kids being motherfuckers, he was not ready to make that sacrifice.

He made it through one game and was in the lobby waiting for another when Miz logged out, and then in private chat told him quietly, "Game over, brother. Go talk to her."

Eedric clenched his jaw and palmed the buttons of his controller with force enough to break them. Finally, he tossed it aside and ripped the headset from his head. When he turned back to Adrianne, he saw that she was standing by his table, a thick tome opened up to the bookmarked page in her hands. He had not even heard her move.

"You might not want to read that," he said before he could catch himself. "Too many hard words for you."

Adrianne looked up at that. There was hurt. There was disbelief in her eyes, perhaps even fear. But she held up the book with one hand and he saw that it was a vintage annotated edition of the Tuyunri *Almanac of Life* that Ria had lent him. Acting on instinct, he sprinted up to her and took the book from her hand; rescued it, in fact, from the precarious way she was holding it by the corner of the cover such that the signatures were in danger of peeling right off from the spine. Adrianne didn't notice that. In her other hand, she held the bookmark that had been inside.

"What is this note?" she demanded.

Eedric saw that the bookmark was a slip of paper with the words, "There may be a Ro' 'dal translation of this book now. Please, if you could, check it for me? You may be able to read the words in that version. Yang benar, Ria."

"Who is this Ria?" Adrianne continued to demand, flicking the paper in his face, her expression the most livid he'd ever seen.

Mental images of heavy-lashed eyes peering up at him, of smokey smiles, and of slipping and sliding serpent bodies over a teasing neckline came unbidden to him. Accompanying them were the ringing sound of laughter and the smells of talcum powder mixed with an archaic rose scent. Adrianne's arm clattered with the colliding bangles and charm bracelets she wore, but he found himself thinking of a seashell hanging from twine noosed around another's wrist, wondering at the story behind it.

"She's a friend," he told Adrianne.

It must have taken him too long because Adrianne pressed the interrogation: "I don't know this friend. Where did you meet her? From your history class?"

Adrianne was referring to the private part-time degree he'd told her he'd signed up for. "To while the time away between shoots and castings," he'd explained.

There was no degree. Somehow, he'd managed to keep up the farce by picking imaginary classes that clashed with her own at the local university. In that span of time, he had gone down to see Ria, which was as good as any history class.

Nothing ever happened between him and Ria. There was just talking, of whatever topic came to mind, swinging easily from the profound—discussion of politics, sharing of past lives and moments—to the mundane—food, weather, him ranting about other people. There would also be silence, when neither wished to speak. Why he had skulked about had everything to do with the circumstances of Ria's existence: from her past deeds to her lack of documentation, making her, by law, an illegal dweller within the country. Why he had felt that meeting her was a transgression...that had everything to do with the nature of—no, mainly the reasons for his continued visits to her. It had moved from intrigue, to simply being glad that he had a companion as unique and knowledgeable as she was; to having a friend besides Miz; someone with whom he could have a fresh conversation. But of late, his eyes fell involuntarily to her lips and watched the play of expressions on her face, not believing that the moment and the woman before him were even possible.

A thousand times he'd come to think himself as abnormal for admiring the greenish sheen of her snakes' bodies as they teased her skin with their tongues. Yet in a thousand others he thought he knew her, only to be presented with a new angle, given a new perspective of the ways of the world, of its peoples, of the counter-corners people were made of. He sought blind spots in her every day: giving her a new picture on his tablet, letting her listen to a new song that she would immediately be able to sing along to, presenting her with a new chapter of a book on philosophy or a story in a newspaper. She was quick to learn and was always able to fill in the gaps of what she didn't already know.

Her inquisitive way of cocking her head to one side, of letting her snakes fall across her face and over her shoulder, and that rare open smile she showed in her unguarded moments sometimes caused his fingers to twitch. It was as if there was a fishing line attached to each tip, a line that someone would jerk every time, every *time* a hinting ray of light shone through her grey façade.

He found himself examining the dress racks of department stores and boutiques, wondering what size she wore and how he was even going to find out such a piece of information without being called out. When he was not with her, he found himself staring at his phone at night, wondering what she was doing at the moment; wondering *how* she was doing, and he had caught himself thinking, "I shouldn't text her too soon. Don't want to seem desperate."

To begin with, she was more likely to be communicating via carrier pigeon than a phone. And yes, he was desperate. For her approval and her regard; hell, for her to think about him as much as he was thinking about her.

"Yeah," he told Adrianne, trying to play at nonchalance as he placed the book carefully on the bookshelf by his table. "She's 58. One of the mature students there. Retired and looking for something to do, you know? She…uh…she's not very good at finding things. In bookstores and shops. So she just needed me to help her a bit." He rolled his eyes, made a show of exasperation.

Adrianne seemed to relax a little at that. "Okay," she said.

"Are you reading this for a project?"

Eedric nodded. "Yeah. Looking at Tuyunri history in Manticura. It is actually pretty interesting."

"What do these two words in Sce' 'dal say?" she asked. He could see that she was trying to be nonchalant as well, trying to pry without seeming suspicious or insecure. Adrianne, who had never shown any curiosity about anything that didn't fall within her areas of interest—beauty, fashion, her circle of acquaintances and mindless entertainment on cable—wasn't fooling anyone.

Nonetheless, Eedric looked at the two words she'd pointed out. "The truth," he explained, translating directly.

Adrianne frowned. "That makes no sense."

"'*Yang benar*' is the Sce' 'dal phrase for 'sincerely'. She is a very formal woman."

"How do you know?"

Eedric considered her anew. Had she asked that question at a different time, under different circumstances, he would have told her that Sce' 'dal was his mother tongue. Only his father made him learn Mir' 'dal instead, the language of the Esomiri that didn't have any use or significance in Manticura so many years after the Occupation. He wondered if this was where things had been wrong with Adrianne from the get-go. He thought he'd hit the jackpot. Her being good-looking and well-groomed was a boost for Eedric's ego, a validation of his sense of self and of his worth as a man. Father and Stepmother had been so relieved when he brought her home. Father had even shaken his hand, clapped his shoulder and given him a winking thumbs-up: his way of saying, "You did well, son." It was all he'd ever wanted to hear from Father and Adrianne had helped him accomplish that.

But it had taken him these two years with her to make him desire companionship, bonding and connection. It would have worked if her world view was such that he could have told her about Mama and the part of his heritage Father had been so adamant about keeping secret, so that Eedric had, what Father always called "prospects".

Perhaps if he had given her a chance, she could have proven to be a companion, someone he could at least live with under the roof of a magnificent condominium apartment. Perhaps. But in his gut, it all still felt wrong. It wasn't just her views on people or the fact that he couldn't bring her to a museum on a date because she would get bored. Or that he was five years her senior and no longer found clubs, with their pounding music and sweaty bodies, appealing. It was that they wanted different things in life: she wanted to go down the route of getting her degree and settling down; and he, after meeting Ria, knew he wanted more than that.

He realised that he had been in his reverie for a bit too long because when he replied, "Miz told me once," Adrianne leaned forward a little as if to get a closer look at him.

"Dri," he began suddenly, using the nickname he'd used when they were starting out, "I think we should take a break." Then he watched as the shock drew over her features like the shadow of a cloud over a sunny field.

Surfacing

Edric felt a sudden pressing need to right himself when he next saw Ria in the chamber, her face turned to the skylight. While he adjusted his jacket and pushed up its sleeves, Ria continued to stare up at what she termed, with a rather amused smile, "the bit of her sky".

When he made his presence known, she greeted him so cheerfully that he was at first caught off guard. He saw that she was wearing the lilac dress he had bought her a week ago. The colour really suited her, though the dress was one size too big, so that she had to tighten the waist by fastening a safety pin at the back. All her snakes, except the dead one, seemed to bounce with her as she bounded up to him.

She was radiant, and he felt the need to focus on something else. He spotted the contents of the basket she was hugging to her front.

"Wah, not bad," he remarked, gesturing towards the basket. "Wine and fruit basket."

Ria cast only a brief glance down at it. "That is for the recently deceased patriarch of a family, from his children.

The wine cost them half a month's salary. Maybe even more." Ria shook her head sadly. "A waste. The dead cannot drink."

"Maybe they did not mean it for the dead guy?" Eedric suggested, stepping further into the chamber after a cautious look at the other entrance for anyone from the settlement—for an underground type of community, they were pretty relaxed about security even after he had made an appearance. But he could never be too sure. Assassin-type Scerean maids and all.

"Maybe. Not as if that's any better."

She was always doing this, he thought. Swinging from glow to melancholia within the span of a short conversation. For someone who had the power to create statues with a well-placed glare, so much of her was transient to him. It made him want to reach out—that twitch again, of some blasted marionette seeking to disarm him.

"Do you drink?" he asked.

"No."

He lifted a shoulder. "Then it is wasted."

"Fruits rot…flowers too," she put in. "I bring them home, to eat later."

He raised an eyebrow. "Flowers?"

"Fruits," she clarified. "Flowers I leave here to die." She looked around. "Seems right that way."

She was smiling when she turned back to him. "Anyway, I wanted to show you something."

With that she stepped around him and, moving fast in that soundless way of hers, she led him out of the chamber and down a dim, lamp-lit tunnel. He knew the route by heart now and he wondered what more of it was there to see.

However, she came to a sudden stop and, stooping down, told him rather breathlessly, "There, see!"

He looked and saw that in a break between two walls of sentient remains was a hole—newly-excavated, he would guess—just large enough for a person to crawl through. She dropped into a crouch and pushed her basket into the crawlhole before going in after on all fours. Once on the other side, she beckoned him to follow.

"Come! See this!" she urged. "I found it only this morning."

"How?" he asked, gingerly examining the crawlhole and wondering how the hell she expected him to fit through it. "And damn it, Ria. This is too small for me."

"Kicked some rocks by accident," she informed him. "You have to see this. You will like it!"

"More dead people?" He was flat on the ground, stomach down, prone. Positioned that way, he inched through to the other side, getting stuck for just a bit when he was a little past his shoulders and scraping his right elbow on the rough stone in the process of struggling through.

On the other side, he found himself in a chamber that looked like a scaled down version of the main one. It was overgrown with vegetation that had crept in from the outside through a small skylight in the slanted ceiling. There was a stone table in front of an empty alcove, but it was broken right through the middle as if someone had dropped the blade of a headsman's axe onto it. The walls were entirely covered in tiles like the ones lining the tunnel leading to the entrance. The floor was bathed in shadow. Eedric could just about make out the carpet of leaves and the bones of small animals that littered it. There were bound to be bodies too, he thought, and the chamber had a dank smell about it.

Ria was peering up at the wall that was best lit by the sunlight. On seeing him, she gestured for him to join her. She pointed at one tile and he saw the carved image of two figures, unmistakably entwined in intercourse.

"W-why...would I like this?" he found himself asking, turning abruptly to her.

She didn't seem to hear him as she traced the figures with just the tip of her right ring finger, as if afraid to deface the ancient carvings. He watched the delicate finger, watched the hand; though the nails were never clean and in certain light the knobby, bone-thinness of the appendages betrayed her real age. He found himself clenching his jaw, transfixed as if he was watching the finger trace the tender aureole of a nipple. She considered the carving with a ponderous tilt of her head, immersed in some distant thought that he, as always, was not a part of.

And then she said, "I may be wrong but it could be the *tura-*, hmmm, *tura-is rebakara*," as if she was reading it off the image and what she was seeing was not a very clear one, "of the *jar nah-uk'rh*."

"I don't..." he began.

She turned to him with a start, eyes wide from interrupted reverie. Then, just as quickly, the look left her. She smiled sheepishly, lowering her gaze before turning it back to the images. "*Tura-is rebakara*," raising her brows and nodding as if expecting him to understand. "Picture celebration," she explained.

"They celebrate sex by drawing, I mean, carving pictures?"

"Yes!" Ria responded, brightening up.

"Okay..." Eedric went on slowly. "Like an ancient porno... Why?"

"Nothing so crass like your pornos."

"Excuse me. How—"

As if she hadn't heard, "I am guessing from this chamber that the act portrayed is likely a ritualistic one." She paused, considering the picture again and then the symbols on the tiles beside it. "*Tura* means 'woman', or 'one'. It gets more complicated than that, but I don't know all the other vocabulary meanings. But I do know that *tuis* means 'man'. *Tura-is* is 'joining', I think, so it makes sense that it denotes a sexual act."

"Yes, but I still don't get why it's called a 'picture celebration'."

"A different way of writing *tura-is* can also mean 'picture' in Tuyunri. *Tura* is derived from the root word for rock and earth. *Tis* means the sky." She grew quiet and then added, "So, *tura-is* also denotes 'completion'."

The way she looked at him, with that tilted head, the large blinking eyes, it was as if she expected him to know these things. His formal education meant that he was all numbers, business plans and profit margins. And useless knowledge of internet trends, because lectures and slow office days afford you plenty of time to go web-trawling. He felt stupid for knowing nothing, nothing of the things that interested and consumed her. He ought to be intimidated—standard protocol for any female that showed more intelligence than you, or drove a better car, held a better job: pick up sticks, grab the keys and the man-card, and get the hell out. Yet, he felt only fascination and admiration for her.

She said, "I didn't mean to bore you..." What she didn't know was that she could say anything in that smooth, soothing way of hers and he would listen. He didn't tell her that. He asked teasingly instead: "Are you apologising?"

Her only response was to chuckle and shake her head. "Funny thought though."

"What is?"

"Dinya's the slum that they arrested Anten in. What is it about my kind and running to the lower worlds to seek refuge?" she wondered. Then she added, muttering, "Not a good sign."

"Do you—" he began, "do you know why she did what she did?"

"Who?"

"Anten Demaria," he clarified. "That other medusa. Who turned the general and then got—"

Ria averted her face and he thought he saw her shudder. "Executed? A great number of reasons," she told him. "To protect...to preserve... Though I suspect money might be a good reason for why."

"Money? You think she was paid?"

Her orange, reptilian eyes found their way back to his face. In the dimness of this new chamber, they appeared larger than usual. "Anten was from the Dinya Uk'rh slums. The people there couldn't have had much money, and poverty has been known to make one do desperate things."

"This is from experience, I take it?" he dared ask.

"Not myself. But I live surrounded by it."

"But," Eedric went on, still on the subject of Anten and the assassination, "there has to be some political affiliation on her part, right? I mean, she wouldn't just...*agree* to kill someone as big and important as the general. And what,"— Eedric pointed out, finger towards the inscriptions, though they held no connection to the topic—"about the fact that she was just allowed into the Palaçade? Which should be one of the most guarded places in Manticura."

A small smile curved Ria's lips. With a glint in her eyes, she replied, "The same reason that keeps you coming down to see me." Eedric had no time to respond because she went on to say, "And you forget Ormal Din was only a puppet leader."

Eedric's eyes remained on her for a beat before he asked, "So, what's the other thing? The one about the jar?"

"*Jar nah-uk'rh*? Blood Aunt, the Lady in the sarcophagus. Everyone here knows about her."

They stood staring at the tiles, close and almost touching. In the silence that followed, he almost believed that he could hear her snakes gliding over each other and the thoughts churning in her mind. He took to staring hard at another tile, in which a woman with a ferocious visage was riding a body whose head was lost, worn off from the ages.

"I just thought I would show it to you," he heard her say. He felt her turn her head slightly to him and thought she was going to drop it onto his shoulder. He tensed up, preparing himself for the weight and the snakes. She didn't.

With finality, she took up instead her basket from the floor where she'd left it and asked him brightly, "Shall we go?"

But Eedric did not move. He turned his eyes from the tiles and slowly jerked his chin towards the skylight. "Do you miss it?"

"Yes." Steady, blunt. Ria on good days.

He considered her a while before asking, "What do you miss?"

"Trees. Things taller than me that are not walls or..."—she looked down briefly into her basket as if the answer was there—"stone."

"Will you go out with me?"

"Out?" she asked, turning her head a fraction towards him.

He nodded, the movement heavy and serious as if he'd just delivered bad news. He was nervous when he next spoke. "Outside...and out. With me."

He approached. She remained where she was. As he stood close, it was the first time he properly noticed how tall he was, and how much he had to slouch to accommodate her. His entire body stood on a brink. He could almost feel the tension in how conscious it was, of itself and of hers; how she nearly flinched when his hand touched her arm, high up near the shoulder. He kept it there, watching her hair, testing ground before curving the touch into a proper hold. She let him. She was warm and suddenly so painfully, frighteningly real.

"I'm pretty sure being around death as much as you do invites it," he told her. The air felt thick and it was suddenly hard to breathe. "All I'm saying is, you need a break. Come out a while. If you keep away from the main trails or wear something on your head, no one is going to know. Not all medusas need to be in captivity. At least, you don't."

She regarded him mournfully and his hand moved from

her arm to hover over her cheek. Finally, he prised his hand away from the empty touch, to study it as if he was uncertain of what it was.

"You know something? I always thought I was a safe guy—savings, insurance coverage, general degree... Even the kind of girlfriend that I know my father would like," he said quietly. "Then I go and poke my fingers into dangerous holes and expect them to come out clean."

This caused Ria to smile. "Am I one of those dangerous holes?"

Eedric thought about her, about Adrianne, and how it would all play out for him if this—this woman, this *medusa*—were to come to light.

"Very dangerous." And yet, suddenly heedless, he pressed, "So will you go out with me?"

Ria nodded in answer. They got back out through the tiny crawlhole. Ria went ahead, not realising, it seemed, the view she was giving him as he went after her—simple panties, mauve in a conscious effort to match the dress, he thought. *Hoped.*

In the tunnels just before the spiral staircase, Eedric stopped her with a whisper and removed the jacket he was wearing. It was an old hoodie, he mentioned as he helped her slip into it, and thought she might even know the band emblazoned on its front: Hoarsemen—"Because they scream themselves hoarse in every album, get it?" he explained, snickering a little—four of them with painted faces of violent but sickly hues, each expression a different shade of suffering.

She silently pulled the large hood over her head, hiding

much of her face from his view, and they were off, the skulls watching their passing, taking only a moment's rest from their guard when they were engulfed in the darkness of Ria's and Eedric's shadows.

Even if he would not admit it, the skulls made Eedric feel uneasy sometimes. However, walking with Ria to a now-unknown surface made him believe he was past being frightened. After what he'd seen of her chamber, there was a certain reassurance in skeletal remains. Nothing represented death's absolutes like skulls and bones. He could assume every person the skeletons once belonged to had died of natural causes, or from unfortunate accidents. All of the skulls were intact. A few bore holes in their craniums, either from a bullet or someone's lucky arrow, maybe even a spear. Maybe the experts could tell but as far as Eedric was concerned, the skeletons had no features, no written records on them, and so nothing remained of the people they used to be.

As they went up the spiral, he was aware of every inhale and exhale of his breath, every creasing rustle from his jeans, and the plastic footsteps of his sneakered feet. A few times she looked over her shoulder at him, and each time she asked how he was doing, he would reply with, "I'm okay." Finally, she pressed herself against the central stone pillar to let him pass. He stopped beside her and motioned for her to go on. Wordlessly, she slipped past him and made it clear with just her steady look that she was going to take up the rear. He struggled with himself. A few times he tried to speak, thinking he'd found the words, and each time he clammed up having found none. Finally, he just drew a sigh of resignation and took point.

At her touch, light and drawing on the stretch of his back, he stopped and whipped his head over his shoulder to look at her.

"What?" he asked.

She drew back and assured him, "Nothing."

They exchanged not a word more until they were finally outside. The sudden brightness blinded him and made him squint. It was a while before he could take in what surrounded them. She did the same, peering up at the cracks of sky through the canopy, the leaves that moved with the wind, the vegetation emitting the calls of monkeys and the chirrups of cicadas. He had seen and heard it all before, smelt what she must smell then, but it all seemed more vibrant than he remembered. He wondered if it was the same for her too, after all these years. They went down the nearly imperceptible path he always took to get to her, stepping over roots and through undergrowth. They watched their feet as they walked. Above the sound of their movements, he could hear the distinct, continuous buzz of the rainforest around them.

They paused a moment and Ria closed her eyes to take it all in. As if sensing her calm, her snakes were well-behaved in spite of the hood's confinement. One of them slithered forward, over her cheek, then further down to her chin and the nape of her neck. She was about to tuck it back under the hood when Eedric stopped her. He sized it up. The fact that her hair was made of cobras, each with venom deadly enough to liquefy his insides, was never far from his mind. Then he reached up to touch it. Every muscle in him screamed at him to pull away, but he persisted, never once taking his eyes off the snake.

"Wow, it's dry and smooth!" he remarked.

"Like all snakes," she told him.

The snake raised itself and he snatched his hand back. But Ria held it up by the bottom of its head and stretched it out to him, gently telling him to not be afraid. He dared to touch the snakehead she held, daring even to trace the white eye-like marking on the back of its head. A sense of comfort washed over him as he saw her relax into his touch.

The moment passed quickly and she tucked the snake back in with the rest.

"So?" Eedric prompted. "What do you think?"

He watched her squint upwards. Then she answered, "I want to see what the night looks like."

Eedric was surprised, but only mildly. He waited, and it was just like Ria to not offer explanations when she was expected to. In time, he only turned away and smiled. If this was what it meant for her to let go, to forget and to adjust, he would be with her in surviving the twilight hours of the forest.

"I know what we can do," he replied.

He took her hand from within the too-long sleeves of the jacket—found that it was sweaty—and led her down the gentle incline, slipping a few times as they stepped over roots and fallen tree parts. Further down the path later, they were seized by a sense of unbridled freedom, and for a moment they flitted in the jungle, adding mirth to the forest sounds and carelessness to the possibility of discovery. She moved barefoot through the undergrowth, having removed her slippers before they had left the tunnel. Eedric saw that she moved fast and, save for the slightest rustle of the foliage when she brushed against it, did so with barely a sound. She was a fleeting image caught in pieces between green-leafed gaps—a black-hooded figure trailing the bright, flowery hem of a dress, hands cut off by the over-long sleeves, mottled legs opening up in leaps. Her laughter rang through the forest as if she was ethereal. She was breathless when he finally caught her, wedged in between the buttress roots of a large tree. He perceived her smile from beneath the hood, and all the arcs that made her face just what it was; and he believed, for the silliest, most romantic moment, that he was going to have her forever.

In the jungle of the moment, she taught him which fruits he could eat, which he mustn't and how to bring them down with well-aimed sticks. Later they would watch a macaque hunkered in a tree, picking with flexible lips the eatables from the brown shell of a jungle fruit. It exhibited neither alarm nor concern as it peered at them over the meal in its hands. Eedric envied it for its freedom to scratch its balls and eat where and how it chose.

He felt Ria hesitate for a fleeting moment when they came to the manicured landscaping beyond which the visitors centre stood. However, all she did was pull her hood down further and duck her head before letting him lead her towards the cafeteria. She stood just outside of its perimeters while he bought food for the both of them. While he waited for his purchases to be prepared, he peered through the wide open doors at her. She got looks—a man in a bright yellow polo tee did a double take when he saw her face, two women in trekking gear gave her a glance and quickly dropped their gaze, while a little boy stared up at her from where he stood holding on to his small backpack and red-and-blue cap. Ria didn't seem to notice. When Eedric rejoined her with canned drinks and takeaway sandwiches, he saw that her attention was focused on the open field, where children stood upon the shortened grass with their parents, holding on to lines of massive kites streaming entrails against the sky.

He remembered a time when Father was gentle. He would take Eedric out to fly a kite just like that—a dragon form with a tail that streamed spikes—the two of them holding on to the line. Father would be the anchor and Eedric would do his best to stabilise the kite. A memory in pastel, really, soft and very faded.

They trailed away from the populated area, back into the forest, taking the unbeaten paths until they reached an unused road riven with cracks, weeds and lichen. It turned out to be a steep climb up to the old radio towers that did their towering within ageing fences. The disused road ended some ways off and they crossed over the guardrails to the patch of nearly bare ground at the edge of the dead drop.

They sat waiting for the night, Eedric cross-legged and Ria with her body facing his side, mottled legs stretched lengthways behind him. Eedric watched her for a time, waiting for a snakehead to come free, watching the sporadic drops of dark lashes each time she blinked, and the light tremble of her dress' hem when the wind caught at it. Ria said little, her gaze far off and her body held stiffly, almost pensively. He wondered if she was trying hard to breathe—to keep breathing.

He looked down to the view below, to grey roads and nondescript buildings. Manticura was a country of little beauty and he hoped that some, if not all, of that beauty could be poured into that one night just for her.

The night, when it finally crept in, showed no stars, except for the lantern-dotted city that blazed the further it stretched to the dark expanse of an invisible sea. But there was the slightest shift and when he looked to the medusa beside him, to her fuzzy silhouette, he saw that she had her legs drawn up to her, half her body turned to the view and her weight supported on her arms. Her hood had since been thrown back, and her snakes as they moved in their undulating outlines were docile and languid. Contentment was what he felt when he turned back to the view below. They whiled the evening away with the gleeful delinquency of forgotten youth, as they passed a packet of peanuts between them, describing arcs in empty spaces with the shells that they discarded.

Blind

One hour past ten; the lights were already out. Waro was taking stock, and he thought he might have been short on eggs again. Or was it soda? He couldn't remember. People complained a lot about one thing or the other when it came to his shop. Lately, it had been about how much more expensive his cigarettes were than those sold by the street boys in Dream Garden. The licenses he had to pay the Dream Garden suppliers were enough to set him back. And they kept asking for more and more. Those snakes. Said that it was harder to get the cartons past the F'herak-Manticura checkpoint. Said there were ten different kinds of tobacco taxes now across the strait in both F'herak and South Ceras, and that it wasn't the '77s any more, where police officers could be bribed. "How to make money like that?" they would ask. These young people with their smug way of talking and obscene clothes. Waro almost spat into a man's face once. If anyone should be asking how one was to make money in hard times, it was him. *Damn all Tuyun people*, he thought as he ran through the numbers again.

A sound disrupted his counting. Pranksters, drunk ones, he'd thought at first. They knew, these young people from the purple city of sin, they knew he couldn't count like before. They knew he couldn't see so well these days, even for—*especially* for—a Feleenese. However, his sense of hearing had not been dulled by the years.

Something about the sound when it came again made him perk up and listen. It didn't take him long to realise that it was not pranksters he was hearing. Rather, it was the sound of controlled authority; a muffled cacophony of command and fear-breathing protest. It reminded him of the few moments before the morning call in Menkapa, when the Esomiri prison wardens would make their way to the barracks that housed the POWs. It reminded him of the resounding authority in the gritty sound of boots on gravel and the stalking quality of every step. The quiet sounds had always come before the pounding of fists on the barrack doors, windows and half-dead bodies. All above the sound of the wardens shouting in pidgin Ro' 'dal. As it was, sounds of authority were always followed by sounds of subordination. After every wake-up call would come the shuffling of rank feet bursting with sores in cracked, ill-fitting shoes, as the shambling forms of POWs and Feleenese men who had been accused of the slightest crimes poured out from nondescript buildings to arrange themselves in rows in the camp's parade ground.

Back in the settlement, Waro stared out into the dark. The homes within visible distance had no lights shining in them, save for one or two that had a lamp or a lantern lit in their windows. His own shop was lit for about a metre around by lamps hung at intervals from the awnings. It was silent for a while. Eerily so. Then they—the men with their guns—came around to the front of his shop, in their dark blues and bulletproof vests—*for what also, I don't know*—creeping, faces masked behind the helmets they wore. All of them had night vision goggles, which were pushed up to their foreheads to create two more eyes, round and glowing green.

If they had come around from the back, he could only guess that they'd come from the purple city. From the main entrance to the purple city in complete silence. They must have taken out the guards from the gate and gone by the back of the outermost of the eastern homes. Even with what little he could see of them in his shop window, he could see how these soldiers were moving with informed precision. The old trooper in him could not help but feel impressed.

Waro spotted the sweep of mounted torch lights in the darkness beyond, where he knew more squads were cleaning out the homes. He suspected that some of the homes' occupants were already aware of what was going on. Lights went off from behind the blinds and through cracks in faded curtains. The blue-clad soldiers knew the homes were not empty. They knocked hard. When the doors were not opened, they kicked them in. The thumps of their boots on the metal steps of the stacked homes rang through the terrified silence. No one spoke when they emerged with their hands up in surrender, bodies ready to kneel at a bitten command. The soldiers waved people out and then swept through the interiors with the exactitude of men who'd been trained—hardened—for it. Home to home, gesture by gesture, seeking, it seemed, something that wasn't in any of them.

A voice commanded Waro to get down and put his hands behind his head. He returned the steely gaze of one of the soldiers in the shop window. In spite of the man's balaclava, he recognised a fellow Feleenese from the elliptical pupils set within greenish-yellow eyes. And immediately felt betrayed.

"Get on the ground and put your hands behind your head!" ordered the green-eyed soldier, thrusting the gun into Waro's face to make his point.

Waro stared at him with indifference, ignoring the sounds of feet storming up behind him. He continued to stare even as a hand pushed him down to kneel. Someone knocked his television to the ground. It would cost him half a carton of cigarettes to buy a new one from Mat Tong in the Garden trade district.

There was silence as the men searched through his store. Now, kneeling, he remembered that he was running low on instant noodles. Old Waro then stared at the card he had clipped onto the back of his shop counter weeks ago; Watijah's family still hadn't paid him for the groceries they had taken in advance, but for the first time in his career as a miser, he couldn't find it in himself to care.

One soldier was talking to another: "No sign of the objective." Waro glanced up long enough to identify the speaker as the Feleenese behind the balaclava.

"What are we looking for again?" the other soldier asked as he scanned the snacks on Waro's shop counter with the mounted light of his submachine gun.

"Adult medusa. Black hair. Yellow eyes."

The other soldier held up a snack and rattled it at a nearby team member, eyes alight. At the Feleenese's reply, he let out a low whistle. "A medusa? How are we going to handle something like that?"

Waro found himself thinking, *You can't*. He found himself thinking back to the day of his homecoming from the war, when he had taken a wrong turn and ended up in the main chamber of the catacombs, with its statues with the faces of men he could have known, faces of men he could have fought against, who could have been those who had imprisoned him, who had held razors and shorn off all his fur with such violence as to leave bleeding patches of baldness which, in the camp's humid and squalid conditions, oozed from infection.

In that chamber, she had stood among the statues, that snake-girl with the beautiful sister whom he'd tried time and again in an age of freedom to get a look at naked. Tried—perhaps some failures were meant to be. He rarely ever saw her now, but the strangeness of her face's make— the oddly-shaped head with cold, cruel eyes set too far apart—was etched in his mind. She had turned her gaze to him, smiling in the sinister yet reassuring manner of one who knew she held a life in her hand. One of her snakes had a bandaged end. The bandage had been a sickly shade of yellow and was black at the point of the hanging stump, as if she had not changed it in weeks.

All of him had felt frozen, and the memories, the images, returned with terrifying clarity: long, senseless marches and heavy loads cutting into shoulders; stilled Human compassion in the bite of whips on bent backs; his hand diving into the pockets of fallen campmates. In that encounter with Ria, he had remembered the eyes of one of them, flicking to gaze upon him, face half in the mud, mouth opening and closing with futility. Waro had still gone for the quarter of a flatbread that he knew the man had saved from breakfast.

Waro still remembered it all now, some forty years later. He also remembered the first thing she had asked him: "'Bang, you *nak balik*?" There had been none of the lofty control Barani always had. Just the stoic pragmatism of one who had seen too much.

That homecoming day, she had led him home. He would not, *could* not speak of what he saw.

Back in the shop, the soldiers were still considering the task of apprehending Ria.

"There is a specialised squad for that. We just need to know where she is."

The Feleenese soldier's eyes flicked to Waro, who still knelt behind his shop counter in silence.

After a beat, he asked, gun lifting and pointing, "Do you know?"

Waro did not answer at first, wondering if it was betrayal to do so. The girl, now a middle-aged woman, had done him no wrong. Done no one wrong in keeping to the catacombs, not even in petrifying that Cayanese thug Johan. But he thought about the settlement and how it had been the search for her that had led to this raid, this sudden upturning of what had been a familiar, if difficult life. Hers was but one life measured on a scale against hundreds of others. Perhaps she had been a saviour and a guardian once, but she was no longer either of those.

Lady forgive me, he thought. "Catacombs," he said.

The Feleenese soldier perked up. "Where?"

"Catacombs. The statues, she. They all in the catacombs. There for years. All soldiers from the Tuhav. All of them."

The soldier with the snack: "Catacombs? What is he talking about?"

Another in the back: "Why are we looking for a medusa anyway?"

Yet another: "Big shot orders ah. Safeguarding security or some shit."

The Feleenese soldier, however, kept his eyes steady on Waro. "Take us there."

∿

Kak Sab was clearly fretting again, that night more so than usual. She would not sit for long and would not eat more than a few mouthfuls of the food Lan had brought back for the family on his way home from work. If he had been worrying about a lean envelope at the end of the month, he cast the thought aside now, in favour of asking his mother what was wrong. He already knew the answer, of course:

"Your brother, how many weeks already haven't come home."

And whenever Lan managed to get hold of a feeler on the way back from the surface, none carried a message from Sani on them, a message which could have explained why he had not returned for so long.

Why, Lan also wondered with anger, must Sani feel a constant need to stress his family out all the time?

Lan threw his spoon into the fray of rice, sambal goreng and mutilated chicken. He was not hungry any longer. His head was heavy and he rubbed at his eyes, the stony grate of his *tur* scales between his finger and eyelids suddenly annoying him even though they never had before. Sani was the golden child, the one with the best of everything—looks, education, and the opportunities that came with it—and more Human skin than Lan could never hope to see if he were to scrub himself clean of his textures. Sani saw more daylight than the majority of people in Nelroote put together. His hands were unblemished by an indefinite life of hard labour in the mines, hacking at unyielding rock to get at the iridescent minerals, which were the only honest lifeblood of Nelroote. No one asked anything of Sani but to be their paragon and a mother's pride.

But Lan had heard what the elders said, of their runners and feelers who were mostly in their youth, of Sani too: "Stare at the sun too long and you'll become blind." He doubted any of the youngsters would want to return to the dank and putrid underworld. Were it not for the enforcement of its security, Lan was sure the population of Nelroote would already have dwindled to endangered degrees. He knew the Dream Garden families, sometimes even his own father—whose only concern should have been for the lesser residents—sent out people to hunt the deserters. The hunters they sent out were usually Cayanese: the ones with the best noses and keenest eyes, and so fiercely loyal to the hands that fed their every hunger that they feared nothing from the surface. Harsh punishment followed for those who were caught—beatings, torture, and a shaming in the public square near Old Waro's shop.

Their bruised and groaning bodies were left out for three days each time, and served as a reminder that it was best to drop one's head to one's chest and continue eking out a living from next to nothing, so as to not miss the next payment of protection money.

A part of him did not wonder why his brother, addled with lofty book ideas and greater unfathomable theories, would want to be away from this place. Another part was angry that the younger son had had all of life's ease and still couldn't find it in himself to be responsible to his family. And if any of the DG lackeys found him... Lan could only hope that their father would deign to have a say about it. Or Kak Ria. No one dared contradict Kak Ria, if she so chose to put in a word every once in a while.

"And where is your bapak?" his mother asked no one in particular. "So late already, still not home?"

Lan let his head hang for a moment before pushing away from the table. The single leg of the chair that had no crutch tip screeched as it dragged across the bare cement floor of the small house. Kak Sab was peering out the window, into the near darkness of Nelroote's cave night, worrying about one son and not—*ever*—seeing the other who had stayed for her, who stayed and doomed himself to a life of solitude to take care of her.

With a deep sigh, he said, "Lan go look for Bapak."

Bapak was likely at Mesa's Den again, either betting precious money on racing traacs or losing it all in a game of Root Leg. But even that was better than finding his father visiting the prostitutes in Sensa. Lan had never been able to look at his mother properly after that.

Kak Sab didn't answer. Lan looked to where his mother continued to stand by the window. The fatigued way she held herself gave way to rigidity, followed by an expression of curiosity and then sudden, knowing fear.

A face suddenly appearing in the window caused them both to jump, but Kak Sab must have seen the Dream Garden runner coming up to their house because she recovered in a split-second and demanded, "Ah, Wei, where is my husband?"

The wispy Feleenese fought for breath as he spoke and for a while, not even Lan could believe what he was hearing. His father was not coming back. Nelroote was being raided by squads of law enforcement soldiers, no house left unchecked in the hunt for the medusa sisters. And the only thing that was delaying the soldiers' onslaught was the sheer size of the settlement as well as the intricacy of its winding paths and over-building.

Lan digested the news with the slow grind of rusted gears above the deathly stillness of the settlement and the ever-pressing crisis of time. He peered up, first at the dark ceiling, then far off to the pink-hued trio of statues. They remained unchanged—serene and indifferent—making him wonder if he could believe what he never actually saw happen.

He snapped his eyes back to the runner, and stared into the expression of contained terror and perhaps even excitement in the boy's countenance.

"Take my mother," he instructed, unable to keep the defensive, dominating growl out of his voice. He glowered, bringing his face close. He didn't like DG lackeys, not a bit, but he didn't think he had a choice at the moment. "I go find Kak Bara and Kak Ria." He made a cutting gesture, indicating his mother to the boy. "Take her! Go by back ways. Go to the catacombs, to the keramat and hide. Make sure no one see you. Understand?"

The boy nodded, shoulders straightened and chest pushed out. Kak Sab stared at him. Lan thought she was going to start worrying about Sani again.

"Kak Bara is only next door, Lan. We can go together," she suggested, hands reaching out to very nearly take his arm.

Lan shook his head. He half-climbed and half-vaulted out the open window, grabbing the kerosene lamp from the hook by the door as he went. "Go two by two safer, Mak." And then he made a dash around the corner for the sisters' home.

∽

Barani looked up from the book at the sound—a rough snap like the breaking of a hard piece of wood—and sat listening for footsteps outside the door. None came, and the door remained obstinately shut. Normally, she would have sighed and wondered how Ria could spend as long as she did among the dead. However, there was something rather ominous about the sound. Barani sat up straighter, a finger trembling in the cleft between the pages.

Panicked knocking at the door launched her out of her seat to answer it. It opened to reveal Lan's familiar face bathed in the light of the kerosene lamp he was carrying.

"Ah, Lan," she remarked, surprised, "what business, dead in the night knock on people's door?"

She never thought brown scales could be so pale, but that was what Lan was. She wondered what could have riled him so, for Lan was not one to be easily frightened or worried.

Lan appeared positively spooked as he swallowed and

apologised, "Sorry, Kak, sorry. Got a message from Bapak. He asked me to come here as soon as I could."

Barani glanced over his shoulder and saw no one. "Where's your Bapak?"

"Bapak was at…" Here he frowned and gritted his teeth as if at an unpleasant thought. He swallowed it and went on. "Bapak was at Sensa when the police came. Arrested everyone. He just managed to send Wei to us."

Barani could not see herself but she was sure she had blanched. A memory took hold of her, of petrified men and forgotten faces, and of the fear palpitating through her as she and her sister ran from crimes that were bound to condemn them for life.

Suddenly, Barani snapped herself up taller. "And where is your Ibu?" she asked.

"Ibu is with Wei. I ask him to take her to safety."

"You sent your mother with that louse?" demanded Barani. "Why?"

Barani knew the odious Garden runner by unpleasant association. He had appeared outside her door one day, demanding that she pay the ten per cent increase in protection money, just like everyone else. Barani and Ria were exempted from paying anything at all, but Barani had paid him the ten per cent anyway, just to get him to go away. His shakedown, however, had sent his boss into such a fright so as to send her a basket hamper and the money back.

"Bapak sent word. Said to get you and Kak Ria away, said that the two of you must not be found. No matter what. He didn't give a reason."

He grew quiet, his great head downturned. Something

about his stance, the murmuring disquiet belying his solemnity, compelled her to clasp his hard shoulder.

"Like they always say, Lan: as long as your soul lies in your body, every deed will be remembered and every deed with the call to repay." Seeing his incomprehension, she explained, "Your late grandfather felt he owed Kak Ria quite a lot after the war. So he promised us shelter and protection as long as his kin remain alive. Your father has upheld the promise."

Lan's frown deepened. She thought he was going to shake her hand off, angry at what the sisters' past had done to his family. Instead, he gently asked, "Did it have something to do with why you came here?"

Barani's jaw tightened, heart clenching and throat hurting. "Not just that." She would have said more but for a growing urgency to vacate the home she'd known for nearly fifty years. The bustling around the house was all too familiar, but there was little to take and there was even less time. Lan shut the lamp's aperture and they slipped out into the dark just as a white light started to burn on the front of the house. She did not look back to see who they were. She *knew* who they were, only with better weapons and darker uniforms. Yet Barani wanted to believe that once the raiders were gone, there would still be a Nelroote to return to. There *had* to be a Nelroote to return to. The settlement was too established, too large—it would be a bureaucratic and financial nightmare to simply erase it from the face of the country. It was home, *her* home. Raids were supposed to be like culling: they kept populations of undesirables down, *hangat-hangat tahi ayam* only, so that everything that was wrong continued to exist, standing the world precariously on its axis.

Now it was Barani's turn to look back at the one-eyed house, with its gaping door-mouth, as they ran for the wall-houses at the far west of the settlement. Somehow, she'd expected to see chickens pecking in the dirt. But that could not be right, for the ground was rock and they had no chickens. Even if they did, they would have sent the birds scurrying into the undergrowth, where they could at least have a better chance at living.

There was an exit in the settlement that led to Ria's catacombs, named the Gatekeeper's Path, used only to transport the deceased via a tightly narrow corridor to a preparation chamber. The exit was in the southernmost side of the cave, across the way from the walls of the Dream Garden and concealed by protrusions of stalagmites and their ceiling brethren. Unlit and hinted at only by the scent of the incense hung in its mouth and placed on the small altar beside it, the entrance was virtually impossible to find in Nelroote's night-time. To one side of the settlement were the wall-houses, built in step-ups to the cave's rock wall. The lowest rested on the first and bottommost steps, spilling into the main settlement itself, while the highest were held up on tall, sturdy stilts close to the pointed tip of a low-reaching stalactite. Beneath these, Barani and Lan came upon Kak Sab, close to hyperventilating, proceeding very slowly with Wei, who held her hand to steady her and to encourage her to keep going.

Dark shapes in front of them in the kolong caused them all to stop, until a frightened voice quavered, "Who's that?"

"Kak Bara," Barani whispered. "We will go to you. Don't move."

Barani thought she detected the person nodding, slowly and carefully, as if that movement itself could make a sound.

The four crept up to a frozen group of about eight or ten, mostly women and children, their fear palpable.

"My husband—the men told us to wait here and don't move," the woman who had called whispered to Barani once she was near. Barani saw that the Scerean, holding a toddler and a small child, was barely a woman. Her large wet eyes were bright in the shadows, and they considered Barani beseechingly as she spoke.

"No, we have to keep moving or—"

Barani couldn't continue as the pounding of fists on wood and the thuds of boots kicking in doors came to them. Recovering quickly from the shock, Barani signalled for everyone to move. The party crossed the backyards of the houses situated on the periphery of the settlement. They crept under tall and low kolongs alike, around discarded furniture and junk, trying not to trip or hear the cries or desperate pleading. Fuzzy-edged white light searched in the gaps between houses and through windows. Whenever any threatened to shine their way, the group dropped into a prone position, stomachs to the uneven ground, parents pressing palms over the mouths of their children, everyone counting and praying, terrified eyes never leaving the sweeping lights.

Crack down on the crap happening in the settlement's centre of vice, fine, Barani thought. *The Dream Garden is a festering shithole masquerading as benevolent bloodletting anyway. But what business do they have with the lives of people like these? People who live by what they can scratch up by day, they eat in the day, and what they scratch up by night, they eat in the night; desperate to get by while the world above sees them as nothing but the diseased among the diseased?*

Barani's anger at the situation culminated in migraine points around her eyes and head. She could feel her hair tensing, wrapping themselves into tighter coils. She squeezed her eyes shut and pinched at her nose bridge to ease the feeling.

She had barely regained control of herself when brightness swept over her eyelids. She heard someone in the group gasp. Wei cursed. She opened her eyes to blinding light that caused her to squint. Two of the police raiders were peering into the kolong. For a time, everything seemed to be still as the two parties stared at each other. Barani didn't know who was more shocked in the encounter—the escaping group or the raiders who had seen her.

Seen her. Flashes of old images came to her. Barani knew she did not have much time. She had been keeping only one eye barely cracked. Now, she pried them both wide open to give the raiders her deadly stare. And just like all those years before, the men, these soldiers in civil service, froze over into stone. Somehow, something about the whole business of history repeating itself tickled Barani. She started chuckling at first, before it grew into a near manic cackle. The group stared at her, both in fear and with concern.

"Ani," she heard Kak Sab say. "Can?"

Barani's face was wet. She had apparently been crying too. She wiped at her cheeks, replying, "Can, can."

When they reached the Gatekeeper's Path, Barani kicked over the pots of incense, and the others covered up the entrance as best as they could with bits of junk from a nearby trash pile. Barani looked back as she ran, as with every bitter and heavy step Nelroote became a tinier crack in the shadows behind her until, with every lamp they extinguished along the way, it gradually turned into nothing but void.

Uprooted

It was strange, this allowance of touch—strange that Ria didn't flinch away from the accidental brushes of the backs of Eedric's hands, and that she allowed the light flutters of his fingers seeking hers, and later the lacing of their fingers like zipper teeth joining to close a rift. He, on the other hand, didn't seem to think anything of it, grinning goofily when she didn't pull away.

They returned to the keramat together at his insistence. She'd suggested he go straight home after helping her locate the entrance into the quarry as it was already late, but he wouldn't hear of it; said it was only proper he saw her safely "home". They emerged into the keramat, breathing in as if divers from the dark breaking the surface for lighted air. Their hands were still joined and she thought he would let it go, step away, say goodbye. He held on, studying her face in the wavering light of the nearest lamp.

She felt her face twitch when he ran a thumb underneath her eye.

"Got eyelash," he informed her gently, but didn't lift the

thumb from under her skin after he was apparently done. Instead, he ran it along the arc and traced another from the inner corner of her eye to her nose, going down the side of it to lips then chin.

Too late did Ria hear the voices coming from the Gatekeeper's Path corridor on the far side of the chamber. When she turned, she was already seeing the lamp light. There was only time enough to edge away from Eedric's touch as Barani emerged with Lan and about a dozen others including Kak Sab behind her. Bara froze at the sight of Eedric, and in her sister's countenance, Ria recognised the petrifaction's aftermath. In the pain her eyes held and the dazedness that Bara was desperately trying to blink away even as she beheld Eedric. Hysteria buzzed just under the surface of her sister's person. There was none of the aged calm or control that Ria came to realise was a terribly fragile thing. When Bara finally moved, it was to make a dash for Eedric, her hair vicious and alive in a way that Ria had never seen before.

Ria had to move quickly and plant herself between them, forcing Barani to stop just short of an arm's reach of the stupefied survivalist. Bara's livid eyes were so fixated on Eedric that Ria could not help the slivers of fear crawling into her.

"You!" shouted Barani, pointing at Eedric. "This is all you!" There was a tremor in Barani's voice. Tears were welling in her eyes, and she snapped her gaze to Ria. "He was supposed to be gone!"

"He's my friend," Ria said, quickly adding, "and he's just like us."

"Like us?" Barani asked, voice dropping low. Bara took a step forward—Ria took one back—and continued, her voice louder, "Like us? What have *you* been telling *him*"—Bara stabbed a finger in Eedric's direction, though not once taking her eyes off Ria—"that led to the raid on our home?!"

If hearts could voluntarily stop their ceaseless work, Ria's would have done so at that moment. At first she could only stare at the corridor beyond, seeing only the ominous black from extinguished lamps. Then her eyes scanned the party that had arrived with her sister, took in all the frightened and even accusing faces. A protesting hiss erupted when Ria snapped herself around to face Eedric. When she spoke, her voice was a quiet whisper: "What did you do?"

She saw confusion cross his face, followed by a state of knowing panic. "I swear I had nothing to do with this. I was always careful!"

"Was there a reason why you wanted me to go out with you today?" she asked. Escalating in her discomposure, she went on, "I told you about the village, the settlement, where I lived, what I did and you—"

"Ria," Eedric broke in, taking hold of her. "Why would I do that to you? Why the *hell* would I do that to you?" Ria didn't hear the words, only felt the big hands as they continued to clasp her upper arms and the shaking, always the shaking.

"A man like him, they need no reason!" Barani put in. "If anything, position! There's a million like you. They would not have known if it wasn't for him. Now the police going into our homes, rounding people up, bringing to—"

Ria spun round now to face Barani. "Then why are you

here? Why aren't you there, helping them?"

Bara closed up the distance until the angry serpent buzz was right in Ria's ears. "*Why?*" Bara demanded. "Why am I here? I am here, for you. As I have always been!" She heard Bara suck in a breath, then draw back. "And what do you think I should do against all of them? I am *not* you!"

Bara appeared to regret the words the moment they left her. She gazed down at Ria, shoulders heaving before snapping her attention to Eedric, who in that moment had turned his flickering attention from Barani back to Ria. Acting quickly, Ria grabbed hold of Eedric's arm and turned him away so that he would not see Barani's eyes clouding over, all her snakes pointed towards him. Beneath Ria's hand, Eedric's body was already racked in tension. She could feel the pulse in his wrist hammering fast. With this much fear and anxiety coursing through his person, she knew his transformation from his Human self into that of the Changer was imminent. His skin was already glossing over, stretching over elongating bone, as the blood vessels rose closer to the surface, warming her hand. If he proceeded with the change any further, the crowd, now an angry, buzzing thing looking for something, *anything*, to blame, would react, and at the end of it nothing would stand but new statues and the two sisters in a room full of regrets.

"Don't," Ria warned Barani.

Bara thrust her face towards Ria's, hissing through bared teeth to add to the din her hair was already making. Her eyes were clear again, but they burnt a corybantic violet, their pupils squeezed so thin the knots were nearly invisible.

"You would protect him?"

"You have to listen to me, Kak, please. I have been with him every time he came down here. He has not even got close to Nelroote. He has been nothing but kind to me. It couldn't have been him. It couldn't."

As the crowd let out a collective cry of naysaying, Ria could see a fleeting softening of her sister's features, followed by a shot of pain. Then Bara clenched her jaw. Very quietly and steadily, she hissed, "The raid didn't *just* happen." Each cavernous hold seemed to whisper as the silence stretched between the sisters in spite of the incensed murmurs in the background.

"No," Ria agreed, keeping a level gaze on Bara and later appealing to the others in the chamber, "I know it didn't just happen." She looked to each and every one of them. "But ever since that day, this man has never been to Nelroote. It could have been one of the feelers. Or someone who goes to the surface a lot. What we can do is—"

"Like who?" Lan demanded, unable to keep his counsel any longer.

Ria said nothing to his question, but her guilty regard of him spoke all the answer he *didn't* want to hear.

"No," said Lan, shaking his head. Scowling at Ria, he added, "You! You were always the problem here. A murderer and a traitor! They are here for *you*!"

Eedric went fully tense under her hold. Lan started to take a lunge at her.

"No, Lan." Barani's voice was cold, her expression colder. She drew herself up to her full height, but there was a tiredness to her bearing. She kept her eyes steady on Ria's face, her face completely devoid of expression. "Don't come back," she said. Indicating Eedric, she added, "And take that animal with you."

Wei, who had been keeping himself out of the exchange, suddenly stepped from the crowd and appealed to Barani: "We can't just let them leave! You don't know what people like him do!" Turning to the rest of the people in the keramat, he went on, "Keep him here. If they come and they find us, they find him with us!"

There was a ripple of agreement.

Quickly staunched by Barani, who said over her shoulder, "Ria goes. And the animal with her. If anyone disagrees... You will have plenty of friends in this damn room. And I will start with you, Wei."

Ria wasn't aware of how long she stood there, unable to utter a word. Barani seemed so distant then, and so diminished in her line of sight. She only felt Eedric's hand take hers—she didn't even know when he'd come back to himself again—and tug for her to come away with him. She did not move at first.

"I know the catacombs," she said beseechingly. "I have studied them. I have maps. There are places you can hide and one not far from here. Let me do that, at least."

Barani shook her head slowly, but said nothing.

"Please," Ria begged, voice dropping to a near whisper.

There was no response.

Eedric tightened his hold on her and pulled harder. Ria would not take her eyes off Barani. Her sister only returned the look with an impassive one of her own. When Ria finally turned away, the world became a blur of grey-blue and black-lined orange. She could not sense the tunnels as Eedric dragged her through them. She heard not his wet, rapid breaths; saw not the lamps or the skulls that lined her walls. Blindly, she climbed the stairs and only looked up when the damp night air hit her face. Where before it had been rejuvenating, right then it was dead cold. And even the moon peeking between the silhouettes of foliage seemed distant and accusing. The sky that had appeared so vast before was reduced to shards in places where the canopy was broken.

They were still walking when she turned to the man beside her. She had thought he had gone back to his Human state, but she saw that the vestiges of his other form were still in the process of ebbing away, leaving his skin visibly pallid even in the dark of the forest. His grip on her arm was strong enough to bruise.

She had thought she would see disgust in his face. Men like him, they never wanted a hassle, a problem, on their hands. Yet he disregarded the danger of her snakes and pulled her into an embrace. He hoarsely whispered, "I'm so sorry," and pressed his mouth into the side of her neck. His lips were dry, scraping at her skin. "I shouldn't—I shouldn't have—"

She stood stiffly before wrapping her arms around him. His shoulders gave no comfort. Nonetheless, she clung to him.

Drown

Ria clung to him, cheek against his neck as her fingers dug into his shoulders. As if he were an anchoring tree. The feel of her snakes sliding against his skin made him shiver, but he'd come to understand that they were a far better expression of her emotions than her well-schooled features could ever be: a wild buzzing nest in anger, focused regard at the moment before petrifaction, and the nicest complement of undulating waves whenever she was pleased or happy. Right then in haunted misery, they crept away from her, pulling at her scalp in the slow manner of one who wished to leave another who was grieving.

Ria started to draw away. He caught hold of her wrists just in time. There was a surprised hitch in Ria's breathing before she gave him a stare that teetered between surprised and crazed hostility. He held her hands, palms facing upwards in supplication, fingers curled into claws. He could feel the rapid pounding of her pulse, and above it all there was the grating sibilance of her snakes. Everything about her was shaking as she cried. *Cried*, he noted, the sight of it heartbreaking.

"Don't," he managed to say. *Don't*. Don't what? Don't go? Don't look? Don't fucking cry? Even if he hadn't had anything to do with the raid, and knew nothing of the inner workings of the country's government, he might as well have been the criminal here. It would have been easier for her to give him over to the underground people, to her sister who regarded him with so much cold hatred it could have frozen lava. It would have been easier for her to leave him to die that first time round too. He recalled seeing her from the back as the fight went out of her at her sister's renouncement. She had fought for him at every turn and he couldn't even do the same for her.

"Come home with me," he said to her.

A raising of snakeheads. "No."

He shook his head again. "We can't stay here."

"Go then."

He dug his fingers into her arms. "If the authorities don't find you, the people here might. They are not going to be nice and your sister might not be around to protect you." He thought he saw Ria's expression harden and he went on before she could say anything. "And if you fight them, those people will die."

He felt Ria stiffen. Her eyes stared, wild with despair.

"There is nothing you can do any more," he told her. You are no longer anyone's adik, he wanted to say, but couldn't because of the sudden escape of breath from her lips. Her eyes were glistening over again.

"But you can run," he went on. "The life you had before. All those people down there. This raid. There is nothing to hold you back. You're free now."

Ria didn't respond, beyond letting her eyes drop. He took that as a "yes".

A fear-ridden walk to the car park after, they were in his car. Within its dark interior and behind the tinted windows, he felt a little safer. He leaned back in his seat and let out a heavy, tired sigh. He ought to have thought of something better. His house was not the best of places but where else could they go? Hotels were too risky. Miz's place was too crowded and Mama's family flat was a place severed from him by his own neglect. Also, he didn't want to implicate them any more than was necessary. Ria was, by historical precedent, a dangerous fugitive. He *was* concerned about what it meant for his future life if he was ever caught with her. But—he looked over at her—for the first time in a long while, he had someone he really cared for, someone who at this moment *needed* him. And he was not about to run helter-skelter down the road like a frightened pup.

If he was lucky, he thought as he started the car, Father and Stepmother would not even be in when he returned.

As he belted her up, she said absently, "The car smells like you."

He noticed the smell then: his cologne mixed in with the lemon-scented air freshener. The interior was warm from nearly a day parked without the air-conditioning running.

"It's the only thing my father gave me that I actually value," he answered. And suddenly he didn't want it any longer.

Ria nodded and said nothing more, keeping low in her seat. The street lamps cast her in a constant orange light. He found himself thinking how it was no different from the lantern glow in her chamber.

∿

The lights in the house were out when they drove up the short driveway to his spot under the patio. Father's car was nowhere in sight. In a bid to disturb no one, he'd rushed out to open the gates and then bundled Ria into the house as quickly as he could to minimise whatever his neighbours' cameras might catch. If he was lucky, they would dismiss it as him being the immoral son, bringing home some girl he was going to bang without his parents' knowledge.

He kept a tight hold on Ria's hand when the motion sensors flooded the hallway with light, and an even tighter hold when he saw Suri, the family's maid, standing at the end of the hallway, having heard his car and come out to greet him. Suri was a tiny woman, made more diminutive by her oversized T-shirt and pair of worn cargo shorts that might have been his from back when he was a kid. She was only in her late teens but Eedric thought she looked a decade older.

It wasn't the first time he'd brought a girl home, Adrianne or otherwise, but the look on Suri's face wasn't one of discreet knowing. Suri stared at Ria, transfixed. Eedric looked down to see that a snake had escaped from Ria's drawn-up hood and was sliding over her cheek. Being so used to her hair, he hadn't realised it until it was too late.

Suri opened her mouth, on the verge of a scream. Eedric lunged for her, pleading for her to calm down.

"She's not—she's my—" Eedric began, clamping his hand over her mouth. He glanced back at Ria who was hurriedly tucking her hair back in. Slowly, he told Suri, "She needs help. I don't—I can't—" He placed a shaking finger over his lips, while his other hand remained, so tight he felt as if his grip might crush her jaw. But he wouldn't let up. "Ma'am and Sir cannot know, okay?"

Suri let out a squeak and then tried to shake her head.

Eedric was about to say more. The urge to press down harder and make her swear upon her life that she wouldn't tell was overpowering. For a moment, he wondered if the only assurance he could get was to suffocate her in silence—and all he had to do was move his hand a little and hold on until she stopped struggling—but Ria stepped forward.

"What the hell are you doing?" he hissed.

Her only reply was to reach up for his hand and, with surprising ease, remove it from Suri's mouth. He blinked hard. Suri couldn't have appeared tinier than she was then, when she was cowering from him, peering up in terror. His hand had left a pale mark over her mouth and on her lower cheeks. It soon blushed a deep red with the returning blood.

He stepped away, both embarrassed and horrified. Ria gave him only a quick glance before turning to smile at Suri. With astonishment, he listened to Ria explain her situation to Suri, with vulnerability, even kindness, in the old-fashioned cadence of her voice. Suri was a Human in the employ of a Human household; he couldn't guess at any reason why Suri might feel any solidarity with Ria. They spoke a common tongue but were not of a common land. Yet Ria was convincing enough that Suri nodded at the end of it. Perhaps Suri held no love for Father or Stepmother, who ruled her rather strictly. No love for him either, who had done nothing to stop the punishments he knew were meted out to her over the slightest mistake. Who in his own way—in not washing his plates after he was done eating, in complaining when his shirts were ironed wrong, in never washing his own car—was only perpetuating the injustices she experienced day after day.

"Sir went out with Ma'am to party," Suri told him when she finally turned away from Ria.

"That's good," Eedric said. Feeling relieved in spite of what passed before. He added, "Please don't let anyone know. And…"—he took a fifty from his wallet and pressed it into her hand—"something for your help."

He could feel Ria looking at him, but he wasted little time in bundling her up the stairs to his bedroom on the third floor.

"Is that how you surface people always work?" Ria said quietly when they were in the room, door safely locked behind him. "Buy off anyone, any place?"

"It will keep her quiet."

Maybe the indiscretion would come back to bite him in the ass someday, but the way he saw it then, the transaction was merely him bringing someone along if he was to go down with the SS Medusa.

"She seems a frightened little thing," Ria went on to say, her gaze distant.

Eedric checked to see that the windows were still shut fast, the way he always left them. After a quick glance out to the dimly-lit road below and across the way to the neighbour's dark balcony, he drew the curtains tighter and clamped them together with a metal clip from his table for good measure. "Father is strict about work discipline. Suri's predecessor got sent home before her contract ended and...well, Suri doesn't want to end up the same way," he explained, turning back to check that the air-conditioning was on.

Ria stood stiffly in the middle of the room, arms folded, shoulders hunched and head retracted into the hood as far as she could manage, as if afraid to disturb the objects on display in the suddenly tight layout of the room. She was scanning the room. It compelled him to start cleaning: he moved the morning's rejected pile of clothes from the bed to the chair, and then realising that Ria might want to sit on the chair, subsequently shoved the pile into the wardrobe.

Between tidying up magazine stacks, old seminar notes and portfolios, he turned to see her still standing in the same spot, perfectly inert now that she was done assessing her surroundings.

"You can sit down, you know," he informed her.

"Sit?"

"Yeah, sit," he replied, motioning vaguely. "I don't know how long you are going to be here and you don't want to stand around all day, right?"

He expected her to come back at him with a quip about standing stones or a messy room, if not actually sit somewhere. Instead, in a quiet voice filled with apprehension, she asked, "Who is your father anyway?"

Eedric straightened up slowly from where he was half-kneeling and half-squatting on the floor, collating loose photograph prints meant for his updated portfolio.

"Nothing I haven't told you before," he replied. "He's in the chain store business and a part of the Star Malls group. Not much of a family man. He hates my mother and is the reason she died in the first place…"

"Beyond that?" she cut in, gaze flicking from the corner she had been frowning at to him. "He knows people. Important people. You told me once. I remember." Ria spoke with growing disquiet, perhaps even a rising anger. She was holding herself away from him, winding the strings of her person tight, closing up and sealing all entry points. Her stare was unnerving, as it could sometimes be, but it was what she said after that broke him: "Why did you bring me here?"

He regarded her, mouth working to find words.

The portfolio hit the side of his desk at which he'd flung it. "What now? What are you trying to say?" he demanded, going up to her. He made to take hold of her but, something, either the memory of his exchange with Suri earlier, or the fear that she would flinch at his touch, stayed him.

She spoke fast: "How is it all nothing but coincidence? You took me away on the day the police raided Nelroote. You never left, and I thought it was because… I thought *you* were different, because you never changed, because being what you are, being someone like me, meant something to you. Because *I* meant something you! And to think, you were only biding your time; to think, that in half a century I have managed to keep the likes of you away, only to lose everything now!"

He had been moving away from her, to check the windows again, but the accusation made him turn back. And he did take hold of her. He wanted to shake her but he didn't. His grip wasn't even tight. She could have stepped out of it, could have moved away. Instead, she turned her face as if he was something repulsive.

"Ria, look at me," he said, and then once more, shouting, "Look at me!"

She kept her gaze away, her snakes rising to start a flurry, the spreading of their hoods synced with a chorus of warning hisses.

"You don't trust me, do you?" he demanded. "You don't. No one does!"

"I don't even trust myself," she told him.

He threw his hands up, practically tossing her away from him. "Does it always have to be like this? The mistakes of another time brought up over and over? I know I keep saying this but look at me. Look. At. Me, please." He gestured towards himself, fingertips stabbing his chest repeatedly, and so hard he could have pierced skin.

"I may not be good enough. For Father, for your sister. For you! But I am here, Ria. And I am *not* a stone statue."

She looked and he saw that she could see him there. It was strange, but he felt that in that moment, she was seeing him with perfect clarity for the first time since they met. Parts of her begin to unravel. He saw her shoulders droop.

"What will we do now?" she asked quietly, afraid.

Even at a time like that, "we" was a sweet word coming from her. She was everything he couldn't explain and yet nothing he needed to explain. She was a dangerous thing to possess and an equally dangerous thing to let free. There was no medusa outside of captivity because authorities would rather have one than be rid of one. A medusa—two medusas—must be worth something to someone. And in that moment, he wanted to do right by her, whatever it meant. It was with certainty that he told her:

"We sit it out as long as we can. And if my father or anyone else ever finds out, if there is even the slightest indication that they have an idea, we will clean out the drawers, pawn all the jewellery we can get hold of and jump cheap hotels. We will live off convenient store food, maybe even get drunk on cheap beer every night. We keep doing that until we either get caught or reach the end of the road, where we know we're fucked anyway."

Ria lifted an eyebrow, smiling. "Is that supposed to make me feel better?"

"It is what it is. Only, I make it sound classy."

She laughed, in spite of things. He came close and she dropped her forehead onto his chest.

"I don't understand you."

He shrugged and closed his arms around her. "I know."

They stood like that for a while, the silence that reigned around them possessing the quality of a foggy lull right after a battle. In time, he started to say, "Back in the chamber…you—"

He stopped when he felt her arms tremble and her hands grabbed fistfuls of his T-shirt. Guilt welled up in him anew, and he was prepared to drop it entirely when he heard her say, forehead pressed to his chest as if she wanted to lose the words to the floor below: "She was always the perfect one."

"Ria, that's not—"

"She's beautiful and she's strong. She was the one with the plans. The one we all looked to, *still* look to. So many years ago, all I ever wanted was for her to look at me. To acknowledge me. To *see* me. Sometimes I wanted to be just like her. Most times, I wanted to be better, smarter... I wanted to know more; to be more. And when I was better, and when I was more, I would be more dangerous. And when she finally did look at me... We were already so deep in. No light at the end of the tunnel. A part of her had died and I was the one to kill it."

He could not help but consider her with frustrated pain. Bleeding welts that never healed, scars and a life of self-isolation; recalling them all made him angry.

"I know now is not the right time to say this, but you need to let all that shit go," he told her finally.

For a time, she remained quiet. He said no more. He thought that she didn't need to hear any more of the inconsequential things he was likely to say anyway. Then, she lifted her face to him.

"I don't know," she said, "but it is time to try."

He wanted to let her go. It was in a strange turn of opposite intentions that he only pulled her closer, so that her body was flush against his. She did not try to disengage herself. Her thigh was pressed up into his crotch. A twitch and then a movement in reaction to that, and he knew he was going to get hard. He cursed himself for it; for reacting like a hormone-driven boy in the midst of such a crisis.

Never mind, never mind, he thought. His mouth met hers with violence, in a kiss of one who was both desperate and unthinking. His head reeled from the clash of teeth, but he gathered enough of his senses, or rather lost enough of them, to press on with his affections—hands dropping from shoulders to bum, cupping it and lifting her up a little, pressing her hips to his. She was fleshier than he'd thought, heavier and more solid. There was a hint of the coffee they'd drunk some two hours or so before, on her lips and on her tongue; a hint of her usual talcum powder smell, mixed in with the cologne that still clung to his hoodie—scents of him and scents of her.

Take her, take her, take her.

He couldn't have picked the worst of times and he knew she was vulnerable and confused but that was the only mantra drumming through his clouding mind, in this room, this space of his that discomfited her so. He wanted to burn and burn and burn her out so there was no barrier left between them.

His face was buried in flesh. "Fuck your sister. Fuck Nelroote. Fuck this whole entire place," he murmured. His teeth bit skin. "It's just you now. Just you."

He noticed how the skirt of her dress had ridden up her thighs and how one of his hands was gripping on to her flesh, clawing into it; noticed how his left leg had started to cramp. She was so impossibly soft. Her snakes moved around her face in their own coital dance, wriggling and coiling, one body with the next until they nearly resembled braids. He knew then that the precious window would soon pass; that in seconds, she was going to be in control again in her ghostly but overpowering manner.

A car passed, its headlights a pale glow through the curtains that grew and diminished as it went, and then the neighbourhood outside was dark and silent—dark and silent and ignorant again.

He reached out to relieve her of the hoodie, dropping it in a shapeless pile on the floor. He mustered the courage to finally weave his fingers into her hair at the back of her head, working blind between the loosening strands of serpent bodies to get to where the snakes met scalp. With a gentle tug forward, he pressed his lips to her face, near the hairline, ignoring her whisper of "Eedric, no," and whispering instead reminders of "I am here" and "It's okay".

Her breath came out shaking. Out there in the world, she would be considered hideous by people that wanted long porcelain faces and luscious locks; fat by a generation of small waists, flat stomachs and thigh gaps. Once, that kind of beauty was what he had desired, strove for it in the women he preferred and pursued, fed it with his prestige and occupation. But in that moment with her, he was blind to all of it and nothing but lucid to everything that was her.

On his unmade bed, she was so warm that he could not help but let out a pained moan. She laid back, unmoving as he touched her—from breasts to the folds in the furred region between her legs. She responded to him, but he couldn't tell if her grimaces were those of pleasure or hurt. He ought to pause, to check in: if it was all right so soon after a tragedy. But he was so far gone, he couldn't stop. The act itself—a painful barrier to break for her—had to be quiet, bodies kept close, taking breaths in shallow gasps muffled against each other. *She* was quiet. And tight. He finished in a few thrusts. Somewhere in the middle, she'd pulled his chain off—mangled and broken the clasp. The pendant lay cupped in her hand, a fake military dog tag of dull silver that he'd got a long time ago from a shop specialising in streetwear. He'd had it engraved with his name and a number that meant nothing, not his phone number or birthdate.

Just the first combination of six numbers he could think of—156713, was it? He couldn't remember. It had come to be a tribute, a monument to an age of swaggering youth. It meant something different now, something in the way she grasped it as he rolled off her, and the way she stared up unblinkingly at his bedroom ceiling even after he'd returned from washing up.

Blaze

Eedric surveyed the spread on the table, wondering what he could take up to Ria after the meal. He chanced to meet Suri's eyes as she crossed behind Father at the head of the table to get to the kitchen. He nodded and tried to smile, but Suri's wary and dazed expression caused the smile to falter. He cast only the briefest of glances up at the ceiling, imagining Ria sitting two floors up in the corner of his room, wedged between wardrobe and wall. She would not so much as twitch when she was left like that—not move a leg or adjust her sitting position. He loathed the idea of leaving her alone and would rather be in his room pretending to game with the volume turned up real loud than be away from her. But it was her wish that he join his family for a meal that day.

"Nice to finally see you come out of your room, Jonathan," Stepmother said as she reached for the serving bowl of sautéed vegetables. Leaning over, she added with a smile, "Must be that new game, right? I can hear you playing it."

Eedric continued drowning his rice in gravy. He tried

to remember what he could have been playing that she'd heard. *Must be one of the shooters*, he thought, *or a gameplay montage on replay at full volume.* Stepmother would be none the wiser. He was known to be a noisy gamer, raging when things didn't go his way, which was often. He was also known for locking himself in when a game was particularly hard or engrossing; forgoing showers and a change of underwear, eating bread slices right out of the plastic bag.

Eedric came to the depressing realisation of how deep in isolation a person could live even in a house shared with others. He saw clearly now how it had always been this way, how his days were spent in a home that resembled one from pictures—with a lazy ceiling fan, sterile walls and paintings of fruit bowls—but his room was an untouchable sanctuary of relics needing both dusting and a good wash. The family meals were actually pretty few and far between because it was rare that everyone was home at the same time. Even Stepmother would often stay over with her parents when Father was out of town for long periods. He didn't know if he dreaded family meals more because they obligated him to spend time with people he didn't much care for, or because the meals were unfamiliar events to him.

Ria simply didn't exist to Stepmother and Father. She was outside of their plans, their social planes of existences, just as her people were outside of the country's. In another space, another world, she was his inexplicable truth—a warm body against his every waking hour. They lay curled, she a crescent moon against the dark space of him. Sometimes he partook and she indulged him in silence. But it was enough for him to simply lie back, his head cradled in the circle of her arms. He must have missed countless castings and classes. He screened all of his calls and only took the ones from Miz, though he told his friend nothing of the woman sitting by his window, or how he sometimes traced the filter end of his cigarettes over the contours of her, imagining that the smoke spirals were her ghosts leaving through a chimney. How he sometimes sat on the toilet watching her stand with her face inclined to the warm deluge of the shower. Sometimes he wished for her sister back, just so he could see her smile again.

"Yes," he replied slowly—carefully—"still at that new game."

He continued to drench his rice, so that the white became brown.

Stepmother shook her head, amused and, like all of her generation, not understanding the media and technology that ruled her stepson's life.

"You know," she continued, as always perfectly conversational and positive, "I have not seen Adrianne in a while."

Eedric stopped. Then carefully replaced the ladle in the bowl.

"Is she all right?"

"She's all right."

Actually, Eedric didn't know. Last time he was in contact, it was to pick up the box of his things from her house, and it had been her maid he met at the front door. She had handed him the box filled with his T-shirts, a hoodie he thought he had lost, electronic cables and a bunch of other mushy crap he had given her. The maid had lowered her head and wrung her hands by her apron before saying, "I am sorry things not happy any more, sir." Eedric had only shaken his head and told her to take care. He had never felt freer.

"Busy, I think," he felt compelled to add.

He saw concern flit across Stepmother's countenance but Father cut in with a sudden remark, "First Feleenese minister—and a drug raid on the same page."

Eedric perked up at the remark.

"Why is that significant?" Stepmother asked, though even Eedric didn't miss the slight roll of her eyes.

"The raid took place in one of the places where a lot of those people live, of course." Father was casual about it, but there was nothing casual about the derision in his voice.

"Did they say where?" Eedric asked in turn.

Father glanced over the newspaper at him, brows furrowing slightly as he regarded his son.

"Somewhere in the west, near the Layanen Docks."

The surface, Eedric thought with relief.

"Is that all?" he went on, trying to get down the rice he'd spooned into his mouth.

Father folded the paper in half and slid it to Eedric, the drug bust story on top. It wasn't a long article to begin with and Eedric read it quickly, skimming for familiar names and places. There were none and while he could breathe a sigh of relief at that, he couldn't help but feel that there was something inconsequential about the news piece. One couldn't have a drink in the Layanen entertainment district without a ruckus—usually a fight, followed by sirens. The police were almost indiscriminate about who they asked IDs from: anyone with scales, anyone fresh off the boat, anyone who spoke Ro' 'dal with a F'herakian accent, any Human they thought looked like trouble. Eedric actually knew people who went to the district specifically to smoke illegal doses of medicinal winter'gra, a type of plant that resembled tobacco in constitution and appearance, except that it could make you see the world in technicolour when taken in strength with powdered aspirin. There was nothing new about a raid in that shady district. Every time the authorities cracked down on the stuff that went on in the winding paths between the low-rise buildings, there was always someone willing to sell excess rolls of winter'gra under the table as soon as they left; always more girls stepping off the boat at the ferry terminal to take the place of the ones who had been taken away; always more unlicensed cigarettes from across the border going cheap if you only winked at the right bartenders.

The latter pages of the paper reported the usual tripe and diatribes, and half-page spreads of advertisements selling toasters and out-of-date stereo systems. There was nothing about Nelroote or an underground settlement of illegals. Eedric didn't know if he should feel relieved or worried by it. Eventually, he turned to the article about the Feleenese minister—of youth welfare and development. (Of course. As if they would let a Feleenese hold, say, the education portfolio, because you know, ex-army generals knew *exactly* how to teach kids their ABCs.) He found himself gazing down at the elegant features of the man, wondering what the aged eyes had seen that the smile could not utter.

"They just needed to get a face in," he heard Father remark. "I don't want to believe that our youth are going to grow up on policies sanctioned by that man."

"Don't want to, or don't like to?" Eedric found himself asking. Aloud.

Father stared at him before replying curtly, "Both."

"Neither," Eedric countered. "For you, the uncertainty would have done the race too much credit."

"Yes, you're right," said Father, without conviction or agreement, "and I suppose Human genocide is right as well. Betrayal, no loyalty—"

"That shit happened a long time ago!"

"Watch your mouth, Jonathan."

"It was a *war*. Last I checked, everyone in that battalion had the choice to follow. And they practically won it for us, didn't they? Got this country back so that you can still be here, bitching about this. If getting rid of half the Human population is the only way to make sure you live, *you* would do it, wouldn't you?" demanded Eedric.

"Why are you defending them?" Father snapped. "You were not there when—"

"Gentlemen, please!" Stepmother cut in, holding up a hand as she did so. Exasperatedly, she went on, "Henry, we don't always have our son sitting to dinner with us. Can't we just have a civil meal for once? For once! Without all this drama. And keep politics off the table." She shot Father a glare. Then Eedric. "Henry? Jonathan?" she pointedly added. "Do we agree on this?"

Eedric stared as Father sullenly went back to reading. "I guess I should apologise," he went on with mock effusiveness. His appetite gone, he gazed down at his mess of a plate. He rested his utensils beside it with great deliberation before lifting his eyes to look at Father once more. "I just can't help but think that whatever you couldn't get over from all those years ago caused you to let them put Mama down before her time came."

He imagined he heard the faintest hiss around his ears in the muted atmosphere. Even so, he went on. He could not remember a time when he'd spoken up of his own accord at the table, thanks to the attitude drilled into him by Father from a young age and carried into adulthood out of sheer apathy. Now that he was on a roll, he didn't see why he should stop and start playing at being polite.

"What are you talking about?" Father demanded. "Why this so suddenly?"

"Because there are days when I can't sleep at night, wondering if what we did to Mama was right! Days when I lay awake wondering if there was something I could have done!" Eedric cried, fist slamming into the table, drawing a protesting clink from the tableware. "And you," he continued, "I wonder, I *do* wonder, if you are really not this man. That you wanted to do something too, but due to some…some difficulty, some need…some necessity…" He snapped his fingers and then raised his eyes from the lacy tabletop to his father once more. "Some reason why you had to let her die like that."

Stepmother turned sharply to Father. "What is he saying?"

"Tell me," Eedric said as if he had not heard Stepmother, "did she go easily? Did she smile for you? Forgive you? Or did a doctor do the work for you, while you played golf at the Hynes?"

"You were there, Eedric, when the doctor talked about

this. You knew we had to do it."

Leaning forward, Eedric angled his head to get a better look at Father's face, and asked, "I didn't. I still don't."

Father had his head down, staring at his near-empty plate. His voice was gentle when he next spoke with difficulty, "Your...mother...her illness's final stage was...violent. She was hurting nurses and attacking doctors, breaking equipment... They had to call in the police and tase her more than once. That was how bad it had got. Nothing was working. The doctors said she retained no semblance of her Humanity and she wasn't getting any better. They gave me two options. Either admit her into a specialised asylum—hospital—or give her the peace she deserved."

"Henry!" Stepmother gasped.

"Like a sick pet?" Eedric pointed out.

Father looked away.

Eedric believed he had expected the answer. He had thought he would understand, thought he was going to be prepared for it. However, hearing the words, *Father's* words, caused a release, like a fuse box blowing out or machinery that had been performing at optimum suddenly deciding it had had enough and couldn't take any more. His palms met the tabletop; he didn't feel the pain. He could sense Stepmother and, somewhere, Suri flinching, but he could only keep his glower focused on Father.

Father turned to consider him with an expression somewhere between hard and mournful. "You don't know what it feels like when you no longer know the person you're married to. You don't know what it's like knowing your only son is tainted because of it!"

"Tainted?" Eedric said, voice high with disbelief.

"*Extra* effort had to be made to make sure you grew up into a fine young man in spite of it," Father went on to explain, patiently and levelly as if he was explaining a project in a meeting. "If you ever wondered why I made sure you had the best education, the best tutors, and more, wondered why I keep pushing you? It was all to make sure you'd never fall behind, that you'd still be on the same level as your peers. So that you would have everything you needed to break out of it!"

"You talk about it like it's a disease…or a fucking handicap," Eedric pointed out.

Father met his eyes: onyx against onyx.

"It is."

"I am not an investment, Pa," Eedric told him. "*Mama* was not an investment." Disgusted, Eedric pushed away from the table. He was about to make his way to his room when a sudden rush of blood to his head and limbs made him turn back. Something in Father's impassive expression as he evaluated Eedric's condition—condition!—made him want to tear the face off the man, for he, Divines damn him, didn't need it.

But he thought about the woman sitting in his room, severed from the only life she'd ever known.

He thought about her. He continued to regard Father. And then said, "I get it." As an afterthought, he added, almost amiably, "If you read the science pages in that newspaper, you will know they just discovered that survivalists can grow back lost limbs in their temporary beast forms, by the way. And so many are coming forward to help with research."

He shrugged and started to back away. "Maybe all Mama needed was time, Pa. Maybe all she needed was you."

"Oh, Henry…" Stepmother started to say.

Eedric had reached the bottom of the stairs by then. He paused, a hand on the ornate baluster, feeling the coils and curves of the carved flower beneath his fingers. Looking back, he regarded the man who continued to sit in his chair at the head of the table, and thought, sadly, how small he'd become. Eedric threw a glance upwards. He climbed the stairs to this room. He heard Stepmother walking away, her bare feet on the parquet floor an impossible staccato rhythm, and later the front door slamming.

Upstairs in his room, Ria stood in the far corner by the window, peeking out between the curtains. Below he could hear Father calling out to Stepmother intermittently. Then a car started, followed by another, seconds later. Ria turned, uneasy questions already written on her face.

He had thought to reach gently for her. Instead, he grasped her face in his hands and mashed his lips against hers, focusing her snakes to a standstill. They remained a frozen halo around her head when he pulled away, and it was a while before she recovered. He ran the pads of his thumbs under those eyes as if to sculpt out her face with them. He wanted to worry about nothing but that distant day when her face was going to be lost to him.

"I heard shouting," she remarked with concern.

"Nah," he assured her, chuckling. "Just your normal family mealtime conversation."

Ria angled her head. "Normal family conversations do not include shouting."

"Yes they do." He saw that Ria was wearing an old T-shirt that he had loaned her earlier. It was rather big on her, and long enough that she didn't wear any shorts with it. Still, it fell only to a little below the thick of her thighs. She wore no bra beneath it and her nipples showed through the thinned material, themselves dark eyes through the veil of white. He grinned, snaked an arm around her waist, and drew her to him. "The family's away," he pointed out.

However, instead of giving herself over to him the way she had always done before, Ria pushed him away. Gently. Almost sadly.

"No," she said. "This isn't right."

"What isn't right, exactly?"

"Us being like this. I don't—I..." She trailed off and looked to him as if expecting him to finish her words for her. When he said nothing, she continued, "I've...I've cost you so much."

"What, that?" he replied, pointing a thumb towards the window. "It was a long time coming."

He made for the window, peered out of it briefly and then continued: "You have no idea how long I have been keeping it quiet, how much I've wanted to say to my father, to Adrianne, but was unable to. But you..." he said, going up to her and taking hold of her, "you made me a braver man than I have ever been."

Sitting on the corner of this bed now, he went on, "You know what, Ria? You stand up for people. You don't see survivalist or Cayanese...or anything. You see something that needs protecting and you go ahead and do it."

"Not always. And you think that is a good thing?" she asked.

He looked at her. "Yes. Why not? There is too much of sitting around nowadays. The whole 'I won't do anything because no one is doing anything'. Or the 'everything is good so why rock the boat'? If I do something, then I lose everything. Like the 'if shit does not flow out of the showers or your faucets, no one cares where the sewage goes' mentality, you know? So we keep voting for the same people to get into parliament. We keep quiet about social injustice. Because we're all so damn engrossed in what we have and so damn frightened to lose it all. And they know we know it." He gestured at the space around his room. "Heck, *I* know it. I could walk away and live on my own…but when it's all you know, a big house, a car, a maid and a full stomach seems like the air you breathe, you know?"

Ria joined him on the bed, falling back onto it, her legs dangling off the edge.

"And what would it take for these people to stop sitting around?" she asked.

Eedric fell back too, his face level with hers. He shrugged. "For shit to flow through their showers." Quickly, he added, "Not you though."

"Do you…do you think they will stop?"

"Stop what?"

"The raid on Nelroote."

At this, Eedric was quiet. He turned to look at her and saw her looking back, eyes wide with expectation, snakes flowing over his quilt. He could always be honest with her, even if the truth was going to be painful.

"I don't think they will. Not until they find…" He trailed off. After a beat, he reached out and took her hand. "But don't you worry. I have some money and I have savings. We can rent a small, cheap apartment and I can find another job. Run away from all this and make a life somewhere."

He gave her hand a squeeze.

"We can make it work."

Ria said nothing in response, only kept her eyes on the ceiling, listening as he somehow fell into a slumber.

Tracing

The light blue water was cold when she dipped her feet into it. The grass surrounding it was clipped so close to the ground, Ria wondered if Eedric's family regularly got someone to come down to their estate to do the mowing and the gardening. It didn't look like anyone in the family knew how to handle a tool and she was loath to think that those tasks fell on the wretched little Human they called Suri. She looked back at the house and her eyes wandered up to the windows on the third floor. Her thoughts drifted to Eedric, sleeping like a dead log on his too-large bed, beneath his too-thick stuffed blanket—quilt—in naught but a small, thin pair of shorts. For a dead log, he tossed and turned a great deal in his sleep, going from side to front, and then front to back, arms flailing sometimes, and sometimes—too often—seeking Ria out to pull her into an eager, though crushing, embrace. In the days that passed, she had learnt to simply remain still, feeling the turn and twitch of his body as she listened to either the smacking of his lips or the far more entertaining murmurs of his gibberish sleep-talk.

Eedric never woke earlier than nine. Which had been a blessing when she needed to step out before dawn. His arms had been around her, one of them crossed over her chest, hand grasping her shoulder. She had had to inch carefully out of them, worried that for all of his dead sleep, he would choose that day to be alert. He had murmured her name, making her pause in the middle of getting out of his bed. She had looked over her shoulder at him and continued to gaze down upon him for a long while after. It was the first coherent thing he had uttered in his sleep since she'd first arrived. And a part of her had died as she considered what she was going to do to him.

Ria's eyes dropped from the windows to the patio. On one of the woven rattan lawn chairs, sitting with his feet propped up on a footstool, Eedric's father reclined, frozen, a cigarette between his fingers.

They had heard his father's car sometime late in the afternoon. Eedric had been working on a resumé that he'd promised himself to send out before the end of the week. Ria had been watching him work on his computer while she finished off a plate that he had brought up for her. There had only been one set of footsteps moving through the house, each step ponderous and contemplative. A featherlight knock on Eedric's room door had caused them both to freeze, wide eyes trained on the door, then each other's faces. Eedric had been so sure that his father would not speak to him after the episode at breakfast. Neither had dared to speak, and then footsteps were heard again, this time receding, before a door closed and it was quiet again. Henry Shuen must have slipped out from the house before dawn to have a smoke in the early quiet before the koel had even started its call.

The automatic porch lights had been on when Ria came down. She had smelt the smoke before she even saw him. He had not made a sound when Ria came around from behind him. The cigarette had barely left his lips when he started to grey over. So abyssal were his thoughts, or so surprising her appearance, that his expression was nothing more than a casual lift of his eyes. When the last of the smoke had streamed away from the cigarette end of stone, he sat fully inert. A good-looking man, even for his age, with a touch of olden-day class in his shirtsleeves and his hair gel-combed away from his face. Eedric kept saying that he took most of his looks from his mother who, from the photographs he had shown her, was pretty in her own way. However, in truth, Eedric was every bit an image of the father he so disliked.

Dawn had come, merging an orange wash with the leftover blues from a fading night. The cool air that had rested around her like a veil was starting to lift with the sun's rising. Ria walked back to the house, bare feet wet and cold. Just as she was about to cross the open patio doors, she buried her hands in the pockets of the hoodie that Eedric had given her. Within the house, Suri was bustling about, arranging breakfast things on the table that had been set for two. Ria glided past her, taking care not to glance.

She moved ghostly quiet through the ground floor of the house and came through on the other side, finding herself in the driveway where the cars were usually parked. That morning, there was only one.

There were more houses nearby like Eedric's with just as many cars, if not more. In each of these houses, there would be a woman just like Suri. Whether Human, Tuyun or Scerean, local or foreign, they were all the same—young, uprooted, frightened and to some degree, Ria considered as she remembered the girl's easy acceptance of Eedric's bribe, desperate enough to partake of one transgression or other when the opportunity presented itself.

She could sense Suri herself standing by the front door, watching her with fear and uncertainty. Ria allowed herself only the briefest of glances up at the third floor window again. She didn't know what she expected to see. His silhouette, perhaps. Then she moved, unlatching the small gate and letting herself out.

She had not noticed before but Eedric's house was only a few houses away from a forested area. Too sparse to be considered a jungle, but old enough that its dipterocarp sentinels towered like stoic, bushy-haired giants. The area was still an undeveloped piece of land, but already the carpet of ferns before the first line of trees had been cleared, leaving swaths of ugly red-brown lacerations on the ground. But there was something familiar about it and about this whole affair of leaving. The main difference this time was that she was alone. The way that was best and the way it had to be.

Ria stared down the small road, lined with cars and green garbage bins. Bougainvillea peeked over a few low walls while morning glory cascaded down others. Periwinkle grew in small planters. Clustered ixora and flaccid white hands of spider lily decorated roadside bushes. A collared traac lay curled on the roof of a silver car. At the end of this lavish road, the line of trees waited, pillars holding up a partheneon roof of green.

She was not sure where the forest trek would take her. From what little she had seen of the modern surface world during the brief period of surfacing and the drive over to Eedric's house, she could already imagine that the developments that had indirectly been instrumental to her and her sister's flight to Nelroote had taken firm hold of Manticura. What bits of forest that existed now would soon be torn from the face of the land, to be bled red and flattened. Then these would be built over, to become high-rise blocks with their nondescript windows and doors. Or an estate of lavish houses no common folk could afford.

She didn't know. All she knew was that spaces for her to hide in were becoming scarcer and scarcer by the day.

Yet, for much of her life, she had been hidden. First by Barani, then by Eedric. And for what? To protect her. To protect others from her.

That, she saw, was never going to change. For the world seemed bent on making the same things happen, over and over again.

To her right, a gur(ma) roc began to bark. Running from one side of the gate to the other, while growling at her menacingly between barks. The roc's owner came out just she turned to look at it. And all the sleep went right out of him when the last bark burst forth, from a greying animal body.

And Trace

Eedric was woken from a dead sleep by a rough shake on his shoulder. He jolted up into a sitting position. His first thought was that Father had found Ria and there would be hell to pay for the two of them. The two police officers standing by his bedside—both large, hulking Cayanese—confirmed his fears. It didn't take long for Eedric to blink away the last of his sleep to see that they did not appear to be ordinary police officers. They were a little too well-armed: rifles instead of pistols, and equipped with opaque riot shields. They wore full-faced helmets with visors pushed up to reveal steely, dark eyes.

Ria's name was on the tip of his tongue but he did not utter it.

The two officers took a step back and raised their guns to point them at him. His response was to raise his hands in submission. His breathing started to get shallow. He fought to stay his Human self.

"Where is she?" one of them demanded.

"Where… Who?" he asked in turn.

"The medusa. The maid said she was here."

"I don't know what you're talking about," he insisted.

He didn't. And he did. His mind was a flurry. Where *was* Ria? Had she managed to hide? Was she still in the house? Did Suri tell on him? That low class whore.

The officers didn't say anything more. The one who had not spoken took hold of him and yanked him out of bed. He was in nothing but his boxers, but they handcuffed him without even offering him clothes to cover himself with.

"Look," he protested, struggling against the man's hold. "I didn't do anything wrong. I don't *know* anything. I don't even know what is going on!"

They motioned for him to move.

"You can't just come in here like this! Where's my father?"

He saw the officers exchange a glance.

"There is something you need to see downstairs."

Dread mixed with disbelief in a putrid concoction. It rose like bile and caused him to reel. They led him downstairs. One by each elbow. There were more people in the house. Some armed officers and a few more others in office attire, wearing lanyards around their necks. Suri was among them, her eyes reddened with hysteria; she seemed ready to break apart as a woman with a clipboard questioned her with slow, gentle words, yet even at a time like this, she sat on the family furniture with the fear and reverence of one who had previously never been allowed to: precariously on the edge, all weight supported on perfectly positioned feet.

Everyone turned to him as he came down. One man broke free and, with his clipboard in hand, gestured for the officers to take Eedric out to the patio, where a photographer was taking pictures of something in one of the lawn chairs. When Eedric was brought around, he saw that the something had in fact been some*one*. It was the perfect capture of his father, sitting with his cigarette, too serenely poised for what he must have seen.

On Eedric's lips was only denial. Despair rose, causing him to reel. His body went weak. His knees threatened to buckle. A hoarsely whispered "Pa" escaped his lips with the stench of regret.

"Your maid said you brought a medusa over and you sheltered her here for a span of several days," the man with the clipboard said. He was completely impassive, scrutinising Eedric as he spoke. "This morning, the medusa was seen passing through the dining area there before leaving the house. Is this medusa an acquaintance of yours?"

Eedric continued to stare at the statue. His own eyes wide and mouth open as if he were the one to look upon Ria's gaze rather than the older man. He was on his knees, body immobile from shock and encroaching sorrow. In a stretch of more than twenty years, he had never felt more affection for his father than he did then.

He didn't fight it when the officers hauled him up again. He let them march him through the house and to the outside. Out on the road was a chaos of civil defence vehicles, police cars and civilian vans. Near each of the latter, spiffed-up news reporters stood, speaking into microphones as they stared into cameras held by their videographers. Civil defence officials were at various front doors and balconies, breaking locks and climbing in through open windows. Beyond all the activity, every house was seized in unnerving stillness. Not a single one of his neighbours was present among the discord. Eedric didn't have to look to know why.

∿

They offered him a shirt and a pair of pants after his arrival at the detention centre. The centre was situated at the end of an old and long road, deep in an undeveloped piece of forested land. There had been a sign at the beginning of that road; too spick and span and over-designed for the nondescript, single-storey white building they eventually drove him to. Its perimeter was walled in by tall mesh that reminded him of chicken wire, topped by whorls of barbed wire. At intermittent points along the wall stood a guard tower, each with two sentries—one looking out, the other in.

Eedric had sat alone in the back of the van. And alone he'd had time to play the stone image of his father over and over in his mind, as he grasped for a reason as to why Ria would do such a thing. Why she would betray him after all that he had done—and *risked*—for her. Shock gave way to questions before plummeting into despair and then rising to anger. He should have known better than to give himself over to the wiles of tainted women. For all of its lack of passion, *safe* was a far better option than the dangers of sun-filled eyes. *Safe* was what he could have been if he had not gone down that spiral staircase that day, and if he had never gone back like he was told.

By the time the van rolled into the detainees' checkpoint, Eedric was tearing at his face and his hair, banging his head against the enforced walls to bruising, and weeping angry tears unbecoming, he thought, of a man: face crumpled up ugly, nose running snot into his mouth of painfully clenched teeth.

He was searched, and his details taken down. He was fingerprinted, photographed and blood-typed. Because he was a survivalist, his irises were scanned for the records as well. Everything he'd once had to conceal was now open to an organ of justice and preserved for posterity.

They put him in a room without windows, walls painted a light blue, one wooden desk in the centre with a laptop already set up. He was commanded to sit. His wrists were bound and someone offered him water, one of those factory-sealed packets; they had even poked the straw in for him.

Two men came in. Both again in office attire and lanyards. One of them was the Human man from his house, still with the same scrutinising stare. He sat across from Eedric and pulled the laptop to him. The other, a Scerean, stood by the door, a handheld voice recorder and pen poised to note everything he was about to say.

"Okay, Mister Jonathan Shuen," the one across from him said. "I am First Investigator Fents and this is Second Investigator binSonda. We have a few questions for you and you are required by law to reply accurately. Are you clear on this?"

Eedric stared back at him before managing a nod. He was aware of the Scerean officer in the corner behind him, and no doubt every centimetre of the room was being monitored.

The investigation went on after that:

When did he bring the medusa to this address? Exact date—What day was today?

How did he know her?—They talked.

Where did he know her?—Main chamber. Catacombs.

In what capacity are they acquainted?—They fucked. How about that?

What were the events prior to his illegal sheltering of a fugitive?—Eat peanuts. Watch sunset. Sister fucking crazy, tried to kill him.

Fents perked up at that. "Sister?"

"Her sister."

"Can you give us a description of this sister? Also a medusa?"

"How the fuck are they supposed to be sisters if she's not a medusa?"

Fents didn't flinch. Just kept typing, the laptop keys keeping at steady clacking pace.

"You said she tried to kill you. How?"

Eedric glowered at the man and spoke slowly: "You saw how they kill. You don't have to ask me how." He leaned back in his chair and he saw again the image of his father captured in stone. Remembering it shook him again. Less belligerently, he replied, "She might have tried to. Ria stopped her."

"Ria?" Fents spoke up, nodding with some interest. "Is that her name?"

A new pain bloomed in Eedric, only to be exacerbated by Fents turning the laptop to him so that he could see the video on the screen. "Is this her?"

Eedric didn't think he could handle seeing her face. She might not have been there to kill him, but in not being there and in leaving traces of her presence, she might as well have. But the screen did not show her face immediately.

Rather, it showed CCTV footage that they had somehow got hold of in that short period of time. An indoor camera, likely installed to keep an eye on the maid, and it showed the living room from one of his neighbour's houses.

A man was looking through his work bag. A woman stood near him, clad in an oversized T-shirt. They appeared to be talking when something caught their attention from out of the camera's line of sight. The couple only had time to peer in that direction before they froze into stone. A blur went past them and moved to some far room. It was only a few minutes later when Ria's familiar figure sauntered back into the living room. She did not even glance at the couple. Instead her attention was focused on the sofa as she ran her hand over it, seemingly enthralled by the material that covered it. When she was done with that, she walked slowly to the front of the room and peered up, looking directly into the camera.

The features so unique to her, every scar and undulating serpent, came into perfect focus.

Then the footage stopped, fixed on that face.

And Eedric couldn't say a word.

Lucidity

Eedric's eyes sprang open in time to see a new man being shoved into the cell. The door closed with a resounding clank, rattling as it went, like a bad cough. They had not even bothered to remove the man's handcuffs—closed the door, shutting him in, trapping him. And while he stood there without words—wrists bound, face close to the bars—the guard who'd arrived with him and the guard who'd been standing there watching over the lock-up, walked away, not meeting his eyes while he stared after them. It didn't take Eedric long to recognise an unspoken plea. The man turned around in panic as someone called out, "Sani."

The midnight Cayanese who had been mashing heads with the Tuyun stalked over to Sani. Arms spread out as if in greeting, though the smirk he wore was more menacing than welcoming. Altan or Adhan or something was a big man, even by Cayanese standards. His fur seemed to absorbed the shadows of the underground he was accustomed to, with only a sliver of grey beginning from the top of his brows and sweeping down the back of his head. Altan—Eedric now remembered one of the inmates calling him—had given Eedric one hard look when he was first thrown in but had never said a word to him.

Sani was tall and lanky, unfortunate enough to have his *yun* scales concentrated into knobs down his back and to a single arm. He did his best at bravado—chin raised, head held to the side in feigned casual regard.

"Ah, Sani," Altan began, "so long never see?"

"I've been busy."

Altan nodded slowly, though it was more of a gentle rocking motion of his head than a proper nod. His cronies were at his back, matching his every step. Eedric found himself standing. Some of them saw but no one confronted him about it.

"Why? You study so high, you cannot speak to your"—he gestured to those around him—"brothers in our language, is it? Okay, okay"—slow nod, slow nod—"no problem."

What followed happened fast. Altan pulled Sani towards him by the collar of the young man's shirt. Their faces were close—Sani's crossed with subdued terror and Altan's with outright anger—for a split-second before Altan threw Sani deeper into the cell, as easily as if the Tuyun were made of feathers. Sani staggered and then regained his balance, trying desperately to free his armoured arm from the cuff.

"You!" Altan bellowed as he rounded on Sani. Two of his men grabbed Sani by the elbows. Sani fought but could not break their hold. Altan gestured once more around him, at the piss-covered walls, the dark faces of the men in the equally dark cell. "This! Is all because of you!" A fist to Sani's stomach was followed by a brutal uppercut to his jaw; and then Altan grabbed his hair and yanked his head backwards to make Sani look up at him. "You are one of us now," Altan growled. "Have always been, educated or not educated, living,"—a knee in the gut, once—"*and* dead"—again—"and your Kak Ria is not here for you to hide behind like a man without balls, eh?"

Eedric had been about to turn away, somewhat glad that no one thought to blame him for the debacle, but the name caught his attention.

The beatdown continued, and didn't stop even when Sani was on the ground. When the ringleader was done, the rest descended upon him with almost delirious glee. Someone managed to break open Sani's handcuffs, which skidded to a stop near Eedric's feet.

Sani just let them beat him.

There was a time when Eedric would have stood by and watched the hurting of another. However, such a hazing was usually followed by acceptance. In some respects, it could be a kind of love—they beat you so you won't break—the sifting act of finding out who belonged and who didn't. In many odd ways, it was the one who wouldn't lay a finger in the name of peace and mercy who was the outsider, disconnected and dispossessed.

Sometimes to take was to give.

But it was the sound of ripping fabric that set him off. He remembered from a long time ago: Father, drunk, had demanded that Mama be naked, that Mama be what she had always been: a whore. He'd heard it from his room, late at night. Father had been shouting loudly, on one of those nights when he didn't care what the neighbours thought.

Eedric hadn't understood then. He understood it now.

He bounded into the pack. In one smooth motion he grabbed the man who had been straddling Sani's back to slam the young man's head into the cement, and threw the offender against a wall. There he lay crumpled, concussed, dead… It suddenly didn't matter which to Eedric. The others backed away almost immediately, eyes wide and mouths agape. Altan stood his ground, however. He was the only one who could see eye to eye with Eedric in his survivalist's state. He kept his body bent low in a defensive stance, his fixed gaze hostile but discerning. Where before he had been cautious of Eedric because of what he represented—that untouchable surface life able to reduce people like him to redundancy simply by having the right papers, the right amount of money—he knew then why it was really so, why the surfacer's blood had smelled wrong, so very wrong from the first whiff. He had heard about the Changer in Nelroote, but he had not been sure this was the man. Now he was.

Eedric matched Altan pace by pace in a circling dance around Sani's near-lifeless body. The rational part of Eedric told him to speak, but he was beyond speaking; beyond comprehension and comprehending. There was only the call to fight, to…*protect what you can protect; the survival of another above your own.* And that was all that was truly important.

He was the first to attack, but Altan was ready for him, and in a blink he was heels up, head down against the bars, the noise of the impact reverberating amidst a cacophony of hoots and cheers. Altan blocked most of Eedric's initial attacks and came at him with keen counters honed, it seemed, by years of fights in rough underworld life. Eedric had no such experience but every hit made him meaner, added to the buzzing in his head so that all he could see, smell and hear was his opponent. Every successful attack became frighteningly narcotic and with every moment that passed, he adapted, got faster and better, until he was the one landing all the hits, taking few, feeling nothing.

Something told him to stop. Maybe it was the hands that tried to restrain him. Maybe it was Sani looking up shakily at him from where he was still sprawled on the floor. Maybe it was Altan's body slumped against the wall, face smashed into it, arms limp by his sides. There was a laugh, low and guttural, but so strangely sad. It took his fight-addled mind a while to realise that it was actually emanating from him.

With the first jolt of shocking pain, he thought he had been shot. With the second, he fought his body's reflex to jump away, and in doing so he froze up. He thought of Ria's eyes as he fell to the ground, still aware though immovable. For all of their treachery, they were still so damn beautiful.

∽

They brought him to a new cell, where there was bedding for two and a corner for washing up, as well as a standard flush-enabled pisspot. The cell was better lit with a small barred window high up that brought in sounds from the outside—birds, the quiet hum of vehicles coming in and out, people speaking in low voices and smoking too from the smell of it.

"Sorry, 'Bang," the young guard said as he turned the lock of the cell door, "standard protocol."

Eedric wondered if this skinny little Human was the one

who'd tased him. He tried to see what was holstered at his belt but just as he was stepping back, another guard came along with another inmate and asked for the cell door to be unlocked. He felt almost sorry for the little man as he did as he was told with shaking hands, his inferior rank painfully conspicuous upon the epaulets of his uniform. The new inmate they shoved in with him was Sani, still battered but significantly cleaned up.

"Lockup is full," the new guard said to Eedric as if he was trying to explain something. "No more solitary cells. In-processing very busy."

Eedric stared at the man with as much emotion as an unpainted pet rock. "Did you manage to find her?" Eedric asked, his voice level. "The medusa?"

The two guards exchanged a glance, both appearing rather puzzled. Finally, the second one spoke, "All the women are in another facility, sir."

Eedric nodded but said nothing. He didn't move when they left, barely noticing the way Sani slunk past him to sit on the bed, or the way the other assessed him from behind his mangy fringe. He wore a shirt the guards had given him. It was grey and oversized, making him appear lankier than he already was.

"Are you from one of the other settlements?" Sani asked him.

Eedric turned away from the bars he had been staring at to look at his cellmate. He felt nothing but disinterest for Sani even though moments before, he'd very nearly torn a man's throat open for him. All the fight was gone from Eedric and there was only numbness in the aftermath.

"Hey, where are you from?" Sani asked. "I have never seen you before, so you must not be from Nelroote."

"Do you know Ria?" Eedric found himself asking in return.

Something in Sani's countenance changed at the mention of her name. Eedric couldn't tell if it was hope, or joy, or maybe even fear.

"Kak Ria?" Sani replied. "How do you know her?"

Eedric couldn't answer him. He found himself without words to describe either the meeting or the relationship they'd had.

Sani stared at him and seemed to understand. "You're that Changer who came to the settlement, aren't you?" The boy hung his head, shaking it.

Eedric clenched his jaws and turned away for a brief moment. Jerking his head in a vague direction, he went on to ask, "They were going to kill you. Why?"

Sani clenched his jaw and looked down at his feet. "You... I—ah, I don't know how you know Kak Ria, but you...you don't need to know anything about this, or me...or what I did. I know that you just—" He grabbed at his hair as he sighed. "Thank you, man. Really. But..."

"A man might have died today," Eedric said, calmly, almost coldly.

"Thanks, man... But what I did..." Then Sani shot up suddenly. "You don't know what life is like there. You don't know what it's like carrying the stuff in your pocket, the meetings in the dark, taking money, paying... I am only a student. I want to graduate. I want to get a degree and get out of that hole! But every time I want to, every time I tried... It's always—*they* always bring up the old connections. Just because I wanted a better life, I am selfish. Just because I have an education, I am stuck-up."

Eedric's gaze continued to be fixed upon him.

Desperately, he went on: "When they said I should tell them everything, where... What... And who... What can I do, man? What the fuck can I do?"

"You told them?" Eedric asked quietly as the truth began to dawn on him. "*You* told them about Nelroote?"

"What the hell was I supposed to do?" demanded Sani. "With the amount of drugs I was carrying, it would have been the noose for me. I am only a student! I never wanted this!"

"What *else* did you tell them?"

Sani fell silent.

"What else did you tell them?" shouted Eedric as he came in close.

"I—I don't know what you're talking about."

Eedric had him by the collar, had him against a wall.

"They sacked the entire settlement and they did not stop there," Eedric bit out. With slow emphasis, he repeated, "What else did you tell them?"

Sani's mismatched eyes met his, before the former swallowed and then replied, "I told them about...the sisters." Eedric drew him forward and slammed him back. Sani hissed at the pain. Eedric didn't care. "There was nothing else I could say that would save me."

Eedric waited, his heart pounding, blood throbbing in his temples. Finally, Sani all but whined, "They were—they were interested in certain individuals, they said, so I told them about Kak Bara… Kak Ria… Thinking…"

The growl that escaped from Eedric's lips surprised even him, but Sani was too far gone to care. When Eedric released him, he slid to the floor as if melting into a pool of himself, sobbing. Eedric didn't notice. A wildness had seized him but the aggression was without direction. He paced. He bloodied his hands trashing the sink, fluff flew from ravaged mattresses musky with smells of others before him. There was a confused turmoil of what-could-have-beens and failure, and of loss and regret.

He turned suddenly to Sani. He was breathless when he said, "Do you know what you did? My father is dead. An entire estate is dead."

Sani stared at him, his expression a cross between horror and disbelief. "That wasn't my fault!"

"Yes," said Eedric, "but all of that wouldn't have happened if you hadn't told them."

"They said that was what they wanted. Needed. Said they would leave the settlement alone after cleaning it up," Sani explained, reaching an open palm to Eedric. "They said I would be granted immunity!" Softly, he added, petering out as he did, "And protection. For myself, my family. I had to choose. I had…to choose…" He sat back against the wall, tilting up his damaged face and closing his eyes. "They lied."

"Of course they did," Eedric replied and sank down to the floor directly opposite Sani. He knew they'd put the younger man in the cell with him in the hope that he'd finish what Altan had started. He'd always thought Manticura's law and order was the best in this part of the Layeptic. Suspects always seemed to be apprehended in record time, and a woman needn't fear going to a twenty-four hour eatery for supper at three in the morning. Yet, when the people in the system were in some way significant enough, by some order of a shadow, the Manticurean prison was a terrifying nexus to be in.

"Of course they did," he said again, quieter this time. He leaned his head back against the wall.

∿

Eedric found out that Sani had served national service in the same camp as he had, only three batches later. Sani had pursued a liberal arts degree, whilst his family had wanted him to become a doctor. Eedric found that the grass was only greener or browner wherever your feet did not tread: "There is more to see," said Sani about life on the surface. "It isn't perfect. The more animal you look, the more people will treat you like shit, but at least you're not looking over your shoulder all the time. Food don't taste like it's been in a cupboard for ten years. The air's fresher too and you can get educated as long as you have the papers. Sometimes, when I'm up here, I forget about the dead bodies that turn up at the crossing between Mati and Styx every other Monday." He grew quiet, regarding the wall above Eedric's head, where new scratch marks crisscrossed over old ones. "And then I remember that all this is an illusion too, and underground is still where the family's at, the hearts and the loved ones. I don't even know if they're even still alive."

Sani had been punching the walls. It took a long time for the *yun* scales to split and for the skin beneath to break. Blood seeped through the cracks and crevices, like tree sap through wounded bark.

When they called for Sani, Eedric found that he was truly sorry to see the man leave. He had watched him fluctuate between despondency and frantic anger. There was nothing he could do or say to make the situation any better, or to drive away the reality that possessed them. He eyed the two guards standing just beyond the cell door, quelling a sudden desire to kill, to fight, and stood when the other stood.

"Hey," he said to Sani, balling his hands into the pockets of his pants, "your family will be all right."

"Yeah…" drawled Sani. The shadows beneath his eyes were darker than before. Eedric had heard, too, the nights of fretful sleep, full of tossing and turning, of quiet murmuring and the occasional prayer for a family's safety.

Sani held out a hand and Eedric grasped it. He watched Sani being led down the short corridor to disappear around the sharp corner with its tiny window, high up and out of reach.

∿

When Eedric was finally called, he expected to be led to a room for another round of questioning. Instead he was merely led through a series of gates and then down a corridor with a window stretching along one side. The room within was dark so he couldn't see into it, only himself, his face hollowed and gaunt, his hair matted and appearing somewhat sparse as if he had tugged it out in patches. His hands were cuffed. "Sorry, 'Bang, standard protocol," another young officer told him kindly as he clapped the irons across his wrists. *Daripada tadi* standard protocol, he thought.

They took his cuffs off just before a set of solid metal double doors. As they did so, he couldn't get over the fact that just above the threshold of freedom, a pair of security cameras watched their every move, transmitting his every reaction to a networked set of blue-hued screens, the seconds running in a bottom corner tagging breath per breath.

He didn't know which was worse, the seemingly endless transit through a deadened corridor or the sterile room he found himself in later. Two paintings and a potted plant on facing walls directed the viewer's eyes to the glass doors at the far end. In the room of perfect symmetry, Stepmother waited with an officer, both dwarfed by his uncle, whom he hadn't seen in years. He was surprised to see them. Of all the people who he thought would bail him out, he had not expected them.

That surprise gave way to sudden meekness and overwhelming guilt. He desired nothing more than to be shackled again and be turned back to the cell with its scratched up walls where he would await his trial. He could not meet their eyes, and felt himself choke on the incomprehension that was his tongue. More than that, he sought answers, and justice, anything before he was going to accept this revolving door prison with its dirty and convenient ways of getting rid of the people. Only, right then, he didn't know where to begin searching.

Stepmother was the first to step forward but he could feel his uncle's eyes on him, the eyes that were Mama's and his. In a brief glance, he saw the lines on the man's face and jowls that framed it like parentheses.

He could say nothing to the man, and to Stepmother all

he could manage was, "I'm sorry."

Stepmother appeared to be on the verge of tears. For all of Father's shortcomings, Stepmother had still loved him. She shook her head and reached out to touch the edge of his T-shirt sleeve.

On their drive to Stepmother's family home, where he would stay while awaiting his trial, Eedric asked that they stop by his uncle's house so that he could see Grandma—his Nenek. A premonition of bad things to come—imprisonment, exile or the death penalty—called at him to do so. Besides, he also owed his only surviving grandparent a visit.

Stepmother turned the car only after asking for directions. When they were there, she would not go inside with Eedric and his uncle. Said it wasn't her place and that it wasn't right. *She's a good woman*, Eedric thought as he looked back at her sitting in the car, dabbing at her eyes with a pale handkerchief. She had him to put the blame on, but she didn't. She saw bigger pictures while he was blinkered into smaller selfish details.

Seeing that, he turned around and surprised her when he opened the car door again. He reached in and touched her hand, really quickly, before he left.

Nenek was wheelchair-bound now, small and thin, her eyes rheumy, wispy hair worn under the kind of thick knitted cap old women liked to wear. She saw him and greeted him with near-toothless volume, "Ah, Maria *datang pun!*" He had to smile as he took her wrinkled hand in both of his by way of returning her greeting; got on his knees and brought the hand to his nose and lips. He detected the scent of medicated oil on her skin. The flat still smelt like cinnamon and betel nut, and the radio station continued to whisper its oldies and boy band ballads in the background.

"Yah," he told her, not looking up. "Maria is here now."

Severances

Ria waited, perched in a tree a distance away from the open entrance to Nelroote, concealed in darkness. The cold cover of the foliage was laced with dew from the approaching morning. She had not thought to find her way to Nelroote on her own. Even with how small Manticura was, it had taken her a little over three days and many false turns, which had in turn taken her to farms, other lavish out-of-the-way estates, and a military training ground. All of which she had turned away from, because Rose Ville would have served its purpose. The nationwide panic, the questions—there would be no hiding; no burying her under layers of cover-ups and diversions. Not any bloody more.

A sound caused her to tense. She drew her legs up and curled herself into a tight ball against the sturdy trunk of the tree to watch through the gaps in the leaves. There was nothing, perhaps an animal darting within the semak-samun. So she continued to watch, hesitant to approach the entrance until she could be sure whether it was guarded or abandoned.

The first time she had crossed a threshold much like

the one she was watching felt like a lifetime ago, even for a medusa. She couldn't remember Acra's face now. Only that, for a time, he'd meant so much to a girl who'd done terrible things. She remembered the void that existed after a departure; not a void that was all black, nameless and featureless, but one filled with everything that was empty of the departed. She wondered if that was what it was like for Eedric now that she had left him.

After some time, she could hear the sound of booted feet. She waited for the squad to pass—two men in full helmets and dark uniforms, alert as they walked, rifles pointed down and neither of them speaking. They paused at the entrance to sweep their rifle lights down the tunnel within. It occurred to her how easily anyone could have found the entrance. Eedric had. And now these soldiers. All it took was for someone to look. For someone to tell them where to look. At this point, she didn't care who did. Only that what she had planned would come to fruition.

She made her way down from the tree. The last foothold that she missed woke her to how out of practice she was in the whole art of tree-climbing. She fell, and there was no one waiting below to catch her this time. She landed hard on her right ankle, the pain forcing her momentarily to her knees on the leaf-littered ground below. She picked herself up and tried her weight on the injured foot before getting herself to walk.

The soldiers were already turning to her, guns pointed, as she approached. She noticed that they were wearing light armour and helmets with visors of glowing green eyes—fully equipped to be mobile, to move fast and delay the effects of her gaze. But even the most seasoned soldiers could only plan on a fraction of certainties. One of them stared at her down his sight, and that was enough. Her hair framed her face and she was able to cover the distance between them within the milliseconds it took him to start curving his finger around the trigger. The world around her seemed to heave and buckle, wavering as if viewed from underwater.

When the first man started to grey over she turned to the other. He had his face averted, gazing at a miniature image of her within a small circular mirror that he wore strapped to his inner wrist. He could have shot her. He had every chance to. Instead he started to run, to get away, but she caught up with him, rounding his body to stand before him. She almost smiled. She remembered now that she had always smiled when a soldier chanced upon the chamber. She'd thought that smiling was a balm against what she was meant to do. It was no balm, however. Just as breathing the surface air was no boon for those who'd lived all their lives without ever seeing the sun.

She spared the petrified soldiers only the barest of glances before crossing the threshold into the underground. She navigated the dark, scraping her shoulders against the patterned walls on either side. When she finally came to a tunnel deeper in, she was met by the glare of floodlights that had been set up at points along the walls. There had been no guards by the staircase. However, two more men patrolled the northwestern tunnel leading up to the keramat.

Their backs were to her and they had not seen her in the brief moment she had chanced to step into the blazing light. She crept up to them and made just enough noise to make them turn around before petrifying them. Rounding the corner ahead, she saw a few more men poking their rifles at the recesses, sweeping remains from out of them and sending them clattering to the ground. Ria's heart clenched at the sight and sound. Without remorse, she turned those men too. After disposing of two more patrols, she finally reached the keramat.

Ria quickly slunk into the nearest pocket of shadow, very close to the alcove with the sarcophagus. She tried to remember if any of the escapees from Nelroote had carried belongings with them when Barani confronted her days ago, for she had come upon the remains of what had once been a crude encampment. Some of the loculi had been cleared of their occupants and there were beds made out of cardboard and piled-up cloth. The remains of a small fire sat in the centre of the chamber—the dust of charcoal surrounded by skulls that propped up a crooked wire mesh that was already blackened from use. The whole place stank a little of urine and shit, and decomposing food matter was mixed in with the odour.

There had been no guards at the entrance from which she'd come. Only a few strips of police tape that she had easily ducked under. Either she had caused enough of a commotion on the surface to draw attention away from Nelroote, or the majority of the raiding forces were clustered in the main settlement itself.

The keramat, however, was not entirely abandoned. A few police guards were stationed on either side of the far exit and a few more stood by the pillars. Her things were still in their old places—her books stacked in the alcoves, the suitcase in the corner filled with her cave survival needs—but she could sense the mark of someone else's touch all over them. Even right then, there were men and women milling about her chamber, examining things with gloved hands, taking pictures of the various statues and setting up numbered signs by them. The bones of the skeletons she had kept so reverently, even though she held no beliefs, had either been removed or knocked askew in their loculi. The sarcophagus of the *jar nah-uk'rh* was closed and it bore scars where the gold leaf halo and eyes had been scratched out. She could not tell for sure if these transgressions were the investigators' doing or her own people's, in a desperate bid to make money out of selling the ancient gold leaves.

On the ground at the painted lady's feet, Ria caught the glint of the tool that had likely been used to deface her: a small scalpel that Ria had used to prepare the bodies before their interment. She peered above the stone table and when she was sure no one was looking, she darted out to grab it. Wasting no time, she used the momentum of her movement to take her to the far corner of the chamber. There, she pressed herself into the shadows again and waited, heart pounding, to determine if anyone had seen her. No reaction. She was glad that the floodlights the raiders had installed only illuminated the centre of the keramat and the various statues housed within. She looked about her, weighing her chances of sneaking past the party. When it finally occurred to her that she could not, Ria stepped into the light.

A wave of shock rippled through the investigators. The guards were quick to recover from theirs, pulling their weapons free from the holsters. One of them took a silenced shot. Ria ducked behind the massive Cayanese statue in time to avoid it. A few more came and a bullet whizzed past the statue's opened legs to land on the ground near her. Instead of creating a crater in the stone floor the way bullets ought to, the projectile bounded off of it before coming to a standstill. There was a hint of red and she saw that they were not firing bullets. Instead, what had landed near her was a tranquiliser dart. Her suspicions were confirmed then.

With resolve, Ria edged around the statue to confront the guards. They had split up into two groups: one to flank her, the other to draw her out. She met the first and turned them before taking cover behind another statue. The need to take her alive meant they had to get into a position where they could get a clear shot. They had limited ammunition, and the presence of unarmed civilians meant they could not risk any misfires.

A movement in front of her caught her eye. She turned to see one of the investigators backing away from her. However, his eyes were firmly fixed on the display screen of the digital camera that he was pointing to her. She glowered at him. He made the mistake of looking up at her. When his back hit the statue behind him, he and his camera were already stone. She barely paid attention to the man's fallen body before she came out of hiding and confronted the last of the guards. They were quickly disposed of, and a few investigators right after. She caught sight of the backs of the others slipping out of the exit that led to the settlement and the southeastern gate. One of the guards she had turned to stone had his walkie-talkie raised to his lips. There was a likelihood that reinforcements were coming her way, but there was still one more thing she had to do.

At the exit, she paused and cast her eyes over the keramat. Then she turned and started to run.

Only to collide with a body standing at the head of the tunnel.

Ria tried to leap away, gaze already armed to petrify. However, the body grabbed hold of her arms, preventing her from moving.

"I knew when I heard shouting that it was you," Barani said. Her grip on Ria's upper arms tightened and she shook the younger woman as she demanded, "Why did you come back?"

Ria had not thought to see her sister so soon and the sight of her caused Ria to freeze up, muting her. Barani was more haggard than when Ria had last seen her. The floodlights cast her eyes in shadows and deepened the cavities of her sunken cheeks. Combined with her stature and the threatening answering murmurs of her hair, her gaunt appearance made her appear fiercer than she usually was.

Ria's voice was barely audible when she finally spoke: "Kakak."

"You shouldn't have come back!"

"Then where could I have gone?" Ria asked.

"Up there. Make a life with the Changer. Somehow." Barani's gaze on Ria was hard and there was a touch of fear in it. "They are looking for you, Ria. I managed to sneak into the settlement for a bit to get supplies. The raiders talk. Of you. They have been asking questions about you."

"Who told them?"

"Does it matter now?"

Ria nodded, then shook her head. Uncertain. Terrified.

Already wretched. But not at the prospects of being apprehended. "They mustn't find you," she said quietly.

"Better they find me than—"

"No!" Ria cried, cutting her off. "It's not better."

Barani looked at Ria with surprise.

"Right now the world above is looking for anyone to blame."

"Why? What did you do, Ria?"

Ria went on as if she had not heard. "They will take you and they will imprison you. And they will make you take the blame for what has happened."

"What did you do, Ria?!" Barani asked again, shouting now. Fear had begun to creep into her countenance.

When Ria didn't reply, the fear turned quickly to despair as Barani remarked in a quiet voice, "Why does it always have to come to this?"

"I don't think people like us will ever have freedom. Not as long as we still have these eyes of ours," said Ria. Her hand tightened around the scalpel that she had held on to throughout her fight in the keramat. Her arms hung like heavy slabs on either side of her. Every minute passed as a carved word on an epitaph, every moment filled with growing dread. She remembered now the lost statues in her catacombs, helpless on their backs or knees, clutching at the backs of their necks or holding on to snake-bitten wrists—the ones she always made sure to break, to leave nothing of them but feet and pieces of hand in the rubble that she swept off into dark corners. She had heard of other medusas who couldn't even control their powers, petrifying people with every turn of the head, every accidental look. But at least they were not burdened with the guilt that came with the autonomy of bad decisions.

"What we have is a curse," Ria said, stepping up to her sister. "We can be taught to use it wisely but when things get bad, control can be lost so easily."

"You cannot believe that, Adik," Barani beseeched. "You really cannot."

Barani's eyes were truly on her now, wide and violet. They had grown more vibrant with passing time, brightening until they were nearly red. Everything about Barani was perfect, so perfect, and a part of Ria was compelled to keep her that way: beautiful, good and…perfect. Because Barani had every right to be. Beautiful things had every right to be, even if they made all others ugly in comparison.

A dark cobra stretched itself towards Barani's face, pulling Ria closer to her sister. The body of the hooded cobra glimmered in the dark, the snake's predatory silence a loud annoying hiss in Ria's ear. Barani continued to regard her. Nothing about her posture or expression showed any sign of fear or doubt. There was only sadness, and Ria knew she would be haunted by it to her dying day.

It was two cobras, not one, that struck eventually. One to clamp over her sister's mouth and another to sink fangs into her right eye. Barani blinked and drew back in reflex. Ria almost did the same. She wasn't even ready. But how could she be, for such a thing? Barani lashed out a hand to grab Ria by the neck and squeeze. Her own vipers were in a flurry, biting down on the cobras each time they came in to attack, at the same time fighting to tear themselves off her head. Barani uttered no cry, of horror or of pain.

She couldn't have even if she had wanted to, for the venom worked quickly. Still, it required a third snake bite before Barani was properly paralysed, eyeballs rolling upwards, face immobile as her body went slack and her hand loosened from around Ria's neck. Ria dug the tip of the scalpel in then. There was resistance, then a breach. Liquid was spilt, colourless then red. She felt her face grow wet, wet as her sister's was from blood, but she couldn't stop, would not stop. In her mind, she played the memories of every one of her sister's wrongs—the abandonment in the hut, then in the catacombs during the war; all the moments of silence in the stretch of time after, only to have that culminate in her sending Ria away after she had discovered her with Eedric. Fuelled by these memories, she worked the scalpel, worked, worked, worked, completely possessed by the need to divest her sister of their identity's cruel determinants.

When it was all over, the first thing Ria remembered was how her sister used to sing. Every night when Ria was very young. Because Ria believed her voice kept the ghouls and spirits of the dusk away from their house.

She wept then, cradling her sister's head as if it were a baby, the nest of vipers sliding over her arm in loops and esses, intoxicatedly slow. She didn't hear the sounds of people approaching from the tunnel ahead. She didn't hear them stop to regard her with fear and shock while she sobbed out as if she had known no other pain. And there was no other pain.

She did not see the red dot that trembled on her arm before skipping away. Why, she barely felt the sudden piercing pain on the back of her neck, near the base.

Numbness began to spread, leaving parts of her body feeling alien and empty. She wanted to hold on to her sister's body, but she reached back and pulled out the dart, the tail-tip red-and-silver point glistening with a bit of her blood. While she gazed upon it, another pain came, less keenly felt but still there; lower spine. With the last of her strength, she dropped her face onto her sister's neck and whispered her apology into the other's warm skin.

Aegis

Medusa the First died from a beheading, and in a dream Ria saw herself on a rickety stage kneeling before a crowd that stared at her with eyes of the already dead. They appeared bloated and removed, spots of black bloom floating before them like they were an image in a de-silvering mirror. She saw herself in full, her dress hanging limp from her body, the hem coming undone in places. The air that hit her was cold and she regretted wearing a sleeveless dress. Glancing over her shoulder, she saw her headsman, an ample hood obscuring half of his face such that all she could see was a sculpted nose and stubbled jawline. His emotions were indiscernible as he raised his axe to take a swing. Fear rattled through her, keeping her rooted, unable to turn her head and inflict on him the force of her gaze after the initial ineffectual glance. She was finding it hard to breathe, as if her lungs were fighting both the tears and a weight on her chest. Her snakes were lifting from her shoulders and neck, exposing it, to coil into tight curls around her head. She felt the cool line of steel touch her skin above the silver chain of the army tag she wore as if the headsman was gauging where it would land before lifting the axe again. He whispered an apology, said her name in Eedric's voice, so concrete she could smell his cigarettes on it, feel the weight of his touch and of his gestured volatile gaze. Later, she felt buoyant. The people down below turned sideways and in that way went up, then down again, before the sky came over her like a blanket. In the sightless light, she thought she saw the diamond of a kite trailing streamers behind it.

Ria came to slowly. Sensation had returned to her limbs and she could feel her arms wrapped close to her body in bandages, her feet clamped down onto a hard, unyielding surface in what seemed to be the centre of a large and empty room. Her head still felt heavy, her snakes unalive. When she tried to heave herself off, she realised that there were further restraints around her forehead, neck and waist. There was an uncomfortable tightness along her hairline and over the whole of her scalp—it must be a cap, her hair was barely breathing. She could feel the blindfold pressing over her eyes and the bridge of her nose.

This was before the opening and closing of a heavy-sounding door, before the hard voice of a man had begun asking questions about her political affiliations—Manticurean or F'herak, as if she belonged to either—her ambition in creating uprisings, her war contributions, motives... What else, Ria could not remember. Her reticence had angered him and had earned her strikes of fists across her face. Then came the endless wait without food, water, or a means of relieving herself. She was aware of the room's strange smell, as if it had been previously doused in a kind of cleaning fluid. She guessed that it wasn't new, nor particularly used. It had only waited a long time for an occupant. There must have been other interrogations like hers; no country existed without someone's teeth being removed or tongues torn out with hot pincers, and all that usual drama. No birth without blood. No erected monument without a tragic explosion. *Biasa lah.*

Feet moved with intermittent apologetic squeaks across the floor and every now and then she could hear a mechanical click and whirr.

A woman had come next to ask her the same questions, her voice deep and charismatic, reminding her so painfully of Barani's. She had introduced herself as Diyana and called herself Ria's friend, but not before speaking coldly to someone: "You beat women, Officer?"

"She wasn't cooperating, ma'am." *Suara manja*, a voice used to getting what it wanted, belonging to a creature who felt itself entitled to never wiping its own backside.

"Try doing it when her restraints are off and when she is not blindfolded."

"But—"

"We do not hurt our suspects like some Esomiri secret police," Diyana had cut in, biting down on every word. "Do you understand?"

"Yes, ma'am."

There had been the indignant stuttering tap-tap-tap-shrieks of his exit and then nothing, to which Ria allowed her mind to take in the presence of one who had sought to defend even one such as her.

Diyana. Diyana… *Nama sedap*. Ria imagined someone

tall and regal, with groomed eyebrows and full lips painted blood red, framed by a short hairstyle perfectly parted and sleeked down with oil or cream. The suit she wore would be sharp and precisely ironed, shiny buttons down the front of a perfect figure, and a knee-length pencil skirt with a slit at the back. Stockings too, stretched black with the showing beige of skin like a face through a mourning veil. Diyana had apologised for her colleague's behaviour. Ria only rasped, "It's the only time they can beat a *metu'ra*." She had tried to shrug but her shoulders were stiff and the neck clamp got in the way, like a thick, heavy collar coiled up and over with chains.

"You mean, *me-tura*?" Diyana had corrected her. "Snake woman and not…what is the other word? Storyteller?"

"Inscriber." Ria had not got it wrong.

After that, Diyana *suruh ci'ta*, Ria *ci'talah*, throughout which someone had typed away vigorously on a keyboard. They must be recording her too, with those big cameras meant for shooting movies. She had wondered if she would be in colour or in black and white, the date static below, hours ticking, seconds running and running the way she had been running from this very captured state for years and years.

Diyana had been listening without interruption. Now, she spoke up, "We have been looking a long time for you, Ria."

"Yes."

"Your file is a very interesting one, Ria. Kenanga is practically legendary in Manticurean folklore, the disappearing Tuhav soldiers in the Ne'rut rainforest…

military horror stuff the men still tell each other at camps." Ria noticed that Diyana used the old pronunciation for the forest's name, the one that distorted and emphasised the first syllable making Nerut sound like *nye'i'root*. It was an old Tuyunri way of pronouncing words but Diyana didn't sound that old.

Diyana had paused, as if she had been consulting something. Then she added, "And then...Rose Ville Estate down at Dornor Lane. Plus...all those soldiers and officers." After a beat, Diyana remarked, "These are very serious crimes, Ria. *Murder* in fact. Why?"

Ria didn't reply for a while. She felt an approaching warmth and then a twig's prod between her lips and against her resisting teeth.

"Drink," she was instructed gently, and understood that the twig was a straw. She took a long, grateful sip and pushed the straw out of her mouth with her tongue. The distance opened up between them, cold and empty, before Diyana picked up where she left off, "Your history is...incredibly tainted. No matter how we try to..." Diyana trailed off and then sighed. "There are a lot of unhappy people—frightened people, who are demanding answers from the authorities right now. And we need answers, Ria. Why?"

Ria continued to remain quiet.

"And then... What you did to your sister. What were you trying to accomplish?"

"What of her?" Ria asked, doing her best not to appear concerned.

Diyana did not buy it. "Alive."

Ria felt herself breathe a little easier.

"She is in specialist eye care now," Diyana informed her as if by way of reassurance. "We did what we could but she will never regain her sight."

"Who are 'we'?"

"Us, here at the centre."

"I did it so that you would find me. I did it so that there will be no doubt that I was the one behind Kenanga, behind the disappearing soldiers," Ria told her.

It seemed that Diyana had not expected the answer to come as easily as it did, because for a time the other woman was quiet.

"And your sister?"

"To spare her."

"From what, Ria?" Diyana asked, sounding both puzzled and horrified.

"From what is going to come later."

"And what do you think—"

"You tell me. What do you need a *me-tura* for?" demanded Ria. "You said before there are a lot of people asking questions on the surface. People seeking answers. Just look at your officer. He did not hurt me without a reason. He hurt me because he was angry. He was angry…like everyone else out there. The world they know is starting to crumble, because scary things—unexplainable things are happening on the streets. Their *clean*…little streets where not a single lamp has ever burnt out to leave them in darkness at night. And yet now—" Ria paused. "They turned to the government for answers and the government had none. Now that you have me, you can give them what they want and then things will be back to normal."

Ria could almost sense Diyana shaking her head.

"You know we can still use Barani for that, right?" Diyana asked. "The people know what killed all those victims. They have the Internet, some form of general knowledge. Making them all intelligent, it seems. And with the way things are right now…" Here, Diyana gave a dry chuckle. "The pictures are already on social media and citizen news is already making the rounds. But…they only need to know that the creature has been found and dealt with. You *or* Barani. It wouldn't matter to them. The masses are simple, Ria. When their rice bowls are filled and their lives are comfortable and secure again, they easily forget these things in favour of continued comfort. And the fact that you and your sister are so isolated from everyone just makes it easier."

Ria struggled against her restraints then and tried to pull herself off from the hard board, teeth gnashing, spittle flying from between them to dribble down her chin. She croaked a litany of curses, in both Sce' 'dal and Tuyunri, curses she knew Diyana could understand.

The room erupted in a flurry of activity, filled with shouts and metal dragging on resistant floor, and then a shocking wave of pain that did nothing to her but fuel whatever it was that had ignited the sudden violence, and the long-overdue desire to break free and fight. She could feel in every fibre of her person that she would fight. By the Lady she would fight; go into a manic decline just to make all those years of stony restraint, of poise and control, worth it.

Diyana came in close again and spoke urgently to her, "However, we can ensure your sister comes to no harm."

Above the smell of blood and her own stink, Ria detected

the characteristic spicy tang of *yun* scales before Diyana drew away. The other continued to speak: "We can ensure a comfortable life for your sister. Provided you are cooperative."

"Lies!"

"Right now, I'm all you have."

A silent stand-off; Diyana no doubt looking; Ria not knowing where to look. And then: "How?"

"No need for how. There are a lot of things you can help us with."

Ria was still. She barely felt the pinprick on her left arm. She could feel one of her wrists about to tear free. Her snakes were pushing against the cap. She tasted blood and realised that she had bitten down too hard on her lower lip. Her wrists were slick. With blood or sweat, she couldn't tell.

"Do we have your understanding on this, Ria?" Diyana asked.

Ria continued struggling.

"Do you understand, Ria?" Diyana asked again.

Seeing no way to escape and feeling herself already starting to drift away into unconsciousness, Ria stopped and replied mechanically, "Yes."

Diyana must have nodded then. Sadly, because she said, more to herself than to Ria, "*Turni'in, bcir(o)h.*" *Ground above, night below.* The Tuyunri words of prayer that were recited when interring the dead, the only words in their native language that most Tuyuns still knew and still spoke today.

"*Et(he),*" Ria replied. *So it is.*

Measured footsteps diminished into a blind distance before darkness came over her with the unmistakable sound of a closing door. The last thing she was conscious of was her own rambling about swings and courtyards, and names—Erlina and Jyadi, Baslit and Unir, Sara and Ani. Chrysaor and Pegasus. A random list that meant so little to her.

∿

When she was conscious again, she found that she was unbound. She was lying in a narrow bed, upon a thin mattress. The pillow that supported her head was hard, and a coarse blanket had been thrown over her. Her head reeled as she sat up. Her hair hung about her face, moving in lethargic and confused loops. It was a while before the effects of the drug they had injected her with wore off, and still a while more before her eyes adjusted to the dimness of the room she was in.

She was in a cell: four bare walls, a sink and a toilet. No mirrors. The only window was a tiny rectangular hole through which a bare bit of light from outside streamed in. Even if she could somehow squeeze through it, the window was barred—there was no escape. The door to the cell was a heavy metal one with a small slit for looking into and looking out.

Ria was barely on her feet when her cell suddenly flooded with light from the fluorescent bulb above. The light blinded her momentarily. In that moment she heard the door open with a loud protesting whine. After blinking hard from the light's intrusion, she turned to look at the door, expecting to see someone standing in the doorway. There was no one. Only the silence of the darkness beyond.

She waited, thinking this to be a ploy or a trick. When

still no one came after a few long minutes of waiting, Ria approached the open doorway. She had only put a foot out before the area outside was illuminated by vast overhead lamps that reminded her of the ones they had back in Nelroote. She was not allowed to feel too nostalgic, for the sight that greeted her was that of a corridor with numerous other cells like hers. A single level of them; every door ominously black and securely closed. Though even that notion of security soon dissolved when, with a collective whine and groan, all the doors swung open.

The cells' occupants were likely just as puzzled as her to find no one standing at the door because it took some time for the first among them to step out into the communal space outside, disbelieving, bewildered expressions etched onto their faces. There were burly ones and spindly ones. There were those who appeared menacing and those who looked like they could cheat you out of your life savings with a smile. There was a dangerous quality to some of them. And to the others, there was a resignation, as if it was just another day. Ria would say that there was a good mix of the races, however, the demographics tilted heavily to the non-Humans. And they were all men who appeared to have been imprisoned for a long time, by the way they looked around as if they had never seen an open space before.

She recognised no one from among them and knew they were not from Nelroote.

Ria looked to the wall at the end of the rows of cells and spotted a high-up square of black glass, its surface showing only a reflection of the prison space below it. Installed at regular intervals along the walls above the cell doors were closed-circuit cameras, each dark eye pointed in her general direction.

More prisoners had by then emerged from their cells and all of them were looking at her. There was uncertainty in a lot of their expressions; puzzlement as to what she was doing there. Perhaps a few were eyeing her a little too eagerly—too hungrily—and she knew it was a dangerous place for her, *me-tura* or not. She cast a final glance up at the window and thought she could make out the forms of people watching her from behind it.

She did not expect the announcement at all when it blared from an invisible sound system: "Attention, wards. The first to kill the medusa will earn a president's pardon."

This brought new life to the eyes that now cast themselves upon her, even in those who were resigned to their capital fate. She found herself feeling disgusted by this new sport. She had thought, from the clean streets and the ordered stacks of homes, that this country, this Manticura that others had once fought for, that still more had trusted—that this country would have in it a sense of justice, if not for people like her, then at least for the full-bellied people of their middles and those on top.

Yet, at the same time, she was not surprised. She understood. She was not to die that day. In that moment, it felt as if she was no more than a severed head stuck upon the shield that the nation-state sought to build. For what? Against who? Ria realised she was no longer in any position to ask.

Her hair raised itself in preparation. Then she dropped her gaze to the first man who broke out of the uncertainty, and watched as his countenance greyed over at the sight of her, whilst she moved to the old battle-rhythm of a flightless body.

APPENDIX I

PARTIAL HISTORICAL TIMELINE OF MANTICURA

2nd Lt Diyana Zuranisa, PhD, DI01, S/N 08986
Clearance L.8, Call: Primary Investigator
Project #151: Study on Conflict and Historical Diversity
—Management and Integration
Centre for Research on Multiculturalism
Ministry of Social and Community Development
V03. 17 Her. 5116

PROJECT NOTE #02: PERIOD OF HUMAN COLONISATION

4498 CE: First Humans arrived from the lands in the western continents. By then there was already a thriving population of Scereans, Feleenese and Cayanese. The presence of the Tuyuns was generally known, though still considered a myth to the more isolated settlements. In keeping to the nearly impenetrable jungle, the Tuyuns were able to remain obscure, even to the Scereans with whom they made trading pacts.

The Human pioneers numbered a hundred and forty-four—three ship captains each with a crew of twenty, two cartographers, two topographers, three botanists, three anthropologists, and 70 fighting men, builders, and any accompanying spouses. They were all led by a Major-General Kankrow, who had been tasked by the High King of Arlands to seek out new land to occupy and regions within which new trading routes could be secured.

The surrounding jungle was cleared for farming and building, and the wood was used to build houses for the settlers.

4503 CE: Humans made first contact with the Cayanese Yan (Leader). A trade agreement that resulted in the cultivation of the western half of the Anur Delta region was signed within three months of negotiation. The Cayanese proved not only to be good allies but a good provider of sturdy workers as well. Large groups of Cayanese villagers seeking work and fortune moved to the growing Human settlement, where they worked as menial labourers, often in unsafe environments.

Attempts to strike the same agreement with the Feleenese Nes were not as successful. They met the Human emissaries with hostilities and would sometimes attack the Human-owned farms in West Anur, leading to tensions between the three races.

4504-06 CE: Human/Cayanese-Feleenese tensions escalated into open conflict, resulting in what the Humans and Cayanese knew as the Anur War. The Feleenese simply called it the "Massacre". The Feleenese's primarily melee attacks were no match against muskets, and the result was a loss of more than two thousand soldiers on the Feleenese end compared to three hundred on the Human side. Most of the casualties on the Human side were, in fact, Cayanese.

The war ended with the Feleenese Surrender on the 6th of Mist. Feleenese lands in East Anur were taken over by the Humans, and those directly involved in the conflict were put to work on construction in the Anuri Prison Quarries. For years after, it was illegal for Feleenese to own land, vehicles, or weapons. They were not allowed into Krow City and were only permitted to work under Human employers, and only with recommendations from either a Human or a Cayanese.

4510 CE: Human emissaries made contact with the Scereans in Su(Ma) Uk'rh, or Lower Marshland. First contact failed when the emissaries fled Su(ma) Uk'rh upon seeing some of the inhabitants rise out of the swamp waters. (See account, "Dragons of the Lower Marshlands" by Sir Grant Shun.) Shun returned with more armed reinforcements; however, the confrontation did not end in armed conflict.

The hostile flora and fauna in Su(Ma) Uk'rh, as well as its harsh environment and location, made the land's development a very unprofitable one.

Shun and a more adventurous number of his entourage chose to remain in Su(Ma) Uk'rh to study the environment and its people. Their accounts and reports attracted other adventurers from Krow City and countries beyond the shores of Ma(an) TisCera well into the latter years of the 4th Millennium.

Just like their Cayanese and Feleenese neighbours, a few Scereans left the region to seek fortune in the towns that were growing around Krow City. Scereans were the most diverse when it came to appearance, ranging from the dragon-like purebloods to the ones with embedded Human features. Their appearance and odd natures, e.g. moulting and behaviour differentials during temperature changes, made them the most poorly treated of all the races. Scereans away from Su(Ma) Uk'rh often found themselves without work. They were not allowed into public places such as theatres or post offices, much like the Feleenese during the period of the Treaty.

The Scereans created a space for themselves in Dinya Uk'rh, Lower World, which would later be known simply as Dinya, one of the largest "tin-can" towns in modern Manticura up until its clean-up and development in the early half of 5067.

Manticura was pitched as the jewel of the Layeptic. The promise of space, fortune, and beauty drew large groups of migrants. While most preferred to stay in the Human-dominated city centre, significant numbers, particularly those from the lower parts of the North Continents, chose to establish villages and towns deeper within the country, encroaching upon Tuyun territories.

4511 CE: Earliest records of Tuyun encounters began to appear. Contact between the Tuyuns and the Humans was often established by the Scereans in Su(Ma) Uk'rh. (See article, "The Other Marshmen" by Shun.)

An expedition led by botanist Mayren Lod made first contact with the Tuyuns of Ne'rut Uk'rh . (See account, "Shadows of the Deep: First Contact with the Jungle People of Lower Nelroote" by Mayren Lod.)

In the wake of the wars of succession following the death of the Jar nah-uk'rh, or Blood Aunt, the Tuyuns saw a regression to their older state of paganism and segregated clans. The old catacombs and temples were buried and forgotten, leading to accounts of the Tuyun's continued primitivism.

Unlike those of their marsh and coastal cousins', the immune systems of the jungle Tuyuns were not able to fight foreign diseases. An outbreak of the common flu among the expedition proved deadly to the jungle Tuyuns. Whole clans were wiped out as a result. The expedition was considered to be one of anthropology's major disasters, but it led to the creation of an essential first-contact guideline in later anthropological studies.

The term "a Tuyun sneeze" is still invoked to show that a situation will come to a disastrous end, and is a common phrase used to this day.

4728 CE: Governor Abbett Kros' proposal for a unified government was met with opposition from the leaders of the other races, who still lived within largely segregated communities.

4809 CE: Abbett's son, Gransen, gained political backing from the Cayanese and Scerean leaders to form a union. Ma(an) TisCera was renamed Manticura after the chimerical creature that once lived in parts of the North Continents. Gransen Kros, Herkal Din'l, and Tecra binDrun headed the new Manticurean Union.

binDrun's position was contested by his cousin, Sunya rinDrun; however, she purportedly withdrew from the race and disappeared from public affairs after his rise to power. Her withdrawal was followed by the resignations of everyone who had been vocal about their suspicions of binDrun's legitimacy and fairness over the course of his years on the seat.

The Feleenese were invited into the union in 4812 CE, but only joined in 4814 when the old leader was replaced by his young son, Malik Saini, who was fourth in line for the position of leadership. Accusations of nepotism were quickly quelled.

The Tuyuns, the smallest minority in the country, were offered a single seat in the union. Without a proper leader, renowned Tuyun businessman, philantrophist and scholar, Jyani, took up the seat. She was the only woman in the union and the only legitimate advocate for her people's welfare.

In spite of the union, Manticura did not have a unified army. In favour of their individual interests, each race maintained and trained its own army. The Humans had the largest army and the Tuyuns the smallest.

Cross-race liaisons were also punishable by the law of the woman's racial faction. However, interracial pairings between Scereans and Humans were known to be common occurrences before the passing of the law. As a result, pureblooded Scereans became a rare sight in modern Manticura.

4956 CE: The World Union was formed, spearheaded by the countries of the North and West Continents, including the Arlands. Ceras split into North and South Ceras following the Cerasean Wars.

Internal conflict had been festering between the leaders within the Manticurean Union due to the Humans' monopoly of major political decisions. This came to a head when the Tuyun and Scerean leaders staged a coup to remove the Human leader, Thomason Stil, from power. It resulted in a civil war, seeing the Humans backed by their staunch ally, the Cayanese.

Without an alliance, the other races lost the war. The new Manticurean Union only had Human and Cayanese representatives in the seats. Martial law was declared across Manticura.

Across the border, Fel and Cay had since been unified and the new country was called F'herak. F'herak was first a part of Ceras, and later South Ceras after the Cerasean Wars. The leader of the self-governing state began championing for independence after they helped the South Ceras forces win the Juntra Plains bordering the warring halves of the Cerasean Peninsula.

PROJECT NOTES #05: THE MAKING OF MODERN MANTICURA

5042 CE: The New Republic of F'herak split from South Ceras. F'herak extended an invitation to the politically unstable Manticura to join their "F'herakian Imperative".

Seeing the advantage of unified governance based outside of the tenuous race relations, the Manticurean Union accepted the invitation and Manticura attained title as a state of F'herak.

5050 CE: Barani's birth as marked by the first sighting of her in Manticura.

5058 CE: Ria's birth as marked by her founding by Barani.

Manticura was granted self-governance with a largely-Human minor parliament headed by Ormal Din, a Cayanese F'herakian chosen by the F'herakian government. Ormal Din was a retired army general, and for the next seven years Manticura was governed by strict quasi-martial law.

5065 CE: Ormal Din was assassinated in his own home.

His petrified form and those of his personal bodyguards were discovered by one of his maids on a Tuesday morning, 4th of Evernoon. Anten Demaria, the medusa who was believed to be the assassin, was apprehended in the slums of Dinya, one of the most deprived slums in Manticura at the time, in the exact spot where the Covalence Mall stands today. Anten's actions were seen as an act of terrorism by the F'herakian government, causing friction between F'herak and Manticura. Stricter laws were passed, and suffocating regulations implemented.

"Trouble-makers", most of them Human, were removed from the population before they could "disrupt the state's fragile peace".

Nenek began educating the girls on the values of patience and acceptance, and abstinence from using their gaze powers. Ria and Barani attended public school briefly; they were then home-schooled by a woman known only as Cikgu Ramlah.

Anten was put on trial for her crimes and later sentenced to death by firing squad. However, on the day of her execution, the chief executioner ordered her beheading. Leaked footage of the deed sent the state into an uproar as people took to the streets to protest the inhumanity, citing her assassination of what they described as a "cruel warlord" to be a kindly bestowed justice in contrast. (See article, "The Woman Who Sees" by Anonymous in what was then known as the *TisCera Tribune*.)

The Order, then an organization rebelling against F'herakian government, rose to power during this time, rallying the crowds in their push for Manticura's independence.

5066 CE: Tension grew in the Layeptic Region as South Ceras agreed to lend military support to Manticura should they enter war, and F'herak imposed a trade embargo on both states. Panicked exodus of F'herakian citizens from the country saw suffocating crowds at train and ferry stations.

The Layanen Station Massacre took place at 5.30 am on the 12th of Sol. A small band of gunmen fired machine-gun rounds into the crowd waiting for the first train to take them out of Manticura. Sixty were killed and more than twice that number injured. The Order denied any connection to the attack, calling it an independent act of terrorism.

F'herak declared a state of emergency, resulting in further panic at the stations.

At this point, the Union stepped in with the Layeptic Summit, during which both F'herak and Manticura borders were policed by the Union Peacekeeper Corps. Manticura was granted independence mid-5066 under the Layeptic Compact. Both countries agreed to cease hostilities. An official apology was given for Anten's unfair treatment; through an agreement, her severed head was given to the new Manticurean government for proper burial.

5068 CE: Ten-year-old Ria turned Kenanga to stone. Barani turned a few government officials to stone in Ria's defence. The sisters fled to Nelroote.

Discovery of the Kenanga incident led to a renewed interest in medusas. However, the tender political state of a newly-independent Manticura, the pressing need for industrial, commercial and residential developments, as well as the brewing tensions in the north and the west, made tracking down Ria and Barani a low priority.

5070 CE: The North Coalition was formed following a gas attack in Rhesof, with the goal of seeing the world liberated from the extremism of the Eastern former empires.

Ten-year-old Lela Marudin left Nelroote for the surface with her two brothers, father and mother, following a period of difficult illness during which she took on her "Changer" form.

5072 CE: In early '72, Esomiri North Coalition forces made a push east towards the Layeptic Region, where resources of common metals, oil and wood were in abundance. The threat saw the beginnings of a rift opening in the F'herakian parliamentary.

Avoiding the open sea route, their forces took F'herak by surprise via the desert that divided F'herak from Estagur. Manticura, F'herak, and North and South Ceras formed the Layeptic Alliance to counter the attack.

North Coalition forces arrived in Manticura. Henry Shuen, 18, and his friend, Usa Marudin, also 18, as well as a Scerean named Acra, 25, left to join the army.

5073 CE: Usa and Acra died in battle in the same year.

F'herak saw a parliamentary split following party disagreements over peace treaties with the northern forces, resulting in the division of Upper and Lower F'herak.

5074 CE: The Layeptic Alliance fought a two-and-half-year war with the invading Esomiri forces, but isolated from the main Alliance in the north; the Layeptic armies faced a slow decline as communication and supply lines were cut off in key areas, and planted agents ensured decreased support from the people.

The war veterans in Manticura later named the period of fighting as the "Two-Half" or "Tuhav".

Year of the infamous "Feleenese Retreat", where significant numbers of Feleenese troops from the 89th and 151st Manticurean ground troops retreated across the Honour Strait into Lower F'herak. Henry Shuen was a sergeant in the 151st, one of the few who disobeyed the order to retreat.

Lower F'herak and North Ceras continued to resist invasion, while Upper F'herak, South Ceras and Manticura agreed to terms of surrender.

5074-78 CE: Manticura's period of occupation. During this period, Manticura experienced accelerated scientific advancement, as well as rapid development of urban and industrial infrastructure. The great number of Human immigrants from the North Coalition resulted in an increase of the already-significant Human population in Manticura, altering social structures in the nation. Humans gained greater privileges than the other races, with the Feleenese receiving the worst treatment. The latter race faced continued suspicion in light of the "Feleenese Resistance" in both Upper and Lower F'herak, and the pockets of rebel groups working in Manticura itself to push out the invaders.

Ria began her collection of statues in the central chamber of the catacombs, disregarding race or uniform. Many of her victims were soldiers trying to escape capture when they were either unable to join up with, or were cut off from, the mass of retreating forces.

When Coalition patrols began disappearing in the Ne'rut forest, old files on the region were revisited, resulting in the discovery of the Kenanga incident that the young Manticurean government had kept classified from the larger population due to its sensitivity, being so close to the Ormal Din assassination.

The power of the medusa involved in the Kenanga incident was recognised in its sheer magnitude and stealth. Anten had been beheaded on the order of the F'herak parliament so that her head might be brought back for study on the effectiveness of her gaze even after death—thereby finding out if it was possible to utilise the power without the autonomy of the person it belonged to. Acquiring a medusa alive and in secret would minimise the chances of a political incident.

Kenanga's obscurity meant that there were no contemporary reports on the incident, but Usman Kemat's reports identified that there were, in fact, two medusas on Manticura, confirming the suspicions that Kenanga was the work of more than one individual. The development plan was a calculated move to have the medusas within the control of the government.

Covert operations were dispatched into the Ne'rut rainforest to scour the jungles for the medusas. Given the technological limitations of the time and Ria's heightened ability to cover her tracks, her position and by extension her sister's could not be triangulated. Ria grew faster and stronger with each new encounter, and between pushing back the waves of attack on two fronts from Lower F'herak and North Ceras, the growing Feleenese *and* Tuyun threats in Manticura, the occupying Coalition order could not devote resources in pursuit of persons whose existences were based upon a few unverified file reports.

The main Alliance continued their fight in the Northern countries of the North continent, pushing steadily through Rhes and Esom and into the Layeptic region.

In Manticura, the last remaining Coalition forces faced a defeat in Jankett New Town on the morning of the 14th of Grudan, where the Two-Half War Memorial stands today.

Ria returned to Nelroote on the 22nd, bringing the first real news of freedom with her in the form of Waro, who had been released from the Menkapa POW camp on the north coast.

The medusa case was again neglected as the national focus moved to economic and infrastructure rebuilding as well as parliamentary re-elections.

Manticura returned to its old system of a unified, multi-racial government, now simply called the Order. However, a single military was established and there were no racially individualised laws. Each race was allowed a collective that saw to their own race's needs, but every decision made had to first be passed by the Cohesion Ministry.

Manticura's education system saw a major reassessment. All schools, workplaces and housing estates were also to adhere to government-passed race quotas.

5088 CE: Eedric was born as Jonathan Eedric Shuen to Lela Marudin-Shuen and Henry Shuen.

5102 CE: Lela and Henry became estranged due to irreconcilable differences and Henry's affair with his personal assistant.

5106 CE: Lela passed away from a disease that was unspecified by Eedric. Doctors' records indicated it to be lung cancer. Lela's health records also indicated a history of hypertension, clinical depression and borderline general anxiety disorder. These conditions are likely characteristics of her being placed high on the survivalist spectrum, however they were not clearly marked as such.

5116-17 CE: Ria and Eedric met, and carried out a brief sexual relationship. Pregnancy tests on Ria have come back positive, possibly twins of unspecified gender. It is not known how the combined genetics of the father and mother will affect the offspring.

Project journal entry:

At this point, I am unsure as to how we should proceed with Ria's rehabilitation and subsequent integration into the internal security defence unit of the country. My observations and the conversation that I had with her have led me to conclude that she is highly volatile and therefore a security liability. However, I do wonder at how much of a hand we have had in creating her in the first place. Hormonal changes may or may not aggravate her volatility. I personally feel that there might be a better chance of cultivating the necessary values in her offspring. On another note, the window for study and experimentation may now be confined to a significantly smaller timeframe. Note to research team.

APPENDIX II

LIST OF TUYUNRI WORDS

Extracted from *Almanac of Life: An Annotated Edition*
by Prof. Manuet Juros (4914 CE)

A
/ah/
- **(an)** : of
- **ak'er** : ceremony
- **anir** : animal
- **ahas** : excrement ; shit

BC
/b'(uh)k/
- **bcur** : day
- **bcur'in** : "Day above" ; Tuyunri equivalent of "good day" or "hello"
- **bcis** : night
- **bcis'in** : "Night above" ; Tuyunri equivalent of "good evening"
- **bc'ne'** : today
- **bc'jot** : not today ; understood as "tomorrow"
- **bc'jot(h)** : not today ; understood as "yesterday"

D
/oo/
- **dal** : tongue
- **dalla** : fall
- **dallayari** : waterfall

E
/eh/
- **et(he)** : yes ; "so it is"
- **et(hor)** : no ; "as such it is not"
- **(eis)** : can

F
/ph/
- **fel** : cat ; feline
- **fel'nees** : Feleenese

G
/g'(uh)g/
- **g'urk** : idiot ; unfitting
- **g'ukm** : kin (not blood-related); belonging
- **g'jarukm** : blood-kin ; relatives
- **g(nal)** : give
- **g(thur)** : harm
- **gur** : sand
- **gur(ma)** : desert

H
- **(he)** : so
- **(hor)** : such
- **hur** : flesh
- **hurnees** : Humans

I

is-uk : uncle/father– The only existing word in the Tuyunri lexicon that can be used to address an older man or the father of a child.

J

jar : blood
ja'tur : blood-sister
– **(var.) tu'tur** : earth-sister (women who share a very close relation-ship and are not blood related)
– **(var.) ura'tur** : heart-sister (also female lover/partner)
ja'tis : blood-brother (born of the same mother)
– **(var.) tu'tis** : earth-brother (see *ja'tur* and *tu'tur*)
– **(var.) ura'tis** : heart-brother (also male lover/partner)
jot : forward ; north
jot(h) : back ; south
jot(h)ur : death ; dead

L

lay : (pronounced lah'yi) sea
layari : water
layar'in : rain
layer : (pronounced, lah-yehr) sail
layeri : river

M
/heh/
ma : land
masi : big
maura : small
me : snake
meri : flow
metu'ra : inscribe ; carve ; (later) write
me-tura : snake-woman ; or in other words, medusa

N

nah : mother
nah uk'rh : aunt ; "not mother but could be"
na-uk : shortened form for "aunt", usually used to address a significantly older woman
ne' : to
nee : born ; child
– pl. **neer**
nee'is : alive ; living
nees : people ; a questioning gesture or intonation is also a way of saying "who"
nin : tall ; lofty
ni'in : high ; above

O
/r/
(o) : where
oa : place

R
/'oo/

rebakara : celebration (likely a Sumean alteration)

r(o)h : short ; beneath ; low

roc : a species of four-legged reptile that can be domesticated. Has unique control of their body temperatures and a secondary system of adrenaline release that can be activated, making them particularly fast and active. Known to be very loyal; ferocity and loyalty are largely dependent on the way they have been cared for. Life span of 15 to 20 standard nees years.

— **su(ma) roc** : the favoured sub-species among the privileged. The need to provide a substantial sub-aquatic habitat for them makes them expensive to care for.

— **gur(ma) roc** : hardiest of the species. Thrives in (and prefers) dry living conditions. Most of the strays in Manticura are of this sub-species.

— **yun'(ma) roc** : originally a jungle-dwelling sub-species. Smaller in size compared to the other two.

Ro' 'dal : common tongue

ror : many ; common

ru : a point of reference to oneself ; I— It is actually a shortened form of "ru'nee", which is best translated into "see this child". Tuyuns, like the Scereans of Su(ma), refer to others primarily using terms that indicate kinship—"na-uk", "is-uk", "ja'tur", "ja'tis", "nee", "tu'tur", "tu'tis".

rujot : a point of reference to another when indications of kin are not involved ; you (generally taken to be hostile)

runa : home ; permanence

ru'neeura : "I see you in/close to heart" ; a form of greeting between intimates

Runi : name of the clan that unified the various Tuyun tribes under one banner during the period of Tuyun enlightenment, the same clan that led to the building of the Ne'rut catacombs, later known as the underground system of Nelroote.

rut : see

S/C
/se'h/

cay : dog ; canine
cay'nees : Cayanese
cera : hills
ceranin : mountains, or tall hills
sc'r : lizard ; reptile
sc'rnees : Scereans
scer : speak
scer'jot(h) : spoken
Sce' 'dal : spoken tongue (represented as earliest lingua franca)
su : marsh
su(ma) : marshland

T

tis : sky
traac : relatively small domesticated mammal, usually between 25 and 30 centimetres in length, not including the tail. The species is identified by its long, pointed ears that grow backwards from the top of its head, ending with a frill-like finish that resembles those borne by some Scereans. They are solitary animals and can be highly territorial in terms of their direct physical vicinity. However, with training and care, they prove to be good and simple pets for those who do not have the time and energy for a roc.
tu : earth (world)
tuis : man ; also flight or "skybound, apart"
tur : rock
tura : woman ; also earth or "ground beneath"
turam : consume ; eat
tura'is : picture ; also "sexual intercourse" or "joining"
tura'isnee : most intimate one ; "precious person"
Turni'in, bcir(o)h : "Ground above, night below" – Tuyunri words of prayer when interring the dead

U
/oo/

uk'rh : "what is not, yet could be" ; lower or minor
uk'm : "what is most, always" ; higher or major
ura : heart
uram : keep
uram'gur : protect ; "keep from harm"

W
/'ur/

(wre) : on
wre : wear ; "dress in"

(wre)ur' : "to wear on heart" ; Tuyunri equivalent of "thank you"

Y
/'ur/
yun : wood ; bark
yun'(ma) : forest ; jungle
yun'wre : tree

Notes on language:
The premise to keep in writing words of the Tuyunri language is that ancient Tuyuns, before the advent of Human civilisation and the compact with the Scereans, are deeply tied to the natural landscape. Their language is deeply embedded in gestures, particularly when speaking of temporalities, and their perception of the natural order of things. As such, their language is also deeply matriarchal, rather than patriarchal. The earlier point on gestures also hints at a hunter's way of living, in which signals are a preferred means of communication between nees.

There are very few words of abstraction in the Tuyunri. For example, they lack a word for "love", seeing how the sentiment is not a thing that words can easily express.

Symbols and sound:
' : (apostrophe) is akin to saying "un" without opening the mouth ; back of throat
( ) : (parentheses) is a full sound, very similar to saying "orh" with a wide open mouth, embedded within the pronounciations of the words. E.g (ma) will sound like "moah", with emphasis on the "m" and "ah" sounds.

Tuyunri words are very rich with sounds that are derived from the animal calls of the jungle.

ACKNOWLEDGEMENTS

Firstly, a big big thank you to Edmund Wee of Epigram Books for daring to have the Epigram Books Fiction Prize and providing Singaporean novels, which would otherwise be buried somewhere deep in some drawer, or on a hard disk drive, the opportunity to see light. And for giving many a reason to write. Oh, and where do I begin with all the enthusiasm in putting this book out; thank you to Yong Wen Yeu for the beautiful cover design and maps, to Jason Erik Lundberg and JY Yang for the arduous editing and enduring my terrible propensity to be too optimistic about time. Winston Tay and Andy Lim have both done so much in keeping my neurotic self calm through media events and meetings. Finally to Allan Siew for making me look good in the author photograph and to Clara How for being so wonderful during the initial phases, because my anxiety about this whole thing started way back. This is also not to forget everyone else who has kindly contributed in their own big ways to making the prize (and, as such, this book) possible. Thank you, all you awesome people, you!

That said, this book has been a long time in the making. A *long* time. Just ask my PhD supervisor, Jen Crawford, to whom I am indebted for her sharp critical eye and all the positive energies she sent my way while this story was being written up as part of my creative doctorate thesis. I thank her for her friendship and support, *especially* when it came to pushing me to read and share little bits of earlier drafts in various academic domains. I really look forward to the day this book is in your hands.

I would also like to thank the members of my defence committee at the English Division of Nanyang Technological University—Neil Murphy, Daniel Jernigan and Barrie Sherwood—for their thought-provoking questions and honest feedback during the viva. The points they raised were very helpful in the preparation of the manuscript. Daniel was especially strict with me throughout my creative writing journey, calling me out each time he felt I was falling short of my potential. Neil was instrumental in getting me into the division, seeing something in me when my grades barely made the cut, which opened my path to this book in the first place.

The earlier drafts of this novel were read and critiqued by a number of wonderfully helpful people to whom I am deeply grateful: from my peers in my graduate cohort, to the undergraduate students whom I was teaching at the time, and to writer Timothy O'Grady, then one of the NTU-NAC Writers in Residence (International). Thank you for the early feedback.

My family I have to thank for their fortitude through this journey: my brothers have been supportive of and even optimistic about my writing, and my parents, even though they may have differing opinions on the validity and propriety of fiction within a religious context, have maintained an open mind when I chose to pursue a literary path in my education. My most heartfelt gratitude to my mum, Juliah Bte Othman, who has endured so much in her own life to make sure I got mine. I am afraid I may be too rebellious and headstrong a daughter, and she always feared me going out there into the world. But I have only learnt from the best of women.

To Rebecca Yeo, my friend since thirteen and my sister from another mother, thank you for seeing me through the "Wolverine" days, and for making me go out when you know I have been holing up in my room for too long. To Nurul Ain Yahya: So much of the wisdom of this novel was born and sharpened from our lunch and coffee sessions together. *Terima kasih, sahabat, bagi sokongan, dorongan dan suntingan-suntingan kritikal anda terhadap novel ini.*

I also have my colleagues at the Centre for Research on Islamic and Malay Affairs (RIMA), Shariff, Nabilah and the ever calm Diyana, and the Board of Directors—current and former—Mr. Nazzim, Dr Razak, Dr Nawab and Mr Azha Putra, to thank for their support and excitement through the course of this publication journey. No one could be more excited about the prospects this book will have than the centre's projects coordinator, Shariff. And when I thought I was going to be in deep trouble, the Directors have proven to be true champions of achievement within the community by being some of the first to congratulate me on the news. Thank you.

Finally, to my Lydia and Garrus combined, Frederick Wu: if you had not bugged me so much about the EBFP and flooded me with email upon email of publishing and writing opportunities, *The Gatekeeper* would be absolutely nowhere near where it is now. Thank you for having so much faith in everything that I do (except climbing stools with no accident), for coming to get me when I needed a shoulder, and for all the little things that you do to free up the mental bandwidth for creative work. Thank you so much for your initial work on the maps upon which the ones in this book are based. I could not ask for a better supporter, man-in-arms, sounding board of crazy ideas and best friend. *Ru'neeura*.

And to everyone else who, in their own ways, have made this novel possible, *(wre)ur'*, thank you.

PHOTO BY: ALLAN SIEW

ABOUT THE AUTHOR

NURALIAH NORASID holds a PhD in English Literature and Creative Writing from Nanyang Technological University. She works as a research associate at the Centre for Research on Islamic and Malay Affairs (RIMA), where she studies marginalities and the confluence of religious ideas and secular society. Her writing has been published in *QLRS*, *Karyawan Magazine*, *AMPlified* and *Perempuan: Muslim Women Speak Out*. *The Gatekeeper* is her first novel.

INHERITANCE
BALLI KAUR JASWAL

A NOVEL

INHERITANCE BY BALLI KAUR JASWAL

- Winner of the 2014 Best Young Australian Novelist Award -

In 1971, a teenage girl briefly disappears from her house in the middle of the night, only to return a different person, causing fissures that threaten to fracture her Punjabi Sikh family. As Singapore's political and social landscapes evolve, the family must cope with shifting attitudes towards castes, youth culture, sex and gender roles, identity and belonging. *Inheritance* examines each family member's struggles to either preserve or buck tradition in the face of a changing nation.

ISBN:	978-191-2098-00-2
PUBLICATION DATE:	May 2017

KAPPA QUARTET

A NOVEL

DARYL QILIN YAM

KAPPA QUARTET BY DARYL QILIN YAM

Kevin is a young man without a soul, holidaying in Tokyo; Mr Five, the enigmatic kappa, is the man he happens to meet. Little does Kevin know that kappas—the river demons of Japanese folklore—desire nothing more than the souls of other humans. Set between Singapore and Japan, Kappa Quartet is split into eight discrete sections, tracing the rippling effects of this chance encounter across a host of other characters, connected and bound to one another in ways both strange and serendipitous.

ISBN:	978-191-2098-72-9
PUBLICATION DATE:	May 2017

NOW
THAT
IT'S
OVER

a novel

O THIAM CHIN

NOW THAT IT'S OVER BY O THIAM CHIN

- Winner of the 2015 Epigram Books Fiction Prize -

During the Christmas holidays in 2004, an earthquake in the Indian Ocean triggers a tsunami that devastates fourteen countries. Two couples from Singapore are vacationing in Phuket when the tsunami strikes. Alternating between the aftermath of the catastrophe and past events that led these characters to that fateful moment, *Now That It's Over* weaves a tapestry of causality and regret, and chronicles the physical and emotional wreckage wrought by natural and man-made disasters.

ISBN:	978-191-2098-69-9
PUBLICATION DATE:	July 2017

"Direct and bold, yet breathtaking in its fragile beauty." —Gerrie Lim, author of *Inside the Outsider*

THE LAST LESSON

of

MRS DE SOUZA

A NOVEL

CYRIL WONG

THE LAST LESSON OF MRS DE SOUZA BY CYRIL WONG

One last time and on her birthday, Rose de Souza is returning to school to give a final lesson to her classroom of secondary school boys before retiring from her long teaching career. What ensues is an unexpected confession in which she recounts the tragic and traumatic story of Amir, a student from her past who overturned the way she saw herself as a teacher, and changed her life forever.

ISBN: 978-191-2098-70-5
PUBLICATION DATE: July 2017

SUGARBREAD
BALLI KAUR JASWAL

A NOVEL

SUGARBREAD BY BALLI KAUR JASWAL

- Finalist for the 2015 Epigram Books Fiction Prize -

Pin must not become like her mother, but nobody will tell her why. She seeks clues in Ma's cooking and when she's not fighting other battles — being a bursary girl at an elite school and facing racial taunts from the bus uncle. Then her meddlesome grandmother moves in, installing a portrait of a watchful Sikh guru and a new set of house rules. Old secrets begin to surface, but can Pin handle the truth?

ISBN:	978-191-2098-66-8
PUBLICATION DATE:	September 2017

LET'S GIVE IT UP FOR GIMME LAO!

A NOVEL

SEBASTIAN SIM

LET'S GIVE IT UP FOR GIMME LAO! **BY SEBASTIAN SIM**

- Finalist for the 2015 Epigram Books Fiction Prize -

Born on the night of the nation's independence, Gimme Lao is cheated of the honour of being Singapore's firstborn son by a vindictive nurse. This forms the first of three things Gimme never knows about himself, the second being the circumstances surrounding his parents' marriage, and the third being the profound (but often unintentional) impact he has on other people's lives. Tracing social, economic and political issues over the past 50 years, this humorous novel uses Gimme as a hapless centre to expose all of Singapore's ambitions, dirty linen and secret moments of tender humanity.

ISBN:	978-191-2098-67-5
PUBLICATION DATE:	November 2017

STATE OF EMERGENCY

A NOVEL

JEREMY TIANG

Author of *It Never Rains on National Day*

STATE OF EMERGENCY BY JEREMY TIANG

- Finalist for the 2016 Epigram Books Fiction Prize -

A woman finds herself questioned for a conspiracy she did not take part in. A son flees to London to escape from a father, wracked by betrayal. A journalist seeks to uncover the truth of the place she once called home. A young wife leaves her husband and children behind to fight for freedom in the jungles of Malaya. *State of Emergency* traces the leftist movements of Singapore and Malaysia from the 1940s to the present day, centring on a family trying to navigate the choppy political currents of the region.

ISBN: 978-191-2098-65-1
PUBLICATION DATE: November 2017